SP.5⁹⁵

ALSO BY ANTONY SHER

Year of the King

MIDDLEPOST

иона
2, 11. И сказа Господь киту, и
онъ извергъ Іону на сушу.

MIDDLEPOST

Antony Sher

with five illustrations
by the author

Alfred A. Knopf   New York   1989

THIS IS A BORZOI BOOK
PUBLISHED BY ALFRED A. KNOPF, INC.

Copyright © 1988 by Antony Sher

Illustrations copyright © 1988 by Antony Sher

All rights reserved under International and Pan-American Copyright
Conventions. Published in the United States by Alfred A. Knopf, Inc., New York.
Distributed by Random House, Inc., New York.

Originally published in Great Britain by Chatto & Windus, London.

Library of Congress Cataloging-in-Publication Data
Sher, Antony
Middlepost.
I. Title
PR6069.H4556M4   1989   823'.914   88-45764
ISBN 0-394-57436-2

Manufactured in the United States of America
First American Edition

For Jim Hooper

Acknowledgements

I consider myself fortunate that my editor at Chatto is the poet and writer Andrew Motion; his guidance has been invaluable. I would also like to thank Jonathan Burnham at Chatto. When I began work on this book I was initially frustrated by my failure to locate the town in Lithuania where three of my grandparents were born – Plungyan. There was no trace of it in either modern or nineteenth-century Lithuania. It was Mr Rostis Baublys (owner of the splendid Lithuanian Library, which he runs from the front room of his London home) who solved the mystery: Plungyan was the Yiddish name for the town of Plunge; and Mr Baublys continued to supply endless research material. I must also thank the Institute of Jewish Affairs at 11 Hertford Street, London W1. In South Africa, I am indebted to the Isaac and Jessie Kaplan Centre for Jewish Studies and Research at the University of Cape Town; their Oral and Documentary History Collection provided much of the primary research material. My cousin Ralph Sher accompanied me on a return visit to the real Middlepost, where I had holidayed as a child and where he grew up. He was able to explain and name many things both there and at the Calvinia Museum, as did my father, Mannie Sher, who travelled with us. My mother, Margery Sher, has spent many hours chasing up various details, for which I thank her. The book could not have been written, quite literally, without my two typists, Alexandra Patterson in London and Margaret Bray in Stratford-upon-Avon; and finally, thanks to Gregory Doran for providing material on the Russian Empire, Victorian England and ostriches.

MIDDLEPOST

Smous

He was born Zeev Zali – that is the name on his birth-registration papers and it is written clearly, without smudge or error. However, some thirty-five years later, when he made the great journey from his native Litva to British South Africa, his document of identification then bore the name Zeev Immerman. His certificate of entry, completed upon arrival, showed a different name again – Maurice Josif Brodnik. Within a few months he was known as neither Brodnik, Immerman nor Zali, but Smous (rhyming with 'dose') which wasn't a name at all, being the word in the Afrikaans language for hawker or peddler, his trade at that time. When he was reported missing by the firm of wholesalers that supplied his goods, the official police papers carried the curious description of a missing smous called Smous. He often thought how Yiddish the word sounded, despite being Afrikaans, and, of the several names at his disposal, it became his favourite. Since that was his inclination, that is the name by which he should be introduced from the beginning – Smous.

1. CAPE OF GOOD HOPE

Landing

Smous blinked. He was on the other side of the world.

It was best to be certain, so he closed his eyes and waited for the giddiness to pass. Ever since that moment in childhood when someone told him the world was not as it seemed, but round and moving, ever since then he had had sensations like this, sensations of having missed his footing, and of Plungyan, all of Litva, the whole of Russia itself shooting away beneath him, sensations of falling, of spinning, of landing somewhere else. He remembered preferring the idea of an unrounded world, picturing it like one of his mother's onion flatcakes, a pale expanse with small dents and rises. But no, they said it was different. He couldn't say who first told him, or how old he was at the time; his memory was of the place – a field of grass alongside the Babrungas on a day when everything was especially still, the sunlight resting in the water, the shadows heavy on the banks; a scene of such certainty it was hard to credit this news about a whirling, tipping, circular chaos. However, from then on he was to be afflicted with these sensations of giddiness.

It was passing. Now he felt sick. He opened his eyes and squinted into the blazing light. Ocean, horizon, sky; he had been staring at little else for the last three weeks. But there was something unusual this morning. Although it was out of view, he could sense the land over his shoulder, he could smell it, hear it. It was true – they were there.

They must have docked hours ago, for the ship was deserted and silent. He was slumped below a porthole on a corner of the deck, his spine interlocking with a column of rivets. 'Nhhhh . . .' he murmured, shifting slightly, wondering how anyone could sleep in such agony – then remembered last night's festivities, the barrels of ale carried on deck with their supper, and him staggering to this part of the ship so he could be alone when it docked at sunrise. He had a picture of himself standing at the rail, gasping at the fresh black air and laughing, or crying, he couldn't be sure – and having to sit for a moment under the porthole.

But how, he wondered, could anyone *sleep* like this? His back ached, one arm was dead, his neck was drenched in sweat, so were his socks. With his working hand he patted his chest, then looked round, blinking and frowning, as his fingers explored the planks underneath him, behind, on either side. The cloth bag was missing. Definitely missing. Strange. Who would bother to steal that? All it contained was a sliver of soap, one filthy shirt, a stone jar of preserved fruits, and the end of a black bread now so stale you could no longer soften it under the tap on deck. With a little gasp, he checked his pockets, but his money was safe – and the English scroll. 'Stupid fool . . . stupid fool . . .' he muttered drowsily, hoping the thief was still in earshot.

Something touched his knee. 'Huhn?' he said and turned to find that a small grey pile, with specks of blood in it, had landed there. He peered up at the sky; how blue it was here. A seagull was circling above, flashing across the sun like a blade – 'Naa! Naa! Naa!' it cried, before another blood-speckled pile landed on one boot.

Wide awake now, he glared at the bird, with envy as much as anger, for his own bowels had been blocked all week. Wondering if it was even worth trying, he gave them a cautious squeeze – only to be reminded of what had woken him in the first place. 'Tssss!' he whispered and sprang to his feet. 'Yaak!' he cried as his cramped limbs were almost snapped off by the sudden change of position, and then 'Good God!' as his bladder began a deadly, no-nonsense countdown. He fumbled open his trouser buttons, then paused. Was it more decent under the porthole or through the railings, out to sea? He couldn't think fast enough. As a dancing trickle touched his boots, he stumbled to the rails, thrust forward his hips and finally stood there, eyes closed, murmuring 'Uhhhhh . . .' while a thin line arched from his body down to the waters of the harbour, joining the two for quite a while. He listened. Although the air on his face was hot and still, he could hear a wind blowing on the other side of the ship. And distant church bells. Now he remembered someone telling him they would be arriving on the gentile sabbath.

Fastening his trousers, he slowly made his way along the side, passing the iron drum reeking of salted herring, the previous night's supper, and tripping over a half-eaten potato which bounced over the edge of the ship and, after a long pause, plopped into the water below. Now, as he approached the baggage-deck, there was an abrupt, sharp, cracking noise, like a great whip. 'Ohhh . . . !' His trunk – like the bag – wouldn't be there! *'Ohhh . . . !'* He broke into a run and turned the corner. The wind was powerful, a wild shadow raced across the deck making him jump back, while, at the other end, a sheet of tarpaulin, big as a mansion, reared up into the air. *Crack* – it went, then collapsed, revealing a sight which took away his breath. A mountain filled the sky. The Table Rock, which the ship people had been telling them about throughout the voyage. There it was: a giant mass sliced perfectly flat along the top, as if half of it was missing, as if there might be even more somewhere else. Smous never imagined it would be so huge, or so close; he felt he could run across the deck, reach over the rail and lay his hand on its rough, grey sides. *Crack* – the tarpaulin shot up again, blocking out the mountain and the light. He stood transfixed, waiting for it to happen again, when one of the English sailors appeared and began to gather in the sheet.

Smous frowned, trying to remember what brought him here before he was distracted. His trunk – where was his trunk? The flapping tarpaulin had held down a mound of luggage throughout the voyage, but now the stretch of deck was empty, flashing with light and shade. His eyes darted back and forth. Nothing. A child's shoe. Nothing else. First the cloth bag. Now his trunk. All his belongings were gone. 'Actually quite serious,' he muttered, patting his fists on his stomach, unsure whether to stroke or punch himself. 'Only you . . . only you . . . only you . . .' – that's what his mother would have said if she were here; the famous triple curse would have been delivered without hesitation. The first 'only you' was spoken quietly through clenched teeth. Then she would fix her eyes on his greying hair and say again, but more vehemently, '*Only you!*' There followed a deep intake of breath and the third was just audible on a long doleful sigh, ' . . . only you . . .' By this time he would have an alarming picture of himself hanging alone in the sky among the stars.

The sailor had roped down the tarpaulin, and now Smous noticed that the Table Rock was flanked by two smaller peaks, set there as if to frame the astonishing view. The town was miniature by comparison, a white strip gleaming along the base, its buildings joined by the glare of the sun and then broken here and there by dark vegetation pouring down the slopes. Church bells rang out from a dozen directions and he listened, smiling, to the alien music looping over and under the roar of the wind. Taking a deep breath he scanned the deck again and now his eyes fell on a familiar green shape overturned in one corner; the trunk must have been moved when the rest were sorted. He gave a sheepish smile and almost waved, for it was as though one of the family was lying there asleep. A few extra dents, a patch of mould on the corner, otherwise it was exactly as it looked back at home. He bent over and grasped one handle, enjoying the way the old leather exactly fitted his palm, then hesitated, remembering it was too heavy to lift on his own. In Plungyan his father and brother had carried it out of the house and hoisted it onto the wagon; in Mazheik they transferred it onto the train; at Libau there were some cousins to help put it onto the boat; in Southampton an official from the Jewish Immigration Authorities had sulkily arranged for its transportation to the hostel where the travellers spent a few days; and then, oddly enough, it was the rabbi supervising the loading of kosher food who helped carry it onto this ship.

Glancing up, Smous saw the sailor passing with a mop, and dug in his coat pocket. His fingers skimmed over the large thin notes and peculiar coins exchanged for his roubles during the Southampton stop-over, and selected a medium-sized coin. Hoping this was sufficient, he stepped forward and said 'Um . . . ?' Since his only language was Yiddish, further conversation was impossible, but by holding up the coin with one hand while the other gestured towards the trunk and the gangplank, he was easily able to communicate. In vain. Although the sailor responded in English – 'I'd sooner die, cut-knob!' – Smous gathered the answer was no.

The wind pulled and rattled the gangplank as he dragged the trunk off the ship. Its weight grew more and more awkward, shoving at him like an impatient child, until, a few yards from the bottom, it broke free from his straining fist, knocked him aside, and hurtled down to make first contact with the earth of Southern Africa. He followed in a tumbling run, and finally they sat there in a heap, he and his luggage, arrived at last.

There was a dent in the gravel where the trunk had landed. Despite himself, he scooped out a handful and peered at it. 'You get off the ship,' he remembered Lazar saying, 'you bend over, you shoo off a monkey or two, and you can pick up a chunk of gold big as your fist!' He smiled as the grit trickled through his fingers – had he honestly believed it would be true?

Before him was a row of shacks and warehouses holding off the wind, and, like the ship, this area was deserted and silent. There was probably a good reason why no one was about, probably no more mysterious than the day being a sabbath, yet Smous felt uneasy, his eyes flitting back and forth across the black doorways. He started. There was a man standing in one of them. Smous narrowed his eyes. For a few moments the man stayed there, motionless, only just discernible among the shadows, before he stepped forward into the sunlight. Yet the darkness came with him. Although the man was clearly out in the open, with a shadow of his own, it was as though the doorway had not released him, or that the sun, where he was concerned, had lost its power. Smous blinked, glanced to the sky, then back to the man, who moved closer. 'Ah!' cried Smous, suddenly understanding, '– a savage,' then wished he hadn't spoken aloud. The man stopped, his limbs rigid, one heel fractionally raised. Smous held his breath and now they both remained poised, studying one another.

Apart from a sweat-band on his forehead and a loin cloth, the figure was naked, and Smous's first thought was that he had expected savages to be browner; this man's skin had a blue-grey sheen, like woodsmoke, and his fingernails were startlingly pink. Smous had never seen hair like this, crisp and woolly, although the broad, flat bones of the face reminded him of people from the far-eastern regions of Russia who sometimes visited the horse-market in Plungyan.

Strangest of all were the man's eyes, drowsy and solemn, their whites discoloured, as if the darkness of his skin had spread. They met Smous's gaze, noting, in turn, the alien shape of his eyes, like almonds, his soft, peaked cap, the ragged brown beard with traces of red and grey, the long charcoal coat, a boot with bird droppings that held specks of blood.

'Carry?' asked the man in English, pointing to the trunk. Smous shrugged to show he couldn't understand, then, seeing the man reach towards his trunk, lunged for the other end. The man waved him aside impatiently. 'Carry?' he repeated, flicking long fingers onto his chest. 'You pay silver hog?' Smous shrugged, smiled, frowned, nodded his head, shook it – leaving the stranger to choose whichever applied. The man grunted in return, lifted the trunk, swung it high into the air and let it land, of all places, on top of his head. Carrying it like this he led off, and Smous trotted after, suddenly feeling rather distinguished.

They turned into a yard where, to his relief, there was a queue of passengers from the ship winding into a wooden shed, and a group of British soldiers leaning against the wall. With his bearer a respectful pace behind, Smous joined the queue and waited, jigging on his toes. He reached for his cloth bag, remembered it was gone, and quickly checked his pockets again. His travel documents and money were kept in the inside pocket of his coat, while his most precious possession, a letter of introduction written in English, he kept in a waistcoat pocket close to his breast. It was a beautiful scroll of parchment with a yellow satin ribbon, drawn up by a linguist in Telz, and proudly described by Smous's father as his 'diploma in English'.

'Mh-hh . . . ah . . . mm,' murmured Smous as he patted the various pockets, making the man queuing in front glance round. Smous nodded and cleared his throat, then, puzzled by the man's deepening frown, turned away and found himself facing the soldiers along the wall.

You would never imagine these men had just fought a war, and won. People said their opponents, the descendants of the original Dutch settlers, were a race of colossal barbarians, and yet these soldiers, like the sailors on board the ship, were so small and lean, with pink and orange faces, and thin lips, speaking their English in a dozen different ways. One man made it sound a sharp and nervy language spoken out of the side of the mouth, another made it sound slow and flat, a third spoke with hoarse jabbing noises, like coughs. Now an officer appeared and he sounded different again, with tiny, delicate, flickering tones. And how casual they looked, these English conquerors, basking in the sunlight with their bleached khaki uniforms unbuttoned and their curious helmets, like overturned vases, pulled over their noses; how different to the Imperial soldiers back at home, those illiterate peasant boys in massive greatcoats strutting through the streets.

Smous hesitated. Several of the English soldiers were staring back at him, one or two pointing and laughing. The man ahead of Smous turned again and, with a sigh, said 'You are at the wrong place.' He had spoken in English, so Smous shrugged and smiled. The man sniffed and turned away. Suddenly aware that he didn't recognise any of the passengers in the queue, Smous jigged faster on his toes. Now a pebble hit the trunk and one of the soldiers called, 'Jewish immigration – over there!', pointing to the other side of the yard. Without a word, Smous's bearer swung round and headed off. 'They've got it at last!' shouted the soldier while the rest clapped and cheered, and Smous, blushing scarlet, hurried after his luggage.

Across the yard stood a smaller shed with no queue outside and deserted within, although there were signs that a crowd had recently passed through. A bench was pulled away from one wall and there were scraps of paper, eggshells and breadcrumbs on the floor, a pool of liquid and another lone shoe. The place had no windows and was airless. Dust swam thickly in the shaft of sunlight that stretched from the doorway to the battered counter at the far end.

Suddenly a bespectacled face shot up between two stacks of paper and, seeing Smous, cried, 'Oh my, another one! Oh now, dear oh dear oh dear, blow it, blow it, oh dear Lord lay hold of this fine jolly – *where have you been?*'

Smous felt his feet tightening, ready to run, but the man had rounded on his bearer. 'Hi, you!' he said, then dashed from behind the counter and, clapping his hands sharply, shouted, 'Shoo!' The dark-skinned man fled from underneath the trunk, which remained momentarily in the air before crashing to the floor. Now that the clerk was out in the open he was revealed to be in shirtsleeves, and very short indeed. His skull and chin were dotted with colourless stubble, catching the light like sprinkles of dust. He toddled to the door and checked that the dark man had gone. 'You want to watch that one, he'll ventilate your bosom for a fadge-fly tip,' he said, returning to the counter, his head popping in and out of view between the stacks of paper. 'Well, you've landed us with a most grievous problem indeed. Why you weren't with the rest of your people is a mystery I warrant you're not going to help us solve – if I'm any judge of character, you, like all the rest, don't speak a word of the King's English, do you? *No*, despite an apparent intention to settle in this, his colony. Savvy? No, you don't, do you? A fine reason in itself to have stayed with the group I would have reckoned. We had interpreters here to explain your fearsome puckerings, *interpreters*, your own people from the lodging houses up in Harrington Street. Even a very kind fellow with a basket handing out boiled eggs. You could have had a boiled egg if you were here on time, *a boiled egg and an interpreter*! Now what shall we do . . . ?'

Smous was fascinated by the shape of this mouth speaking English in yet another way: it hardly moved at all; instead, there was furious activity up in the nose which bunched and stretched as if it held a tongue of its own. 'Mister Polchard is going to have to lay hold of this one, but he's at his breakfast, and when Mister Polchard is occupied with the stoking of his bodily fires we could be talking about a fair fine wait indeed!' At this point the tiny clerk disappeared completely behind the counter and Smous heard the slamming of a door, which, since it wasn't visible, he presumed to be the same height as the man.

As he stood listening to the distant sound of high-pitched gabbling, he became aware of a putrid odour in the shed and spent several moments scanning the floor, before realising where it came from. He grimaced and plucked at his woollen clothes, damp and itching, but there was nothing to be done. Now his eyes strayed to a picture hanging above the counter. A very old, very round, very severe woman in black glared down; sufficiently like the tiny clerk to be his mother. Odd, thought Smous, to keep such a prominent picture of one's mother at work. Then the invisible door opened and closed again, and the man's face sprang back into view.

'Mister Polchard has been summoned, but which exact slap-bang he has chosen to breakfast at on this particular morn, and how long it will take my glock-witted coolie to locate the aforementioned breakfasting lay, these are questions which the Lord alone could answer, and He, at this precise point in time, dear oh dear, *won't*!' Whatever the clerk had just said seemed to please him, for Smous watched him return to his papers with the hint of a smile.

Why on earth should my arrival cause so tiny a man such enormous agitation, wondered Smous, what is it that I have failed to do, and what will now be expected of me? And what lies behind the little door beyond the counter? Are there to be further embarrassments because I stink so? He thought back to the dockyards at Libau where, before they could board the first boat, they had to strip and go into a large tiled room where water fell from the ceiling like rain. Here they washed while officials, also naked but tremendously dignified, strolled among them in search of lice and ringworm, shouting comments to clothed minions scribbling on the outskirts. When they reached Smous, the officials made several observations, but, because of the water round his ears, he couldn't hear. What might they have said? Hirsute, runtish, tiny hands and feet, buttocks flattened by a lifetime of idleness . . .

A giggle rose in his throat and was swallowed – 'Np!' – making the tiny clerk glance up suspiciously. Yes, they all had faces like this, the naked officials at Libau, the Russian administrators back at home, the overworked Jewish Immigration people at Southampton, they all had these round, unshaven faces with thick spectacles, deaf ears and reciting tongues. Smous feared this breed of humanity more than any other, and, in turn, their contempt for him knew no bounds. The English scroll! – perhaps that might appease the clerk. As Smous drew it from his waistcoat, he saw a flicker of curiosity behind the eye-glasses. The man took the document, unrolled it and, with nose bunching and stretching, read aloud:

KIND SIR OR MADAM, MY NAME IS ZEEV IMMERMAN. I AM TRAVELLING TO MEET THE UNCLE AT CALVINIA AT SOUTH-ERN AFRICA. NAME LAZAR IMMERMAN. I WAS BORN AT THE TOWN OF PLUNGE AT THE IMPERIAL NORTH WEST REGION OF LITVA. I DO NOT SPEAK YOUR LANGUAGE YET. PARDON ME. ASSIST ME PLEASE IF YOU ARE WILLING. I AM ABLE TO OFFER THE LITTLE REMUNERATION. I THANK YOU IN ADVANCE OF HOPEFUL FOLLOWING ASSISTANCE. FAREWELL KIND SIR OR MADAM.

Looking up, the clerk contemplated Smous for several long moments, while, behind his head, the framed portrait of his mother in black added her own terrifying scrutiny. 'Please listen to me carefully,' said the man finally, assembling pink fists in the fractional space between chin and counter, 'because I shall tell you this once only and not in duplicate. My day has been long, my spirit is coopered, and it is not yet mid-morning! So I couldn't care a fadge who you are, whither you are bound, or from hence you hail. *Plunge* is not a hughey of which I have heard, despite nine long years at this desk dealing with you and your kind, but it is, nevertheless, one which you might find yourself mizzling back to, before the gun on Signal Hill fires one o'clock this fair fine Sunday. Savvy?'

Smous gazed back, frowning. The English scroll seemed not to have made any impression. Apart from anything else, the clerk had continued to speak English despite the information that this was not a language Smous understood. He glanced at the document. It looked so splendid and official; it was his *diploma in English* – what had gone wrong?

'. . . so in the meanwhile you may cease blocking my view, if you please.' The clerk waited, then cried, 'Sit!', clapping his hands sharply, '*Sit!*' – making Smous stumble back onto the bench that was pulled away from the wall. He perched there, glancing round him, stranded in the middle of the hot dusty shed.

'And we hardly require this little fakement littering our desk!' said the clerk, flinging the scroll at Smous. It caught on a current of air and floated briefly like a kite, the light glowing through the veined parchment, the yellow ribbon trailing gracefully; then descended with little swoops from side to side, landing neatly on his lap, from where it was slowly returned to his waistcoat pocket.

The Linguist

It was one of those days when there was scarcely any light at all. Night had eventually given way to a vague wet greyness and now, just past noon, darkness was already falling.

They were grateful their journey from Plungyan to Telz was almost over, for there had been few forests to hold off the sleet. Smous's parents were huddled on the front of the wagon, Froi Immerman with her white goatskin shawl pulled over her head, Her Immerman with an enormous purple handkerchief secured on his streimel hat to keep the fur dry. Smous lay on the back, crammed among his father's goods: rattling boxes of thimbles, needles, clay-pots, ice-hatchets, children's shoes, nuts, raisins, spices. His long charcoal coat was wrapped tightly round him, though he was hardly aware of the cold. In over thirty-five years (none of the family could be precise about their age) he had never set foot outside the Plungyan district, even when it had been easier to do so; the permits for today's trip had entailed lengthy applications and hours of queuing. Peering over the sides of the wagon Smous saw that the lowlands were exactly as people had described, open and bleak, shining with mud. Even in warmer seasons there was always a watery glint here, for the tufts of yellow sedge were like sponges and a slight mist would linger in the hollows of peat and moss.

Telz was a disappointment. It was a city after all, so he had been expecting something far grander – not these dark, ragged streets clinging to the hills above Lake Mastis. Chalk scrawlings covered the walls: signatures, sums, obscene drawings, as well as the inevitable anti-Jewish slogans and marks. The roads were crowded and hostile, everyone hurrying in different directions, gasping from the cold.

Smous was horrified when, on arrival at the linguist's house, Her Immerman forgot to remove the purple handkerchief from his hat. He resembled a simpleton at the best of times, dumpy and short, his mouth fixed in a desperate grin; how could he not realise that the handkerchief made him look even more foolish? Fortunately the linguist was a man of great civility who bowed his bald head in greeting (an almost Oriental gesture repeated whenever he was addressed) and led into the warm interior, inviting them to discard coats and headgear. Now it was Smous's mother who became embarrassing, when she refused to part with her soaking shawl. She was fearful of the stranger stealing it and self-conscious of what she wore underneath. A quilted jacket in mauve velvet, embroidered with metal thread and beads, it was her best garment, but since its last airing years earlier it had grown too tight, and her stocky frame was bursting through. Eventually she was persuaded to relinquish the shawl, and followed the men to the linguist's work-table, tugging at the jacket with small white hands.

The place had no rooms, but was a light, high space heated by two glazed stoves, with a crude staircase leading up to a bench-bed high in the rafters, where the sleet rustled on the roof.

Having never before entered a gentile home, the first thing Smous noticed was a different smell. The houses of his people always held a faint scent of cinnamon, while here it was of wax. There were candles and sticks of sealing-wax everywhere to be seen. The walls were stacked with books and these looked waxen, the spines blackened and soft; and the linguist himself, with smooth yellowish head and stained smock, looked as though he was made of wax – wax or parchment, the other predominant material of his trade.

'Polish, French, English, Italian, Russian?' he chanted, gesturing for them to sit round the long table.

'Yiddish,' replied Her Immerman. The linguist hesitated, then gently raised his arms in surrender. 'Oh?' said Her Immerman, though he was not unduly worried; unlike his wife and son, he had learned two other languages from his life as a trader. 'Litvak?' he suggested next, only to regret it instantly. It was the only moment when the linguist was less than courteous. He dropped his eyes furtively and gave several brisk shakes of the head. Although Litvak was his own language, it was officially banned by the Russians, and while you might use it freely in rural areas, here in Telz you only spoke it with people you knew well. 'Russian then,' said Her Immerman quickly, giving a panting laugh and choking on the stiff collar Froi Immerman had insisted he wear.

Smous watched, intrigued, as the two men began talking a language that both loathed. The linguist pronounced it with much splashing, as though cleansing his mouth as he went, while Her Immerman's grins grew broader and wetter, and one eyelid started to flicker. His sentences were broken by a short dry cough.

'Uh-uh! . . . My son, yes? . . . Go ride, ride, ride, far, far, far . . . uh! . . . Africa, yes? English Africa, yes? . . .'

Froi Immerman shifted impatiently. She was in agony – from the tight jacket and, worse, because the men were speaking a language she couldn't understand. Her younger son reach the other side of the world on his own? Impossible! So why throw away money having a document drawn up? She had explained this to her husband a thousand times, but it was one of those rare occasions when he was determined to have his own way. So was she. However, sitting here now, unable to comprehend a word, she began to wonder if she had not lost this battle. She slowly raised one fist (her fingers were always clenched) and stroked the crown of her head, where the hair was thinning, then sat forward, nodding, as though following the conversation.

'. . . and my son . . . uh-uh! . . . must show . . . authorities, English authorities . . . who he is, where he go . . . uh-uh! . . . in English, yes? You write in English – for my son?'

Smous watched the linguist turn to look at him as he had already done several times, and wondered if the man found it odd that someone of his age, with grey in his hair and beard, should visit today with his parents and say nothing for himself, but sit fidgeting with tiny hands, scuffing tiny feet along the floor. He tried to sit still, but this felt even more juvenile. The man smiled. Smous liked him.

At last all was explained, and the linguist's turn had come. As if about to start a conjuring trick, he held up a piece of his finest parchment for their inspection. Froi Immerman whispered, 'Don't like it!', while her husband nodded eagerly and rubbed his hands. The linguist now began to sharpen his quill; this was done on the side of a broken bottle, scraping the feather to and fro along the sharp edge, with a little ringing noise. Smous murmured to himself, recalling that time long ago when he and his cousin Issy had tied broken bottles under their shoes to skate on the river. It ended with Issy cutting his hand and the blood seeping into the ice where it remained trapped, shaped like a red phantom, a fleeing figure, which fascinated Smous for weeks.

The quill was sharpened, dipped and raised. Without looking up, the linguist sat poised, a small smile on his lips, awaiting dictation. For a few moments Her Immerman's eyelid vibrated so wildly he couldn't see, then he subdued it, took a deep breath, thought of the correct Russian words, and began, with a cough. 'Uh-uh! . . . Kind sir or madam . . . uh! . . .'

'Kind sir or madam . . .' repeated the linguist quietly, in English, as he wrote.

'I'm having him put "Kind sir or madam",' was relayed in whispered Yiddish to Smous and his mother. The former nodded in approval, the latter went 'Ffh!', then Her Immerman continued in Russian. 'Uh! . . . My name is Zeev –' He stopped abruptly, eyes bulging.

'My name is Zeev . . .' repeated the linguist, in English, calmly bent over his work, while Her Immerman turned white and, out of the corner of his mouth, whispered to his family, 'His *name*!' Immediately the problem was clear and horrifying and they cursed themselves, even Froi Immerman, for not anticipating it.

Immerman or Zali?

Because the law demanded one son from every family to serve twenty-five years in the Imperial army, a practice had begun of registering all but the firstborn under different surnames. When Smous was born, his elder brother Elie had already laid claim to the family name Immerman, so he was given the fictional name Zali. But which to use on this document? Smous would be travelling to Southern Africa so he could establish a foothold for the rest of the family. Since they would all arrive as Immermans should he be established there as Zali?

By now the linguist had looked up with a respectful but baffled smile. Why was there a delay at this junction? How could the man have forgotten his own family name? The friendly, smiling face terrified Her Immerman. Although not Russian, the linguist was gentile and not to be trusted; the Immermans had broken the law – the penalties were severe. He desperately needed to consult his wife who would surely know best, but any further whispering would make the whole business even more suspicious.

'Immerman!' he suddenly blurted, then began coughing rapidly and buried his face in cupped hands. He didn't want to see his wife's expression, didn't want to know if he'd made the wrong choice. Smous gulped. Was this a good idea to go abroad with a different name to the one he had used all his life? On the other hand, it was a relief to be legitimate at last. It was done now anyway; the linguist was already inscribing the word 'Immerman' with beautiful, curling strokes of his quill.

Smous shrugged, sat back and had just begun to relax when he noticed the dictation stop again. A faltering conversation in Russian followed for some minutes before an explanation was provided in Yiddish.

'We don't . . . uh-uh! . . . know what to call the birthplace.'

'Plungyan!' retorted Froi Immerman impatiently, thinking her nerve-racked husband had forgotten the name of their town.

'No, but you see, *they*, the Litvaks, call it Plunge . . . uh! . . . the Russians call it Plunjani . . . uh! . . . it's only us that call it Plungyan.'

'Well, this document is for *us*!' she snapped, now unable to believe his stupidity.

'No, but, well, is it? Actually, it's for the authorities in Southern Africa and they're English. Now what do they call it? . . . uh-uh! . . . D'you see my point?'

Froi Immerman was stumped. She showed this by tutting irritably and turning away. Her husband swivelled in his seat, as though hoping to find the room filled with counsellors, but there was only his son – gazing back with those sleepy eyes, that perpetually raised brow.

'You see,' continued Her Immerman, looking at Smous, but talking to himself, 'my choice would be Russian. I mean they're a great nation like the English . . . uh-uh! . . . so if any version is known in Southern Africa it isn't going to be the Yiddish, it isn't going to be the Litvak, it's going to be the Russian! Now that's just common sense . . . uh! . . . isn't it?' Smous was about to agree that it was, when his mother decided to rejoin the conversation, using hushed tones and glancing at the linguist, convinced he was secretly following their conversation.

'It should be the Yiddish,' she said. 'Plungyan. That's where we're from. That's how we know it.'

'But that's the last language anyone will know in Southern Africa!' said Her Immerman, slightly louder than he intended, directing an apologetic look to the linguist and giving a panting laugh.

'Yiddish!' whispered his wife.

'My darling, I'm forced to disagree here . . . uh-uh! . . . it's so obvious that it should be Russian, it isn't even common sense any more, it's a must. After all –'

'Yiddish!'

'My dearest, Russian.'

'Plungyan!'

'Plunjani!'

Sweat began to glisten on Her Immerman's forehead. She was doing it again, speaking to him in that voice, staring at him in that way. What did she want of him, how had he failed her? They had been so happy until a few years ago. Then she began to change, growing distant and tense, with a frown like a scar, growing harsh, like everyone and everything, like the world these days, growing unrecognisable.

'Darling . . . uh-uh! . . . Plunjani, please.'

'*Plungyan!*' cried Froi Immerman with such vehemence that one of the buttons finally shot off her straining jacket and scuttled across the table. Watching the linguist return it, that polite smile on his lips, Her Immerman wanted to scream. To be arguing in front of such a learned man while keeping him waiting at the same time, this was unbearable. He suddenly swung on his son. 'What do *you* think? You're the one who's going – it should be your decision.'

Smous was flabbergasted. He couldn't remember his parents asking his opinion before, about anything. To have to make a choice now, in these circumstances, with both of them counting on his vote, was a terrible initiation. Like that nightmare he sometimes had: a uniformed figure would burst into his home to murder either his father or mother, leaving the choice up to him. As he looked from one to the other now he realised he had only one option, ludicrous though it was.

'Plunge,' he said.

'Plunge?' said his father.

'*Plunge?*' said his mother.

'It's what they call it here in Litva,' Smous protested nervously, 'that's where we're from – Litva. Might as well use the Litvak name – Plunge.'

There was a moment's pause while both parents gazed at him despondently, then his mother said 'I don't care, you and your father want this document, not me. *Plunge?* Only you . . .' and withdrew from the conversation; while his father, looking hurt, relayed their decision to the linguist. He, in turn, looked surprised and flattered, then gave his deferential nod and proceeded to write the name of their town in the illegal version used by his own people – 'Plunge'.

Squirming in his seat, Smous gave a little laugh. 'You know,' he whispered to his parents, 'isn't it amusing to think I'm going to be carrying a document that has my surname and my birthplace written in a way the authorities here wouldn't like? All I can say is, God forbid if I have to turn back!'

His mother's head shot round. 'If you're thinking of turning back, do us all a favour and *don't go!*'

Smous's cheeks turned red. He felt winded. How could he have been so careless as to walk into that one, virtually to confess he wasn't up to the journey? He watched a ripple of satisfaction pass over his mother – a shrug of her shoulder, a twitch of her mouth, the fists unclenching for the first time since they arrived – until her whole being was slightly rearranged, as if she'd straightened a tablecloth.

The rest of the document was dictated without further hitch. After silently cursing himself for a long time, Smous flicked his head abruptly – a gesture he often used to change the pattern of his thoughts – and leaned on the table, watching the linguist work, admiring the way the man bent over the parchment with such care, never spilling a drop of ink, each stroke of the quill like a caress, the feather dancing under his nose. Then Smous's gaze drifted to the walls of books, and he sat staring at their soft black spines, wondering if there were bricks or planks beyond them, or only more books – different stories, lives and languages, poems, songs, a host of words holding up the roof. He wondered if any of these books contained the ancient heathen legends of the Litvak people, legends which Her Immerman had learned on his trading excursions and recounted to his children when they were young.

Smous's favourite was the one about the forests. It was believed that somewhere in the deepest reaches of the forests, somewhere beyond the dark firs and wild oaks, the tanglement of ivy and berries, the bushes of cherished rūta, here began an animal kingdom where great herds and flocks lived, as in Paradise, on a beautiful sunny plain. But no man could ever make his way there. The forest itself mustered all its might and terror to prevent him.

Glancing back to the linguist, Smous remembered how shocked he was to learn that the Litvak people – people like this gentle, charming man – were now accusing the Jews of destroying the sacred forests. Did the Litvaks fear that the Jews would reach the fabled land beyond the forests before them? Or that the Jews would finally reveal no such place existed?

Feeling giddy, Smous shifted in his seat and flicked his head.

When at last the linguist was done and had blown the last trace of powdered eggshell from the parchment, it was handed to Her and Froi Immerman for their inspection. Smous peered over their shoulders to see what the English language looked like. It bore the closest resemblance to Litvak, with the same joined, travelling curl to it. Hebrew went in the opposite direction and the letters had an ancient, ornate weight to them, as though carved in stone. Yiddish letters were identical but often written without the dots above and below, so seemed more forlorn. Russian letters, on the other hand, had busy, jagged shapes, like insects.

A Carriage Ride

'Mister Polchard – oh my, oh now, thank the Lord you have arrived!'

'Mister Theed – declare yourself – *what* is the matter?'

A man had appeared in the doorway of the shed, blocking out the sunlight; a huge round silhouette with a bright triangle glowing in the middle, which, as he moved forward, was revealed to be an enormous napkin with yellow splashes, tucked into his collar. Like the tiny clerk, this massive figure was bespectacled, unshaven and in shirt-sleeves, but there was a difference, a flamboyance to his untidiness. His black hair hung in long flopping strands, his moustache was stiff with wax, and a cluster of teeth held one side of his mouth in a little smile.

'I have relished few breakfasts more than that from which I have been summoned this morning, Theed,' he announced slowly, 'one of old Pa Gommie's finest curried mussel pies, one of Mommie Gommie's sweetest little sugargirls standing by to soothe away those enteric upheavals which might ensue. Nevertheless, here I am, ready and able for duty, eager only to discover that neither you nor your faithful coolie runner saw fit to exaggerate when coining the following summons – "A matter, Mister Polchard, of the gravest urgency and import!"'

'No indeed, Mister Polchard, no, no, you just lay hold of this, please do,' said the little clerk, pointing to Smous who jumped to his feet. 'Another one!'

Polchard had already glanced at Smous and didn't bother to do so again. 'And it would be the very acme of delusion, would it, Theed, to hope you might have completed the documentation unaided?'

'Oh! Now then, well, yours is the authorisation required, Mister Polchard, yours is the mauley they –'

'Forge it!'

'Forge it?'

'Forge it! How long is it now that we have worked together, Theed?'

'Oh! Erhm . . . I believe it to be a ninth anniversary we anticipate, Mister Polchard, yes I do believe so, on erhm . . . on the thirteenth of –'

'Nine years. And in all that time you've learned so little about the artistic side of our work. You look at this pile of papers and what do you see?'

'A pile of papers, Mister Polchard.'

'Exactly. Whereas I am persuaded by an image of trees felled, cut and shredded. You look at this quill and what is it to you?'

'A quill . . .'

'I see the bird on the wing snatched from the blue by the huntsman's arrow. Here is ink – what are you seeing?'

'Erhm . . . a dark fluid for writing with?'

Polchard leaned on the counter and indulged in a few private moments of despair, passing the back of one hand across his bristly chin with a sound like someone sawing. Smous had watched the exchange with interest. Since the arrival of the large man, the small one had shrunk, his terrible gaze growing timid, his voice lighter, his gestures fidgety. Now Polchard turned to Smous. 'Sir, welcome to His Majesty's Colony, the Cape of –'

'Pardon me, Mister Polchard,' said Theed, appearing round his superior's waist, 'but not a word of English does he speak!'

'I don't believe I was asking him to speak, Theed, I was asking him to listen. There is music in every language for all to hear.'

'Yes, Mister Polchard, sorry, Mister Polchard.' Red and white blotches flowered on Theed's face as he shrunk a few more inches; Smous wondered whether he began each day as a very tall man.

'Now,' said Polchard, 'does he possess any identification, Theed?'

'Ah!' exclaimed Theed, seeing his chance, 'no, he doesn't, Mister Polchard, why, you've touched on the very nub of my problem, the very reason why your assistance here was so imperative. Not a scrap of identification does he carry, neither on his person, nor in his baggage, both of which I have fanned rigorously . . .' Theed worked hard to unleash his imagination; this, after all, was what his superior always asked of him. 'What with the hostilities of war only recently ceased and the deluge of notification we have received, well, I need hardly tell you, notification alerting us to the danger of shake-lurks and other undesirables, I was forced to view this out-of-twig character with the utmost fear and caution. Were my opinions sought as to his true identity I could only hazard a guess and shudder. Thus I felt compelled to send for your good self and . . .'

'*Dung!*' intoned Polchard. '*Dungg! Dunngg!* Your brain, Theed, produces dung faster than Pa Gommie's curried pies.' He took Smous by the elbow and transported him to the counter. 'Sir, if it is true that you have landed on our shores like an orphaned babe, without name, address or history, allow me to invent these for you.' He bawled out instructions and Theed quickly handed him an official form. 'Look at this,' cried Polchard, thrusting the paper under Smous's nose, 'these are the colonies, sir, where we are compelled, alas, to function twelve calendar months behind the rest of the civilised world. Look, look! ". . . year of our Lord, one thousand nineteen hundred and *one* . . . pleasure of *Her* Majesty the *Queen* . . ."'

He sighed and set to work on the document, updating the number of the year and altering the gender of the monarch, wielding his quill so that the tip sprung around the page, sending fine trails of ink in every direction. 'Why, they have even failed to send us a pictorial representation of the new sovereign yet!' he said, one thumb jerking Smous's attention towards the framed picture of the elderly woman in black. 'What are we to do?' demanded Polchard. 'We can hardly turn the glorious little black pudding to the wall and be left without any reigning monarch at all, no dear me, hardly, hardly – when that happens we will be, as Theed here might say, right coopered! Thus we are forced instead to serve under a ruler who has since departed this world, as at the foot of a smashed idol, a god discovered to be false, and we must continue to do so, blithely, foolishly, haplessly, until one day there will arrive from Westminster a parcel adorned with the finest decorations the postal service can bestow, a new portrait will be hung, and sanity finally restored.'

He looked up at Smous's bemused face, its moustache and beard framing a glazed smile, and took pity. 'But what is this to you? It is a new identity you were promised and which you now crave. Let us dally no further.' He took Smous's form in one hand, the quill in the other, and moved along the stacks of paper on the counter, peering down at random. '*Family name?* Let's see, yes here's one – Brodnik! *Forename or names?* You can be . . . Maurice Josif! *Age?* . . . Fourteen! You are fourteen again, Maurice Josif Brodnik. *Native of* –? . . . Poland!' and so on, until he had completed the form. Then he pushed the quill between Smous's fingers and guided his hand across the paper. 'A most bravura mauley, Mister Brodnik!' he cried, signing the form himself, then pounded it with a rubber stamp and tossed it to his assistant. 'Over to you now, Theed, yours to do with what you must, yours to enumerate, duplicate, stack, package and file!'

Taking Smous's arm again, Polchard grabbed the green trunk with his free hand and conveyed both beyond the counter to the door which Smous had earlier imagined to be minute and foreboding, and which was now revealed to be completely ordinary – until Polchard flung it open to reveal another sudden, breathtaking view of the Table Rock. Both men were blown backwards by the wind.

'Go forth, Mister Brodnik,' cried Polchard, his cheeks flushed, his lank hair streaming behind him, 'go forth, a new identity is already yours and a new land awaits you. And now we must part and hurry in our separate directions, you to a promising future, I to a cooling breakfast!' Smous and his trunk were pushed through the opening, and the door slammed behind them.

He found himself in a different area of the dockyards, busier than before, and criss-crossed with railway lines and dirt tracks, all leading in different directions. Uncertain which path to take, he chose the nearest and set off, dragging his trunk behind. Above him, the gulls gave their mocking, warning cries – 'Naa! Naa! Naa!' – the birds were in such numbers the sound was overwhelming, like crashing waves. His path ended at a wooden platform with a pulley. He turned to the right, only to encounter railway tracks, turned to the left, took a few steps, stopped again, looked around him. Everyone else was going about their day with very definite plans, pushed by the wind so that they looked even more determined; stevedores wearing fezzes and carrying large hessian sacks, soldiers on horseback, a man blowing a tin trumpet and pushing a cart heaped with glittering steenbras fish, a group of Oriental sailors hurrying by squeaking and chattering, a herdsman with goats.

Seeing the Table Rock loom above a line of warehouses, Smous decided to use it as his marker. As he set off, the wind whipped away his cap and, before he could even think of giving chase, it had disappeared. 'Tscheee . . .' he muttered, then shrugged and moved on, passing a colossal ship afloat on a timber framework with a swarm of half-naked workers crawling over it. Their women squatted nearby, passing round a bottle and fingering their skirts above bruised legs, grinning at the stranger who dragged his trunk by. Sweating and panting, Smous crossed the dockyards, dodging trails of dung and rotting fish on every path, or the cats crushed and split in the cart-tracks. Finally, turning by chance down an alleyway, he emerged onto a road beyond the harbour area where a grassy hill led up to the town and the giant mountain beyond.

The road was protected from both sun and wind. No one was about – there was that stillness again, as when he woke on the ship, as when he disembarked. Across the road stood a tall, thin tree with a fan of leaves at the top, which he recognised from illustrations of biblical scenes. A palm tree. Staring at it, he perched on his trunk and thought, How odd there should be a tree from Palestine here.

He sat still, breathing heavily, watching beads of sweat drop from his nose into the grey wool of his trousers. He looked at the seagull-droppings on one knee, frowning at the specks of blood, then at his finger nails, the brown freckles on his hands, his wrists, and thought how stupid to have worn his best cuff-links for the journey – they were rusting. Now he closed his eyes, held his breath, and listened to the silence.

It's like being invisible, he thought, it's as if I don't exist here yet. I could walk for hours in any direction and not bump into anyone I know. A whole part of me has vanished. That part made up of what everyone else thought, how everyone else saw me, that part saying 'Sorry . . . sorry . . . sorry . . .' down every street, in every room – that part's gone. Now it's me, really me, me alone in my head. 'Only you . . . only you . . . only you . . .'; remembering his mother's words he gave a gasp, and a little smile.

There was the sound of hooves. He opened his eyes. Nothing had changed, the road was still deserted. Again he heard the hooves. They stopped, took a few steps, stopped again. Now very slowly, a horse plodded round the corner, pulling a two-wheeled hooded carriage with the driver asleep inside, arms folded across his whip. Noticing some weeds, the horse stopped to graze. The bones shone through its pinkish-grey hide, its knees were swollen, its hindquarters sloped, but the expression on its emaciated head was tranquil and wise, quite beautiful. The carriage was skeletal also, with dry wood and metal showing through the blue-and-gold paintwork, and the hood hung in tatters. But here there was beauty also, for the driver had threaded wild yellow flowers through the frame.

Smous glanced to the palm tree across the road, the tree from Palestine, and wondered if there was a sign in all this. Unable to think what it might be, he sighed and stepped forward.

'Sir . . . your honour,' he said, then cringed at the sound of his voice on this alien street. But the man remained asleep, his face hidden behind one forearm. His clothes looked like cast-offs: huge grey corduroy trousers and a faded black serge jacket with high brocaded collar, which might once have belonged to a ship's officer. 'Sir,' said Smous louder, rapping his knuckles on the footrest – '*Sir*!'

'Only . . . save my soul!' shouted the driver suddenly, one arm shooting up with the whip and his boots crashing into a pile of bottles on the floor. The old stallion started, rocking the little carriage, and, confused by his blinkers, bit at the air, while the man continued to moan in a strange voice, his eyes open but unseeing. 'Oh, dear merciful God, we are visited by the hounds of Hell!' As Smous leapt back, throwing up his arms in surrender, the man finally came to and cracked his whip above the panicking animal – 'Rest it, van Riebeeck, you galloping knobber – rest it, it's a customer.' Although the whip never made contact, the horse instantly went still, blowing wet drops through its nose.

It was difficult to say how old the driver was. His hair was either blond or grey, falling in a boyish fringe across his forehead, and his purplish features were criss-crossed with a mass of pale freckles, stubble and old scars. His nose had been broken many times, leaving eyebrows and nostrils arched, and the impression of a permanently dazed sneer. He chewed at his tongue, then slipped it round his lips.

'Pardon . . .' he said at last, 'pardon the beast, he was always backward, but now that he's old – I'm driving blackmeat and glue. Get rid of him tomorrow, finished, that's that, no fretting, no frutting, and so we does, and so we does.'

Before someone else started gabbling at him, Smous decided to offer the English scroll. 'Hmmm . . .' said the man, peering at it, 'this is a lovely pamphlet, very nice,' and handed it back. 'Now then, what're you asking? Trip round the peninsula? All the sights, views of the harbour, the Grand Parade and Castle, old St Georgie's Cathedral, Government House, thrills, spills and all the frills, a fine old trip, a ream old day?'

Smous hesitated; he thought he'd noticed the man reading the scroll upside down, but couldn't be sure. Waving it in the air, he asked, 'So, you can take me to my uncle?' The man nodded eagerly. 'Really?' asked Smous, 'it's not that far?'

'Good, good,' replied the driver, 'and then this afternoon, maybe a trot out to the suburbs, see the fine old toffkens, vineyards and orchards. There's a lion with three legs someone's got on a chain.' Confident that they were in accord, Smous smiled and said 'Excellent.'

'Good, good,' said the driver, 'money no cause to fret, uhn?' and when Smous shrugged, he concluded, 'Good, good, no fretting for you, no frutting for me, messy, muddling, piss and pus, leave it till the end. If you've had a fine old trip, a ream old day, you can come a bit over, if not we call it the usual, and a fairer bone deal you could not ask!' His voice was rasping, his accent a curious mixture from the local streets and the curling, buzzing Dorsetshire tones his parents had brought with them long ago. He clambered down onto the road and, cursing at the weight, lifted Smous's trunk into the small carriage which also groaned in protest. Now Smous clambered into the vehicle and found a space for his feet among the bottles, while the driver heaved himself onto the bench, virtually closing him in.

'Go on, van Riebeeck!' cried the driver, cracking his whip in the air. As they jolted into motion, he spoke over one shoulder: '. . . our beast, you'll have observed, is named after the great Dutch sea captain and discoverer of the Colony in the year sixteen hundred and nn-nh . . . for today, you too are going to discover the fairest Cape in all the world, and all its fair old sights . . . its treasures . . . trickshens and trackshens . . .' Here he began wheezing and bent forward, rocking himself, the reins slipping loose in his hands. Alarmed, Smous peered round the man's black serge jacket, but the old stallion seemed to know the way on his own, turning up the hill, stretching his neck into the wind and beginning to climb.

Smous sat back grinning. Despite the dilapidated vehicle and its peculiar driver, he couldn't believe his luck. This was how he most wanted to enter the town, in his own carriage. He squeezed the worn, rounded handle of his trunk, as he might someone's hand, and thought of the Russian Bible – the unclean Bible – pressed against one inside wall. He had succeeded in smuggling the book into the trunk while his father was packing it, despite a moment of panic when one loose page fluttered down near Her Immerman's foot. But Smous had snatched it in time and folded it into one waistcoat pocket, where now – his fingers quickly checked this – it still rested. For years he had hidden that Bible, ever since his brother first gave it to him, secretly, when they were children. It was filled with exquisite, hand-coloured engravings, and those images of ancient spectacles evoked a strange feeling in Smous, a sort of magnificence, a sort of loneliness, which drew him powerfully. He had sought these sensations in real life, but always in vain – until now. He pictured himself entering some walled biblical city, perhaps triumphantly, perhaps in a cage, it didn't matter, there was glamour and pity in both. Now he heard an odd sound above him, a tiny ringing, and found a small rusting bell hanging from the hood, shaped like a pair of cupped hands.

They reached the crest of the hill where the field of long grass gave way to neat lawns and then burial grounds, gentile crosses and monuments stretching away into the distance. 'Pardon us this . . .' muttered the driver, 'It's the war . . . don't ask me why they couldn't just bury the wounded out on the veld . . . instead they've got to bring them back here, some just bits of leg and scut-hole, to stink up these lovely views.' He spat at a tomb they were passing. 'Scumming army! Pick you up and throw you aside. Three long years they give you their trade, never known anything like it – "Take me here, take me there, money's no fretting, we're on the randy and you're a ream old thing!", then the next minute they say – "Right, that's it, war's over now, pop off, tiddly-oo, chew up your danglers and sit in the salt box!" They're bitches, bastards, gashfarting sluts!' He passed a hand over his face, collecting his features in one grasp, and removed a film of sweat. 'Anyhow, your tour picks up from here on . . . all the sights and sounds, colour and cheer . . .' He slumped forward, and, to Smous's amazement, began to snore.

So they continued towards the town, the driver sleeping and waking, snoring and mumbling, the old stallion seeming to mumble also as he chewed on the bit, and Smous gazing at his new land, alert and suspicious. Nothing was familiar. The very sensation of riding in a carriage was different to home. The roads were shaped differently, sloped at different angles, and were made of a thick red dirt which the wind lifted in great sheets, clogging his eyes and ears, crackling in his teeth. The houses were built of stone, not timber, so the shape of every gateway, window and door was different. The gardens overflowed with strange trees, gaudy flowers, monstrous shrubs that surely were made of wax or leather, and some that looked like pin cushions. And the people that he glimpsed – they looked so different. It was very odd: every one of them, old and young, men and women, was remarkably handsome. A race of perfect specimens? It was days before he could work it out – everyone lived in so much sunlight here their skin had changed colour, darkening beautifully, like the savages, enhancing the plainest features.

As they progressed into the town, the roads deteriorated, gouged with holes and pools of mud. Smous's jaws were shaken open and remained so, gawping at the sights around him. There were granite buildings, five, six storeys high, with carvings on their sides, massive pillars, towers with giant clocks, round domes like the cupolas on Russian churches. Several buildings flew the English flag, and some had colossal wrought-iron words protruding from their roofs, shuddering in the wind. Because it was the sabbath the streets were mostly deserted; a brown-skinned girl in a straw boater selling flowers, a beggar so crippled it looked as if he was crawling up through the board-walk, one or two starving dogs on the prowl, shop dummies with their faces pressed to the windows watching Smous arrive. And now, bearing down on them, an immense black monster, shaped like a bug, with feelers clutching at webs in the air. A tramcar, which they said you only found in Moscow or St Petersburg! Unable to bear any more, he lowered his gaze and stared at his green trunk – at least that was recognisable – and listened to the ringing of the small bell, letting himself be rocked by the lurching, shuffling motion of the ride.

He looked up. They were parked in the middle of a vast market square, deserted except for flocks of pigeons hunched against the wind. The carriage driver was staring out across the empty space with his fixed, dazed sneer. He sighed, beckoned his passenger towards him and began what sounded to Smous like an incantation: 'The Grand Parade – famed round the world! The Saturday morning sales – what colourful sights to behold! . . . pity you're here on a Sunday. See the Castle – where the Governor rules! See the Opera House – an evening of artistry! . . . I know the brother-in-law of one of the ticket sellers if you're –' He stopped suddenly and stared at Smous as if seeing him for the first time. 'Fine and bone if you're just visiting, uhn?' then began to make mocking noises out of the side of his mouth, popping and grating his tongue. Smous frowned. 'You Japanese?' the man asked. 'Serbian? You're a Turk, aren't you? You're one of these Turkish Ottomen there's been talk of, aren't you?'

Recognising the rising tune of questions, Smous offered the scroll.

'No good showing me your pamphlet again, old mate,' said the driver, 'would I be doing this arse-jellying job if I could read? Stupid glock!' Now he buried his head in his hands. 'Sorry, sorry, but I need refreshment. How would that suit you – refreshment and refurbishment before we go any further? Hard to find this early on a Sunday, but I know a little slap-bang up Orphans Lane, with a ream old view of the harbour for you. Don't suppose there's any chance of some push yet? I mean, how've you fancied the tour so far?'

Smous shrugged emphatically to show he couldn't understand a word. The man rubbed his fingers together. Payment already? – wondered Smous – is this it, are we at Lazar's? I thought they said he lived in a different town. Puzzled, he looked round the deserted, windy square.

Then he heard the noise of a shunting train, and, turning to his left, saw puffs of smoke rising from behind a row of buildings. All was explained, he'd been brought to the railway station so he could continue the journey by train. Grinning broadly, he fished in his coat pocket and produced a handful of the foreign money, inviting the driver to select the right amount.

'Rut-a-Boer!' said the man, pocketing several notes. 'That's more than kind, friend, you won't be sorry, promise you, day to remember . . .' Smous wondered if he was being cheated, but there was no way of checking, so he nodded his thanks and rose, expecting the man to make way. Instead the driver threw back his whip, narrowly missing Smous's eye, and bellowed, 'van Riebeeck – *mecks!*'

Smous was hurtled into his seat as the horse bolted through the nearest flock of pigeons. A blast of wings, and the carriage went dark with flapping shadows. Smous gasped as he realised one of the pigeons had been scooped into the cramped space with him. For a few moments he and the bird fought, shrieking at one another in equal terror – then one of his wild punches made contact, sending the pigeon over the side, and Smous fell back, recoiling with disgust.

By now they had left the square and, with new, astonishing strength, the old stallion charged up towards the mountain, which flashed into view, green-grey rocks between the white of the houses. What on earth is going on, wondered Smous – did I miss something? Did that bird bring a message? Has the war started again?

They hurtled round a corner to find the road ahead a chaos of holes, planks and scaffolding. 'Gaah – udders and scuts!' roared the driver, reversing the carriage wildly, the horse bucking. 'Everytime you look round they're building something new, can't leave anything alone, got to rip it up, break it down, burst and bugger it, build, build, build 'til we're half way up the scumming mountain and rut the drivers, and we docs, and we docs! They're sluts, they're bastards, they're titfisting glocks!'

Above Smous's head the small bell rang wildly as they rattled along narrow streets with peeling walls, smashed windows and choking smells. Glancing down, he saw a litter of dead puppies along the gutter, pink swellings in the black mud. They turned into an alley cut off from the sun, but with a bright slab of mountain rock at the far end. As they hurtled straight for it, Smous wondered if they might smash through, into some luminous cave, the source of this gale perhaps, for the wind had never felt more powerful.

Suddenly a headless torso flew round the corner and came straight for them. The horse gasped and stopped dead. 'Hell-hounds!' screamed the driver and ducked, so it was Smous who was hit in the face.

'Yaaark!' he shrieked, enveloped by a stench of sweat and wine, then, tearing at it wildly, found a piece of clothing in his hands.

'Haai, where's that damn-bladdy jacket now?' called a voice, echoing down the alley. Another voice was singing loudly. A group of men had appeared at the corner, swaying in the wind.

The carriage driver turned to Smous and said, 'Throw them their bastard rag as we pass, I don't want trouble.' Smous leaned forward, eager to understand, but they had already surged forward. The men spread-eagled themselves against the walls – all except one, a scrawny figure in a yellow shirt, who lost his balance and, in a slow, almost graceful way, fell in front of the horse. It screamed and tried to dance in the air, but the falling man shot under its hooves and hit the wheels behind, bringing the carriage to an instant, shuddering halt. The horse looked between its legs, shaking its head, frustrated by its blinkers, while the driver flapped his reins wildly, as if still at full gallop, desperate to be gone. There followed a peculiar stillness broken only by a repetitive bump and a tinkle of the bell as the horse pulled forward, the wheels strained to lift over the body, the carriage rose up and rolled back, rose up and rolled back. Everyone watched this happen, transfixed, the men spread along the walls, the driver and Smous hanging over the sides, until at last the horse gave up and, like everything else, went very still.

'Don't know this drag, to say fair . . .' mumbled the driver eventually, 'that was my worry.'

Smous shifted in his seat to peer round at the man's broad back and, feeling as if he was watching a puppet show, saw the heads of the men lift as one to look at the driver. They were half-castes, their skin patched and bruised, crumpled canvas suits hanging from their lean bodies. Now they vanished from Smous's view as the horse, sensing danger, lifted its tail and eased out a green turd. The tail descended again as the driver addressed the men – 'Do we need a doctor?' He waited, then when nobody said anything asked, 'What's the damage?'

The heads looked down underneath the carriage, then back at him, but remained silent. The driver was chewing his tongue and seemed to be swallowing pieces of it.

'Better go for the Law as well, d'you think?' The men said nothing.

'Right –' said the driver, rising, 'I'm off to fetch a doctor then . . . and the crushers . . . and anyone else who can lend a hand.'

'Why?' said one of the men suddenly. Smous shifted to see the speaker, a tall man with a savage hare lip, his shirt marked with old blood-stains.

'Why? Why?' repeated the driver. 'Why . . . because there's been an accident.'

'Crushers will be all your chommies,' said the tall man.

'I haven't got any chommies in the crushers. Far from it, trust me please! I hate them. Like you do. You hate them, I hate them.'

'Sit down, mister.'

The driver sat and swallowed heavily. The wind was buffeting him roughly, the tall man staring up, whispering, 'Aai . . . Aai . . .', his mouth a mess of fangs and gum.

Smous knew there was going to be violence, yet felt calm. In normal circumstances, if he could speak the language, he would be forced to step in, to take sides, but in this present situation he felt absented, invisible behind the driver's square back, and safe. However, at that very moment his protector leaned forward and said to the men, 'Look, what if my passenger stays here with you while I go for help? How's that? Then you know I'll have to come back. And if I don't – you've got him, no fretting. He's Turkish. Very rich. Me? – I'm poor. All my life, poor. Like you folk.'

'Aai . . . Aai . . .'

'You're going to hurt me. Please don't hurt me.'

'Aai . . . Aai . . .'

At that moment the driver spotted some horsemen passing the end of the alley and called out to them in an odd voice, half screaming, half whispering, as though hoping the group round the carriage wouldn't notice, 'Help . . . help me please. They're going to hurt me!'

The riders paused, then turned into the alley. Smous shifted again to look at them: on the first horse there were two English soldiers squashed together, their uniforms dishevelled, their hair wet and dirty. A second horse and rider remained behind them, blocked from view.

The front soldier was a squat, hefty man with a bulging moustache. 'Morning,' he said, grinning down at the group.

'Morning, Master,' muttered the half-caste men.

'Or is it evening?'

'Master?'

'Looks like your Saturday night never ended.'

'Master?'

'Us too. All night. Hunting on your mountain, shooting some of your monkeys, stoking some of your bitches –'

'Losing some of our horses . . .' giggled the young soldier hanging round his waist.

'Rejoicing,' said the squat soldier.

'Because we're sailing home,' giggled the younger, then sang:

> 'But now discharged I fall away
> Then rise with a swell, spurt with the spray
> To land on her hillocks, shoot straight up her lane
> Look for me now in Thamesfontein.'

'*You're* not sailing home, Gant!' said the squat soldier, 'not when they discover you've lost a prad, a mare prad, army issue, fit for light transport, formal parades, active service, manure-supplying, foal-bearing, and a filthy old frot when nobody's spying! They'll never let you sail home, never-ever-a-glimming-gain!'

The young soldier burst into a fit of giggling while the first said, 'He's laughing now. Wait 'til he's dry,' then turned to the carriage driver – 'Who's trying to hurt you, darling?'

'There's been an accident, but I'm blameless . . . one of them threw themselves in front of my beast, nothing I could do.'

'Has he ghosted?' asked the soldier, squinting under the carriage, and when the driver shrugged, he barked to the younger soldier, 'Gant!'

'Boneham?'

'Dismount my mount 'fore you lose him and all, and go and see if the glim-mucked Hottnot Bastaard has ghosted.'

'Boneham!' replied the young soldier as he tumbled off the horse, then slipped in a puddle, crashed into the wall, giggling all the time. He glanced under the carriage, and stood to attention. 'Ghosted, Boneham, ghosted good and proper – ghosted, wiped, stopped, drained, defunct and dud – dud as Boerseed in the morning mist.'

'Dear oh dear. We fight a war, Gant, three long years, sacrifice body and soul, lose arms, legs . . .'

'Prads.'

'. . . and for why? To protect the Colony and her sons. And what happens? They start ghosting one another in the streets like they're in a rat-pit!' Now he addressed the group in the alley, jabbing one thumb over his shoulder towards the second horseman, still hidden from view – 'There's a soldier here, bravest man in the world, they gave him a medal this morning, or yesterday morning, or whenever-the-shatting shit! – he's risked his life for you lot and you're sicking in his proud face.' He shouted over his shoulder, 'Roddis!'

'Boneham?' replied a calm voice from behind.

'There's a slit here who's ghosted a poor little Bastaard. What d'you want me to do – kiss it or close it?'

There was a shuffling in the alley as the second horse made its way through. The squat soldier bawled, 'Saluting the hero, Roddis, to the front – S A L U T E!' and his two fellows executed a smart salute, while the half-caste men did a sheepish version, the carriage driver tugged his fringe, and Smous, not wishing to be impolite, scratched his eyebrow. In the gloom it took the civilians a moment to register why there seemed something odd about the new soldier's shape, then they gazed in amazement. He was a taut, black-haired man carrying a rifle, and except for boots and spurs, totally naked. His mare was stripped also – no saddle or tack, but gripped by the mane. Her eyes were dilated and her body damp and shivering. The group had only just recovered from the first shock, when their exploring eyes discovered another: a small, star-shaped metal was pierced through one of the man's nipples, and a ribbon of dry blood led down his stomach into his loins.

When he spoke it was in a quiet, dry voice: 'You're admiring my medal? One of last night's pox-boxes wanted to keep the uniform, so she repinned it. Doesn't hurt. More than you'd want. That aside, not a scar. Look.' He held out his arms and legs like a clockwork toy. 'Not a scratch. Three years. Not a slash. I've been into the fires of all damnation. Not a burn. Commanding officer told the garrison yesterday morning at the presentation, "This man's courage is beyond belief." But I fancy he was selling them soft. Anyhow, thought I'd have a ride round and show the Colony before we sail away.'

He slowly drew his spurs across the mare's belly. She shivered and he restrained her. Glancing down, the carriage driver saw that the animal was dripping with blood, and winced. 'What's the matter?' the naked man asked. 'Don't you like it when I do this?' Again he worked his spurs, this time plucking a fold of skin away from the belly and ripping it slowly.

'Wish you wouldn't, sir . . .' mumbled the driver.

'Oh pardon me I'm sure, tra-la-la, who, oh who, shall cast the first stone?' he said, and gently nudged the driver's whip with the end of his rifle.

'Never used it on the beast, sir, never touched van Riebeeck.'

'Why not? Only a beast, as you say.' He suddenly placed his rifle into the old horse's ear and said, 'Here one moment –' A tremor went round the group as he pulled the trigger; there was a small click. '– still here, the next.' He threw the rifle to the squat soldier. 'Boneham, reload my rifle!'

'Roddis!' shouted Boneham, complying, while the young soldier giggled and chanted:

> 'Instructing the laddies when firing their lead
> And naming their weapons, the old sergeant said
> Up here's your rifle, down there's your gun
> This be for slaught'ring, that be for fun.'

The reloaded rifle was tossed back to the naked man, who took aim at the driver, very slowly and carefully. 'And under what name would he who buggers beasts go calling?'

'Miller, sir.'

'Sounds like a Boer name to me – Muller.'

'It's Miller, sir. *Mi*-ller. English. My folks were among the first lot of settlers, sir, in the last century, sir . . .'

Smous no longer felt safe behind the driver's back – a shot would tear through and hit him. By shifting six inches to his right he could remove himself from the line of fire, but that would attract attention. His mind was racing: if I sit here, I'm going to be shot by accident, and if I move, he'll shoot me deliberately. Either way I'm going to die and I don't know why, or even what's going on. My family will never know what happened to me. In fact, they won't even be able to trace me ever arriving here, because that entry form wasn't filled in properly, I know that. He felt giddy, he needed to clear his mind, but even flicking his head was too bold a move. Despite the madness back at home, there had only been one occasion when he was under threat – one small, terrible occasion – otherwise it has taken a journey across the world to land in the firing sights of a lunatic. He had often wondered what it would feel like. Now he knew. Small, insect-like noises escaped from the corners of his mouth.

'They've passed away, sir,' the driver was saying as the barrel of the rifle brushed his nose, 'both dear folks, sir, carried off by the smallpox, sir.'

'Not the great pox?'

'No sir, smallpox, sir.'

'You're not diseased then?'

'No sir, no diseases, sir.'

'Nor a Boer?'

'No sir, not a Boer, sir, no fretting there. I hate them. Like you do. You hate them, I hate them. And if you –'

'Not diseased, not a Boer, not glock-witted in any way?'

'No sir, no glock-wits in my –'

'Then why are you wasting my time?'

'Sir?'

'You've ghosted a Bastaard. Who could care less? Some old, fat, lushington settler sinning with a savage, thirty, forty years ago, a dribble up her pox-box in the last century and you want me to care? Do you know how many beloved I've lost in this war? Englishmen. Young strong Englishmen. Not half-breeds, not half-made Hottnot Bastaards, but Englishmen. Do you hear what I'm saying? Englishmen, Englishmen, *Englishmen* . . .'

'Sir –'

The naked man suddenly swung his rifle towards the nearest wall and fired it. The shot resounded in the narrow space, the horses and Smous screamed, a hole exploded in the plaster and a window shattered, showering glass onto the group of half-castes. They leapt into the air and tore down the alley as the young soldier sang sweetly:

> 'Tis the last goodbye, take your place in the line
> Go and do your duty, Jack, and I'll do mine . . .'

Smous had felt a smaller explosion in his trousers and wondered whether his constipation was cured. He dared not move to investigate.

The naked man was looking at the carriage driver with glassy eyes. 'Hook it,' he said.

'Can't sir, wheels are stuck on the body, sir.'

'Please . . .'

He lifted his rifle and aimed at the driver again. Miller lashed his whip across his horse who bellowed in surprise and rage, terrifying the other animals; then it leapt forward, effortlessly lifting the carriage over the body, and galloped down the alley. Smous twisted round to peer through a tear in the hood – the two horsemen were already riding away in the opposite direction, the young soldier running after them, stumbling and laughing. The man who had been knocked over lay sprawled in a puddle; his head was twisted back, stretching the skin of his forehead and pulling one eyelid open, so that only the white of the eye watched the departing carriage. For an instant – despite the gathering distance, despite the lurching ride – Smous saw the face clearly, and peered closely into that open white eye. Then he flicked his head to shake away the image and sat back heavily. He had not, as feared, filled his trousers, though there was a definite wetness.

They turned the corner onto a road with the mountain towering up one side, shacks and a church on the other. Miller stopped the carriage, trembling and puffing. He muttered apologies to the horse, then twisted round to Smous and said, 'Fearful thing, uhn? Never ghosted anyone before. I . . .' Suddenly the heavy sacks round his eyes prised apart, revealing their contents for the first time – small and green, rather beautiful – as he stared at the man's jacket still in Smous's lap. 'What do you want to keep his rag for?' he demanded. 'Are you sick in the brainbag? They'll butcher us dry – his friends, his family, the crushers, everyone – ding it, *ding it*!'

The man's wild gestures were so explicit Smous needed no translation, yet he hesitated, staring down at the fawn sailcloth jacket. It seemed such a cruel thing to do, to hurl it away like rubbish. He could smell the man on the cloth, he could feel the shapes of coins in the pockets, some tobacco, a key, pieces of paper. He thought about finding the man's family and presenting the jacket to them. They would weep and thank him; he would be a hero.

'Ding it!' screamed Miller. 'You stupid Turkish titting bastard, what are you waiting for – ding it!'

Smous sighed and lifted the jacket over the side, letting the wind take it.

'. . . rutsucking Turkish clown,' muttered Miller, and flicked his reins. 'Go on, van Riebeeck!' – then his hands tightened, checking the horse. He had directed a final glance to the alleyway and seen an extraordinary thing – the man in the yellow shirt whom he had knocked over, the man he had killed, staggering into the sunlight and snatching his jacket as it flew past. Miller gazed in disbelief, wondering if this was an apparition. Obviously not, the man had tumbled over again and was propped on all fours, slowly shaking his head. 'I didn't ghost him!' whispered Miller, breaking into a huge smile.

Smous had seen the man also and, like Miller, his mouth hung open, grinning. Now they both clambered from the carriage and approached the figure, who was struggling to stand.

'I think the world came and fell on me,' he said as they drew near. He was a thin, ragged man with bony shoulders so hunched they almost met under his chin, making him look back to front. He was clearly no stranger to accidents: half of one nostril was missing, he wore a stained bandage on his neck, and there were bald patches among the tiny curls which dotted his head like a swarm of ants. When Miller asked if he was all right, he made nervous, shushing gestures to his lips, as if to say, It doesn't matter, please don't worry – then examined himself and found a lump swelling on the side of his head. He prodded it and yelped. A little spray of blood shot out of his mouth, followed by a tooth which he caught in mid-air. 'Walaa!' he shouted and laughed, then opened his mouth wide to reveal a toothless upper jaw; the gum was black, speckled with grey and orange.

'Soon there's now none left,' he said, tapping the lower teeth, 'that's how I'm hoping. It's luck, hey, Masters?' Then he sunk back onto his haunches, mumbling, 'Dull skull . . .'

'Where d'you live? I'll take you home,' said Miller.

'Nay, Masters, Masters is kind, but Masters mustn't.' His fist was clutched round the tooth, while the forefinger shushed his lips, pointed vaguely at the two men, danced in the air.

'Come on,' said Miller roughly, embarrassed by his own charity, and hauled the man to his feet while Smous arranged the jacket over his thin shoulders. One on either side, they accompanied him to the carriage where Miller thrust him in front of the horse, saying, 'Look, van Riebeeck, our souls are saved from the eternal scumming fires,' but the old stallion looked unimpressed, as if this man surviving his trampling was further proof of his failing powers.

Miller squashed his two passengers into the carriage, and clambered onto the bench. The newcomer shifted uneasily in the confined space, his finger dancing around, touching the carriage hood, the small bell shaped like cupped hands, Smous's trunk, Miller's back. 'Haai, Masters, smart cart Masters have got to take Gommie home. Down Roggebaai Strand there lives my lady who we call the Mommie Gommie, she's going to give you a drink of hospitality, 'cause the Masters are such kind Masters.'

So they set off down the hill, back towards the sea, all three thinking about the accident and its unexpected outcome. Every time Smous smiled at Gommie, the latter ducked his head and put his finger to his lips, as though saying, Please don't let me disturb your journey. Turning away, Smous stared out towards the ocean flecked with white spray. He could see the dockyards and tried to work out which ship was his. It was odd to be heading back in that direction. Perhaps he was meant to go home now. Perhaps his journey was complete. Perhaps it was simply intended that he should come all this way to participate in a strange miracle: the killing of the nervous man sitting next to him and then his return to life. It wouldn't be surprising. Smous had always expected his destiny to be filled with such things.

Heroes

When he opened his eyes he found it there, all around him, the universe, the whole universe, him at the centre and everything else within reach. And it was a universe filled with treasure, scent and light. It had walls, this universe, like a walled city, walls to keep him safe; though at this moment there was no danger beyond. Giants were singing, gathering round, showering him with more treasure. He tasted a piece of it. Beautiful, the hard shape breaking easily on his tongue and coating it with syrup. He peered over the wall of the universe and saw a small hill with soft, fine, reddish sides, shifting in a breeze from the gathering of giants.

This was Smous's earliest memory. He had just turned three.

As the singing finished, Froi Immerman said, 'Come, if you people want to eat tonight I need this to mix the milcheka.' She lifted Smous out of the basin, emptied the sweets into a bag, and collected a lock of his hair from the little red heap. Later she would add it to the ringlet woven from the other children's first haircuts.

As Smous grew older his childhood duties were few but strenuous. Every evening, Sunday to Thursday, there were cheder classes, held in a shed behind the teacher's house. It was laid out with long, narrow desks, a battered copy of the lessons fastened to each place, the pages giving off a sour, metallic smell from generations of use. There was only one Bible, around which the boys crowded, and some, so the joke went, learned how to read Hebrew not only from right to left but upside down as well. Their teacher was a pink frog of a man, Pinchvinch, so named because of his favourite method of punishment. One clammy hand was probed into the clothing of the guilty party to search out their most sensitive spot – nipple, underarm, or the soft skin between inner thigh and privates – where the nails of his forefinger and thumb would lodge; the victim would then remain impaled in front of the class while the lesson continued.

Even more terrifying was the synagogue. Here Smous would have to stand for what seemed like hours, a dark sea of adults rocking above him, the men muttering and whimpering as they bound themselves in the black strips of their tfillen, the women separated in an upper gallery, gazing down, and always that noise of the Torah rolling open and closed, like the creak of a heavy door. Smous was puzzled that everyone else seemed to regard the Bible as a charter of torment and stricture. Surely they were missing the point? It was a storybook, full of spectacle and of adventures even more thrilling and preposterous than the old Litvak legends which Her Immerman recounted from his travels. As far as Smous was concerned the Bible had been written, quite simply, to inspire his games on the banks of the Babrungas.

Plungyan was shaped like a wagon wheel, with the market square in the centre and the streets radiating out like spokes. The northern radius was the Jewish quarter, discreetly contained by the Babrungas River to the right and a glade of white alder to the left. But as the glade grew into a forest, so the boundaries became less distinct, and, further still, the dark green light and muddy tracks gave way to open fields sloping down to the river – before the railings of the vast Dolrogusky estate appeared on the landscape to limit things once more. It was on one of the open, wild fields that Smous and his cousin Issy Immerman spent long afternoons enacting stories from the Bible. This was a game Smous had devised, so he claimed first choice of story and character; and he was always drawn to the heroic figures. He would be David while Issy would be a plump and diminutive Goliath, snivelling every time the sling was loaded. Or Smous would be Moses and Issy Pharaoh, smitten by whichever plagues Smous would improvise from their surroundings. For Boils he'd plaster Issy with lumps of mud; for Darkness he'd blindfold him and invariably push him into the water; favourite of all was Frogs, since these were in real abundance on the marshy banks and pushed down Issy's back by the handful.

Issy was well known as the biggest blubberer in town, so Smous ignored the constant whimpering, the slime hanging from his nose and chin like thawing icicles. But every now and then he would have to cope with 'Issy's Face' and that was a different matter. The crying didn't stop when Issy put on his 'Face', but what made it so frightening was that his eyes seemed to retract – the closed lids, the whole bulge of the eyeball pulling back and flattening, sucking into the skull, while his mouth stayed half-open and he made little popping noises in his throat. There was nothing to be done when this happened. Smous had tried it all: scoffing, shrieking abuse, singing lullabies, sticking his finger in Issy's ear, but he was utterly beyond reach. 'Issy's Face' only ever lasted a few minutes, then he snapped out of it himself, but it was enough to impress Smous. Did the old prophets go into trances like this when God warned them of plagues or floods or the cities of sin? Was his cousin being shown such things? The end of the world, or the fabled land beyond the Litvak forests, where only wild animals lived, or maybe the Litvak spirits called laumés, or Jewish ghosts and dybbuks. Whatever the visions were, Issy had seen them again and again, and it was the only thing about him that Smous envied.

Issy lived alone with his father, a doctor and a leading figure in the Jewish quarter. Onkel Lazar had been one of the rare Jewish students to continue his studies after cheder at the government school, progressing to the Yiddish University at Vilna, and returning eventually with diplomas of distinction and an imposing top hat which he always wore, indoors and out, day and night. Lodged between his huge flapping ears, it gave his head the appearance of a tall ship sailing around on the undulating silver curls of his beard. There was no Russian who could make Smous's family feel more inadequate; Her Immerman was, after all, a humble trader barely able to read, or afford, the newspapers. Smous would watch the familiar top hat sailing through the air above everyone else, and imagine his uncle was God Himself, that omniscient, bearded Presence worshipped so fearfully in the synagogue.

Issy's mother and two sisters had died in one of the fires that were the scourge of the timber-built town. It happened when Issy and Smous were eight, but years later Smous could still clearly remember the mourning rituals. How extraordinary to see the adults tearing their clothes – deliberately – and leaving their hair unbrushed, and sitting on the floor. It was during one of these shivah sessions that Smous first saw Issy do his 'Face', and when it first occurred to him that his cousin was perhaps seeing ghosts – of his mother and sisters.

The fire was a mystery. Lazar claimed it had been started by rampaging, drunken soldiers, but, since this was long before such things were commonplace, Smous's parents refused to believe his story, putting it down to his fancy, *university* mind; they stuck instead to a version where Tante Selma spilled heated goose-fat over an open stove. Smous preferred the story about the soldiers. It seemed perfectly feasible that the Russians should punish Lazar. He might be able to sail round this part of town looking like the Almighty and terrifying everyone in sight, but the Russians wouldn't be impressed. They had their own, greater gods.

So when it came to their games on the banks of the Babrungas, Smous bullied little Issy with a sense of righteousness, a sense of power, rare and mysterious; a thrilling sense of what it was like to be Russian.

For the rest of the time, Smous's role in life was as subject rather than as ruler, particularly at home where there was a real live hero sharing the same bedroom. Elie, his brother, possessed everything Smous coveted: three years' seniority, the family name, huge front teeth (Smous's were minute) and a truly inventive mind. Recently, for example, Elie had started to wear a smudge of coal dust on the end of his nose to shorten its hooked shape and so de-Jew himself. While it wasn't entirely successful – in fact, it just attracted attention and made Elie look like a Jew with a dirty nose – Smous found the idea astonishing. Elie devised the coal blob because he had started studying at Count Dolrogusky's Musical Academy, and, of all his brother's achievements, Smous most envied his access to the Russians and their summer palace.

In Plungyan you could always tell which day was the first of summer because the Dolroguskys and their retinue would pass through the town en route to their holiday residence. Leading the procession were grand coaches lacquered in black and green with red wheels, gilded oil lamps, ivory door handles carved like butterflies, squirrels and chameleons. The heads of the family rode in these vehicles, invisible behind patterned insect nets. Next came open carriages and troikas with nannies and the younger children – blond dolls in white sailor suits – who hung over the sides shrieking and pointing at the locals; then came wagons carrying supplies for the summer and the rest of the servants, footmen, cooks and maids, who travelled in best clothes and assumed airs; finally, bringing up the rear, was a small private army, packs of hunting dogs, wolfhounds and laikas, and, on one occasion, a wheeled cage with a small albino bear. For ten minutes or so the colours and perfumes would transform the market square of Plungyan into the centre of Moscow, before the procession passed through the town and disappeared into their estate.

No more would be seen of them for the rest of the summer. The estate was so huge that the Russians could walk, ride, hunt and swim without ever stepping beyond the carved railings which ran along the boundary. Then, on the last day of summer, the procession would pass through the town again, but travelling in the opposite direction and without the noise and glamour of before. The family heads were now invisible behind velvet curtains on the front coaches; the children were encased in their autumn furs, weighed down and grumpy, and the servants looked exhausted.

The Dolroguskys' great love was music and when in residence they held a musical academy which admitted, even encouraged, local Jewish children like Elie to bolster a symphony orchestra which played in the garden during outdoor luncheons and dinners. Smous listened to these concerts from a particular spot along the railings where he could just glimpse the pearl-grey palace as he marched up and down to the tunes, or stood dazed, the music washing over him, nourishing his dreams of heroism and splendour. Elie told him he was hearing both 'the great Europeans' and 'the Russian masters' and Smous was in no doubt which he preferred – the Russians. Their sounds were headier, full of clanging and chiming, with giant harps and deep rolling drums. The thought of his own brother sitting among these people, helping to produce their pagan sounds, was almost unbearably exciting.

Sometimes Elie would return from these feasts bearing pieces of rich, sticky black cake in a damask napkin, and the brothers would secretly devour these in their bedroom, while Elie told Smous how the Russians lived: of their gilt icons (Smous always heard the word 'idols'); of a religious holiday when they exchanged eggs made of silver and jewels; of perfumed curtains scenting the rooms with every breeze; of smoked mirrors, naked statues, and doors so grand a twelve-year-old needed both hands to open them.

On one memorable occasin Elie described a favourite pastime among the Dolrogusky servants: mimicking Jewish behaviour and speech. 'This is what we look like to them,' he said, burying his head in his shoulders, gesticulating wildly with his arms, then rubbing his hands together in greed. '"Oi-yoi-yoi, business schmusiness, what a to-do, such a carry on, do me a favour!" They also say that we torture our animals in the most unspeakable way when we slaughter them, that we then smear their fat on our hair and on our bodies to keep warm, which is why we look so slimy, that we drink human blood, and that, all in all, our hygiene stinks.'

'And does it?' asked a breathless Smous.

'Probably. But worst of all is how we breed.'

'Breed?' Smous gulped. 'What? How?'

'Prepare yourself,' warned Elie. 'The man puts his fruit in the woman's mouth and then after a while she swallows it, and then a year later she vomits out more Jewish babies.'

'She swallows *his whole fruit?*'

'Ach, you fool! His seed. She swallows his seed.'

Smous's eyes grew wide. He had never been clear about this description, 'fruit,' having spent hours examining his own organ without detecting the resemblance, but now to discover there was *seed* involved also – they'd be telling him next he could grow lots more! And for a woman to put this fruit in her mouth, to swallow this seed, and then vomit out babies; it was challenging news.

'Jewish copulation is what the Dolrogusky servants call it,' declared Elie.

'Jewish copulation,' repeated Smous slowly. 'Jewish copulation . . .', again and again, fearful that he would not be able to remember this exotic phrase.

But he was never to forget it.

When Elie was given a violin of his own to take away for practice, the Immerman household erupted. 'These people are jumping up and down on our faces – *Zetz! Zetz!*' screamed Froi Immerman, 'and you're parading their goods round my house,' gesturing towards the manufacturer's inscription on the belly of the violin. Everyone leaned forward to peer at the gilt Russian words winking back at them, while Her Immerman shifted from foot to foot, uncertain whether it was shame or pride he felt. There was no doubt Elie had changed since he started visiting the Dolrogusky palace; he would mimick the family strangely, rubbing his hands greedily and pulling at his nose; but if the Russians liked him, if they could offer him a better life – surely that was a good thing? 'I want it out, *out*!' cried Froi Immerman, now threatening the instrument with her fists. 'I'm not having any Russian words in this house!'

'No Russian words,' repeated Elie, smiling, then took the violin to his bedroom, ' – right.'

Smous hurried after, then watched open-mouthed, marvelling at his brother's imagination, as the Russian lettering was gently sliced away with the razor Elie had recently been given. 'Here, you want a Russian foreskin?' asked Elie, offering him the sliver of gilded spruce, and Smous pulled away screaming, making his brother laugh.

To appease Froi Immerman further, Elie promised that he would only practice the violin in the bedroom, and as softly as he could manage. Smous would watch him sitting cross-legged in one corner, trying to play the violin with the bow just making contact; his hunched secretiveness suggesting it was an experiment with some kind of forbidden magic, the coal dust on his nose now looking like ritualistic paint.

'Now listen,' he would whisper to Smous (for some reason he lowered the volume of his voice as well), 'this is the second movement of Mozart's Sonata for Violin and Piano in C Major, you'll just have to imagine the piano . . .' (Smous couldn't think what a piano sounded like, so he imagined the look of one) ' . . . it's incredibly hard to play at the best of

times, terribly hard to play as quietly as this, but "such strictures are good" –
this is what a gentile would say – "it'll make one even better."' However,
after several hours of this tiny sawing and plucking, Elie's fingers would be
blistered and bleeding, causing Smous to wonder whether these Russian
exertions were not some form of torture, a punishment for being Jewish
perhaps? On the other hand he could see his brother's mind expanding
daily, he could *see* it. Elie was already unlike anyone else Smous knew, even
more cultured than Onkel Lazar whose boisterous knowledge lay in other
areas. Where was it all leading? Was Elie like Moses, living in splendour
among the Egyptian oppressors, until one day he would turn against them
and lead his family from Plungyan to a promised land? Or was he a Samson,
seduced by Philistine decadence, shorn of his strength, and in the end
capable of only one massive act of destruction which would bury himself as
well? Either way, Smous held the highest hopes for his brother.

Then, without warning, it was all over. Elie reached thirteen and a
decision had to be taken about his future. The Dolroguskys were so
impressed by his talent they offered to sponsor his education at a larger
music school in St Petersburg, but Froi Immerman refused outright, and
her husband was forced to agree – their son was too much of a stranger
already. It was time for him to come down to earth and join the family
business, trading round the villages. To Smous's astonishment, Elie
accepted the decision in silence – although it was a strange, disturbing
silence. The only comment he made to Smous was, 'They'll be sorry', but
refused to say who or how, leaving his younger brother confused and
fretful, fearing the Samson option had been chosen; and it suddenly lost all
glamour.

When Elie visited the palace for the last time he was given a farewell gift
which had to be brought home smuggled inside his shirt – his mother
would have needed only one glimpse to drop dead – and then, inside
the seclusion of their bedroom, he showed it to a trembling Smous. A
collection of Old Testament tales, written entirely in Russian!

Smous tried to make the appropriate gasps and grimaces of horror, but
in vain. The book was too beautiful. Its crimson leather binding was not
so much embossed as carved – you could dip your fingers into the furrows
and hold the rises in your palm – which made the pages seem to swell
beneath, and these were edged in a reddish gold, so that from the side the
book looked like a chunk of brass. Elie stroked the Russian title. 'It's an
unclean Bible,' he said, grinning in that way which had begun to frighten
Smous, 'and it's yours,' then hurried from the bedroom. Again Smous

searched for the terror he was supposed to feel, but again he failed, for now, flicking through the pages, which fell from the hand, thick and soft as cloth, he discovered the most astonishing thing – the Bible was illustrated.

Up until then he'd relied on a few woodcuts in Pinchvinch's cheder class as inspiration for his games with Issy, but these were frustrating: crude black outlines which you were expected to fill with your own imagination. The Russian Bible, however, had been illustrated by someone who was able to put onto paper all the varied and separate movements, dimensions, angles and space, sunlight and shadows of real life. Despite the Russian captions, the scenes were so perfectly drawn Smous could recognise them instantly, and the images exploded in his mind – whether the massive spectacle of the Red Sea Parting, or the small details like the beards on Assyrian warriors, worn oiled and wrapped in silver bindings, or the shockingly naked breasts hanging from the Queen of Sheba's handmaidens as they knelt before Solomon. But best of all was 'The Great Fish Vomiting Out Jonah Upon The Dry Land'. In spite of its tremendous size, the fish was able to lift itself right out of the water and lean towards the land to release Jonah. He rode out on the column of vomit, as on a bucking horse, legs gripped on either side, his face showing suitable surprise. From a hole in the monster's head a spray rose into the sky, though whether this was steam, sea water or more vomit the otherwise brilliant artist had failed to make clear.

Now Smous could think of nothing else. He was determined to create the scene in his games with Issy. But how? The image was far too fantastical to hold in his head, and he dare not remove the book from the bedroom, where it was hidden under a loose floorboard. It took several months to summon enough courage for the next step.

One hot afternoon, with Elie safely away, now learning to be a trader with their father, Smous stole into the bedroom and, with trembling fingers, carefully tore out that one page. As it came away in his hands a giant shiver passed through him. He was dismembering a Bible, a holy book, and yet one written in Russian, owned by the Dolroguskys, and probably priceless. Could anything be more wicked? He slipped the torn page into his jacket, hurried from the house and ran to the riverbank, certain that at any moment the hand of God, or Count Dolrogusky, Froi Immerman or Pinchvinch, would grasp the back of his neck.

The countryside had never seemed so frightening before. Down every track, under every bush, in every shadow, there lurked werewolves and laumés, or strange heathen gods with snakes and rainbow girdles. Those heavy slanting-stake fences, like barricades, how easily you could be impaled on their vicious, splintery ends. The tall fields of rye and šienas, turning dark or light as the clouds moved in the sky, how easily a child could be dragged into them, and from there into the forest, deeper and deeper, to that hidden land where only animals lived and all people perished. And the shrines at every crossroad, some with little closed doors (what was inside?), the wayside chapels, the crucifixes nailed on trees, these were terrifying to see; the writhing Christs and grieving Virgins, those rough-hewn mallet faces, those gouged eyes staring down at the road, demanding to know what a Jewish child was doing here.

Miraculously, Smous made it to their special field. Issy was waiting at the usual place, next to a collapsed water-mill which was occasionally used by shepherds or beggars. As soon as Smous saw its dark, round shape he knew it would be perfect for the Great Fish and set to work converting it, shouting the afternoon's plans over one shoulder. There was little point in showing Issy the picture since he couldn't see properly these days – he had started wearing pebble-glass spectacles and hadn't adjusted to the huge magnification yet; also they were too heavy and only stayed in place when he scrunched back his neck and wrinkled his nose, meaning that he could never look downwards, and was forever tripping or bumping into things.

The gaping doorway of the water-mill was perfect for the Fish's mouth, the little window served as an eye, even the mysterious jet from the head was easily achieved by lighting a fire in the crumbling chimney. The interior of the mill was black, damp and reeking: exactly, in fact, as he imagined the belly of a Great Fish to be. The only thing which remained beyond their invention was the gush of vomit, though Issy seemed quite relieved about that, and Smous had to be content with hurling himself out of the doorway making choking, gurgling noises.

There was a soft breeze brushing the field of long grass which became the ocean on which Jonah sailed to escape the Lord. Smous, of course, portrayed the prophet while Issy portrayed not only the entire crew of the ship, but also the voice of the Lord once Smous had been gulped into the hut. Issy's assumption of the Divine Presence was done by pulling his shirt over his head and summoning up an astonishingly deep voice, sounding not unlike his father Lazar. For a while Smous grew angry, wishing he had God Almighty for a father rather than the coughing, winking simpleton back at home; but his gloom passed, and when they had finished playing, many hours later, it was hard to deny the game that afternoon was the best they'd ever had.

It was dark by the time he reached the house and everyone began shouting the moment they saw him – delayed punishment, he assumed, for tearing the unclean Bible. He had forgotten it was Friday and had missed the weekly trip to the bath-house with the men, never more necessary than today, since he was coated in mud and grass-slime from the countless Great Fish vomitings. 'You can stay like that for another week, I don't care,' muttered his mother and then delivered her triple curse, 'only you . . . only you . . . only you . . .'

In the kitchen also were his two married sisters and their babies. 'My poor little darling,' said Sima to her infant, cupping her hand over its tiny nose, 'that you should have to smell such a disgusting boy so soon in your life!' However, it was his older sister, Golda, who made the most devastating remark; she looked at him steadily and said quietly, 'You're going to have to stop all this playing soon, you know, it's *puerile*.'

A few months later Golda and her family would move from Plungyan, settling in the town of Shkud twenty-seven miles to the north, and only returning once or twice a year, at Pesach or Rosh Ha-Shanah, or perhaps for a special occasion like Smous's bar mitzvah, Elie's wedding, Issy's a few years later, the circumcision of their firstborn sons. But for the most part she and Smous became strangers. Later in life he could only bring to mind the vaguest picture of Golda: a stocky figure like their mother, but with a rounder, sadder face and with hair worn in the Litvak style, plaited round her head like a wreath. And he would often think how odd it was that he hardly knew his older sister and yet a chance remark she once made changed his life.

'You're going to have to stop all this playing soon, you know, it's *puerile*.'

That evening continued in a routine way: the men returned from the bath-house, everyone trooped off to synagogue and then back to the house for the Shabbat rituals and meal, but Smous was in shock. 'Puerile' was not a word he understood, but the rest of what Golda said needed no explanation. 'You're going to have to stop all this playing soon, you know . . .'

That night Smous learned a new fact of life – to do with the passing of time – and he spent the meal trying to absorb the information, studying the adults around him in the wavering candlelight. His two sisters had certainly gone from childhood to adulthood without so much as a sideways glance; although still only in their teens they had babies of their own, plump bundles in their plump arms, and tended to sit heavily in their chairs, like the old women. Smous found both of their husbands peculiar:

one was round and bald, and laughed loudly at anything said by anyone, except Smous, while the other looked like a very thin, very mean crane and walked as though crushing eggshells. Next to Smous's parents at the table sat his ancient grandmother, his mother's mother, whom everyone called the Old Girl. She lived in a small dark room half way down the passage and only appeared at meal times. Her mouth was so sucked in it looked as though she carried a small lump under her nose, not unlike a dwarf's fist, which punched back and forwards as she chewed her food.

Finally there was Elie, already changed out of all recognition. Smous couldn't work it out: Elie had threatened that '*they* would be sorry', yet he was the only one who seemed to be suffering. He had grown bloated and sneering, boasting of his ability to drink any of the older men under the table, and grotesquely mimicking Jewish behaviour in a way which was doing little for his popularity in the town. 'Life is like a child's undershirt,' was his latest catchphrase, ' – short and soiled.'

These then were the adults, whose ranks Smous was invited to join.

He felt sure there must be wonderful things in their lives which were, so far, being kept hidden from him. The fact that they only showed their exhaustion, bitterness, worries – this was probably a test of some sort, daring him to investigate further. Otherwise they would all be playing on the banks of the Babrungas, that much was perfectly obvious. Nobody would choose to live as they did.

The next day was the sabbath and games were not allowed. Then on Sunday afternoon he made his way at the usual time to meet Issy, his heart very heavy. As his cousin was easily upset, Smous knew he would have to be brave and not break the news until afterwards. They considered playing Jonah and the Great Fish again, but there had been a rainstorm and more of the water-mill had collapsed so that it now looked nothing like a Great Fish, and Smous bleakly wondered if it ever had. Instead, they played Abraham and Isaac. Issy made the usual fuss as Smous forced him to stretch out on a flat stone, covered him with the sacrificial kindling and prepared to stab him; then the ram in the thicket was discovered – they used a half-eaten beaver – and offered up instead. The air was thick and hazy that afternoon, and a listless atmosphere hung over their game.

At last they were done, and had collapsed under some bushes. It was late and the afternoon was growing cool.

'We're going to have to stop playing like this, you know,' Smous said suddenly, 'it's puerile.'

Issy looked up with a start, so that the heavy eyeglasses dislodged from one ear and swung across his face, hitting his nose. Then, rearranging them, he said, 'Yes, my father was saying just that. Fine with me.' Smous was amazed – Issy was happily prepared to forgo these wonderful afternoons, he showed no regret, needed no persuading or consoling, and, worst of all, the decision had already been sanctioned by Uncle Lazar, God Himself. Smous suddenly noticed how big Issy's eyes were behind the pebble-glass. Adult eyes. Issy had already joined them! Fighting back tears, Smous told him the spectacles made him boring, that they were always covered in sweat and squashed midges, that if he wasn't careful he would grow up into as repulsive and hated a figure as Pinchvinch, that his mother and sisters had obviously deserved to die horribly in a fire, and that his father did too. Smous tensed as he saw 'Issy's Face' appear, those adult eyes sucked back, the popping noises starting in his throat – then Issy tore off the spectacles and stumbled away across the field. Smous sat alone among the cool, long shadows; the evening smelt of grass and of churned, black soil. He had a vague memory of a basin full of sweets, and heard the distant sound of a walled city crumbling.

In those moments he felt he'd made a terrible mistake, as though he'd been tricked into joining the adults and their lives of misery. He could never have imagined that some thirty years later he would be travelling to join Issy and Lazar on the other side of the world; or that on the voyage, standing alone on the deck early one morning, the air and water coloured in pale, fresh greys, he would actually see a Great Fish rising up from the deep – colossal yet weightless, a sort of dream, showing itself to him only – and that it would spray its jet of steam, water or vomit into the sky, tempting him to jump over the side and be eaten, which he almost did, so unique was the vision.

The Sugarhouse

An enormous woman sat crying on the sea shore.

'The Mommie!' cried Gommie, scrambling out of the carriage before it had stopped and loping through the wind towards her. She rose to her feet and they ran into one another's arms with a crash which left him spread-eagled across her front as if he had run into a wall.

She covered his head with kisses. 'Oh, you bastard . . . you gave me such a damn-bladdy fright, you bastard, you damn skukking bastard . . . how could I have lived without you?' Suddenly she dropped him from her arms. 'What are you playing at, hey? One of your slack-arsed, dull-in-the-skull chommies comes running in, says, "Haai, the Mommie, listen here – your man's dead!" I say, "Waalaa!" He says, "Jaaa, he's fallen to his death under the wheels of a cart!" I say, "Waalaa – it's never!" He says, "Jaaa, he's fallen headlong into the morning paper!"'

Gommie's hand danced around in the air, shushed his lips, pointed vaguely at the huge egg which had swollen out of the side of his head, as he said, 'Nay, but it's a true story – I was dead!'

'Hey!' She clouted him across the face. 'Don't start your skukking silly talk with me, hey?'

'Aai – don't!' he said, hitting her hand away.

'Don't what?' she said, clouting his face again. 'Don't what?'

'Don't, man! My head's still sore, man!'

'And my head's still sore crying for you,' she shouted, changing to a kicking attack. 'I've spent all our years together crying for you!' He attempted to scramble towards some steps leading to a wooden dwelling suspended on stilts above the beach, but she was there before him and kicked him towards the sea instead, the brown fat rippling over her body with each mighty swing of her leg.

In the carriage, Miller's hands opened and closed around the reins. The sensible thing would be to ride away as quickly as possible; on the other hand, Gommie had spoken of a grateful wife and a drink on the house. He wished life was simpler. From behind his back, Smous watched the fight in horror: had the nervous man survived the carriage accident only to be beaten, kicked and drowned by this female giant? Her hair was cut as short as her husband's, giving her a brutal, masculine look – until one of her immense breasts heaved out of the thin cotton dress. She picked up a length of kelp and, holding it like a whip, stood on the shore line blocking her husband's return to dry land. 'Right,' she shouted to him, 'I'm listening.'

Gommie was up to his knees in the surf, trying to defend himself with his little shushing finger. 'But it's a true story. The world comes and falls on me, I'm lying there dead – I'm so dead I can see myself lying there . . . I'm now floating like a ghost looking down at me dead.'

She started to cry again. 'What are you saying? Why do you talk useless like this, what's this bladdy-fool nonsense now?'

'I was given a lucky break. Look.' He held out the tooth he had saved from the accident. 'Swear to die, swear by God, it's a true story.'

'Swear by God? You never said two words to God before now – you think He cares if you swear by Him now?' She charged into the surf, lashing at him with the kelp.

'Not on the head, please – it's still sore . . . if you touch the head, you skukking bitch, I'll have to slay you dead!' He shrieked as he fell back into the churning water, 'I'm back, back from the dead! What more do you bladdy want?'

When the spray settled, Smous and Miller were surprised to see husband and wife in one another's arms, crying together and rocking in the wind. 'All our lives,' she was sobbing, 'all our lives you give me grief – that's all you ever give me, grief and a sore heart. We've got a good business, but you've still got to cheat and lie and thieve and you can't say two words but your tongue's blue with nonsense. It makes it hard for me, man!'

'But why?' he sobbed in return, 'why can you never ever believe me just one time? I'm telling you a true story. Ask them,' he said, pointing to the carriage, 'ask the Masters, they're the Masters who grabbed me from the jaws of sure and certain death.'

Miller and Smous tensed as the woman turned towards them and waded out of the surf. 'What's the story, gents?' she asked sweetly, one hand wiping away her tears, the other taking hold of the carriage wheel.

Miller cautiously told the story, summarising the original accident and greatly embellishing the rescue of Gommie. As Smous listened to the foreign language babbling on and on, he felt himself relaxing. There was nothing he could contribute, he was absolved from all responsibility and invisible again. From his viewpoint through the carriage hood, all he could see was the woman's one naked breast still hanging free, and a stretch of beach beyond it. In a morning already filled with sights utterly new to him, here were two more, a breast and a beach. As for the breast, he felt a familiar urge, to reach out and investigate the private parts of strangers, saying, 'So what's this you're keeping so secret, hmm?' Then, to his surprise, he saw someone else's hand grab hold of the breast; it took a moment before he realised that the hand was her own, pouring herself back into the dress. 'Come,' she was saying to them, 'I must thank you gents properly for bringing this slup-eyed fool back to me,' and she moved away, leaving Smous with a clear view of the dimpled beach.

Miller leapt from the carriage to hurry after her and the soaking Gommie. Smous hesitated, wondering if it was safe to leave his trunk, but the others were already climbing the wooden steps up to the blue-and-green slatted house above the beach. It was simpler to follow than to stay, so he followed.

The group reached a balcony draped with sheets drying in the wind. 'Sorry about all this, gents – it was a busy Saturday night,' said the woman, pushing her way through them, 'but you show me another sugarhouse in the colony that can brag this many sheets . . .'

Smous found himself inside a cloud of billowing linen; a smell of laundry soap, a glimpse of holes and tears, faint stains – then a girl's face blew into view. Totally bald, with a mouthful of clothes pegs. He thought these were fangs, and jumped. She turned away and vanished behind the sheets. Blinking, Smous followed the others through the doorway.

The room beyond was large and shadowy, lit only by reflections of water through the many windows, reminding Smous of the way snow lights a room from below – except that that was a still, dead light and this was fluid. The walls moved also, hung with curtains which shifted constantly, restlessly, in the wind; and a smell of stale tobacco, wine and cooking spices was carried on the draughts round the room.

The woman led the way through a maze of chairs, crates and old sofas, tin drums and barrels serving as tables. A few women and girls sat around in the gloom, barely distinguishable from the furniture.

'Hey!' she said, suddenly coming across a group of naked children on the floor, 'your daddie's not dead after all.' The children didn't look up – they were busy torturing a chicken, tightly bound with hemp. The eldest boy was sucking deeply on a pipe, an intent frown on his brow, his hands cupped over the bowl, as in prayer. The woman kicked him sharply. 'Hey, I said your daddie's not dead.' The boy took the tumble without a sound and looked up through clouded eyes. He seemed not to recognise his father.

'It's all right,' said Gommie, 'leave them.'

'No bladdy respect,' said the woman to Miller and Smous, 'those are our smallgoods,' and led on. Gommie slipped the tooth from the accident into his son's hand, whispering, 'Luck.' The boy pressed it into his pipe and pulled at the smoke.

The group reached an alcove where thin shafts of sunlight flickered through the rattling shutters onto a cane table around which they gathered. Smous darted for the window seat, concerned the others shouldn't smell him, shouldn't know that he wet his trousers when the soldier fired his rifle in the alley. He peered down at the sea splashing beneath him and felt he was flying.

'Pappie, look, Gommie's not dead after all,' said the woman now to an old, grey-skinned man who arrived at the table with bottles and glasses tinkling in his frail hands. Miller licked his lips eagerly and tried to help with the unloading, but the old man had been distracted by the woman's remark. His head shook with palsy as he squinted at Gommie with loose, syrupy eyes.

'Funny,' he said, 'there were all the signs we'd lose someone today. The sad dog next door was crying when I woke up. And the cupboard drawer was left open with the sheets showing. Yahm, funny. So – maybe it'll be me.'

'Then we'll see if we can spot the difference,' said the woman, chuckling, 'give us a damn-bladdy drink before everyone dies dry. I call him my Pappie', she informed Miller and Smous, ' . . . because he turns up one day and tells me that's what he is, but who can ever say with damn skukking Bastaards? My Mommie told me my Pappie was a slave and these don't look like a slave's hands to me.' She grabbed the old man's hands just as he was about to fill the glasses. Miller bit his lip in frustration.

'I was a slave,' said the old man, 'I was a wigmaker slave. So, wigs are soft on the hands.'

'I wouldn't have had a wigmaker slave for a Pappie, I wouldn't have had a little damn-bladdy Malay wigmaker – I'd have had a gorilla from Madagascar with some of the jungle still in his pants!'

'Yahm, well, you got me.'

The woman bubbled with laughter and rubbed one wrist through the fingers of her other hand, making squelching noises with her tongue.

'Skwoosh, skwish, skwesh,' came an echo from above them. Everyone looked up, except Miller, who snatched the chance to pour a drink. Hanging upside down from a beam on the ceiling was a grey parrot with a red tail. 'And that's His Majesty,' said the woman.

'He can say "Oh my!" like the English,' said Gommie. 'Listen.' He threw a peanut to the bird, shouting, 'Oh my!'

'Skwoosh, skwish, skwesh', said the bird, ignoring the nut which landed on Smous's upturned face.

'He's been saying that all morning,' said the woman. 'There was this Greek sailor here last night who likes to have the bird in the room when he's pumping a sugargirl. A few nights before there was a rain storm so then we had to listen to the damn thing saying "Drip, drip, plop, plop" all the next morning.'

'Or maybe that was just a different sailor,' suggested Gommie, grinning.

'Can't it fly away?' asked Miller, refreshed by the drink.

'Oh, ja,' said Gommie, 'we had to break one of its wings.'

'Skwoosh, skwish, skwesh,' said the bird.

The old, grey-skinned man had finally succeeded in pouring the drinks. 'This is Mommie Gommie's perfume, gents,' said the woman, holding up a glass of the opaque, oily liquid. 'Best Hottnot hot tot in the Colony.'

'And listen,' said Gommie, 'you mustn't listen to the stories that we put dead cats and puppies into it, hey?'

'Nay,' laughed Mommie Gommie, 'those we save for the curries.'

The old man lifted his drink with both hands, and, holding it towards Gommie, proposed a toast: 'So, cheating the Devil!'

'Cheating the Devil!' repeated Gommie smiling, and touched the lump on his head.

'Cheating the Devil!' said his wife and Miller.

'Cheedidah!' said the parrot.

'Cheemmm . . .' mumbled Smous. Everyone looked towards him and Miller quickly explained, 'Turkish.'

'Ah,' said the others. They were used to every nationality passing through their home and, knowing better than to attempt conversation, abandoned him to silence. The old man wandered off back into the shadows, and the others settled down to drink and talk.

Watching their mouths, Smous wondered what language the Gommies used. It was as though they were singing rather than speaking; the sounds swooped through the air, bouncing and snapping. He cautiously sipped his drink, then had to swing away so that nobody could see his eyes water. Through the blur he noticed a figure enter the room – the bald girl who had been pegging sheets on the balcony. She wandered listlessly among the furniture, with downcast eyes and open lips. The shape of her head was remarkable: its crown was flattish, the line curving outwards to wide, sharp cheekbones, then tapering to a pointed chin. Like a diamond. Although she was no taller than a child, her body was adult, clearly visible through a thin, turquoise dress. Her skin was a dusty yellowish-brown, quite different from the hazel-coloured family around the table.

Suddenly the naked children surrounded her, pinching her calves and biting her ankles, crying, 'Speak like the beetles, speak like the birds!'

Mommie Gommie shouted, 'Leave her! How would you like it if I did that to you?' grabbing the nearest child and biting it on the arm. 'Now give her a smoke and leave her alone!' The oldest boy passed over his pipe unsteadily, and the bald girl squatted on her haunches to smoke, making the short dress ride up and reveal her thighs. Smous glimpsed a fold between them, either flesh or cloth. He swallowed a giggle – 'Np!' – then turned back to the table sharply, unable to stare as he had at the breast on the beach. He gulped his drink and tried to focus on the group round him. Miller was holding forth:

'Forty-odd years I've been driving, so nobody can tell me about accidents. First of all, what folk don't realise is that it's much worse for the man driving the vehicle than the pedestrian he's crashed into – it's much harder for the driver to get over the shock, see, and then he's so cut up, before you know it, he's crumped someone else. Still, it's part of the job – you're going to smash a few folks' limbs, you're going to put out an eye or two, and we does, and we does, no point fretting on Sundays, but I've never ghosted anyone, and I just want to say I'm happy we can all be sitting here now because fate came up with a bit for us all today . . .'

'Just as well,' Mommie Gommie chuckled, 'a lot of the crushers use my sugarhouse – they'd have tracked you down, given you to me, I'd have torn out your insides, and given my children an air-bladder to carry at their Daddie's funeral.'

Miller gulped, and raised his glass. 'Cheating the Devil!'

'Cheating the Devil!' said the others, and the parrot.

' . . . Ifs and buts – that's accidents,' continued Miller as he refilled his glass, hoping such familiarity was in order, '*if* I hadn't picked up the Turk for a tour of the Colony, *if* my usual drag hadn't been blocked by those bastard repair works, so on and so forth . . . you can go back and back with the bitching ifs. Through the whole morning, last night, yesterday afternoon, day before that – I mean, take for example, *if* my stupid, scumming folks had only stayed put in England all those years ago . . .'

'I was just mecked,' said Gommie.

'What?'

'Meck-necked and slup-eyed – that's me – that's me again and again! So I fell under your cart. What's that got to do with the Turk or the repair works?'

Miller hesitated. He had been warming to his theme – the illusiveness of destiny – a discourse he had given many times over the years and which always won people's respect and pity, their generosity, their awed silence at the very least. He made a farting noise with his tongue and glared at Gommie who was sitting forward, rocking in his chair. Mommie Gommie turned to her husband with a despairing sigh and said, 'The man is talking wisdom, Waalaa! Not facts.'

'Oh, wisdom,' said Gommie and threw the nearest bottle into the air. It landed with a crash and the parrot said 'Skwish!'

'Hey!' said Mommie Gommie, 'what you bladdy-well go do that for?'

'Wisdom. I'm slupping too much again,' said Gommie smiling, his eyelids blinking rapidly.

'And since when did that give you grief?'

'Since now. God's given me my warning and I'm heeding it.'

'And what all this skukking talk about God all of a sudden?'

'He's shown me the error of my ways. Everyone schemes they know me by heart. I walk down the street and you can now see it in people's eyes. They look at me and think they know everything. "Give him a drink, give him a smoke, end of the story." Why do they think that when they see me? I don't think that when I see them. I think they're full of changes, ups and downs, surprises, all the everythings. How can they be so sure just because that's how I was yesterday that's how I'll be tomorrow? I can be anything, anything they are. All my life I've been stealing from them because they never saw me coming – it's so easy, man, it's like laughing. They must be careful, I'll climb into them and never get out – I'll slay them all, they must watch out – they don't know me by heart.'

'Stealing?' laughed Mommie Gommie, 'he'll take a vase of flowers out of a window and call it stealing. And even then he'll get caught and I'll have to pay off the crushers. Slaying? He'll set his dog on an old beggar asleep in the gutter and he'll call that slaying.'

'How come you're so dead-damn sure?' demanded Gommie.

Mommie Gommie yawned and stretched. 'Don't start, hey?'

'"Don't start, hey?" How do you know what I'm going to start or not?'

'Because I'm the one who does know you by heart. But I love you all the same, so have another drink and shush, hey.'

Gommie paused, glaring at her, then frantically mimicked shushing himself, and turned to the others. 'Who else would marry such a damn-bladdy fat and ugly person, hey?'

She blushed – her brown skin bruising – and bowed her head, pushing up her lower lip until it kissed her nose. Gommie sighed, pitying her, hating himself, then shrugged, found a drink and gulped it down. 'Cheating the Devil!' he shouted and poured himself another.

'Cheating the Devil!' said the others.

'Cheedidah!' agreed the parrot.

Smous glanced up at the bird hanging from the ceiling. He could have sworn he heard it speak several times, yet he wondered if this was the drink, which was spreading to the tips of his fingernails, making them feel heavy. Then again, he thought, these people are laying on so many novelties, I wouldn't put this past them – a talking bird. He looked away from the parrot and immediately heard it whistle. His head shot up again, expecting to see the beak pursed forward, but the bird's face was as blank as before, one frozen, yellow eye fixed on him. He stared hard at the beak and caught a glimpse of a busy, wet, human tongue within, stumpy and black. Disgusted, he looked away and this time heard the bird go, 'Tsk, tsk.' He sat drinking and frowning, wondering whether this ghost-grey, upside-down creature really could be mocking him? Now, as he looked around the table it occurred to him that everyone might be joining with the bird in some huge practical joke: they didn't understand this babble they spoke any more than he did, but were pretending they did, pretending to talk – but if you looked closely you could see what was really going on; the nods, the raised eyebrows, the smiles, you could clearly see it was all just a conspiracy to humiliate him. Perhaps because he was Jewish, perhaps because he was stinking and had wet his pants? Suddenly everybody laughed, confirming his fears. He took a larger gulp of his drink and, through the bottom of the glass, watched them turn towards him.

'Give – me – your – pamphlet,' said Miller slowly and loudly, and when Smous shrugged he mimed unrolling something and reading.

'Ah!' said Smous and produced his English scroll.

'Ag, no,' said Mommie Gommie, 'now who the hell can read?' She scanned the room and bawled, 'Koos – you in here?'

'Ja, miss.' Across the room a pale hand rose out of the shadows. A man was sitting on the floor between the knees of a black-skinned woman who was patiently plaiting his shoulder-length blond hair into the same style as her own – long, tight fronds – which reminded Smous of the earlocks worn by Pious Ones. Now, as the man waved to them, Miller and Smous noticed he didn't have any legs. The position on the floor was his full height.

'Hullo there,' he called, 'the name's Koos Visser. You've heard of the Boer War? Well, I'm the Boer. That's why we lost.' He gave a wheezing laugh. The black woman stopped plaiting his hair and said, 'Yoh, Koos, I warned you what I'd do if you told that one again,' and hit him hard across the back. His little body fell forward, hit the floor and sprang back like the branch of a bush, while he wheezed with delight.

'That's Mister Visser,' explained Mommie Gommie, 'very smart skull. Was even at the university before the war. He says his legs was shot off and torn off and tortured off by the English, but he's such a bladdy-fool joker you never know if you must believe him or nay.' Visser wriggled free from between the black woman's legs and scuttled across the room, the stumps of his legs opening and closing like a claw. He collected a chair on the way and flicked himself into it, arriving at the table the same height as everyone else, grinning and panting. With his hair half-plaited and his heavy straw beard, his head looked lop-sided, but his young face was finely shaped and its light sharp.

'What is it that wants reading and in what language?' he asked. The scroll was pushed towards him. 'English? Ag, what a lovely language, lovely people, always so nicely turned out from top to tail – lovely haircuts, lovely saddles – ja, oh so polite, talk about the weather, call you "sir" even when they're prising off your toenails.'

'Nobody wants to hear your war stories again, Koos', said Mommie Gommie, 'just read the skukking words.'

'Quite right, quite right, what could be more boring than my war stories? My war jokes I suppose.' He grinned at Miller and Smous, then bent over the latter's scroll. '"Kind sir or madam" – see how polite the English language is? "My name is Zeev Immerman . . ."'

Zeev Immerman. Even though the pronunciation was distorted, these were the first words Smous had understood since arriving in the country, and he had a sudden pang of loneliness. He fingered his empty glass and Mommie Gommie filled it, asking, 'What's the man's name again?'

'Immerman,' said Visser.

'Sounds like a stutter,' laughed Gommie, 'im–mer–mer–mer . . .'

'Calvinia!' cried Visser. 'He's heading for Calvinia. Wise choice, Mister Immerman.'

'Your part of the world, Koos,' said Mommie Gommie.

'Ja no, I'm a bit further over Beaufort West way. But it's a beautiful part of the world, the Little Karoo. A wasteland, a wilderness, but beautiful. Like in the Bible. God's wilderness. Now, where does Mister Immerman hail from originally?' he said, returning to the scroll.

'Turkey,' said Miller briskly.

'And yourself?' asked Visser suddenly turning to him. 'Mister . . . ?'

'Miller. No, I'm from here.'

'English?'

'No, no. Wish I was.'

'You wish you were English?' asked the Boer with a polite smile.

Miller blinked. 'Uhn . . . no, I said I wished I *wasn't*. My folks were. Stupid glocks! Me, I hate the English. Like you do. You hate them, I hate them. No, I'm from here, I'm South African.'

'And where was your heart during the war, Mister Miller? If you'll pardon a person asking. Where was your South African heart during the Anglo-Boer War?'

'War? Ifs and buts,' said Miller, laughing slightly, wondering why he felt threatened by a man who, if the need arose, would be unable to give chase.

'Nobody wants to talk about the skukking war, Koos,' growled Mommie Gommie.

'Quite right, quite right,' said Visser, his eyes twinkling, 'we were talking about the Karoo. Now – in the war, Mister Miller, the English fought us for the Karoo amongst other places, although they have no chance of surviving there. Drought – year in, year out. God's wilderness. You've only got two choices: you must either become a god yourself, or a beast. And, with due respect, Mister Miller, the English haven't got either in them. You're all so very jolly damned civilised.'

'I was born *here*,' protested Miller.

'On the other hand, me and her,' Visser pointed to the bald girl with the pipe, squatting nearby, 'we're another story altogether. Ja, we're from the wilderness.'

Mommie Gommie stretched over and drew the girl up into her lap, saying, 'Koos travels upcountry for us and found her there . . .'

'What else can the poor war-wounded do?' said Visser, grinning.

'We've only had her a few days. Haven't even thought of a name yet.'

'She's from Bushmanland – just north of where Mister Immerman is heading.'

Smous heard his family name again and looked up. The fat woman had the bald girl in her lap, and was stroking her. The girl's diamond-shaped face was blank, its light dull, her body rigid – except low on her ribs, where she panted. As the naked children gathered round her, Smous involuntarily pulled his knees away from the nearest little girl – there was mucus hanging from her chin, and pink sores on her brown back. The children's heavy eyes flickered with curiosity. 'Make her talk like the beetles,' they cried in slurred voices, 'make her talk like the birds.'

'Ag, you know she won't when we ask her,' said Mommie Gommie, 'she'll do it on her own when she wants.'

Visser smiled. 'The children are making a common error, Mister Miller, Mister Immerman. Because she's so well adapted to living on the land and *with* the land they think of her as a beast. Never, it's not so. There is still an enormous gap between her and even the highest of the brute creations. And actually what I find interesting is her relationship with animals. Because she and her people have never farmed them, they are capable of the most atrocious cruelty.'

'How? What?' cried the children.'

Visser looked at Mommie Gommie. 'I told you I found her wandering round the veld. That's not true. There's a story . . .' He stretched over to the girl and gently removed the pipe from between her fingers. Now when he spoke it was in a quiet voice which made everyone lean forward. 'I was staying on a friend's farm. Her little band had been raiding the livestock, so we mounted a commando like in the good old days when the only wars we had to fight were with the Bushmen. Commandos like that are illegal now, so you mustn't tell your friends in the garrison, Mister Miller . . .'

'I haven't got any –'

'I'm sure you haven't. My little joke, forgive me please. Anyhow, I just went along for the ride, strapped to my horse there, wearing more tack than him.' He wheezed with laughter. 'Now, when Bushmen are in danger of being overtaken with stolen livestock, they do a terrible thing . . .' He paused to take a deep puff from the pipe.

'What? What?' cried the children, hopping up and down.

Visser let out the smoke in a long, thin stream. 'They riot on the stock.'

'Whass' mean?' asked the eldest boy.

'Mutilate them.'

'Whass' mean?'

'Hurt them. Viciously.'

'How? What?'

Visser smiled teasingly. 'Anyhow, as you can imagine, the farmers in the commando were a little bit upset to see animals they had raised so carefully – not an easy job in that part of the world, nê? – to see them mutilated so savagely. Ja, so when we tracked down the thieves to their village, we rounded them up . . . I say we, but of course mean they, the rest of the commando. My disability exempted me from such strenuous activities. I was just an observer to the events which followed . . .' He paused to puff again at the pipe.

'What happened? What happened?' screamed the children, 'were they all skukked and popped?'

'They would have been. Great sin would have been committed that day, no, that's for certain. But the penalties and fines imposed by the English are so severe now for that sort of thing, the commando was forced to show restraint.'

'Awww,' the children groaned.

'Ja, I'm afraid so. Instead, they simply rioted on the Bushmen as the Bushmen had rioted on the livestock, and inflicted injury for injury in the time-honoured biblical tradition. A few of the children and the older girls, like her, were exempted and distributed among the farmers, otherwise the rest were all rioted on, in one way or another.'

'Rioted – how?' asked the children in hushed tones.

'Ag no, don't ask me, I'm too squeamish. I had to look away. As she did, too, of course, sitting behind me on my horse where she was also strapped now – we were like a big gift tied up there together. So, thanks to the civilising influence of the English, no life was taken that day. Blood was, of course, spilled, but no life, thankfully, was lost.'

'And won't they pop later?' asked the eldest boy. 'From all the blood?'

'I wouldn't have thought so, no. They'll adapt to their disfigurements as they've adapted to all the other hardships in their part of the world. You have to admire their tenacity, it's remarkable.'

'Why doesn't she want to go back to them?' asked a little girl, 'why doesn't she run away from us?'

'She doesn't know she can. She has no idea where she is, so how can she run away? From where? To where? She only knew her own territory – the few surrounding miles where her little band lived. She knew those people and perhaps a few of the neighbouring bands. Beyond that, even other Bushmen wouldn't speak the same tongue as her. Do you know what the Bushmen call themselves, what their word for themselves is?'

'What?' asked the children.

'There isn't one.' Visser wheezed with laughter. 'They have no word for "Bushmen" because they don't think of themselves like we do. Like I'm a Boer and you're a Bastaard and Mister Miller's a . . . South African. Everyone beyond this girl's little band, now so distinctively branded by the commando, everyone else, every other Bushman tribe, all the other native nations, all of us lot here and indeed all the people in the whole wide world, all are strangers.' He gently returned the pipe to her fingers, as all went quiet. The group round the table imagined that they were in the presence of a being from another planet, and felt inspired by it. Mommie Gommie wondered if there was any exotic Bushman blood in her own past; Miller tried to imagine what the girl would be like to touch; and the children tried to imagine the wounds on her family.

The sudden silence drew Smous back to the table as surely as the endless babble had sent his gaze drifting away. Now, he saw the bald girl look up for the first time and rest her eyes on him. The light in her face was so particular that, like the others round the table, he thought, It's like looking at the moon. Then she opened her mouth and, fearing she would greet him, he quickly looked away.

' . . . Immerman . . .'

Hearing his family name, he searched among the group for the speaker.

' . . . near where you're going in the Karoo, Meneer Immerman . . .' It was Visser, now speaking in Afrikaans. Smous was intrigued by the new, guttural sounds, and for an instant thought he was hearing Yiddish with a foreign accent. ' . . . The mountains are so big they make the Table Rock look like a pebble. And the sky. The sky is so damned big there, man, day and night. A person can ride for miles in the moonlight. God, the freedom it gives you! I was born there, Meneer Immerman, so forgive me if I'm a little biased. You must give my love to Calvinia,' he said and gently touched that word on the English scroll.

Glancing down, Smous saw two large teardrops fall round Visser's finger onto the parchment. He stared with horror as some of the words began to disintegrate into little black puddles, and instantly heard his mother's voice in one ear: 'We spend a fortune having the document done nice for you and what happens? – the first legless cripple you meet, you lend it to him for a handkerchief! Only you . . .' But then, snatching back the scroll, Smous realised it was not Visser crying, but Gommie.

'Right,' Gommie said, wiping his eyes, 'we're going there.'

'What? Where? Who?' asked Mommie Gommie.

'Calvinia. With Mister Im-mer-mer.'

'What for?'

'Farming.'

'Farming?'

'Start a new life.'

'You haven't got the education to farm, you damny-bladdy fool!'

'What education do you need? You reach down and grab hold of the ground. It's in our blood, in our Hottentot blood.'

'My blood,' said Mommie Gommie, stretching languorously, 'my blood is the yellow blood, the cruel, yellow blood of a handsome hunter from Bushmanland.'

'Ja, well on your mother's side then,' said Gommie rising. 'If you don't want to ding along it's up to you. I'm going to pack.'

Hoping Gommie was heading for the outhouse, Smous shot to his feet. Mommie Gommie reached up and pulled him back, saying, 'Don't worry about my damn-bladdy madman. He's just slup-eyed, he's not going dinging with you to the Karoo, don't worry.' Smous sat, breathing heavily, wondering if the others could tell how drunk he was.

'So, uhh . . .' Miller said and pointed to the bald girl, 'what's she doing here then?'

Mommie Gommie gave a bubbling laugh. 'Having a holiday by the sea.'

'No, I mean, when we arrived she was hanging out washing, I mean, is that the only work she does here?'

'Nay. But she's still wild, man. Be like trying to pump a cat or seagull!'

'Or a chicken,' said Visser, as one suddenly scampered noisily across the table, 'which can be very pleasurable. If you're stranded on a lonely farm.'

'Ag, Koos!' laughed Mommie Gommie, and tickled the girl's smooth head. 'We had to shave her when she arrived,' she told Miller, watching his purple face grow hotter as he stared at the girl, 'covered in lice and goggas, smelling old, like the veld . . .' She stopped, watching the man's puffy, scarred features turn his longing into something painful. 'Hey!' she laughed, 'Ag *siss*, put it away.'

Miller looked up. 'Huhn?'

'Your face was hanging out, man.'

He dropped his head and muttered, 'So, what're you asking?'

'Ag, no, man,' she said, but Miller dug out the notes Smous had paid as the fare, and asked again:

'What're you asking?'

'I'm telling you she won't be any good.'

'Funny thing to say. You'll talk yourself out of a customer.'

'What do you know about me?' she asked sharply and then watched intrigued as the hefty man looked away, ducking his head, easily cowed, muttering under his breath and scooping up the notes. She laughed at him. 'Hey, don't look so sad, mad and bad, chommie. You're going to get your heart's desire, your dream come true, I just don't want your money.'

Miller peered at her suspiciously. 'Why not?'

'Owe you a favour for helping my madman. If your idea of slappy-happy times is a wobble in the dark with a wild animal then be my guest.'

Visser laughed and said, 'Hell, you're letting the Mommie off lightly.' Miller glanced around shiftily.

'What's the catch?' he asked eventually, 'the ins and outs? What's the if and the but this time?'

Mommie Gommie laughed. 'You must trust people more, man.'

'How do you know? You don't know anything about me either.' He felt confused, excited, unsure whether he was getting what he wanted or being mocked. 'I don't need nothing for nothing, no fretting on that score, so don't pick me out, just don't pick me out – fair enough?'

She looked at him calmly – he was more familiar now and bored her. 'Look, it's not a favour – it's a present. We'll do some feeding and then you'll go to paradise – if you want – or maybe nay, it's up to you, we must just all flop free, hey? Jaaa, Waalaa, happy times, happy times!'

The old grey-skinned man had arrived at the table with a rattling tray of food; pots of steaming rice, bowls of curried mince, crisp pastries shaped in triangles and plaited snakes. Mommie Gommie pushed the bald girl off her lap, and began to dish out portions. Miller chewed his tongue, deciding it was best to say no more, and sat back. Smous, meanwhile, was shifting to the edge of his seat, the juices almost spilling from his mouth. He had not eaten since the previous night. It was only as his own plateful arrived in front of him that a terrible question arose. *Was the meal kosher?*

Kosher? He realised with a shock that he knew very little about the subject. It was such a common fact of life back in Plungyan, and so totally the domain of the womenfolk, he had no more cause to question it than to ask, 'What's in the air today?' Staring down at the meal now, he knew well enough not to eat the meat, but what about the rest? Was there such a thing as kosher rice? Steam rose from the plate in spicy aromatic wisps which curled flirtatiously through his beard and into his nostrils. He felt ill. Days of enforced fasting lay ahead unless he could find a solution.

At that moment the old man returned to the table with a plate of bananas to chop into the curry, a fruit which Smous had never seen before. 'Yellow sausages,' he said quietly to himself, 'that's it, I'm finished,' and staggered from the table.

'Where's Mister Immerman going?' asked Visser.

'Slup-eyed,' said Mommie Gommie, her face a balloon of food.

Smous wove his way through the clutter of furniture to the doorway. Outside the wind had dropped and the rows of sheets hung in suffocating stillness. He fought his way through them roughly, forgetting he was on a balcony – and in the next moment found himself flying through the air. He had time to smile and think – Silly thing to do! – before hitting the beach below. He looked at the imprint his face had made in the soft sand: there was even the trace of his moustache turned upwards in a smile. It's like snow, hot snow, he thought, and struggled to his knees. The sun felt as if it was leaning on his head with all its force. What was I going to do? Why have I come out here? he wondered – then remembered, clambered to his feet and stumbled into the shadow beneath the house. It was as cool as diving under water. He leaned against one of the wooden supports and urinated into the sand, murmuring, 'Uhhhhh . . .'

He delved into the crotch of his underclothes and squeezed the linen. It was so drenched in sweat he couldn't locate the patch he had wet when the soldier fired his rifle in the alley. He sniffed his fingers. Still difficult to tell, everything smelt fetid. 'Too bad, who cares?' he said and gave his bowels a quick squeeze to see if there was any sign of a breaththrough there. 'No,' he concluded, 'and with days of starvation ahead not much hope for the future either.'

Making his way back into the blazing sunlight he struggled out of his overcoat and slung it over one shoulder. Far along the beach he could see the dockyards, even the ship which had brought him all this way. He wondered whether to walk along the beach and ask if they had any kosher food left, but it was too far away. Raising his hand he found he could hold

the distant vessel on his palm like a toy. For three weeks this was the whole
world, he thought. He stared at it, recalling the family of Pious Ones on
board who insisted on cooking their own meals instead of eating with the
rest of the Jewish passengers, refusing to trust that the food was truly
kosher, even though the loading at Southampton had been supervised by
an English rabbi and there was a special kitchen in the galleys. Instead,
this family sat on the deck boiling water and concocting soups out of
lumps of goosefat, onions and matzos they had brought with them.
Watching them, people would shake their heads and say, 'They give us a
bad name, no wonder the sailors think we're animals.'

And here I am, thought Smous, starving but not eating – just as
ridiculous. He strolled over to the carriage to check his trunk and noticed
that the horse was suffering in the heat, its neck drooping, its tongue
hanging out. He looked round for water and saw the ocean, so staggered
towards it, knelt down and cupped his hands. How cold it was – icy cold.
How could that be, in this heat? It felt so refreshing, maybe it was
drinkable? He brought his hands to his mouth and had just choked on the
taste, when Gommie's face popped round his shoulder. The man was
carrying a small canvas bag and his eyes were flickering wildly.

'That's right. Slup, man, slup,' he said, 'whole sea to slup dry. The
Mommie says slup, everyone says slup. One time I go work on a fruit farm,
the man doesn't pay me with money, he pays me with tots of brandywine. I
say, "How'm I going to buy things for my children with tots?" He says, "At
least they'll have sweet dreams – slup, boy, slup." You should see me and
my chommies slup. Yells bells, jur-ruh! Watch out – The Red Links!' He
showed Smous a small red tattoo on his wrist, a cufflink. 'Silly, hey? Like
children and soon we're old men. Know what the latest thing is? Don't use
knives any more, nay, the latest thing is dogs – sharpen their teeth. Bite a
hole in your head so you can see the sky. Clever, hey? Who thought of
such a damn clever thing? Me. Anyhow, the crushers came and shot the
dogs. Don't matter now. I'm coming with you, packed my bag and brought
a Bible for us. But look –' He lifted a thick, battered Bible out of the bag and
opened it, showing a large hole scooped out of the centre. Smous thought of
the Russian Bible, the unclean Bible, and of the day he'd torn out Jonah
and the Great Fish, then quickly flicked his head.

'Someone's been carrying things in here,' said Gommie in disgust, 'a
sin, hey? What's so secret a person must carry it in a Bible? Tots? Dogs'
teeth? Bad sin. They'll get sick. Maybe it was me. We're all going to be
sick if we don't move on to the Karoo.' He rubbed the lump on his head

like a magic stone. 'Either God's made me sick already, or He's growing me a new head. Hurts, man. Hurts with all the new thoughts I'm thinking – I want to go and tell her how it hurts, but she'll just say, "Nay, huh-uh, no, it doesn't hurt, I've heard them all before, all your new thoughts. I know you better than you know you, slup, man, slup." So, we'll just have to go without her.'

Those eyes, quivering and winking, those desperate grins, the jerky, coughing speech – it could be Her Immerman. Smous rose and fled, stumbling, across the beach to the steps.

He found the sugarhouse filled with Oriental sailors, Mommie Gommie sitting in the middle, head in her hands. 'The sooner that damn-bladdy Chinese ship sets sail again,' she was saying, 'the happier I'll be. Right,' she said, rising to her feet, 'how many of you today?' One of the sailors held the fingers of both hands together in a little fan, and another man added three more. 'Thirteen?' she said. 'I should keep rabbits instead of sugargirls, you lot would never know!' She turned and bawled across the room, 'All right, how many are at work today?'

The black-skinned woman with plaited hair rose to her feet. 'Don't know,' she said lazily, 'some came in and went to sleep.'

'Sleep? *Sleep?*' shouted Mommie Gommie as she stormed across the room and walked straight through the wall. One of the sailors leapt into the air and hurried after her, also to be swallowed by the wall. Smous stared at the spot, blinking, then realised the place was hung with curtains; they looked solid without the wind to agitate them. He wove his way through the chattering sailors back to the alcove; the children were screeching, chasing the chickens round the furniture; the parrot was rocking excitedly from the ceiling, whistling, squeaking and purring.

At the table Miller was clutching the bald girl's arm. 'Will there be enough tail for them all?' he asked vaguely in Smous's direction. Smous smiled, shrugged, and sat. Visser looked up from the remnants of his meal and grinned teasingly. 'I knew there'd be a scumming catch,' muttered Miller. 'Ifs, buts! Ins, outs! Fret, frut! Tricks, tracks!'

Smous found the bald girl staring at him and again had the feeling she was going to speak. He looked away sharply and drank from his glass, wondering if there was such a thing as kosher alcohol.

Women and girls, young and old, black, pink and brown-skinned, yawning and stretching, drifted into the room from doorways behind every curtain. Then Mommie Gommie crashed back into the centre, followed by the Chinese sailor who was jabbering excitedly. Ignoring him, she grabbed the nearest child and said, 'Climb across to Mister and Missus Gool's balcony and if they've finished feeding, ask if their two daughters can come and do half an hour's work.' The child scampered away towards the doorway. 'But only if they've finished feeding!' bawled Mommie Gommie, then turned to the jabbering sailor. 'Right. I've maybe got twelve for you, maybe, maybe, but that's the bang-stop-finish. Nothing I can do about it. So maybe one of you is going to miss out, or maybe two of you is going to share. Up to you.' The sailor was hopping up and down furiously, shouting in Chinese. 'They don't understand,' said Mommie Gommie with a despairing sigh and sat at the table.

Miller was fingering the bald girl's arm. 'Look,' he muttered unhappily to Mommie Gommie, 'if you need her, if it's not a bone thing that I . . .' He chewed his tongue, cursing his parents for teaching him their English manners. Before Mommie Gommie could reply, the sailor leaned on the table, and, struggling to form the word in English, eventually said, 'Cheats!'

'What did you say?' asked Mommie Gommie, swinging towards him.

'Cheats!'

'Haai, who's a cheat, you skukking Chinese bastard?'

'Cheats! Cheats!' shouted the sailor. 'Cheeees! Cheeees!' echoed the parrot from the ceiling.

Mommie Gommie rose to her feet, towering over the Chinaman. 'Hey, nobody calls me that!'

"Cheats! Cheeees! Cheats! Cheeees!' cried the sailor and the parrot.

'Say that once again,' she roared, 'and you're out. I don't need your skukking business, hey? I don't need you stinking up my place with your knobs like bamboo splinters and your eyes like babies' pussies. Now I'm doing my best to get you a dozen sugargirls, and if that doesn't fit your plans – hook it!' Cowed by her noise, the sailor returned to his fellows and they conferred in their own language:

'What's the matter?'

'There aren't sheets on the beds and every time I say sheets in English she gets angry.'

'We'll do without.'

'Have you seen how dirty the beds are?'

'Keep the girls underneath.'

'Ah, but so boring.'

'Shing-shung-shoo-shoo, hing-hah,' mimicked the parrot.

'It talks Oriental!' shouted Smous, and everyone turned to him, amazed to hear him speak for the first time. 'It did! I saw it . . . I'm sorry, I'm sorry you can't understand me, but . . . a talking bird, it's incredible, believe me, I've never seen anything like it.'

'Gezz-in, gezz-in, klei-klei,' said the parrot, now imitating the Yiddish sounds, and the children screamed.

'He also wants a girl,' said Visser, laughing. 'Hee-aww, hee-aww, hee-aww' sang the parrot. Mommie Gommie threw a plate at the bird, but it swung out of the way effortlessly.

'Oh my!' cried Gommie, pushing through the crowd of sailors and girls, and stood underneath the bird. 'Say *Oh my*!, Your Majesty . . . *Oh my*! . . .' But the parrot went still, staring at him with one eye. 'Stupid fool,' said Gommie and sat next to Smous, clutching the canvas bag. 'Ready whenever you are Mister Im-mer-mer, next stop – Calvinia.' Smous shifted away from the strange man and poured himself another drink, wishing he could eat something to soak up the liquid. He struggled to focus his eyes.

Visser's face was leaning in, saying, 'The Mommie will give you a girl if you want.'

'Sure,' sighed Mommie Gommie. 'Help yourself. Skukking Chinese bastards.'

Miller could bear it no longer. 'But what about me?' he whined.

Mommie Gommie looked surprised. 'I thought we said you'd have the wild animal.'

Miller's face lit up. 'You mean it's still a bone deal?'

She shrugged impatiently. 'Trust people more, man.'

Visser kept grinning at Smous. 'Well, Mister Immerman, anything here that takes your fancy?'

Smous knew from the man's face what was being offered, so he replied, 'Thank you, but I'm saving myself till marriage.'

The children crowded round him, screaming, 'What did he say? What did he say?'

One of the sugargirls dislodged herself from a sailor's clutch to enquire 'Boys – does he prefer boys?' She had a husky voice and hairy arms.

Visser laughed and asked, 'Chickens? Maybe he likes chickens? They're the best, man. What you do is this: you carefully trap the head in a cupboard drawer, then you put your . . .'

His face disappeared from view as Mommie Gommie clouted him off his chair, laughing, 'Ag, Koos, you kill me!' and presented Smous with a

Cape of Good Hope 75

view of her toothless gums bunched together like a pink sandwich. Next to her the bald girl opened and closed her mouth like a fish. Visser's head shot back into view, wheezing with laughter, the children screamed, and the Chinamen ran among the girls, selecting their partners.

Who are these people, wondered Smous; though he was sure of one thing – they were not as alien as they had seemed earlier. This was not the first time a crowd had made him giddy with their signalling arms and grimacing faces, groans and grunts and sighs of approval, the trading of shoves and touches, making contact, missing chances, spelling things out, dropping a hint, everything made simple, nothing made clear. For much of his life he had felt confused by this, ever since that evening on the banks of the Babrungas when Issy fled home crying and he was left sitting alone on the cool, churned field. Ever since then he had found himself peering suspiciously at jabbering crowds like this one, working themselves into such a frenzy that eventually they froze in mid-air, like a huge cut-out, still and lifeless, screaming silently, waiting for him to step in and either lose himself or rescue them.

He struggled to his feet, eager to know what would happen, but was distracted by a movement beyond them. The curtains on the walls were shifting as the wind started up again; some were thick and velvety, others of fraying silk, there were string curtains and ones made of wood and bark; all began to move according to their weight – the heavy ones slowly, the thin ones in agitation – so that a curious procession began along the walls.

Then one of the shutters behind him blew open and a gust of blinding sunlight filled the room. As he fell backwards, Smous caught a glimpse of the grey parrot turning white on the ceiling, one startled eye fixed on him . . .

'Oh my!' it said finally.

Plunge

'Southern Africa,' Lazar announced, 'although, as I say, it's still only a notion.'

'What?' said Elie.

'Why?' said Her Immerman.

'Where?' said Smous.

Lazar dismissed his nephews with an impatient glance. It was hard to believe they were men in their thirties; one was a drunken clown, the other a half-wit. He turned his imposing, ship-like head with its towering top hat and undulating beard towards Her Immerman who was lying, face down, on the bed. 'Are you asking me "*Why* Southern Africa?" or "*Why* go at all?"'

'Uh-uh!' Her Immerman gave a succession of tense dry coughs to allow himself thinking time – when it came to his elder brother he always needed to answer carefully. 'Both,' he said eventually.

'Well . . . addressing myself to the first and more valid question, "Why Southern Africa?"' said Lazar in his lugubrious, gravelly voice, then paused to press a glass vacuum-cup onto Her Immerman's naked back, while removing a cooled one with a loud pop and handing it to Smous, who was heating them over a candle.

'Do you want this one reheated?' asked Smous, and when no answer came, he tossed it, rather carelessly, into Lazar's huge leather bag where he heard it crack. Grimacing, he peeped down into the clutter of instruments, phials, jars of leeches, cotton swabs, a small folding tray of sawdust used to catch blood – then looked to his uncle, but, as always, the man was too busy talking to notice anything.

'And the problem is this,' Lazar was saying. 'America, which is where the hordes are clamouring to go, of course, has restricted its immigration quota, or so they tell me in the letter from the Embassy, and there's a waiting list as long as your arm. So the real question is – apart from America, where else is there?' Negotiating his way around the bed, he now encountered the chess board on the mattress, the glasses of corn-brandy and Elie's knees. 'Excuse me, are we in a sick room here, or the tavern?' he asked testily.

'Oi veh,' said Elie, grinning, 'pardon me for breathing, such a carry-on when the doctor's at work – doctor-schmocter, do me a favour – we're talking about a major scientist here.'

Lazar sighed impatiently. Whenever Elie had been drinking he would start this offensive Jewish mimicry, learned years earlier from the servants at the Dolrogusky estate. Lazar deliberately bumped into the chess board, upsetting the pieces, and continued, 'Where, one asks, where else is there? I mean, one doesn't want to go to Palestine and sit in a tent with a camel for company and a Turk for a landlord. Personally speaking, I'd rather take my chances in the jungles of Africa where – or so I hear – you get off the ship, you bend over, you shoo away a monkey or two, and you can tear a chunk of gold big as your fist out of the ground. As to your second question, "Why go at all?", I can't believe you're serious. You only have to read a newspaper and look around to see what's coming our way.'

Her Immerman's eyelid began to flicker, and he quickly rubbed it, covering it from his brother's stare. He was neither in the habit of reading newspapers nor of looking around with more scrutiny than was polite. Suddenly to hear talk of America restricting its immigration quota because of 'clamouring hordes' trying to go there, seemed out of all proportion to anything that was happening in the Plungyan area. He hadn't heard of anyone leaving – *who were these hordes?* On the other hand, to discover that his own brother had been investigating these matters, even corresponding with the American Embassy, that was very odd, very odd indeed. He shifted uncomfortably on the bed and asked, 'How . . . uh-uh! . . . bad is it?'

'Oh please,' said Lazar, 'the pogroms in . . .'

'No, I mean *me*,' whined Her Immerman, 'I'm dying here.'

'Ach, it's a summer fever,' said Lazar, removing another cooled vacuum-cup and handing it to Smous.

'Do you want these reheated?' asked Smous again, but again received no reply.

'I mean,' Lazar said to Her Immerman, 'why am I telling you? You're the one having a new tax slapped on you every day. You're the one queuing three months for a permit to tour a district you've been working all your life. In case you're a smuggler! In case you're secretly destroying the sacred Litvan forests! All these things we're accused of.'

'Cut down the trees,' chanted Elie, speaking in Litvak, 'cut down the forests, and Litva will be no more – aye, cut down, cut down!'

'And all these refugees we see drifting through from the East,' continued Lazar, ignoring Elie, 'it's like watching the exodus from Egypt.'

'*Exodus*! Why do you always have to blow everything up?' said Her Immerman. 'Exodus. It's only one or two . . . uh! . . . and they're not refugees, they're beggars.'

'Of course they're beggars,' said Lazar, 'after what they've been through. They're beggars *now*, but what d'you think they were a few months ago? They were bankers and lawyers.'

' . . . Uh-uh! . . .' coughed Her Immerman. 'Who says they're even Jews?'

'Oh, come along now,' interrupted Elie, grinning. 'You think we'd tolerate non-Jewish beggars in Plungyan?'

Lazar was losing patience. 'The pogroms in –'

' . . . never reached *here*,' said Her Immerman wearily.

'Pogroms, schmogroms,' chuckled Elie, ' a few nuisance-makers get a hiding, do me a favour!'

Lazar knew better than to confront his nephew in this mood, but could resist it no longer. 'There's only one nuisance-maker I can see in this vicinity, my boy.'

'My boy, my boy,' echoed Elie joyfully, rubbing his hands in mock greed. 'I'm just a little trading man like my father here, bartering with nuts and thimbles round the countryside – how do you see me as any nuisance?'

'Excuse me,' said Lazar, copying Elie's rubbing hands, 'what's this supposed to be? You think it's funny – you're a middle-aged man with a family – please, it's so childish. I don't do that with my hands. Who does that?'

'I do,' said Elie. 'Oh dear, you think maybe it's too Jewish? You think maybe I'm giving myself away? Looks like I'm one of the Pious Ones perhaps. Dear oh dear, oi veh! You think maybe assimilation is the answer? Hmm, maybe. I tried it actually, years ago, with a little blob of coal dust . . . here – ' he touched the tip of his nose, 'shortens the nose. Used to wear it to the music academy. People said it looked silly, but what do they know? And my sister too, now that I think of it, Golda, she has the right idea. Wears her hair like the Litvak women. You know, plaited like a wreath. Yes, maybe you're right. Our women should start putting their hair into wreaths, we should start putting coal dust on our noses, grow back our foreskins, and we'll be laughing.'

'He thinks life's so funny,' said Lazar to the others. 'I don't find it that hilarious, but then maybe he hasn't seen what I've seen –'

'Oh, good, yes,' said Elie, 'let's compare suffering.'

'I'll never forget that night, that terrible night . . .'

'And here we go.'

' . . . when I lost my darling wife, my dear, dear daughters, may they rest in peace, when I lost them in that terrible fire – it was then I had a foretaste of the calamities now befalling our people.'

'Excuse me,' said Elie, 'but I always thought the fire was caused by Tante Selma spilling goose-fat while she was cooking. Nobody told me you had an anti-Semitic stove.'

'Elie, please, you're talking about the night I lost the lights of my life.'

'The lights of your life?' muttered Elie, 'maybe that's what started the fire.'

'What did you say?'

'I said: please go on, I wouldn't dream of depriving you of a story you so love telling.'

'*Love?*'

Elie's blotched skin was darkening and his smile had frozen. 'You worship it, adore it, revel in it, carouse and roister with it, you love to prise it open like an old whore's fishcake, love to put your nose in it and wallow, but then pain and suffering is your chosen profession so maybe you're just a good Jewish businessman.'

'What are you saying? Ha?' Lazar turned to his brother on the bed. 'What is he saying?'

'Please, please,' whined Her Immerman, 'no fights please . . . uh-uh! . . . I'm dying here – my son comes round to play a little chess, my brother comes round to heal me, and all of a sudden there's a room full of torturers . . .'

Smous found another vacuum-cup being handed to him, asked slowly, 'Do-you-want-these-reheated?' and when again they ignored him, placed it carefully in Lazar's bag and left the room.

The passageway was dark and narrow. He passed his grandmother's room and heard the familiar scratching, rustling noises within, like a large rodent in its nest, then strolled into the kitchen where his mother was working at the table, her eyes vacant, loading stone jars with fruit to preserve for the cold months ahead. Scuffing his feet through the straw on the floor and ducking his head to avoid the hanging baskets of potatoes, he walked to the doorway which led onto the road. The afternoon was bright but cool. There was no longer that summer smell in the air, that smell when the fields of šienas are cut, and laid in the sun, and turned. Now the smell was of milk and woodsmoke. The Dolrogusky procession would soon depart through the town, their finely shod horses clattering across the cobbles with an echoing, shivery noise which instantly made you think of winter. Smous prised a splinter from the doorframe, peeled it into a blunt edge and sat down to pick his nails.

It was an unusual kitchen, on the front of the house and without windows, but a stable-door kept half or fully open whenever the weather permitted. This had become Smous's place to sit, on the bandaged milking-stool – a remnant from when the house was a barn – which he had claimed as his own some twenty years earlier when he first settled in the doorway. He had often required to explain this peculiar vigil; the question 'What are you waiting for?' was asked again and again over the years, but no reply was ever given. He didn't have one – until today. Lazar had supplied it, put into words things he had always felt. For, unlike the rest of his family, he didn't need to be convinced of the danger threatening them and their people. He had tasted it.

He smiled, longing for someone to pass now, sneer and ask, 'What are you waiting for?'

'Oh – don't you know? The end of the world.'

There had never been any prospect of Smous being one of the rare Jewish children who graduated from cheder classes to the government school. And since there was no room for him in the family business (Elie already having joined their father, and the wagon only seating two), he found himself at the age of thirteen without direction in life. It was then that he first perched on the milking-stool in the kitchen, wondering what to do with his days. When no answer presented itself, the act of pondering became in itself his routine – week after week, month after month, as, very gradually, like the dough forever baking in the oven behind him, so too his body began to creep and stretch into new shapes, developing just enough insolent weight to settle back on the stool. He found an old pillow to soften the seat, began storing books underneath, bags of roasted nuts and, during the summer months, a jug of cherry juice covered by a square of muslin hung with beads.

'A fool grows without rain,' people began to comment, or, 'If you lie on the ground you cannot fall' – sometimes warmly, sometimes not, sometimes to his face, mostly not.

As the family grew more fretful, Smous grew more relaxed. The doorway had become an interesting place to sit. You became aware of the smallest modulations of every hour, of every day and month, of the slightest change in the weather and in the seasons. Or, at other times, it was hypnotic and you lost all sense of time passing.

One moment it was early Sunday morning, and Glown, the travelling sign-writer, was setting off for the week, his paints and powders in a bag, to tour the surrounding district; the next moment it was Monday evening and the Jewish Volunteer Fire Brigade were practising their drill, unrolling the perishing canvas hosepipes, bickering among themselves, or else with the householders for not keeping the walls watered and stoves guarded; now it was Wednesday morning and the horse traders were using that road as access to the weekly market in the town square, and for half an hour there would be rumbling like thunder, and the doorway was filled with sweating horse flanks, beating tails and slow-falling turds; and now it was Friday afternoon and Glown, the travelling sign-writer, was passing again on his way to the ritual slaughterer two houses down, carrying a hen which had been given him as payment, the bird looking outraged as it travelled upside down to execution; and Smous would sigh and think, another week gone – how time flies.

Then one day, in the same way that, years earlier, in a basin of sweets, he had suddenly woken into childhood, so now he happened to pass a mirror propped on the floor while the wall was cleaned; and because of the singular angle of the glass he saw his reflection anew. An adult stared back, an adult with heavy eyelids and stubble on his chin. Then his mother whisked away the mirror, saying, 'Excuse me, Your Excellency, but some of us have work to do.' She replaced it on the wall, muttering, 'It's wonderful to think I gave birth to a Russian count who doesn't have to work for his living, well, it's a miracle actually, God be praised, we've got Russian royalty in the house, go – quick – go tell the Dolroguskys they've got family down the road.'

Smous was exceptionally proud of the hair sprouting from his chin. It grew bushier every day, showing on his face like a mysterious and wonderful sign, a mark of his uniqueness, for it was thicker and darker than any of his contemporaries' – even Issy's. His cousin and childhood playmate was presently surviving the anti-Semitic rigours of the government school with courage, winning one diploma after another, and had exchanged his boyish fat for a tall, muscular build, his clumsy eye-

glasses for delicate gold-rimmed ones which magnified his eyes astonishingly. Issy might have bigger eyes than anyone they knew, but Smous had
the bigger beard, and he never tired of preening it in his cousin's
presence. He hoped it was obvious to Issy that, as in their games on the
banks of the Babrungas, he was still planning a life of biblical heroism, as
prophet, warrior or whatever, the sort of life where a dark and hefty beard
was clearly more vital than any diploma.

Smous's earliest memory often came to mind these days, that
wonderful moment of waking from infancy after his first haircut, of
discovering the universe to be filled with treasure, scent and light, with
him at the centre and everything within reach. Much had happened since
to discourage him, and, in moments of despair, he sometimes wondered if
that haircut had not been, as in the story of Samson, a way of mutilating
his strength. If so, it was now returning for all to see, and on his chin.

Not everyone was impressed. His father decided that such a full beard
on a fourteen-year-old boy – or was he fifteen? – might simply be final
proof that they had engendered someone very peculiar indeed. At
mealtimes he would glance repeatedly at Smous; glances that were meant
to be surreptitious, but the flickering eyelid was like a trapped insect in the
room, constantly buzzing at Smous's face. And the neighbourhood
children would laugh and point as Smous passed, a runtish boy with a
beard, like a midget, or some freak you might see in the travelling gypsy
sideshow. And then the beard came to the notice of a Russian soldier.

It was a drizzling, blowy Sunday morning in October, just after the
New Year. Smous knew something was wrong because Glown, the travelling sign-writer, had not passed the doorway, setting off on his week's
travels. When, a few hours later, he still hadn't appeared, Smous
decided to stroll round the corner to his house.

He found it had burned down during the night, killing the whole
family. The Jewish Volunteer Fire Brigade had fought the flames
bravely, but in the end it was a sudden thunder storm which extinguished them. Glown's body had been dragged out of the house and was
lying in the soaking gutter. How many times, Smous wondered, had he
watched this tall, bony man pass the kitchen doorway – and look at him
now. Hair, skin and clothes had all melted into the same black, sticky
substance. He had suffocated to death and his lips were still
pushed forward, like a fish, kissing a cobble on the road. Smous stared
and stared. He relished such things, any accident or fight, any letting of
blood – so long as he could watch in safety – he relished it, and hated

himself at the same time, wondering what it meant, this appetite. It came from deep within him, from something he didn't understand or know about, from long ago, perhaps even before he was born; he didn't like to think too much about it.

One of Glown's relations, an elderly aunt, was describing the fire to three Litvak policemen, who were guarded by a Russian soldier – the current practice when the police visited the Jewish quarter. This always bewildered and amused Smous: the police needing protection! From whom? His people – his cringing, apologetic people?

The Russian soldier was young, only two or three years older than Smous, with the flat head and heavy hands typical of the peasant boys recruited for service in Litva. He strolled around, stamping his feet to shake off the effects of last night's drinking, coughing incessantly, his chest clogged with the dark oily tobacco they had been smoking. For a moment he stood and listened to Glown's aunt claim that the fire was started by labourers from a nearby farm, mentioning a woman who had been touring the streets yesterday selling baby snakes as protective charms. Then the soldier turned away irritably and began pacing again, stamping and coughing. These houses were always burning down – small wonder, look at them, timber walls and straw roofs – and these people were always accusing everyone in sight, wailing and screeching.

His wanderings took him over to where Smous stood huddled in his charcoal coat. What a strange creature, thought the soldier, such tiny hands and boots, can't be more than a boy, yet with a full beard. Frightened by the way the Russian looked at him, raising that flat head like an ox, with dull, aggressive curiosity, Smous gave a small shake of his head. It was meant to show sympathy – for the dead family, and, more, for a gentile soldier summoned out on this damp Sunday morning. But the other misunderstood, thinking it was some kind of complaint, and, aiming for that beard, spat in his face. Smous was flabbergasted, then went cold, the smell of the saliva making his head reel. There were flecks on his lips. It had been so casual, there had been no warning, the soldier had simply spat and strolled on, his cough momentarily calmed. Smous dared not wipe his beard, for fear of provoking the Russian further, though he never glanced back.

In front of the mirror at home, Smous stared at the yellowish-white drops suspended on his beard, his proud, first beard. Then he clawed at them, making it worse, meshing them into the hair, releasing their stench all over again.

It stuck in his head, this stench, there was no getting rid of it, no amount of washing helped. It was as though the soldier had kissed him, a violent, stinking kiss, and Smous couldn't bear the thought of that. All intimacy was alien. Even the family kept a certain distance from one another; this was the way in their community. His mother would kiss him before going to bed, but aiming more for ear than mouth, and the men only ever shook hands, as though holding one another at arms length. As a child Smous grieved over this, but now he liked it. Much better to leave some space between you and other people, to stay back from the plans churning round inside them. And as for marriage, love, desire, that sort of thing, here he simply thanked God for blessing him with quieter instincts than other men. They seemed cursed with a craving that was insatiable and deadly. However much they might cover it with laughter, it was clear to him they were in pain, all wanting women they couldn't have. He wanted no one. He could imagine nothing more terrifying than this act which obsessed everyone else, and which he had witnessed, secretly, in the forest once or twice – mistaking it at first for a Litvak heathen rite. People twisting into one another, crying, feeding on one another's necks and faces, sucking at one another's saliva. Did women taste sweeter than that Russian soldier? He doubted it. But perhaps 'Jewish copulation' was different – shooting your seed directly into the woman's mouth. At least that way you could look away while it was happening; at least that would make it a little more civilised. He hoped he would never have to find out.

But now the soldier had kissed him, and the stench of his saliva stuck in his head, a savage, intimate stench, warm and fatty, it stuck there.

Smous never told anyone what happened that morning, fearing they would accuse him of provoking the soldier, which, he now realised, maybe he had: simply by being there, simply by being alive.

He became fascinated by all rumours of anti-Jewish violence, rioting and looting, which reached Plungyan, and which most other people, like his father, chose to ignore. As the years passed, his beard growing longer and his haunches fatter on the milking stool, he lost interest in stories of heroism, the biblical stories that preoccupied him as a child; now he revelled in the stories of disaster, of cataclysm, of mass annihilation: ' . . . And all flesh died that moved upon the earth, both of fowl and of cattle, and of beast, and every man: all in whose nostrils was the breath of life . . . died.' Here lay a new, terrible glamour. How terrible if all his people were to perish, but how marvellous – everyone vanishing together, failing together; not just him alone, framed in a doorway for all to see.

'What are you waiting for?'

  'Oh, hadn't you heard? The end of the world.'

  He longed for someone to pass so he could say this – but no one did, on this cool afternoon in later summer with his mother filling jars of preserved fruit and the men arguing in the bedroom about Lazar's plans of emigrating to Southern Africa. Eventually Lazar lost patience and stormed out, collecting a handful of sour cherries from one of Froi Immerman's jars, popping them in his mouth and pushing past Smous without saying a word. People had grown used to him as a permanent obstacle in the doorway, like a fault in the architecture, and had long since stopped greeting him. Smous watched his uncle lumber away down the street carrying his huge leather bag, the thinning light catching the sheen of his top hat and a stain or two on his frock-coat. All went quiet. The world could not be more peaceful. Its end still seemed a long way off.

  The winter which followed was severe. For months and months a kind of madness hung over Plungyan; in the way that bright, sunlit air could cut your skin; in the way that snow never stopped falling, squashing the town flatter and flatter as roofs and roads reached towards one another, then touched and closed, and the whole world went white. In the afternoon, when the sky grew dark and the snow-covered land began to shine, it was as though things were turning upside down for the night; and Smous would remember the story they once told him of a tilting, rolling, spinning universe.

  His family held their breath that winter. They had always feared he would become the town idiot (to many he already was, sitting in his doorway) and now he grew even odder, more remote, muttering to himself and constantly flicking his head. Behind one ear he took to wearing a sprig of rūta, picked in the summer and pressed in the Russian Bible. When challenged, he replied irritably that it was time someone purified the rūta. The Litvaks might regard it as their symbol of maidenhood, but anyone could tell that its spicy scent was the least virtuous thing on earth. But now that he had dried the sprig and squeezed out its lewd odour, it was finally clean enough to wear. He disappeared for hours, sometimes straying to the frozen banks of the Babrungas – now out of bounds; sometimes roaming the town at night, developing influenza and terrible frostbite, a black mould creeping over his skin.

He would stray into the graveyards where only the tops of the headstones reached above the snow like grey tongues and fingertips; and he would circle these for an hour or so, then suddenly stop, wondering where he was and what he was seeking. Or else he would go into one of the many unfamiliar synagogues (his family only used the one for the trading community) and sit in the blackness, listening to the crowd of beggars and madmen who were allowed refuge at night, moaning and shivering. On one occasion he felt someone's warm, damp breath near his ear and a voice whispered, 'What are *you* waiting for?' Smous grinned in the dark; even here they were asking the same question, but at last he could give the answer.

'Oh, hadn't you heard? The end of the world.'

'Ei!' cried the voice. 'Another one!'

With spring came the startling news that Lazar had booked passages to Southern Africa for himself, his son Issy and pregnant daughter-in-law, Nava. They visited the Immermans for the Shabbat supper one Friday to break the news, and Lazar delivered a long, carefully prepared speech about the violence and looting all around them, to the east in central Russia, to the west in Poland; repeating familiar tales of mass emigration to America and introducing new, bewildering topics like a Zionist Congress in Paris and talk of a Jewish state in Palestine.

Smous sat chewing his moustache and glancing at Issy, now a doctor like his father, with the same undulating beard and weary, impatient eyes. They were the only things Smous could still recognise on him, those eyes, magnified by the pebble-glass; it was impossible to believe the rest of this giant had once been a plump and tearful boy you could torture for hours on end. But, those eyes – every now and then, as Issy nodded confirmation to Lazar's words, he would blink and hold them closed while his lips parted and he made small, popping noises in his throat. 'Issy's Face!' It had always been such a mystery, what Issy was seeing in those visions: ghosts of his dead mother and sister, dybbuks, the end of the world? Now it was solved; he had been shown another Exodus of their people.

Around the table, lit by the sabbath candlelight, a circle of stunned faces listened to Lazar: Her and Froi Immerman, her white fists clutched on her lap, Elie, his wife and children, Smous's sister Sima and her family. Only the Old Girl took no notice, sucking at her soup spoon with loud squeaks, making Lazar glare angrily as he delivered his great tale of doom.

'Wait a minute, wait a minute,' said Her Immerman eventually, 'uh! . . . all right, so I've listened to an hour's horror story, so now what?'

'Now what nothing,' said Lazar. 'I'm just telling you why we're going.'

'That's not what you're doing,' said Her Immerman, the twitch in his eye vanishing along with his little cough, 'you're telling me that because you've decided to go, everything round here has to have gone mad.'

'Oi, I'm telling you,' said Elie, grinning, 'the world is mad already, my boy.' Smous watched a flash of impatience cross Issy's face and prayed for Elie to shut up.

'What do you mean?' demanded Lazar, ignoring Elie.

'This is typical of you,' continued Her Immerman, now turning white, 'All our life, you have to be right and everyone else is crazy . . .'

'What are you talking?'

'I'm not talking, I'm asking – I'm asking, who are you to come running in here saying the writing's on the wall and the world's on fire? Just because you've read a few articles in the newspaper? Means nothing to me and I'll tell you why . . .'

'Nu?' interrupted Elie, 'for why?'

'Because everyone knows they only print two things in those contraptions – fiction and politics.'

'Fiction and politics,' chanted the Old Girl, pairing the two as her son-in-law always did, with equal scorn, 'curse of our times,' while Lazar stared at Her Immerman, flabbergasted.

'Well?' said Her Immerman defiantly, 'isn't that what the papers are full of: fiction and politics?'

'Well, of course they –' Lazar started to answer.

'Tell me I'm wrong. Go on.'

'Of course they print *politics* in the newspapers!'

'There you are. And fiction.'

'They're inclined to exaggerate a little, now and then, yes.'

'Thank you.'

'That doesn't mean these things aren't happening.'

'How do you know they are?'

'Everyone knows, except you.'

'Then why isn't everyone leaving?'

'They are!'

'Huh!, where from? I haven't seen anyone go.'

'Oh, for God's sake!' – it was Issy interrupting now – 'every Jew in Moscow has been expelled.'

'How do you know that?' cried Her Immerman.

'It's in all the papers!'

'Thank you. Point proved.'

Issy banged his temples in frustration while Lazar lifted his eyes to Heaven and growled through closed teeth. Elie meanwhile clapped his hands, applauding his father, saying, 'Oi veh, fiction and politics, schmiction and schmolitics, I'll tell you something for free.'

'And you, shut up!' shouted Her Immerman, rounding on him. 'All day long in the wagon I have to listen to that stupid voice you put on, and your stupid laugh. Who are you laughing at? You're laughing at yourself.'

'That's all right,' said Elie, smiling. 'Maybe if you all . . .'

'Never mind us all, it's you. You talk as if you've got nothing to do with us. Just because once upon a time, a hundred years ago, the Dolroguskys gave you a few fiddle lessons, you think you're better than us?'

'If you like.'

'Never mind if I like, I don't like. I'm ready to burst with all your shit!' Elie put his chin on his chest and shook with silent, painful mirth, while Froi Immerman's head shot up.

'Excuse me, excuse me,' she said. 'What word did I just hear?'

'Shit! Shit! Shit!' shouted Her Immerman. 'Shit and fuck and fart and piss and Jesus Christ our Lord!'

'I know worse ones,' said the Old Girl. 'Fiction and politics.'

'Shut up, shut up, shut up!' said Her Immerman close to her ear, then turned back to Lazar. 'I've got eyes in my head, I'm not as stupid as you've always believed, you may be older, you may have gone to the university, you may have a brain swollen like a mountain, but I'll tell you your fortune now, my boy – cards on the table now, all right? – we've got a few extra taxes, a few pass-laws, a few people get attacked a million miles from here . . . so? Terrible thing. That doesn't mean one's got to go running away to start monkey-farming on the other side of the world. What for? Breaking up the family, deserting all your patients, deserting your birth place, your town, your country. We've got a decent life here. Why do you have to come running in, twisting our heads? It's a disgrace, you're a disgrace, the whole shitty business is a disgrace.'

There was a long silence broken only by the tiny noises escaping from Elie's nose as he stifled his laughter. Then the Old Girl looked up, her fist-like chin clenching and unclenching. 'What's all the fuss please? I'm this, you're that, it's holy, it's unclean, it's heathen, it's gentile, it's morning, it's evening, it's Russian, it's Litvak, it's freezing, it's thawing – they've all got their hardships. The way you people speak you'd think you invented it all. Put aside your newspapers please and go back to your Bibles. It's all in there, all happened before, thank you very much. Nobody's invented any new troubles.'

'And so?' demanded Her Immerman, toying with the huge breadknife. 'Yes? So? *And so?*'

'No, she's right,' said Lazar, seeing his chance, 'ours is a history filled with calamity. Don't I know it. Maybe . . .'

As his voice started to tremble, Elie said, 'And here we go!' fairly loudly, but Lazar pretended not to hear.

'Maybe I'm leaving because of that terrible fire when I lost my darling wife and daughters, the lights of my life, your own dear sister-in-law and nieces, may they rest in peace – I still can't bear to think about it, despite all this time. God! I see death day in, day out, but to think how my own dear ones were murdered by a gang of marauding Cossacks . . .'

'Cossacks?' said Her Immerman. 'Wait a minute, no, no, the fire was caused by Selma spilling goose-fat over the stove.'

'You were there?' enquired Lazar, stretching the last word into a little tune, his brow darkening.

'The fire was caused by spilt goose-fat,' repeated Her Immerman, avoiding his brother's gaze.

'Wouldn't it be lovely to think so? All the fires round here are domestic accidents. Such incompetent cooks we breed in Plungyan.'

'I don't care about the other fires, your fire was . . .'

'That's funny, it was *my* fire and you're suddenly the principal witness?'

'Nobody's interested in the clever remarks,' persisted Her Immerman, though his eye was beginning to flicker again, ' . . . uh-uh! . . . because everyone knows the fire was caused by . . .'

'Cossacks!'

'And please notice,' said Her Immerman, turning to the others, 'it isn't just soldiers any more. Now it's Cossacks, the full works, wild horsemen with the big moustaches, drawn sabres and all the trimmings . . . uh! . . . grow up, Lazar, it was goose-fat, *goose-fat!*'

'It was Cossacks.'
'No – goose-fat.'
'Cossacks!'
'Goose-fat!'
'COSSACKS!'
'GOOSE-FAT!'

The two brothers faced one another across the table, their eyes locked, their faces red, yelling at one another – 'Goose-fat! Cossacks!', again and again, 'Goose-fat! Cossacks!' – until the words lost all meaning and became two snarls of abuse. In the end it was Issy who stopped them – jumping up, thumping the table and thrusting forward his face with its flashing, magnified eyes. 'Please,' he cried, 'you're talking about my mother and sister here. You're churning up their graves, you're fighting with their bones, stop it, let them rest in peace for God's sake!'

The two older men went silent, leaning on their knuckles, panting. Now when Lazar spoke it was with a new, quiet, ominous voice.

'So all right, call me a coward, tell me I'm running away, that's been my experience of life, take it or leave it. As the Old Girl says I've got thousands of years of persecution and exodus bumping up against me. So, go on – I stand before you – here he is again, shoot him down, the wandering Jew!' and with that he wandered calmly from their line of fire, departing the house, followed by a smirking Issy and a tutting Nava, leaving the family dumbfounded, except for Elie who still shook silently with laughter.

'It was goose-fat,' said Her Immerman eventually, 'which . . . uh-uh! . . . which caused the . . . uh! . . .'

'Of course it was goose-fat,' said Elie, 'but it has to be worse. The worst. He loves the tragedy, loves the calamities, loves the suffering. You all do.'

'Again with "you all",' said Her Immerman in a hushed, confused voice, ' . . . but I'm sure it was goose-fat.'

'It *was* goose-fat,' confirmed Froi Immerman, rubbing his shoulder with her clenched first. '*Hust, hust*! It happens all the time.'

'Yes . . . uh! . . . but if he's going to start making a fiction out of something like that, which happened to his own dear loved ones, I mean . . . uh-uh! . . . what about everything else he tells us?'

'I thought you didn't believe him anyway,' said his wife.

'Yes, but . . . uh! . . . I mean . . . uh-uh-uh! . . . I mean, what are we to think or do?'

'Sizzle, sizzle,' said Elie, grinning, as he stuck his fingers into the flames of the sabbath candles, and held them there, unflinching, while they turned black. 'Sizzle, sizzle, sizzle . . .'

The rest of the community received the news of Lazar's departure with disbelief. Dokter Immerman was such an essential and remarkable figure in the town, no one could believe he would go. Even after he closed his medical practice and sold his house, people still refused to accept he was leaving; inventing all sorts of rumours about his retiring, or moving to a smaller house. When the day of departure actually dawned all were caught unawares and had to gallop into Mazheik with farewell gifts. In a fit of extravagance someone even hired the Jewish band, who were found in the tavern, sobered up, bundled into a cart and driven to the Masheik railway station.

So it was that Lazar, Issy and the pregnant Nava finally left their family and friends, waving merrily from the carriage window (inside they were knee-deep in gifts of breads and cakes, silver candle-sticks, ornate plates and brocaded purses filled with coins) while the band played bitter-sweet tunes and everyone wept their eyes out. Her Immerman had been most certain that his brother wouldn't actually go, and now felt desolate as the train disappeared from view into a tall forest of spruce, his bad eye flickering slowly to the last stirring melody from the band. However much his elder brother had always intimidated him, he relied on Lazar, not only as a doctor, but in all things. What was he to do now?

In the months which followed, Her Immerman watched events around him with more attention and less comfort. Now, every time there was a rumour about a fire starting mysteriously, or a procession of new vagrants through the town, or new punitive taxes and permits, he would frown and ask, 'Where's all this suddenly coming from?' Then one afternoon Elie got drunk and marched to the Dolrogusky Palace demanding to see the family. When even the oldest of the gate-keepers failed to recognise this bloated, purple-faced man as the boy who had once been the star pupil of the musical academy, Elie produced proof: his old violin, which the Dolroguskys had given him. But he had forgotten that, long ago, to appease his mother, he sliced away the Russian lettering. 'Oh, sorry . . .' he said, giggling, to the gate-keepers, 'seems like I circumcised this little Russian baby by accident.' The men beat him so savagely they destroyed the sight in one eye. From then on that eyelid hung slack, just showing a sliver of pinkish-grey. 'The Immerman vampire,' Elie would joke, but no one laughed.

*   *   *

Almost a year after Lazar's departure, a letter arrived bearing a strange purple stamp. It had English words, and a picture of an unfamiliar deer standing on grasslands. With shaking hands, Her Immerman read it and then passed it round his family.

My dearest brother,
   Much to tell and little time to tell it, life here is so hectic and full. Issy and I have recently joined the medical practice of a charming old Polish gentleman called Lipschitz who is, poor fellow, on his last legs. We're trying to treat the patients and learn their languages at the same time. If we succeed, and don't first fatally bleed someone who only came in to have a quinsy lanced, it could prove a profitable concern.
   But first things first. We have settled in a small town called Calvinia in the Cape Colony, and it is a delightful, quiet backwater not dissimilar to our own dear Plungyan. It has a surprisingly substantial Jewish community, mostly from central Russia, and even a charming little makeshift synagogue. Although the surrounding land is very barren, almost like a desert, the town itself is altogether a civilised habitation with no signs of monkeys, lions or tigers. Indeed, the only threatening natural force is the heat which is something to be believed. It's like living all year round in the Plungyan bath-house. Fortunately they have the most ingenious cooling sheds, the size of rooms! The luxury leaves nothing to be desired. A dear Froi Katzeff, a widow from Moscow, is our housekeeper and she maintains two savages as servants, so actually we have a staff of three, hard to believe, yes?
   The local population are mostly of Dutch descent and although our intercourse with them has been limited, they seem a warm and hospitable people with an impressive knowledge of the Old Testament as well as their own. They seem totally receptive to our Jewish community in their midst, and even draw parallels between your troubles back home and their War of Freedom here with the ruling English government. Fortunately the hostilities are mostly far away, though there was apparently a small and ferocious battle just fifty miles away at a settlement called Middlepost. Politics, I hear you cry! Well, you'll be pleased to hear that I can't read the newspapers here yet, which is just as well since there is so little time for leisure.
   What free time I have, I devote to my darling granddaughter born

shortly after our arrival. To tell you the truth, I think Issy was more than a little disappointed it was a girl, but as I told him, they'll have plenty more, I'm sure. The child is called Esther, aptly named, a child for our joyful future.

I hope all is well and life there is still kind to you. With God's blessings for good health and prosperity.

Your loving brother,
Lazar.

One evening, a few days later, Her Immerman brought a chair out of the house and carried it across the road to where Smous was sitting with a glass of cherry juice, enjoying the last of the sunshine. Nothing was said for a long time; the older man's face was grim and his twitching eye fairly still. He took the glass from Smous's fingers and sat drinking, half-whistling, half-singing one of the old songs through his teeth; then he threw the dregs of the glass onto the cobblestones and watched the red drops go grey in the dust. Smous blinked, remembering a childhood game on a stretch of frozen river, a trickle of blood, shaped like a fleeing figure, trapped for weeks in the ice. He blinked again, while Her Immerman sang:

> 'Play that lovely tune for me
> The Sherele they're all dancing
> I'm in love with a pretty girl
> But I dare not go romancing . . .'

When it became clear his father would never take the next step, Smous said, 'If it's any help, I think I know what you've come to discuss.'

The other nodded slowly, then said, 'It's such a vast distance to go, isn't it?'

'Very far.'

'To go on one's own.'

'Yes.'

Her Immerman glanced at Smous, unable to gauge his attitude. 'You remember that story the Litvaks used to tell me . . . uh-uh! . . . of their . . . what was it? . . . an animal kingdom beyond the forests, their Paradise . . .'

'On a beautiful sunny plain,' prompted Smous.

'That's the place. Where no man has ever been able to reach.'

'I remember.'

'Well, it's even further away than that.'

'Hm!'

'Of course we could have a document drawn up . . . uh! . . . in English . . . all the whys and wherefores. To carry on one's person at all times. Elie says he's heard of someone, a linguist in Telz.'

'Sounds like a sensible precaution.'

'If one was going to do a journey like that.'

'If one was.'

'To establish a sort of foothold.'

'A foothold?'

'Yes, a foothold, in a manner of speaking. So that others could follow. I mean, it was easy for Lazar – there were only three of them, and he could afford their passages. I mean, there's so many of us, there's . . . uh! . . . us and the Old Girl, and Elie and his family, and your sisters and their . . . uh-uh! . . . well, it goes on forever.'

'It'd need quite some foothold.'

'It'd need a hero,' said Her Immerman glumly and, when he saw his son's eyes light up, turned away quickly. He was still unconvinced that he should abandon everything here, everything he knew, and had devised a way of covering himself: sending out the one member of the family whose absence would scarcely be noticed. 'Yes, so . . .' he said, 'so . . . what . . . uh! . . . what do you think?' The question was asked painfully slowly, almost sucking back each word onto his tongue, half praying that Smous would run screaming down the road, sparing them any further investigation of this lunatic plan.

Instead Smous said, 'It's what I've been waiting for. All my life.'

Together they went into the kitchen across the road to break the news. They could not have chosen a worse moment. An old lady from their synagogue had just left the house, having told Froi Immerman that the meat she bought the previous day, and was now cooking, had been discovered to be black-market and was not guaranteed kosher. She was required to throw it out, to purify her iron pots in scalding water and to smash all earthenware crockery which had been in contact with the suspect meat. When Her Immerman broke the news about Smous, his wife seemed not to hear, but said quietly, through white lips, 'How am I going to replace all these things if I smash them?' She was holding a large clay pot, a favourite, black and blistered with use. Staring at it, she said absently, 'Send the family fool across the world to start a new life for us? That sounds like a good idea. Whose was it?'

'Mine,' answered Smous quickly, seeing the terror in his father's eyes.

'Only you . . .' said Froi Immerman three times, then suddenly lifted the pot high into the air. Smous sprang back, thinking she was going to murder him – but she hurled it onto the floor, the red clay bursting into view like flesh ripping. What shocked Smous most was that she was crying, and he had never seen her cry before.

'Over my dead body . . .' she said, very quietly and in earnest.

Cape of Good Hope

A fly was crawling on Smous's lips. He blew it away with a small sigh and half opened his eyes.

There had been a talking bird, a man with no legs, Oriental sailors, naked children with pink sores, a bald girl opening and closing her mouth, but now the place was deserted. Which place? Where? The room was completely unfamiliar. He had been in a blue, shadowy, smoky room: this was bright, with yellow dust swimming in shafts of light. He heard water and thought he must be on the banks of the Babrungas, but then, slowly recognising the ocean smell, decided instead he was on board the ship sailing to Southern Africa.

Now he noticed a brown-skinned man with a lump on his head sitting opposite, clutching a bag of belongings, jigging nervously in his chair, staring at him intently. Smous remembered an accident in a carriage, a man being dead then alive. Confused, he sat up – a swarm of angry flies exploded into the air, rising as one from the uneaten food on his plate. Smous remembered a non-kosher meal and endless glasses of an oily drink which clogged every corner of his head.

The nervous man shushed his finger in front of his mouth, apologising for disturbing Smous, then leaned forward and whispered, 'Just to say whenever you're ready, hey?'

'What?' said Smous, hearing the foreign language again.

'I've forgotten your name,' said the man.

'What?'

'Something like a stutter,' said the man as Smous stared back, frowning; 'Mer-mer-mer, something like that.'

'I'm sorry?'

'Anyhow, whenever you're ready, just say the word, sorry to wake you, hey, sorry, hey?' Gommie moved off his chair and began to pace around the room. It was the same place as before, Smous now realised, but the shutters had been opened and the balcony had been cleared of the sheets, letting in the late afternoon light and the sea breeze. Gommie led his eye through the maze of crates, tin drums and chairs to a sofa where the huge, fat woman was sprawled asleep. He knelt next to her and nudged her arm.

'Hmmm?' She tilted up her head, one cheek squashed in sleep, that eye still closed.

'You awake?'

'Hm-mm.'

'Is that yay or nay?'

'What you want?'

'You coming with us?'

'Hmmm?'

'The Karoo.' She smiled lazily and pushed away his face. 'Don't,' he said, 'head's still sore. Comes and goes.'

'Me too. A hot, hot day.' Only half awake she began to kiss him gently round the head, hardly bothering, yet with tenderness, while Smous watched, wondering if the two were husband and wife, or mother and son? Then his gaze drifted away . . . the movement of curtains around the walls was calmer than he remembered. He stared at their stately procession for a long time, trying to piece the day together.

Now one of the heavier curtains bulged into the room, and two people pushed through – the carriage driver and the bald girl, he walking tall, she with difficulty, legs bowed outwards. What's happening? Something's happening, Smous thought, suddenly feeling more alert. The Gommies were laughing with the driver who blew out his chest and hitched up his trousers, while pretending to be embarrassed, flapping his arms to stop the fuss. Next to him, not much higher than his waist, stood the girl, obviously in pain, though it was held in, her face squeezed as though she was about to fart. 'Np!' – Smous dug his fingernails into his palms to stop himself giggling. He thought, whatever's going on, all I can say is thank God it isn't me standing there, thank God I didn't let them take me into the rooms back there.

The girl started to speak, soft sounds flowing between the clicking and snapping of her tongue. 'He harmed me, he shamed me. I am another man's wife, not his. I am the wife of Kgototxe, and the mother of Bo.'

'Where are the smallgoods?' laughed Mommie Gommie, her head propped lazily on one fist, 'they love to hear her speak.'

The girl took a few steps towards her and said, 'Take me back to my people now. Please take me back.'

'Ag, shut up,' chuckled Mommie Gommie, 'if you want to say something to me, first learn to speak.'

The girl looked at the woman's heavy, bloodshot eyes and knew she was wasting her words. She scanned the room and saw Smous. 'I've watched you,' she said, 'your face is peaceful. Will you take me back to my people?' Smous bit his moustache, stifling his laughter – her clicking tongue sounded as if she was urging him on, as you would a horse.

'Now where are the damn-bladdy smallgoods?' said Mommie Gommie, peering under the furniture. 'Ag shame, they'd've had a happy howl!' Her face set abruptly as she noticed how awkwardly the girl was walking. 'Haai, Mister Miller, what did you go do to her?'

'Nothing . . . I don't know . . .' Miller muttered, blushing and beaming, as he found his glass among the debris on the table. 'She's small as a child . . .'

The girl shuffled towards Smous. He watched her mouth opening and closing like a fish drowning in the air, and shook with silent laughter. 'Help me,' she said, suddenly reaching for him. He shrieked, leapt into the air, and scurried away, making everyone else guffaw.

Then Mommie Gommie heaved herself off the sofa, scooped the girl up into her arms, turned her over and attempted to lift her dress. The girl struggled to keep herself covered, saying, 'No, it shames me.'

Miller watched this pensively. 'She's so shy – it's a funny thing,' he said, 'when you think they all run around bare in the veld. She doesn't mind if you see her . . . you know, the top half, but it's her scut-hole specially she seems to think is the old Lord's greatest creation.'

'Koos could explain it,' said Mommie Gommie, wrestling with the girl. 'Where is he?'

'Gone,' said Gommie, 'gone like a mad crab across the sand.'

'Stop it, you stupid damn thing!' shouted Mommie Gommie to the writhing girl. 'I'm trying to help you, I won't show them everything – as if they care.' The girl was hushed by the loud noise, and went still, her eyes glazing, as the woman carefully lifted up her skirt. Smous stopped giggling and stared, braver than before, thinking, they're all looking, so can I – it's all right to do that here; but all he glimpsed was her yellow thighs and a watery bloodstain that looked like orange dye.

'Tsk!' said Mommie Gommie and carried the girl on to the balcony, where she stood rocking her, enjoying the breeze. 'Going to be a lovely evening, gents,' she said over one shoulder and disappeared from view, climbing down to the beach. They drifted after her, Gommie, Miller, and finally Smous, coat slung over his arm, feeling as though he was made of air – the sleep, the drink still rocking his balance, the lack of food – feeling that he could watch these people unobserved, circle round them, inspect them when he wanted. He was content with the way they ignored him; he would learn about them in his own time, take from them what he chose, remain mysterious in a way that was no longer irritating, as the people at home had thought, but powerful.

Down on the soft, warm sand the group spread out: Miller went to hug his horse, his forehead pressed against it, standing like that until the surf slid round their ankles, filling his shoes; Gommie said, 'I feel better now,' to no one in particular and began to scan the sand for valuables, waddling along with his legs arched wide, elbows on knees, head between them; and Smous watched the woman bathe the girl. Each time her loins were dipped, her body arched in pain while her face remained oddly detached. Mommie Gommie said, 'It's good, good, the salt water will make it better, good, you stupid thing, *good*. Say it with me now, start to learn, look at my mouth – gooood . . .'

'Gooood' – Smous's lips also formed the word silently, tasting the English sound. 'Gooood,' he whispered to himself several times, before he noticed Miller and Gommie sauntering away along the shoreline and drifted after them.

'I've had one of the best ream old days I can remember,' said Miller to Gommie as they walked.

'Lucky I had one at all!' laughed the other.

'Lord yes. To think . . .'

'Jaaa . . .'

The sun dipped and for a while the world became weightless. All events felt concluded or postponed. Miller lifted the bottle brought along from the sugarhouse and declared, 'Cheating the Devil!' – then drank, watching the sunset in the oily liquid above his nose, the oranges, pinks and greens pulsating slowly. 'Drinking in the day, as the saying goes,' he chuckled, passing on the bottle.

Smous drank walking backwards along the sand, trailing his coat, gazing at the Table Rock and the two smaller peaks flanking it on either side. Litva was such a flat country, it was wonderful craning back your head to see the edge of things. I'm here, he thought, as he had done often during the day – I'm actually here! He stopped in his tracks. The Litvak's fabled land, their Paradise beyond the forests, beyond the reach of man – it was *Africa*. That's what they were describing. An animal kingdom on beautiful sunny plains. Africa. And he, Smous, had made it there.

Grinning broadly, he set off after the men again, while they began to talk and link their plans to his:

'When are you taking Mister Thingie to the Karoo?' asked Gommie.

'Huhn?' said Miller. 'No, all I'm taking him on is a tour of the Colony. Well, I *was* – it's over now.' He turned to Smous and asked, 'That all right, you had enough? Enjoyed the tour?', and when Smous responded with his usual uncomprehending smile and shrug, Miller sneered and said to Gommie, 'He probably understands, you know, they all do really. One time I was driving this Norwegian . . .'

'So how's he travelling on?' asked Gommie, nodding towards Smous.

'Who knows? Not our worry.'

'It's my worry, I'm going also.' Gommie glanced away. He had assumed the two men were travelling on together tonight, and it was essential he left *tonight* – before Mommie Gommie realised he wasn't joking or talking his nonsense, before people started questioning him about it, before he thought too clearly about it himself, before any of that happened he needed to be gone.

'You're still thinking of joining him?' asked Miller, smiling.

'Ja,' said Gommie absently, his mind racing. He didn't need Miller, but he did need Miller's horse and cart – what was the sly way of asking the next question? Unable to think of anything better, he said, 'You fancy it?'

Miller laughed and asked, 'And what would we do out there, up north, in "God's wilderness"?'

Gommie closed his eyes – here they were, the questions. 'Farm,' he said.

'My family never had much fortune with farming.'

'All right – mining then. All the gold and diamonds, copper, all the things they're now finding up there.'

'Nowhere near the Karoo.'

'All right – then we don't know. Good. No damn plan in this dull skull! Good. Over to God. It's His wilderness, let Him sort it out.' He saw Miller's mouth start to open, knew he would make some clever remark about God, so quickly said, 'Hey, pass the bottle, man.' Then he laughed. 'That's why I have to go. I don't want any more to slup, but you've got the bottle with you, so we slup . . .'

'I know what you mean,' said Miller, 'and it gets so you don't feel it no more . . .'

'That's it.'

'Still . . .' said Miller and lifted the bottle to his lips.

'And everything's like that. Round and round and round. Gommie, Gommie, Gommie, they're all shouting. What kind of skukking name is *Gommie*? Sounds like a child and I'm soon an old man. Priest that uses our sugarhouse, gets slupped one night, have to throw him out, he says, 'We will civilise the native nations, but the trouble with you Bastaards is you can only go backwards with each year.' Round and round each day and backwards with each year. Nobody leaves me alone, everybody knows me too well. I know me too well.'

'I know, I know . . .' said Miller passing the bottle, 'same with me, I know me too well.'

Gommie sighed and drank. 'A man could make a new start upcountry.'

'Or it could be worse.'

'Never.'

'Well, good luck to you, my mate. Any thoughts of running somewhere else I'll keep in my head, little dreams, just enough to get me through this bastard, itching life, but I'll tell you one thing, if I started running it wouldn't be any deeper into this scumming country, but home.'

Gommie turned to look at him. 'I thought you were born here.'

'Was. I'm talking like my folks used to talk about their lives. Always "going home", always somewhere else – the rolling chalk downs and the dear old water meadows, everything such a dear green colour, and the dear mist and the dear snow, ah how dear it all was, ah how it made the heart ache so. Stupid glocks!'

'England?'

'Mm.'

'Like all the soldiers and sailors talk. Makes you feel like you're living on a road and everyone else is tramping over you on their way somewhere else.'

'That's right. I was brought up with the idea that here was nowhere, but that one day we'd "go home". And you know what? It was the only thing my folks were ever right about. They should never have left in the first place. They were like you, always running somewhere else. Trouble is you take your scut with you. And they were made of it, scut, brought up in it – farmers in Dorsetshire, well, I say farmers, they were just labourers on a farm, some bastard place, name of Stubhampton, hog farm, farming some old swine, name of Wessex-bastard-Saddleback. That was them, thick and poor as swine scut, treated as swine scut, bottom of the pile, yesterday's swine scut they were, couldn't get no worse. But it did. The farms are failing because of some bastard French Wars, don't ask me what French Wars have got to do with the price of Stubhampton-Saddleback-swine-scut, but the labourers are starving and rioting and every bastard thing. So they hear about this settlers boloney, how the government is offering free passages to the Cape Colony, quit-rent farms when they get there, all the ream old trickshens and trackshens. So they're like you, think it's better somewhere else, so they come out here with their eyes wide and stupid, oh how good life was going to be now, oh, oh, oh, how they boasted and bragged in the letters back home to the rolling chalk downs and the dear old water meadows, in the letters someone else had to write for them because they were so swine-scut-stupid! That was them – they'd brag and boast, but inside the house they'd sit like two little mice going mad in a corner. Lot of the English are like that.' He passed his hand slowly over his face, collecting the features in one clasp, and squeezing them.

'Anyhow, they get given this piece of rubbish land in the Cradock district, where I was born. What did they know of farming in that part of the world, of the droughts, the diseases the crops are going to get, the insects? Less than me who's staring out of the window thinking I've been born on the moon. The only thing they know about is swine. So they keep this old hog, treated it like a king, there were times when we'd starve and the scumming hog was lying there like a fat king – something for them to boast about, you see, it was the one thing they'd made work. I hated that hog. It had a sort of smile on its face. Anyhow, in the end they had to give up the farm – by then they were just grazing locusts and growing dust – so they sold it for a fart to some bastard Boers who probably turned it into a paradise, yes, they sold it all – except the hog. That came with us in the cart, so my folks could show it to the authorities, show them the bitching hog, and say, "Look, we did well, didn't we? No fretting. But now we'll just pop back home if that's all right with your worships . . ."'

'They brought the hog all the way back here?' asked Gommie, clapping his hands.

'Trying to, they were. Half back to Cape Town, sleeping for the night on a mountain pass, we were attacked by baboons. First time we'd ever seen them. I can remember my mother's words – "Oh dear merciful God, we are visited by the hounds of Hell!" and she was right, that's where I was – Hell, not the moon. God never made baboons. Two faces – one on the scut-hole, the other growing straight out the shoulders, running and barking and biting like dragons. My father lost half a hand, the cart was tipped over, all our things went into the ravine, horse ran off . . .'

'And the hog?' asked Gommie, breathless.

'Now that was the only good thing. They tore it to shreds, tore the smile off its face and ate it. So, my folks end up here in Cape Town with nothing left to boast about to the authorities, just crying, "Can we go home now please?" – and the men said, "Rest sure you can, my good people, soon as you've paid us back for our farm that you've sold off to the Boers." So – while my father does his julking in the jail, my mother works her old paps flat, this job and that, and when he comes out we get that piece of finery I still drive, because it looks good for boasting, see, and so we live in it, all three of us, three little mice shivering to death at night, and in the day my father drives people around the bay, saying, "Look, look at the fairest Cape in all the world, isn't it marvellous, aren't we the lucky ones?" – trying to earn enough push to get back to the rolling chalk downs and the dear old water meadows so that we'd never have to see the fairest farting Cape again.'

'And did they get back?'

'They got the smallpox.'

'Ag shame. Never got back to the rolling water meadows.'

'Never did. So, that was them and this is me. Still waiting.' Miller stopped walking and stared across the beach: sand, sea, sky were all turning grey and becoming one. 'Keeps me going anyhow,' he said. 'Who knows? Maybe I will get back one day.'

'What's the hold-up? Why don't you go?' asked Gommie morosely, feeling he'd lost all chance of Miller's carriage for his trip north with Smous.

'Huhn! You know how much they charge for the bastard fares?'

'If that's your worry, you're worry-free. We'll scheme you onto a ship for nothing. We don't just have sailors for our customers. Nay man, a lot of the captains also. We'll scheme you onto a ship tomorrow – maybe you'll have to slave on board, but you'd still get back to England.' Miller stared at him intently, but Gommie seemed to be serious; his tone was matter-of-fact, his eyes fixed on the sea, his mind elsewhere. 'Ja,' Gommie said with a sigh, 'we'll get you there – sing-a-ling-ding – and then people will start asking you what they're going to ask me about the Karoo. And now what? Now what are you going to do? Ja? Hullo, we're waiting, some answers please.' He turned to Miller. 'Well, and what will you do in England?'

'In England . . .' Miller laughed. 'In England you do anything you choose.'

'Ja, and so what're you going to choose?'

Miller opened his mouth and then stopped, trying to think of an answer, surprised one wasn't on the tip of his tongue. For a long time his lips remained open, as if he might speak at any moment. Then he slowly closed them, set his features into their dazed sneer, and turned his head towards the ocean. He saw a clear image of himself – boasting to strangers during the day, shivering at night in his carriage. 'And we does, and we does . . .' he muttered. 'Yes, you're right – this is me for good. Never knew . . .'

Gommie's eyes flickered – he hadn't meant to be *right* about anything. He held his breath and waited, then, beginning to tremble, said, 'Mister Miller, when do we leave for the Karoo?'

'Did I say I was coming along?' asked Miller.

'Isn't that what you've been telling me – all the whys and wherefores? How you tried Cradock and that was no good, how you can't go back to England, how you've messed it up here, how all your life there's been devils chasing you – locusts, baboons, however you want to call them – and how today you won? Me too. First time today. Isn't that what we've been saying all day?' He lifted the bottle and grinned. 'Cheating the Devil! Our luck has changed, Mister Miller, we're the skukking swine who're still smiling, and that accident this morning, when you almost slayed a man and I was almost that man – that stuck us together – tight as the old nun's sugar-purse!'

Miller looked at him, wishing he could be certain the man was as much a fool as his wife said. He chewed his tongue and cursed – he'd been so happy ten minutes earlier – why was there always a catch? Then he thought seriously for the first time about travelling up north with this peculiar pair, and was surprised to find the notion appealing.

'When do we leave?' asked Gommie again.

'Look . . .' said Miller, 'maybe we can talk about it . . . I don't know. We'll sleep on it.'

'Mister Miller, Mister Miller,' said Gommie, gripping his arm, 'if we sleep on it we wake up and find Monday morning – *Monday morning*, Waalaa! – the old never-ever time. Now come on, you show me a man who's ever, *ever* done anything brave on a Monday morning.'

The two men looked at one another, steadily holding one another's gaze in the dimming light. Miller thought, if it doesn't work out I could always hook it; Gommie thought, if it doesn't work out I could always steal his horse and cart; but for the moment they smiled at one another.

Gommie lifted the bottle and, after a long pause, Miller nodded and said, 'Cheating the Devil.' Then they shook hands and turned to look at Smous standing nearby, swaying drunkenly, marvelling at how quickly it was going dark – in Plungyan the evening light would hang in the sky for hours; and the two men thought, if it doesn't work out we can always take his money and lose him, but for the moment they slapped him on the back, grinned, and Miller said slowly, 'We're-going-to-take-you-to-Calvinia.'

Smous smiled and shrugged, then, suddenly remembering, pushed his lips forward and said, 'Gooood.'

'See,' said Miller turning to Gommie, 'told you he could understand us all along.'

As Gommie put back his head and laughed, Smous noticed an extraordinary thing: the few teeth remaining in the man's mouth, on the lower jaw, were a perfect miniature of the three mountains above the bay, now showing in massive silhouette against the purple sky; the broad flat Table Rock in the middle with the two sharp peaks on either side. In astonishment Smous pointed to Gommie's teeth. 'Rut-a-Boer!' said Miller, 'yes, it's a marvel.'

'Wha'? Wha'?' cried Gommie as the two men held open his jaw, gazing inside.

'A marvel, a right ream and bone marvel!' said Miller.

'Wha'? Wha'?'

'You've got the whole of Table Bay in your mouth – there's the Devil's Peak, there's the Table Mountain and there's the Lion's Head. Perfect.'

'Ag, what's this shit you're throwing me now – I know my mouth,' said Gommie, pulling away from them and squinting at his reflection in the bottle. 'Jur-ruh!' he cried. 'It's a true story – the Table Bay, the whole damn thing in my mouth. There they all are, even the Lion's Head, exact. Haai, my mouth never looked like that before – must be because of that tooth I lost in the accident.' He started to laugh and hop around on the sand. 'You know what it is, gents . . .' he said, spluttering and gagging as he tried to keep his mouth open and talk at the same time.

'What?'

'It's because . . . today I'm the man with a mouth full of Good Hope.'

'Mouth full of Good Hope . . .' said Miller and opened his own mouth wide to roar with laughter, '*Waaaah!*'; and Smous laughed also, delighted that he'd noticed it first. The three staggered around in the sand, yelling with joy. Every few moments Gommie showed them the view in his mouth again and each time they found it funnier. Now Miller splashed some of the liquor over Gommie's jaw, saying, 'And you know what this is?'

'What?' screamed Gommie.

'The Cape of Good Hope in a rainstorm. *Waaaah*!'

'Cape in a rainstorm!' shrieked Gommie, backing away, choking and gagging. Then, his laughter stopping abruptly, he said, 'Mister Miller, is it true the Lion's Head was a volcano long time ago?'

'True, true,' shouted Miller. 'Why, are you going to make that tooth explode? *Waaaah*!'

'Because, it's just . . . they said it was an old volcano.'

'It's not such a young tooth. *Waaaah*!'

'A dead volcano . . .'

'Kill the tooth! *Waaaah*!'

' . . . and it doesn't feel dead to me.' In the same moment both Miller and Smous noticed how still Gommie had become, and they stopped laughing, Smous balanced on one leg. 'There's a lion's head in mine,' said Gommie in a tiny voice, 'going to go up any second. Ooo, aina! Take it out, pull the tooth before it roars . . .' He steadied himself, aware that he was talking what his wife called his nonsense, and tried to shush the thoughts away with his finger – in that instant he felt the carriage wheel go over his head again, then the bruise inside exploded and he saw a blue curtain fall across the horizon as the sun sprang back into the sky. He fell foward onto his knees, leaned over slowly and put his face in the sand.

Miller and Smous stood on either side of the bowed figure, both transfixed. Smous was watching Gommie's ribs, waiting for them to move. Two, three minutes passed before the thought crossed his mind – mind you, with his face in the sand like that, he couldn't breathe even if he wanted to – so he bent forward and touched the figure. Gommie toppled over very slowly, with a small sigh, which made both men lean forward hopefully. But a film of sand covered Gommie's face, even his open eyes, making it seem, in the grey light, that maggots were already at work. Miller looked at the pale face and remembered the soldiers riding into the alley after the accident, asking, 'Has he ghosted?' He swallowed hard. Gommie had been killed, as everyone thought, killed earlier that morning, and his spirit had stayed with his murderer for the day . . .

Smous fetched some sea water in his hands and splashed it over

Gommie's face. He did this three times, then stopped and thought, for some reason I did that three times. Now he remembered the reason: the Pious Ones believe every time you sleep it is a form of death and so when they wake they wash their hands three times. Smous frowned and thought, what is that to me? I am not a Pious One. Odd thing to do.

Washing Gommie's face had done nothing to change its ghostly expression. Smous sighed and was covering Gommie with his overcoat when, without a word, Miller suddenly turned and ran back along the beach. Uncertain, Smous trotted after. They quickly reached the sugarhouse, and, seeing Mommie Gommie and the bald girl still sitting in the dusk light, their feet in the surf, Smous expected Miller to stop and explain what had happened – but instead the man rushed straight past, leapt into his carriage, and, in an instant, had driven away. Listening to the small, ringing bell grow fainter, Smous slowed down. His trunk was still on the carriage; had the man gone for help, would he be back? Then he saw the alarm on Mommie Gommie's face and knew one thing for certain: he would be blamed.

Smous turned in a circle, then doubled his speed as he heard pounding, splashing feet behind him and looked over his shoulder to see the woman's massive bulk lumbering through the dim light. The bald girl was following, running with difficulty, legs bowed outwards, but with surprising agility. He ran on, passing the dark heap of Gommie under his overcoat. Glancing back, he saw the woman stop, but still he ran on, and on, for what seemed like miles, until he tripped in one of the waves sliding on and off the shore in the blackness, and fell. He clasped his hands over his mouth, stifling his violent panting so that he could listen in silence.

When at last he felt sure nobody was following, he tore down his trousers, squatted on the sand and released his terror. He was crouching there, hugging his knees, when it suddenly struck him – his overcoat covering Gommie's body – *all his money was in it*. Everything was lost. His funds and his trunk. Everything. Could it be? Earlier that day, when he woke on the ship and discovered his small cloth bag stolen, he ran to the baggage-deck fearing the trunk would be missing. Now it had come true. What was in it? His mind raced back to that last morning in Plungyan. Along with clothes, blankets and dried food, his father had filled the trunk with the oddest assortment of goods from his wagon: an ice-hatchet, a pair of wading boots, two pairs of children's shoes in different sizes, a box of thimbles, a lady's long-fringed shawl – all of which he kept telling his son 'might come in handy some day.' At the time Smous found this absurd, it

made him blush, it was his father behaving like a simpleton again. But
now, now it was terrible that those goods, those precious goods, six
months earnings at least, that they had been stolen. And without the thief
even wanting them, not even knowing they were there. Miller would open
the trunk and throw half of it away. The thought was unbearable. Smous
flicked his head sharply. And all his father's money, those funds collected
with such difficulty . . . He flicked his head again. What else, what else
was gone? 'Oh no!' he whimpered – the Russian Bible. That was the last
thing to be packed, by Smous himself, fetched from under a floor-board
in the bedroom and secretly pressed down the inner wall of the
trunk.

But now he remembered something else, the one loose page which
fluttered down near Her Immerman's foot, almost giving the game away.
That one page torn out years earlier: the illustration of Jonah and the
Great Fish.

With frantic fingers Smous dug in his waistcoat pocket and found it
safe. He had brought it out only once before, during the voyage – when
he watched a real Great Fish rise from the deep like a dream; he had
brought it out to compare them. And the picture which, before, had
seemed so perfect, then looked flat and lifeless, meaningless marks and
scratches, a nonsense compared to the shape resting in the water below
him, dark and complete and colossal.

Smous drew the illustration from his waistcoat and unfolded it. The
beach was too dark for him to see clearly, but he put his nose to the paper
and just caught a smell of home, a musty, resinous smell. He filled his
nostrils with it again and again until there was no trace left.

This illustration, and the English scroll in his other waistcoat pocket,
his 'diploma in English', at least they were safe. 'Thank you,' he
whispered.

And what of that man, that odd little man with teeth shaped like the
mountains above him? He would be alive now if Smous hadn't arrived this
morning and hired that carriage. It was a strange thought. The whole
sequence of events was strange – the man dying, then coming back to life,
then dying again. If he had known, known that it was his last day, known
that he was being given a second and last chance, what would he have
chosen to do with it?

Smous grimaced and flicked his head.

How warm the night is, he thought instead; how interesting that it
should be hotter here at night than during the day back at home. Winter

was starting there when I left just three weeks ago, and here it is summer, how interesting, how different. Here I am in Southern Africa, how different everything is, how different life will be from now on . . .

The figure came springing out of the darkness without warning. Smous was just rising to his feet and buttoning his trousers, thinking that, at least, the dreadful event on the beach had cured his constipation, when he was leapt upon – and he screamed in a voice which he had never before heard from his throat, so high and icy was the sound. The figure muttered something, but he was panicking too much to notice that it was a pleading voice with a clicking tongue, belonging not, as he imagined, to Mommie Gommie or her husband's ghost, but to the bald girl from the sugarhouse. Smous fought her off, striking her wildly across the head, shrieking in a terrible falsetto, then tried to escape across the beach. She leapt again, this time bringing him down on his back, and straddling him. They landed in a patch of light from a nearby boat, a yellow-green glow on the sand, and, finally, he saw who it was. Now, as she spoke, leaning close to him, the look on her face was so clear he was able to understand her words without translation.

'Help me,' she said.

2. KAROO

Smous the Smous

'It's a smous.'

'What?'

'A smous,' repeated the farmer, deliberately not raising his voice.

'What?' From behind the screen door his wife's measured tone warned that she couldn't hear him, that she had told him so before, and that if he didn't speak up she would ignore him.

'A smous is coming,' said the farmer, even quieter, smiling to himself – he relished their latest battle, and if she persisted now, she would forfeit the luxuries stacked on the cart travelling towards them.

The man was sitting on the front step of his house, holding a butter churn which he'd spent most of the morning trying to repair. He liked to wear his floppy, mustard-coloured hat low over his eyes and to tilt back his head when he considered the world, as he did now, studying the little group on the road. It seemed to him there was a distinct similarity between the driver of the cart and his white donkey – both were slumped in the heat, heads drooping, as though moving in their sleep; the animal's steps were dragging badly, the man's boots hung off the small cart, skimming the ground. The short girl walking behind them, though, seemed fresh and alert, moving with an easy stride, her hands dangling over the ends of a long stick she carried across her shoulders. The farmer calculated the distance she had walked, their journey from the previous farm, and thought, as he often did, how tough these Bush-people were.

Actually, the girl had been riding on the cart until a few minutes before the group came into view. Smous always insisted she ride alongside him whenever they were unobserved, although this had been forbidden by his employer, the wholesaler Kottler.

The girl's hair had grown back since her days in the sugarhouse but was still short as a boy's, which Smous found even odder than her baldness. She wore the same turqoise dress as on the day of her escape, and Smous the same shirt, waistcoat and grey woollen trousers, all threadbare now. His face and hands were now the colour of rust, and his hair, beard and fingernails had grown long. On his head was a battered straw hat found one day alongside the road, its crown missing – which the girl repaired with a nest of grass, paper and string. In spite of the shade from the hat, Smous kept his eyes half-closed these days, squinting at the glare of the Karoo, which made him look aged and disagreeble.

At the moment he was particularly depressed by the sight of this farm, the last habitation before the land became totally barren. The farmhouse, the workers' huts, the shearing sheds, all had been built from the same stone and mud, orange blocks protruding from the orange veld. There were no trees. Two windmills provided the only break from the monotony of squat buildings and low bushes, lifting the eye, gratefully, into the dazzling blue sky.

The white donkey shuffled into the yard and came to a halt, sighing, as if certain that no reward would be offered for its long and punishing labour. The farmer set aside the butter churn and rose to his feet.

'Haven't seen you for a while, my friend,' he said to Smous in Afrikaans, 'how goes it?' and extended a massive hand.

Smous shook it, and said 'How*areyou*?' in English, the inflection shooting upwards at the end as when he first learned the greeting, which he believed to mean 'Hello'.

'No . . . good . . . thank you,' replied the farmer, switching awkwardly to English, 'and how are you?'

'How*areyou*?' said Smous again, still shaking the man's hand.

'No, it's good with me,' said the farmer, frowning slightly, 'and you – how are you?'

'How*areyou*?' mumbled Smous again, smiling wearily, thinking how irritating this ritual was, you always had to say hello again and again. Chuckling indulgently, the farmer was about to lean sideways and prop himself on the donkey when he thought better of it – the animal was so exhausted it couldn't shake away the flies feeding round its eyes. The farmer shooed these off with a wave of his hand and then, groaning softly, watched them return.

'I . . . tell her . . . you . . . here,' he said. Smous smiled vaguely, he had exhausted his vocabulary for the present. 'Told her you're here,' repeated the farmer, reverting to Afrikaans, 'and she always likes buying from you, but she's having a little bit of a mood today. Watch.' He tilted his head towards the house and, only fractionally raising his voice, said, 'Your smous has arrived.'

'What?' came the tight reply from within.

'Your favourite smous, the smous called Smous, Meneer Smous himself, he's here and waiting for you.'

'What?'

'See,' said the Boer to Smous with a grin that was spotlessly white from the brackish water in his wells. His build was powerful but awkward: short legs under a heavy belly which pulled him forward, long hairy arms and heavy hands. The low brim of his hat seemed to press his features into the centre of his face, and the jaw jutting into the light was huge.

'What have you got for her today?' he asked, pointing his boulder of a chin to the boxes and sacks on the cart. Smous eagerly leapt from his seat, dust tumbling from every crease in his clothes, and flipped open a row of lids, revealing buttons, thimbles, sewing and knitting needles, cottons in every colour.

'Ja, ja, oo-ja, she'll like these,' said the man gleefully, 'just what she wants.' He tilted his head towards the screen door again. 'My little lamb, there's a lot of nice bits and pieces here for your sewing basket.'

'What?'

'You must come and have a look.'

'I haven't heard a word you've said,' said the clenched voice.

'Then how do you know I'm talking?' retorted the farmer. This silenced the voice and the man twanged his braces with pleasure, momentarily dispersing the flies from round the donkey's eyes. 'She's in a hang of a state today,' he told Smous, who smiled and nodded vaguely as he untied the sacks on the cart.

'Gooood, hmm, gooood?' Smous asked as the aroma of coffee and tea rose into the hot air, but the man's mind was elsewhere.

'There's the culprit,' the farmer said, jabbing one thumb towards the butter churn, 'she tells me it's my fault the thingie's leaking butter between her toes. No fear, no – the only mistake I made is taking her on a visit to old Pienaar's farm a few months back. There she sees this new butter churn they've got, all varnished wood, and with, you know, a shiny brass band around the rim. Ever since then ours has started leaking. Perhaps someone has been sliding in a knife and jaggling it about, hey? Oo sonny, listen – a person must never take them visiting, they're always going to covet something! You want my advice? Take them to church for communion once a year and call it the end of the story. Anyhow, as the old people say – they who dig the grave fall into it themselves. I'm going to fix this thingie so she'll still be churning butter in it on Judgement Day. And she can stop talking to me altogether, you won't find me complaining. I love the silence. She's the one who'll go mad first. *Shh!*' he suddenly whispered as the screen door creaked open. An old, barefooted Hottentot woman stepped into the sunlight, wiping her hands on her dress.

'The Ounôi says, Baas Andries, your food is ready,' announced the woman, 'and will Baas Andries be wanting it inside or out here with Baas Andries's friend?'

'Not my friend,' growled the farmer, 'I'm not planning to do any hell-damned needlework, nê?'

''s Baas.'

'And tell her she'll find me having my food at the usual place – at the head of *my* table.'

''s Baas,' said the old woman and returned inside, the screen door shuddering behind her.

'Oo . . .' whispered the farmer, his great chin throbbing, 'she's really asking for it today. Next time you come calling I may have some goods to sell to you – a wardrobe of woman's clothes, a selection of shoes, a bonnet for church. All right, my friend, good to see you again,' he said absently, shaking Smous's hand, and strode into the house.

Smous was left standing alongside his goods, one hand still extended in mid-air. Surely that could not have been goodbye? It had taken him all morning to reach the farm, it was inconceivable they had travelled all this way only to turn back now without selling so much as a button!

No, I must wait, thought Smous, he's told me to wait.

He looked to the girl, but she hadn't been paying attention. She was squatting nearby, her arm propped on her knee, the fist clenched on her forehead to shade her eyes. All Smous could see were her thick lips moving slightly, chattering to herself as always.

Now he turned to the donkey as if it might offer some explanation, but it was even less help, standing there with downturned mouth and self-pitying eyes. Such a pale and abject creature, it could only be gentile – Smous had decided that long ago, and it was one of the reasons why he loathed the beast.

But I'd better water the wretching thing, he thought, and moved over to the barrel on the cart. Now the girl's eyes flickered towards him. It was often like this – she seemed to anticipate his actions. He wondered if there was going to be another of her outbursts. Whenever she saw him feeding or watering the donkey she would confront him angrily, saying, 'How can you waste precious food and water on animals? Animals will find their own food and water. It doesn't matter that you don't give any to me, I will find for myself also. But keep it for yourself – you have to work hard, you need strength. Was there ever such a stupid man as you!' Although the language was incomprehensible, her outburst would throw Smous into confusion. After all, she was a native of the land, she must know best about local animals. Perhaps these donkeys, like camels, could survive without sustenance for long stretches of time? He didn't realise that she had no experience of domestic animals, that every passing horse terrified her, its huge weight thudding across the earth like a charging beast; and he dared not consult the other smouses for fear of looking a fool. Meanwhile the wholesaler Kottler always provided food and water for their long trips with clear instructions: 'For you and the white ass, mm?, not you and the dark arse.' Perhaps the girl was simply envious?

Smous stood at the water barrel now, eyeing the girl, eyeing the donkey, uncertain what to do. Slowly he opened the lid and raised a ladle of water to his lips. It was hot and tasted of wood. He lowered the ladle, eyed the girl, eyed the donkey. Should he water it, should he not? Should he leave the farm, should he stay? He stared at the ladle, watching the dregs evaporate in the sunlight, and suddenly it had happened again, the thing that was always happening these days – he couldn't move, his body was stuck.

Rising through the stillness was a less familiar feeling, a prickling of fear and anger, of hatred: hatred for the farm, the farmer, the farmer's invisible wife, the girl, the donkey, the cart, the goods, the ladle in his hand, hatred for everything, *everything*.

On the morning after his first day in the Cape of Good Hope, wandering in dismay through the streets of the town, Smous had met one of the other passengers from the ship, a man called Mindel who had relatives already settled in Cape Town. Although perturbed by the bald girl at Smous's side, Mindel nevertheless took him home, providing a hot bath and kosher food to break his fast. When Smous mentioned his destination was Calvinia, Mindel's relatives were able to offer more help. They knew a firm of upholsterers that supplied furniture to a wholesaler in Ceres, a town on the way to Calvinia.

Two days later, Smous and the girl departed from Cape Town in unexpectedly grand style; seated in two capacious armchairs on the back of the furniture wagon, among a clutter of tables, stools, and one gigantic wardrobe. With their backs to the Hottentot driver, they watched the three mountains of Table Bay dwindle into the distance until they were so

small they looked like the teeth in Gommie's jaw, and Smous shuddered –
then the mountains slipped from view behind a bump in the road and
never reappeared. The luscious orchards and vineyards around Paarl
and Wellington led up to a rocky mountain pass drenched with mist and
waterfalls. Here they came to a white stone cottage where the driver paid
a toll of threepence per wheel to an officious English soldier who then
declared them 'free to enter the interior of His Majesty's Colony.' From
then on the landscape gradually flattened, the mountains lowering into
hills, the boulders into rocks, the trees into small grey bushes; the patches
of earth between turning red, everything drying and hardening under
the increasingly fierce sun.

The wholesaler in Ceres, Kottler, was a German Jew, short and
round, with orange hair and freckles, who walked with his arms folded
across his back, the fingers of each hand embedded in the red flesh of
the opposite elbow. In this way he strutted around his store which was
cavernous and dark, smelling of spices, maize, coffee and tea. These
were ranged round the walls in deep wooden boxes with tin scoops
half-buried in the mounds. On varnished counters stood weighing scales
and glass jars; above were shelves with rolls of wallpaper, numbered
cardboard boxes, stationery, medicines, children's toys. The furniture
from Cape Town hung from the rafters, casting odd shadows on the
sawdust floor below.

Kottler listened to Smous's story – of how he had lost all his
possessions and funds – with a patient smile. Then, at the end, he closed
his eyes and fluttered the lids teasingly.

'Sure, sure, I believe you, sure, others wouldn't. Others would think
you're one of these fools who come dancing into the Golden Land with
their pockets empty and their heads full of crazy ideas, mm?, find
themselves a nice little bushgirl concubine to do a little sinning with,
away from the eyes of their family who'd otherwise drop down dead so
help me, mm?, and then when they start looking for all this gold they
find only sand, and then they're in trouble, dreaming time over, welcome
to the real world, mm? That's what others would think. Not me.'

'It's not like that,' interrupted Smous, pointing to the girl, 'we're just
travelling together.'

'Of course you are,' exclaimed Kottler, 'for the conversation. I could
tell right away – you play chess at night in the bedroom. She sleeps at
your feet, don't tell me . . .'

'Actually she does.'

'Please, no more, my heart's breaking. Others would faint. Not me. As far as I'm concerned all I know is you're a Jew, I'm a Jew, you're in need, I'm going to help you. So, what did you do back home in Litva?'

Smous chewed his moustache. I sat in a doorway, he thought, I'm very good at that. I'll sit in the doorway of your store for you, tell you how the weather's changing. Instead he said, 'I was a trader. With my father. Round the villages. Assorted dry goods and notions –'

'Say no more, you're hired, problem's over, you'll do the same for me, mm? Smousing we call it here. I run a few donkey-and-carts, little sideline, travel round the outlying farms, piece of cake, make your fortune in no time, and then you'll be able to travel on to your uncle in – ?'

'Kulvidya.'

'*Calvinia*,' said Kottler, correcting Smous's pronunciation with a smirk. 'Calvinia, mm, show your uncle his new niece-in-law, a few little mulatto toddlers, say to him, Onkel dearest, look – I've been doing missionary work among the savages – watch him do backward somersaults you wouldn't think a man of his age could still manage. Good, so, there we are, problems solved, mm?'

However, there were a few points Kottler had omitted to mention.

The donkey-and-carts were hired, not loaned, to the smouses, and it was also the practice for them to buy their goods at a nominal price from Kottler and then sell them at a profit. When Smous reminded the wholesaler that he had no capital to start with, the man waved him aside, saying, 'Please don't – you'll make me sick with sadness. Go, start work, we'll discuss it at a later date.' At the end of the first week Smous was presented not with a salary or his profits, but a bill of debt explaining that he owed J. Kottler & Son one week's donkey-and-cart rent as well as the wholesale cost of his goods. This amounted to four guineas exactly, against which J. Kottler & Son would generously subtract the seven shillings and sixpence which he had earned during the week – although they were, of course, entitled to this as well. Even without much nose for business it was clear to Smous that he had entered a form of slave labour. But he already owed the man so much there was no choice but to continue working for him, which doubled his debts by the end of the second week. How would he ever reach Calvinia at this rate?

He wished now he'd paid more attention back in Plungyan to the family trade. Perhaps his father or brother would have found a way of selling Kottler's goods with sufficient speed and profit to overtake the mounting debts, but Smous discovered he had little talent, and even less appetite, for the world of commerce. He had only to hear talk of wholesale and retail, outlay and overheads, and his senses would cloud over as if he was listening to one of the foreign languages of the land. In practice, the work was even more confusing. Bartering was a nightmare to him, with all its play-acting, and Smous would often accept any price nominated by the purchaser, even below the wholesale price – anything to be done with it!

If only, at the very least, he had watched his father tend their horse back home so that he would know what to do with Kottler's little white donkey. Animals terrified Smous. They looked at you with their human eyes, showing what you thought was warmth, or indifference, or even hostility, yet they always surprised you. For most of the time the donkey seemed the most servile beast in Creation. Then suddenly, without warning or reason, it would open its jaws and bellow: an unearthly, pumping bellow which froze Smous's heart.

'We're both miserably enslaved,' he would sometimes say to the donkey as they travelled along, in an attempt to endear himself, 'miserably enslaved, you and me both, but with such great things waiting to burst forth. Maybe that's why I hate you so much, we're too similar. Still, one of these days . . .'

In the meantime he and the beast shuffled from farm to farm, each nursing their miseries.

Smous had made no effort to learn the languages of the land. He told himself this was because he was far from certain he'd be staying. He knew two place names: Ceres and *Kulvidya*, five words in English – Howare*you*, Gooood, Yes, No, and Bye-bye, and only one in Afrikaans, Smous – his trade and new name.

The Boer farmers had experienced great difficulty pronouncing Immerman. It sounded to them as if the middle of the word was missing. They reminded Smous of the Polish race, with the same thick flat features, and he found them a hospitable people, though with little curiosity in foreign cultures; so, after a few cursory stabs at saying his name, they surrendered. 'Ja, well, never mind, hey, we'll just call you Meneer Smous.'

Smous liked it. You only had to say it with a 'sch' and it sounded Yiddish – *schmous*. He would coin a new Yiddish word, he decided. Here at last was a part of the job which appealed to those distant dreams of glory: I am not just a smous, he thought, I am *the* smous. Future generations of smouses will have to look back to me, the great grandfather smous . . . There will be a statue of me in Ceres, bestriding a rocky terrain, one hand holding my hat against the glare of the sun, the other outstretched, holding a fistful of buttons and threads, the forefinger pointing into the uncharted wilderness where no smous had yet gone smousing – *Smous, the smous . . .*

The screen door on the orange mud farmhouse shuddered open and the farmer leaned in the doorway, his huge chin glistening with animal fat. He had been watching Smous from inside the house. For an hour the small bearded man had stood next to the water barrel on his cart, one hand holding the ladle, without moving a muscle. 'You all right?' the farmer asked. Smous looked up at him with dull eyes, sweat pouring from his face.

'Listen here,' said the Boer, 'sorry you've come all this way for nothing, hey? But she's not coming out, my little wifie isn't, you must just accept that. Hang of a state she's in back here.' A shoulder of mutton flew out of the darkness and thudded against his skull. He let out a growl, his neck bulged, then he paused and gave a clenched smile. 'So . . . Meneer Smous, my friend, now you must get going, for your own sake get out of this heat at least . . .' and he closed the door.

I don't think they are going to buy anything, thought Smous, perhaps I should get going. He replaced the lid on the water barrel, slowly walked to the front of the car and clambered on to his seat. Flick the reins, he told his hands, click your tongue, he told his mouth. Nothing happened. He couldn't move again.

Out of the corner of his eye he watched the girl dart over to the shoulder of mutton and, without brushing off the grit, tear at it with her fingers. Holding the shreds inside her mouth, she chewed with her strong back teeth, looking as though she was forcing her fingers down her throat. She caught Smous glaring at her and held out the meat towards him. He shook his head impatiently, how dare she offer him such unclean food? How dare she eat like that – like a lunatic?

Ever since that night on the beach when the girl begged for his help, she had been at his side, and he still didn't have the vaguest notion who she was, where she was going, or what she expected of him. She was simply *there*, loading and unloading the cart, helping whenever she could, asking nothing in return, providing for herself without complaint. She was always *there*. They mystified one another equally. The girl found Smous's travels particularly odd: he would repeatedly lead her in the direction she sensed home might be – where the land grew more barren – but then he would always turn back, retracing their steps, returning to the town, only to reload supplies and set out again on the tantalising route. Sometimes, overcome with confusion and frustration, she would frown so fiercely that her young face was covered in wrinkles, the skin loose as a reptile's. Then Smous would have to look away, glancing as he did over her body in the turquoise dress. Her buttocks protruded in a shelf as pronounced as her breasts. The shape was odd, almost deformed, yet far from repellent. She unsettled him, deep in his gut, and, unable to name the feeling, he wondered if one day he might do her some harm.

Watching her eat now, he heard the sound of a pulse, thought it was his heartbeat, then realised it was in the air – the heat, throbbing and ticking.

'What the hell-damned blazes are you still doing here?'

Smous stared at a nerve twitching on the donkey's spine and didn't look up. He heard feet scuff across the dust and a shadow fell across him. 'I'm talking to you, my friend. You've been waiting out here for two hours now. Two hours. What are you waiting for?'

As Smous lifted his head, the farmer started – the skin around Smous's eyes was purple and his cheeks were two white blotches. Smous, in turn, was surprised to see the Boer in his underclothes. The flesh of his chest, arms and legs was yellow and soft, in contrast to the leather-brown of his head and hands. He's all in separate pieces, thought Smous, and struggled with an impulse to knock the figure over and watch it break apart. He glanced down at the open box of knitting needles near his elbow.

Now the sound of a woman shouting came from within the house, then the rattling of a locked door. 'We're having a little lie-down now . . .' explained the farmer quickly, ' . . . because of the heat. So nobody's coming out again this afternoon. Understand me? So, go!' As the Boer turned back to the house he noticed the girl gnawing at the shoulder of mutton. 'Hey!' he shouted. 'And who invited you to lunch?' He made a sudden movement, spreading his legs and crouching, as if to pick up a stone. She dropped the meat and scampered over to the cart.

'Don't do that to her . . .' Smous heard himself whisper hoarsely and felt his feet jerk beneath him. I'm going to rush at him, he thought in shock, but didn't move.

The man was standing at his doorway staring back at Smous incredulously. 'Why aren't you going?' he bellowed – then, without waiting for a reply, ducked towards the ground, this time collecting a stone, and sent it slicing through the air. '*V'ts'k!*' he hissed. Perhaps the stone had been aimed at Smous – it hit the donkey instead, who sighed.

Even a blow like that can hardly stir the miserable creature, thought Smous calmly as his hands tightened round the reins. 'Bye-bye,' he said courteously to the farmer, and 'Ck-ck' to the donkey, then watched the girl's head swing towards him, misinterpreting the sound as always, thinking he was trying to speak her clicking, clucking language. 'Stupid fool,' he muttered as they wheeled round the yard and headed down the road.

'And I mustn't see you on my land again, you hear?' the farmer was shouting. 'I've seen the smouses go mad before. You come to our land, you understand nothing about our climate . . . that isn't the sun, that's Satan's eye hanging in the sky, man! What do you know about it? Just keep away from me, you keep away from my land, you keep away from my woman – you hear?' Another stone rang against the side of the cart and then there was silence. Smous presumed the man had gone back indoors. He didn't bother to look back.

As they travelled down the road, Smous heard a tinkling sound, and, glancing over his shoulder, realised he'd forgotten to replace the lids and tie the sacks. White buttons were jolting out of their boxes, spilling over the side, and reels of cotton sprang away, unravelling into the bush. The girl walking behind made no effort to retrieve the goods, but lifted her diamond-shaped face towards Smous, her eyes shining brightly. There she was again, reading his mind – for if she had stooped to pick up so much as a single button he was ready to shout, 'Leave it!' He enjoyed the squandering of his goods – the falling buttons glinted in the light like coins – he couldn't sell anything, so what difference did it make?

They were approaching the end of the farm property. A gate in the rough wire fence led onto a white dust road and the veld beyond. Always, on previous visits, as the donkey pulled the cart onto the white road, turning right to start the long journey back to Ceres, Smous would lean in the opposite direction, following the line of the road to the left, to the north, a thin white strip disappearing over the horizon, stretching across the Little Karoo, leading eventually to Calvinia.

But today as they reached the gateway and the donkey automatically turned right, Smous lowered his eyes, watching the animal's vertebrae shining through its hide. He listened to the shuffling, scraping noise of beast and cart, and tried to settle back for the journey. With any luck they would reach Ceres by the following evening . . .

Theft. A surprising topic, he thought, to while away the hours. 'Theft,' he muttered aloud, 'all right, let's discuss theft . . .' The girl glanced over to check that he was talking to himself, then settled into her stride and began her own chatter.

'Now there's theft and theft,' Smous said. 'I could reach down and pick up that rock and no one would mind. On the other hand, if I made off with the donkey and cart, Kottler would mind terribly, and yet they're almost as worthless as the rock. I mean, what have we got here? A bag of bones and meat . . . a few planks and nails hammered together. You'd be hard put to cry "Thou Shalt Not Steal!" about such paltry nothings. Still, there is the merchandise, I suppose.' They banged over a rock on the road and another load of white buttons, coffee beans and needles sprang into the veld. Smous smiled. 'Won't be anything left of them to steal, so that's not a problem . . .' He checked himself and wondered what he was contemplating – why this thought of theft? You're in a most peculiar mood today,' he said to himself, feeling a tingle in his spine, then flicked his head sharply to change his thoughts. Now he suddenly remembered Miller driving away from the beach in the twilight with the green trunk that Smous's father had filled with his goods; he thought of the Russian Bible inside, which he had treasured all his life; he thought of his overcoat draped over Gommie's curled body, all his funds in the pocket; he thought of the small cloth bag stolen even before he woke on the ship; he thought of the last three months in Ceres being robbed by Kottler. '*Yishh!*' he exclaimed. The anger rushed to his head like alcohol and he almost lost his balance.

He stopped the cart, jerking violently at the reins. 'That was theft!' he shouted at the donkey. 'That was why I'm entitled to do anything I want – they've hurt me as much as they're going to.'

'Who's they?' he heard the donkey enquire politely.

'Never mind who's they!' he snapped in reply, '*you're* they, you pathetic, gentile, half-formed shadow of a thing. You're they!'

Smous stiffened, suddenly aware that he was alone; the girl wasn't behind him, he felt sure of that. Narrowing his eyes and pretending to scratch his neck, he glanced over his shoulder and, sure enough, she was about a hundred yards behind, squatting on the road, her stick resting across her shoulders, as if waiting for him.

She knows what's going to happen next, even before I do, he thought in amazement, swallowing hard. He could hardly breathe, see or hear, his body was like a shell, hard and tight.

'Thou Shalt Not Steal!' commanded the donkey.

'Say that to my face!' hissed Smous and pulled one of the reins, forcing the animal's head round to confront him. Instead it simply shuffled in a complete circle until the cart was pointing in the opposite direction, towards the open Karoo.

'That's more like it,' snarled Smous, and slapped the reins on the animal's back, urging it into a trot. In an instant they had drawn alongside the girl, who rose to her feet, her face breaking into a tremendous grin, the first time Smous had seen her smile.

'Yes!' she shouted, leaping onto the cart. 'Yes!', laughing, as they swiftly passed the gate to the farm and headed out into the veld. 'Yes, yes, yes!'

Smous started to laugh also – the girl's joy was the most extraordinary thing; now she would throw open her jaws, the cheekbones sharp as knives, her eyes popping, her skin translucent; now she would clap her hands over her face and whimper with pleasure. Then she stood upright on the rocking platform, put her hands to her neck and tore open the turquoise dress. It came away in her hands like paper, shredding across her breasts and arms and gathering round her waist, so that now she wore a full turquoise skirt. She waved her bare arms in the air, flicking her wrists as though they'd been untied, rolling her head and crying, 'Hoooooow . . .' then spat out a mouthful of dust with a grin that said, What a fool I am!

Smous thought a frog had landed on his lap. Good God, he thought, blushing scarlet, this really is a very unusual day. He stared at the girl's breasts, more like varnished wood than flesh, first sloping down, then abruptly curving up with large, dark nipples, charcoal brown on her yellow skin. A long shadow fell from one breast across her stomach, the sharp point touching her belly-button and flicking away, to the motion of their ride. Where the dress had been covering her skin it was a golden yellow, while her face and arms were the colour of apricots.

'Funny thing, all this time and we haven't been introduced,' Smous said to cover his blushing, yet unable to stop ogling the golden breasts. 'Your name, what's your name?' Puzzled, the girl looked down to see what he was staring at and found a cluster of turquoise threads caught on one nipple. As if kneading dough into a point, she gathered the threads in her fingers. Smous gasped. 'A name, a name for you is what we must . . .' he started to say, but she tossed the threads into his gawping face with a laugh, and shouted:

'Thank you – you're taking me back to my people, back to Kgototxe and Bo. Thank you, thank you!'

Smous's tongue caught on the delicious turquoise threads as he heard himself say, 'Golda!', his sister's name springing to mind, shockingly, while he gazed at the girl's nudity; Golda, his sister, who had stopped his childhood games twenty, thirty years ago, Golda, whom he could only remember vaguely, with a round sad face and hair plaited like a wreath – now a new Golda, a Golda with golden skin, golden breasts, a golden Golda.

The girl laughed and said, 'I thought I heard you call my name. It is Naoksa.'

'That's right,' Smous agreed eagerly, 'Golda!' He spluttered on the turquoise threads round his tongue, then blew them over his shoulder into the cloud of dust, tea leaves, coffee beans and glinting white buttons which fell from the little cart into the wilderness around them.

Karoo

It happened about an hour later and without warning.

Smous had momentarily turned his gaze from the road to steal his umpteenth glimpse of Naoksa's breasts when he felt the cart lurch. Swinging to the front he was in time to see the donkey take a nose-dive into the dust, before being catapulted from his seat. In the next instant he was spreadeagled on the animal's back while the girl landed neatly alongside, on both feet, as if she had been preparing for it. She pointed down at him, clapped her hands, and whooped with laugher.

Smous sprang up, glowering. He couldn't bear her mocking him, not with her standing there like that, half naked. 'I laugh only because it is a little misfortune,' she assured him, 'you are not hurt, so it is good to laugh' – but he had already turned his back.

His straw hat had landed across the donkey's ears, slanting down over its nose, as though the animal had flopped down to bask in the sunlight. But Smous was less comforted by the sight underneath: the donkey's eyes were closed, the jaw splattered along the ground, lips and teeth tangled, blood trickling from one nostril. It's all right, he told himself, it only tripped and banged its head, got a bit of a nose bleed, give it a moment to recover, it's collapsed before . . .

He swatted his hat against his leg, releasing a puff of dust, and looked around. The white road proceeded in a perfectly straight line towards a distant range of hills that were the same pale blue as the afternoon sky. The air was cooling. 'Must be about four o'clock,' he said aloud, and was startled by how clearly his voice travelled across the flat landscape, almost like an echo. Naoksa lifted her chin, but he shook his head dismissively and then coughed as dust showered from his hair. He turned in a circle. Under his feet clusters of earth, which he thought were pebbles, popped and disintegrated. The veld looked no different from before – perhaps the low bushes were yellower – but, because he knew no farm lay over the horizon, it was quieter.

Naoksa strolled over to a lone thorn tree a hundred yards away, and circled it, prodding her stick into the ground. 'I thought I saw *bi* leaves here,' she said, 'but no.' Smous listened to her chewing, clicking voice travelling across the open space. The sounds were so clear, so intimate, that, for a moment, he felt he might finally understand her language.

While she's gone, he thought, I'd better revive the donkey. He prised off the lid from the water barrel and, after gasping at the level inside, hoisted it off the cart and hurried to the stricken animal. He placed the lid near its bleeding nose and had just started to pour when, as if by magic, Naoksa was at his side wrestling with his arm. They both shouted at one another – 'No, no!' said the girl, 'Now just a minute!' said Smous, before a splinter from the barrel tore into his hand. The next instant he was drenched in water and the empty barrel was rolling away in the dust. 'Look what you've done!' cried Smous, but Naoksa had leapt forward and was sucking the water from the folds in his shirt and waistcoat, her tongue darting from place to place. 'My God,' said Smous as he found the small warm body burrowing in his arms and his fingers touching her naked back. 'What are you doing?'

'Quick, quick,' she muttered, pushing his shirt sleeve into his face, 'drink before it goes!'

'Kg-g-k!' said Smous as his forearm crashed into his nose, and he staggered backwards, his eyes stinging.

'Quick, quick,' she said, ducking down and planting her sucking lips on the folds of his trousers.

'Hi-iy!' squealed Smous as the insistent, darting mouth travelled across his buttoned flap, then he shoved her backwards and bellowed again, *'What are you doing?'*

She stood back, licking her lips and panting. 'Take off your skins,' she said, 'we must squeeze them,' and advanced with outstretched fingers.

'Now listen here, young lady,' said Smous, 'can we please get one thing clear . . .' then found he didn't know what to say, so waved his arms, trying to calm her. But the sight of the last drops shaking from his sleeves drove Naoksa into a frenzy again. She darted at him, but again he sprang backwards.

'Oh . . . oh . . .' she said, running in a little circle.

'Please calm down,' said Smous, beginning to panic; he recalled her mouth sucking harshly at his body through his clothes and felt giddy. And her eyes, why were they blazing at him like that above her golden breasts?

'I've told you to squeeze out your skins,' shouted Naoksa, 'why don't you?' She waited for a reply, but saw only his timid, uncomprehending frown. 'Are your ears as stupid as your eyes?' she asked.

'Look . . .' he said, his voice wobbling, 'we need this donkey up on its feet.'

'This animal . . .' said Naoksa, once her eyes had followed the direction of his finger, 'this animal will be dead before sunset.' To demonstrate, she grabbed the animal's ears and bounced its head on the ground – it spluttered softly. 'So why did you waste water on a dying animal?' she demanded, eyebrows raised high.

'May I please ask you something,' said Smous suddenly. 'Why do you keep talking to me when you know I can't understand a word you're saying? Hmm? What's the big idea?'

'What?' said Naoksa.

'Ye-e-es!' jeered Smous, but inside he was trembling. She seemed so sure about everything, while he doubted every instinct. He tried a different tack. 'Look,' he said, pointing along the white road, and speaking loudly. 'We – need – donkey – to – take – us . . .'

'There,' she interrupted, also pointing, 'we must go far, far, far. Perhaps we will come to the place where people end. Then we will need water. Now I have to find it although we had all we needed.' Glaring at him she added, 'You make work,' then turned on her heel and strode into the bush.

'Wait,' called Smous unhappily, 'where are you . . .?' but she clearly wasn't going far; already she had found something and was stabbing angrily at the ground with her digging stick. With a heavy sigh Smous looked down at the donkey. He noticed there was a gash on one hind leg, caused by the crash. The thin white hair gave way to a large notch of red meat, brimming with guzzling flies, making the leg look alive and dead at the same time. He wondered where the flies had come from – the air seemed free of insects. Perhaps they had travelled with them from the farm? Now he saw a column of large brown ants arrive around the edges of the wound. Another column was already excavating under the thin tail. Yet another was proceeding across the dry green tongue into the mouth. The donkey was barely able to flinch in protest. 'Ei! Ei!' whispered Smous as he bent over and began to sweep the ants away. For twenty minutes he battled, with less and less success, as reinforcements arrived from every direction. Then an odd brushing noise made him look up. Several large dark birds were circling slowly. The sun had started to dip towards the hills. Night would fall soon, and suddenly – he knew that from experience. 'Right,' he said decisively, and rose to his feet.

He looked across to where the girl was digging. 'Uhm . . . Golda!' he called, thinking how silly this name sounded now; 'Golda . . . Golda . . . we're going,' he called, feeling as though he was back in Plungyan summoning a child from its games.

Rummaging through the half-empty boxes and sacks on the cart, deciding what to take, he discovered that a chunk of bread and a strip of dried meat were all that remained of his food supplies. Something else to have considered before setting off into the wilderness, he thought angrily, then quickly crammed the food into his mouth before Naoksa returned. He filled his waistcoat pockets with the few coffee beans and tea leaves left in the sacks, and finally embedded a handful of sewing pins into the collars of his waistcoat, thinking, It's what my mother would do in this situation.

Naoksa had rearranged her torn dress, knotting the ends between her breasts and creating a sling under one arm, loaded with whitish tubers. She offered him one. He gulped down the last of his own food guiltily, then gave a harsh laugh, saying, 'Pardon me, you don't seriously expect me to eat that filth, do you?' She shrugged, chopped the tuber into a pulp with a sharp stone and drank the milk, squeezing fistfuls into her cupped palm. The moist remains were used to wash herself, rubbed over her face, neck and breasts as though it were scented soap. Smous watched through narrowed eyes. You're even odder than I thought, my girl, he reflected, then cleared his throat loudly. 'We're going now,' he announced and walked two of his fingers along the rim of the cart. She nodded and rose. 'Right, come along,' said Smous and turned to go.

'Your arrows,' said Naoksa.

'What?'

'Your arrows,' she repeated, 'you almost forgot your arrows,' and pointed to the box of knitting needles on the cart.

'You want me to take those?' asked Smous, and when she nodded emphatically, he gathered up a handful, muttering, 'Right, we'll take along the knitting needles, fine, we might want to run up a few pairs of mittens along the way, who knows? Anything you want, anything you say . . .' She watched him intently – she had often seen him bartering with these bright, silver arrows, but had never been able to locate the bow. There was still no sign of it now.

'Right,' said Smous, 'let's go.' He walked a few yards along the road, aware that she wasn't following, then stopped and turned. She was staring after him with a puzzled expression. 'What now?' asked Smous through clenched teeth, determined to avoid another bewildering conversation.

'And all this meat?' said Naoksa, pointing at the donkey.

'Yes, that's a donkey,' said Smous, 'a dying donkey. Say goodbye to the dying donkey and let's go.'

She watched him beckoning her away from the beast, unable to believe her eyes. Who was this person – shaped like an adult, with grey in his hair, yet knowing nothing, like a child?

'Oh please,' whined Smous, 'what is the matter now? The donkey's dying – yes, it's very sad, but there we are. Perhaps if you'd let me give the poor thing some water it wouldn't be dying, but you always know best, so there we are. All right? So now we'll have to walk and we must walk now, *now*, before it gets dark,' and he beckoned her again.

'You'd leave all this meat?' she asked in a hushed tone, then her eyes began to blaze. 'You are more stupid than any other living creature there is!'

Smous rested his chin on his chest and closed his eyes. It's happening again, he thought, I'm having an argument with a half-naked midget savage – how do I get myself into these situations?

'Man!' shouted Naoksa, startling Smous into a wide-eyed stare. 'We cannot leave all this meat!'

He strode back and stood facing her across the donkey. 'All right,' he said quietly, 'try and explain to me what it is you want.' He waited expectantly, but so did she. 'Well?' asked Smous.

She frowned and said 'Go on, kill him and we will skin him together.'

Smous's shoulders shook with mock sobs. 'I don't know what you're saying,' he whimpered.

She backed away from him, appalled. 'You're like the man in the story,' she said, 'the man who is only half a man, the man who is only an arm and leg joined together, hopping out of his mother's sack, needing many wives to succour him,' and she began to hop on one leg, singing mockingly:

'I am but half a man
Yet I have many wives
Wherefore being no man
I am yet a great man.'

Oh God, thought Smous, I knew she was mad, what am I going to do? Naoksa tried one last time. She pointed determinedly at the donkey and mimed shooting it with a bow and arrow. 'You want me to kill the donkey?' asked Smous, repeating her gestures. She nodded slowly, a humourless smile on her lips, as one who had finally communicated with a stubborn child.

'Why . . . ?' Smous started to ask, but then, glancing down at the donkey, the reason was clear: giant shivers passed over the small white body as a million jaws chewed at it. He couldn't leave the animal in such torture. 'How am I to do it?' he asked Naoksa, gesturing hopelessly. 'How? How?'

She stared back incredulously, then gave a sigh. 'Your arrows,' she said, pointing down to his hand.

'You want me to kill it with a *knitting needle?*' asked a horrified Smous. 'You do it,' and thrust the needles towards her.

'I must not touch them,' she said shaking her head, more amazed than ever, 'if I touch them I will rob you of your skill and luck, weaken your heart.'

'Ye-e-es, not so brave now, eh?' scoffed Smous. 'Big with the mouth, but not so hot when it comes down to action.' He caught sight of a heavy stone at his feet and, without further hesitation, lifted it, turned away his head, and thumped one of the knitting needles into the donkey's neck. 'AAAAK!' shrieked Smous and, turning back, discovered one thumb shuddering on the crown of the needle, the nail shattered, the flesh white. The needle was nevertheless driven deep into the beast's neck.

The donkey slowly raised its head and stared at him with bulging, milky eyes. It opened its mouth into a dreadful scowl, stretched out its tongue – on which ants were still at work – and bellowed so loudly that both Smous and Naoksa leapt off the ground, and the ants flew through the air like bees. The animal's cry was strangely human, but then, as if prepared for another, the noise was like machinery, squeaking and grinding. With the stone held high, Smous stepped forward to drive home the needle and silence the terrible racket, but as his shadow, sharpened by the setting sun, touched the writhing beast, Naoksa screeched, 'Beware, your shadow must not fall on a dying animal!'

Smous went cold. He abandoned the stone, threw aside the remaining needles, and, grabbing Naoksa's wrist, dragged her down the white road, despite her shouts of, 'The meat, the meat, your arrows and the meat . . . !'

Behind them, the donkey kicked wildly and struggled to stand. Its pumping cry rang out, terrifyingly, magnificently, again and again, as if to haunt every living being within earshot.

Sucking his squashed thumb as they ran, Smous glared at Naoksa and swore vengeance.

The Racing Stone

He had been racing the stone for over two hours and it was winning.

Mustering his strength he succeeded in taking one pace with his right leg. He would have to wait before the left was ready to follow. In the meantime the stone fixed its grim, cold gaze on the horizon and, with the tiniest scraping sound, glided ahead.

The contest was upsetting Smous deeply. Perhaps it was the presence of Naoksa on the side of the white road, following the race intently. In her hand was a burning tuft of grass. She had started the fire some way back, sitting on the ground, her feet restraining a length of softish wood while her furiously rubbing hands drilled into it with a harder twig. Then she had carried the fire, adding fresh fuel each time it started to die.

I know what you're up to, thought Smous, I know what you're planning for the loser; and he succeeded in dragging his left leg alongside the right. He noticed with pleasure that her fire was dying and that the next bush was quite a distance off, a tiny smudge on the blank earth. Far, far away there was a single hill shaped like a top hat, with a single cloud above it. Otherwise the sky too was blank.

All three were stationary – Naoksa, Smous and the tortoise. Smous listened to the silence. 'Trrrrr,' he heard. He glanced around nervously, then cursed himself for almost losing his balance. That wouldn't do, he thought, play right into her hands – and her arms, her breasts, her shameless breasts, and those buttocks sticking out, like more breasts. 'Trrrrr.' He knew it must be a cricket, but couldn't locate it. 'Trrrrr.' This time he thought he saw a movement on the road, no more than a shifting of white on white.

Smous glanced at Naoksa. The fire had reached her fingers, the smoke curling round her thumb, but it didn't seem to hurt. Not surprised, thought Smous, the sun has no effect on her either, she's some demon from another world, a dybbuk, I knew that long ago, that's why she's so tiny . . .

Suddenly Naoksa sprinted to the next bush, uprooted part of it and added it to the fire. The sound of her steps across the crusty surface carried to Smous in minute detail, and reminded him of someone running on frozen snow.

'Cheat . . . cheat,' he croaked, 'we haven't reached there yet.' Right, he thought, if she's going to cheat so am I. He bent over, ignoring the wave of dizziness, and lifted the tortoise. Immediately its neck and legs disappeared, giving him a terrible fright, and then a foul-smelling liquid rinsed over his thumb with the blackened nail, and down his sleeve.

He fell back into the white of the road.

When he opened his eyes he found his worst suspicions confirmed – he was being burned alive by the devil girl. He could feel his skin roasting and could smell acrid smoke. Turning his head he saw the tortoise upside down on the fire, its neck and legs wriggling in the shimmering vapour.

'You too, hmm?' said Smous. 'So we both lost.'

Naoksa was squatting next to the fire. 'Food will soon be ready,' she said cheerfully, and stoked the twigs. 'It's good food, it arrives with a cooking pot already on its back.'

When Smous opened his eyes again she was bent over him trying to force a piece of sticky meat into his mouth. 'You must eat,' she was saying. 'You've been without food for a day now.'

'I have something to explain,' Smous said weakly, but she took advantage of his opened lips to shove in the meat. He propelled it back into the air and continued:

'I'm not really expecting you to understand this, not expecting you to have any regard for the customs of my people, but the thing is this throughout these long and miserable months the one piece of self-respect that I've been able to hold on to is my faith, and the one good thing you can say about Kottler is that he sees to it his smouses eat kosher. Now . . . in our law it says we must not consume any creature that walks without cloven hoof or swims without fins or scales. Now, that stone . . .' he pointed to the sizzling black shell on the fire, '*that*, as far as I can see, is one big uncleaved hoof. And now that it's upside down you can also clearly see it swims without fins or scales. So, do you see? The food you are offering me is not just unclean, it is Sin itself – Sin made visible.'

He struggled to his feet. 'We'd better get going,' he said briskly, 'Kulvidya won't wait forever.'

Paradise

Now when he opened his eyes he was in paradise. It looked, as he had always expected, like the illustrations which the Russian artist had drawn of Palestine; above his head was a cool grove of palm trees with doves circling and the sky bathed in golden light.

So this is what it is like to be dead, he thought happily, this is what all the fuss was about.

His mouth was full of delicious water. He swallowed gratefully. Naoksa came into view, blocking out the trees and light. Her cheeks were bulging. She put her lips to his. Again his mouth filled with an exquisite taste and again he savoured it. He felt one of her breasts brush across his folded hands and thought: so this is Jewish copulation, another big fuss about nothing. It was exactly as the Dolrogusky servants had once described it to Elie, a passing of seed into the mouth.

Naoksa lifted her face from his and settled back. Smous was intrigued to discover her alongside him – so, there was no linking of loins at all in this method. 'You look so surprised,' she said, smiling, 'perhaps you thought you had died and now you've come back to life.' She laughed. 'It is impossible. Rest, and I'll tell you why . . .' She waited until his frown had vanished. 'This is the story of how death came to people –

'Long, long ago, the moon saw how frightened people were of dying, so she sent an insect to them with this message: As I, in dying, live again, so you, in dying, shall live again. The insect set off, but he got lost many, many times. Then he met a hare who wanted to know what message he was carrying from the moon. When he heard it, the hare thought – this is an important message, I must carry it myself and be a hero. So he left the insect trailing behind and ran off, far, far ahead. As he ran, he practised the message again and again, but he was too excited, too much in a hurry, which is always bad, and he got it mixed up. By the time he reached the people, the message he told from the moon was this – I, in dying, live again, but you, in dying, will come wholly to an end.

'When the moon heard how the hare got her message all wrong she took a stick and hit it – so, so, so! – making the cleft in his nose and lip which remains to this day. And then the hare hit the moon back – so, so, so! – making bruises and scratches on her face, which also remain to this day. See –' she pointed to the sky where a full moon was beginning to shine brightly. Smous frowned. That golden light, wasn't it sunrise? Very unusual to see the moon so clearly in the morning.

'So it was a big mistake,' laughed Naoksa, clapping her hands, 'if the right message had reached people we would never die, never never, but only sleep for a few hours each day like the moon. Do you wish more to drink?' Her face dropped momentarily from view, and when it reappeared her cheeks were filled. She pressed her lips to his and transferred the water. This time he found the sensation sickening. But then, he decided, copulation was bound to take a bit of getting used to . . .

Wait a minute, he thought, the Dolrogusky servants said the woman takes the man's seed into *her* mouth, something's wrong here.

He pushed Naoksa aside and sat up, his mind racing, trying to work out, first of all, whether he was dead or alive. Or both, like Gommie on that first day in Southern Africa.

'Did you not hear my story about death?' asked Naoksa, her head cocked, as if listening to his thoughts. 'You hear so little.' She was kneeling astride a dark hollow in the sand, her fingers touching one end of a long reed which descended into the hole. Putting her mouth to it she drew up another mouthful of water, which this time she swallowed herself.

Disgusting, thought Smous and swung away his head.

They were in a dry river bed with a line of bushes on the far bank holding off the featureless, biscuit-coloured land. On their bank was the palm grove, an impenetrable cluster of trunks and leaves, the roots crowding greedily into the same small underground spring. The sand in the river bed was shaped in flowing liquid forms, yet it was bone dry, and the road travelled straight through – clearly the river itself was seldom an obstacle. Nearby to where they sat, the white line of the road was interrupted by a deep furrow which led across the sand to Smous's heels.

'Paradise . . .' he muttered irritably, 'the Litvaks were so frightened the Jews would get there first, through the forest. Paradise. Palestine. Africa. And look at it.'

The golden light was dimming. He blinked. Had that been a whole day?

'Lie back,' said Naoksa, fanning her palms downwards, 'we have fire and this is a good place to rest for the night. There is nothing to fear. I made an offering to the spirit of the river before I started to dig. All is well.'

Puzzled, Smous lay back and fell asleep. Naoksa looked at him, intrigued by his orange skin with its odd, bland smell, like milk, his loose hair, his tiny hands and feet. She wondered who he was. In the trees above them, doves began to call as night fell.

April

The next morning when Smous woke he peered at the dawn until he was certain there was to be no abrupt dimming of the sun nor rising of the moon. Then he sat up, feeling fresher than he had since starting the journey, two, three days ago – he couldn't be sure exactly.

After curtly refusing the berries and beetles which Naoksa offered as breakfast, he concocted his own: grinding a mixture of the coffee beans and tea leaves from his pockets and chewing the powder. Although the taste was bitter it set the blood tingling round his head and brought him smartly to his feet, saying, 'Ready for anything this morning!'

Clambering out of the river bed, they discovered the white road now pointed its certain finger towards a range of mountains on the horizon. Within a few hours they were standing at the bottom of the gigantic slope, and began to climb. The road snaked up in gentle loops from side to side, lying mostly in the shade. Elsewhere boulders were scorched purple by the sun. Smous fainted twice and was revived with draughts from Naoksa's water bottle – the charred tortoise shell with blocked legholes – and they sat peacefully until he felt strong enough to continue.

The sun was at its height when they reached the summit, but there was a breeze to cool them. A bee hummed by and a butterfly hovered over the long silver grass. Smous left the road and clambered over the stones towards the edge of the mountain so he could look back at the view. Munching his bitter mixture of coffee and tea, he felt trouble-free and reckless. The small flat rocks clattered under his feet like a roof of tiles, while the larger ones clanked suddenly, slightly, as though the whole mountain beneath was unstable, as though the whole world might tilt at any moment, tilt and twist and turn. He reached the edge.

Smous had never stood so high. It seemed as though his entire journey lay stretched out beneath him. The white road led his gaze across the great yellow-grey plains which he assumed to be the whole Karoo; a pale sheen in the middle he thought was probably the white-washed homes of Ceres, and further still, in the lightest haze, he fancied he could see the three mountains of Table Bay. The blue beyond them was surely not just sky, but the great ocean he had traversed, and finally, if he had chosen to really narrow his eyes, he was in no doubt that Plungyan itself could have been glimpsed for an instant.

Of all the people at home it was his old cheder teacher Pinchvinch, that pink frog, who he hoped was staring back.

'Pinchvinch, you monster,' he called, 'look at me – always bottom of your class, standing on top of the world now. Listen how well I've remembered your idiotic lessons,' and he began to recite in Hebrew: '"Moses went up from the plains of Moab unto the mountains of Nebo, to the top of Pisgah, that is over against Jericho . . ."' He filled his lungs and shouted each of the names, rejoicing in their exotic sounds, '" . . . and the Lord shewed him all the land of Gilead, unto Dan . . . Napthal . . . Ephraim . . . Manasseh . . . all the land of Judah, unto the utmost sea . . . and the Lord said unto him, This is the land I sware unto Abraham, Isaac and Jacob, saying, I will give it unto thy seed."'

'My seed, my seed . . .' ruminated Smous, still unsure what the word meant, but, unbuttoning his trousers, wondering if Naoksa could see him from the road, half-hoping she could, 'I give my seed unto this new land!' he shouted, arms held wide, watering the sky below him. 'So, take a good look, Pinchvinch – look at me now!'

Flushed and grinning, he returned to the road where Naoksa was crouched over a sheep's skeleton. 'This is not an animal I know,' she said, frowning. 'I think soon we will find people.' He nodded and said, 'Mmm. Probably a deer, is it?'

As they set off, Smous prepared for the descent; they had, after all, climbed up the mountain so now there would be the other side to climb down. But no, the whole world, it seemed, was one step higher. The land stretched away without dipping as far as the eye could see, the low bushes greener now, with honey-coloured hills in the distance.

They had been walking for about an hour when Naoksa suddenly stopped. She crouched slightly, tensing her neck, while her breasts slowly stiffened – Smous couldn't help noticing this – as she said quietly, 'There is a man.' Smous followed her gaze, but could see nothing. 'Perhaps it is not good,' she said after another few moments, then whispered, 'Come,' and took his arm.

He shook free, saying, 'Don't start your nonsense again.' The afternoon was so bright and clear, the air so pleasant, there couldn't possibly be any danger ahead. In an instant Naoksa had disappeared into the bush and Smous was alone.

He walked on, listening to the powdery earth crunching underfoot like snow, thinking that the silence around him was like a winter's day in Plungyan: except for your footsteps, an absolute silence for long stretches of time. His trousers scratched past a bush and he heard a cricket jump. 'Trrrrr.'

Now he could perceive a speck on the road. Stopping, he glanced into the bush. Naoksa was invisible. Amazing, he thought, for the bushes were no higher than his knees. He continued along the road, watching the speck slowly grow into a miniature figure.

If God is looking, Smous thought, He must be seeing two little dots on this great open space, like two ants, weaving towards one another, and He must be puzzled why we're heading together – just because of this joke of a road – when there's all the space in the world to pass one another by.

'Hast thou not dropped from heaven?' the stranger asked as they drew close, so close their noses almost touched, and when Smous looked baffled the man gave a little sniff and supplied the required response himself: 'Out o'th'moon, I do assure thee. I was the Man i'th'Moon when time was.'

He was a savage – his face, hands and bare feet the richest brown colour – yet looked like an Englishman with some rank in colonial administration. Below the shadow thrown by his khaki slouch hat was a well-trimmed moustache and mutton-chop whiskers, and he wore a linen suit and waistcoat which, although faded and odd-buttoned, had been cherished, while his open-necked shirt was white and starched. In one hand he carried a black umbrella, neatly furled, and in the other an old briefcase with only one strap remaining, the polished buckle winking in the sunlight.

'April is my name,' declared the man, smiling broadly and extending his hand, 'though one must hasten, sirrah, to embellish this information with the humblest request that you may see proper and fit to employ the Boer pronouncement of my name, that is, U*prill*, rather than the British pronouncement, *Ay*pril, which, it was my tremendous startlement to uncover, may be used in the christenising of a golden girl or lass, but not, no, no, for a fine heart-strong gent such as I!'

The stranger's manner was so gracious that Smous found himself standing smartly to attention as the handshake continued. 'Mind you,' April confided with a twinkling smile, 'it could have been worse, it could have been rather very damn worse indeed. On the day of our capture and christenising some of my fellows fared sadly, sadly, sadder still. For heaven's sake, good sirrah, consider bearing the names of November, December or January, woe betide, as some did, oh yes, the almanac was bared of leaves that goneby autumn day. Or consider the name of Wednesday, or Saturday – consider the master asking, "Where's Saturday today?"' He threw back his large head and roared with laughter, his face seeming to explode: huge white teeth, flashing eyes, shades of chestnut, bronze and ginger rippling across his cheeks and forehead, making it impossible not to beam warmly in response.

Now Smous offered his English scroll. 'Credentials, credentials,' said April, 'you are a fellow with my heart, sirrah,' and unrolled it. The linguist in Telz had served the Immermans well, for despite the saturation of sunlight over many months, the parchment retained its sheen and the inscription was clear – except where Gommie's tears had fallen that day in the sugarhouse, reducing the name of Smous's birthplace to 'Plu'.

April looked up with bright eyes. 'Immerman, your honour,' he said, 'I record from your credentials that you have journeyed from afar, "a world elsewhere", as the great poet puts it in one of his serious playpieces – but which world where? Perchance my first imprint of you was correct? Perchance this saying here – "I was born at the town of Plu at the Imperial Northwest Region of Litva" – is no less than a province of the moon. Is't so?'

Smous smiled and nodded graciously.

'Bravo, bullseye!' shouted April. 'You love a legpull too, you rotter you! A province of the moon indeed – indeedeedoo! And why not? How else could you be standing here with all of the Karoo behindst you and no honourable transport in view, if not by stepping off the moon's end one perilous night as she rose over Ganaga Pass towards the strange impatience of the heavens? There are more things in heaven and earth than are dreamt in our philosophies, and yet we are such stuff as dreams are made of. A hopeless complexation! So, dear friend and mooncalf, your origins we will toss to our dreams, but as to your declared destination, Calvinia, this is simpler stuff and here I hope to provide benign assistance, for it lies but fifty miles north of my present humble homestead, the nearby trading post and settlement called Middlepost – or Middelpos – as the Boers say.'

Smous blinked; among the welter of sounds he thought he heard a familiar word. 'Kulvidya?' he asked.

April stopped and passed his open palm across his face, muttering, 'Stupid, stupid, stupid . . . Forgive me,' he said, ''tis a common folly I confound again and again. I never think to be giving the other chap first choice of tongue, for mine, you see, breeds so many. As well as the English, I have the gift of the gab in the Afrikaans, the High Dutch, the Bantu – many, many tongues there – the Hottentot, a smuttering of the Bushman, and some Arithmetic too.'

'Kulvidya?' repeated Smous hopefully.

April frowned and consulted the scroll. 'Ah!' he cried. 'Forgive your potty servant once more, all is finally explained – it says here clearly, "I do not speak your language yet." *Yet?*' He winked at Smous. 'When, then? Eh, mooncalf? Perchance tonight when mother Moon rises and sheds her magic light? How simply thrilling! Allow me to be present, allow me to host you for the evening, pray. I too am behunting magic tonight, magic for my Muse . . .' He tapped his long fingers on his briefcase.' So let us magic the night together, and then on the morrow, with you, no doubt, fluent as I in the languages o'th' land, why tush!, you will come to meet my masters in Middlepost, and thence to Calvinia.'

'Kulvidya?'

'Calvinia!' said April with a cheer, 'already we hear one another clear as the trumpet's alarum! Calvinia, Calvinia! Fie, sirrah, fie – your travels and tribulations are o'er, for I shall host you favourably galore. Now, fear no more the heat o'the sun . . .' and he unfurled his umbrella with a loud 'Whop' and held it over Smous's head, his other hand offering the road ahead as a carpet onto which they might step.

Intoxicated with his good fortune, Smous was about to set off when he remembered, said, 'Oh, excuse me . . .' and, scanning the surrounding bush, called, 'Golda . . . Golda.'

'Golda?' enquired April, 'what a charming name. You are not utterly alone then, Golda. A child of the sun no doubt, as you of the moon,' but his smile dropped as Naoksa rose from behind a nearby bush. A shadow passed over his face, blue-black wrinkles springing up around his eyes and nose. With a harsh grunt he dropped his briefcase, abandoned his grip on the umbrella, which fell like a hood over Smous's head, and swung both fists above his head. 'Are there others?' he asked in a new, hoarse voice.

Smous peeked from under the umbrella and said, 'It's Golda . . . there's nothing to fear.'

'Are there others?' repeated April tensely.

'We're friends,' replied Smous.

'She is your servant?'

'We've been travelling together.'

'What language is that, pray?' asked April, sidetracked by the Yiddish sounds.

'Golda.'

'Golda – is a language?'

'Golda. My friend Golda.'

'Golda is her name or your language?'

'Golda . . .' repeated Smous timidly.

April frowned. 'Summon her please,' he requested, and when Smous shrugged, he turned to the girl himself and called, 'Golda!' Naoksa didn't move. 'Hey, girlie!' shouted April, now in Afrikaans. 'Over here, now,' jabbing his forefinger to the ground at his feet. Still she remained rigid.

'Golda . . .' called Smous gently, beckoning her. 'It's all right, he won't hurt us. Come, it's all right, come.'

Naoksa stepped over the bushes and approached slowly, her dark eyes fixed on April. 'Dog of the wind!' he scoffed in Xhosa. 'Foot of the baboon!' and flexed his knees suddenly to frighten her. She tensed, then crept behind Smous.

'Why do you choose such rubbish as your servant?' asked April, struggling to remember his manners. 'These are not people, no, no, verily no, these are little things that go under the grass, understand? These are fleas, understand? Her menfolk shoot you with their poisoned arrows – *Zoop*! – you look round, no one is there. You die without knowing who it was, where it came from. Where's the honour in that? *Yeha-bah*!' he shouted hoarsely, and dragged Naoksa from behind her protector, shaking out her sling so that tubers, tortoise shell and berries tumbled into the dust. 'Which is your tribe?' he asked in one of the Bushman languages he knew. She stared at him silently. 'Your tribe?' he said, trying another of the languages, 'what tribe?' Again she was silent. He propelled her away from him and, speaking both in English and Afrikaans, said, 'She's not from anywhere near hear, no, no, she's wild, man, we must surely find you a very much more excellent servant.'

Smous dropped to his knees and helped Naoksa collect her scattered belongings. Who was this man? One moment he seemed the most refined gentleman, the next he was like an ape with bared teeth and loose, waving fists. April, in turn, was amazed to see Smous helping the girl. 'Sir,' he said, reaching for Smous's shoulder, 'pray, do not undignify yourself so.' In that instant his fingers touched Smous's waistcoat and a current shot through him. 'Shhew!' cried April leaping backwards. He stared at Smous wide-eyed. Perhaps this small stranger with the unfamiliar clothes and matted beard really was a being from another universe? 'There is a world elsewhere . . .' he whispered to himself and then, even quieter, in Afrikaans, 'May the Father, the Son and the Holy Ghost protect me.'

'I'm sorry . . .' said Smous, grinning sheepishly, and showed April the sewing pins embedded in his waistcoat collar.

'Ah, yes . . .' said April, not entirely convinced that the current was so easily explained. 'So,' he said, 'if your honour Immerman sir chooses this lowly rubbish as your slave, so be it, the world is very strange as Christ is my saviour!' He twirled his long forefingers round his ears. 'We have an old man of her kind living near Middlepost, name of Bok, a dratted cad in my opinion, but perhaps he will elocute her for our favourable illumination forsooth. That is for the goodly day tomorrow, but now, before the sun hath made a golden set, let me oh please entertain you to high tea refreshments.' He turned to Naoksa, growled the word 'Fire!' in every language he knew, and then finally, in exasperation, demonstrated with his hands.

'Ah – fire,' said Naoksa, and drew her firesticks from a knot in her dress, grumbling, 'another fool, he doesn't know the word for fire.'

'It's like wandering in the belly of a bullock,' muttered April in Xhosa, then retrieved his umbrella and held it over Smous's head. 'Follow me, please,' he said with a charming smile.

Leaving Naoksa to prepare the fire, April led Smous across the veld towards a range of rocks. Again his manner changed, falling silent as he scanned the ground, his large nostrils prickling. At last he found what he was seeking – a pile of animal droppings linked together like tiny sausages, which he separated with his fingers and inspected. 'If you will be so kind,' he said to Smous, handing over his briefcase and hat as he set off at a swifter pace, furling the umbrella in readiness. Smous noticed that the tip had been hammered into a cluster of metal splinters.

They reached the rocks and, sniffing rapidly, April led towards a flat stone stained yellowish-white and reeking with musky scent. From there he quickly located the mouth of a lair. Inserting the umbrella and most of his arm, he made contact with something inside, swivelled his shoulder as if unscrewing a cork, and then, with a sudden grunt, withdrew the umbrella. Entwined on the metal cluster was a shred of greyish-brown fur speckled with blood. April peeled this off and, mumbling impatiently in Xhosa, inserted the umbrella again, jabbing it fiercely before swivelling his shoulder. 'Ah-hah!' he exclaimed. 'A very palpable hit!' and withdrew the umbrella. This time the twist of fur on the tip was still attached to its owner, an adult dassie, kicking wildly and gnashing its teeth. It looked to Smous like an obese rat without a tail. April took hold of its short hind legs and swung it above his head. The dassie made momentary eye-contact with Smous, a glance which said, let's hope this doesn't look as stupid as it feels, before its skull exploded against a rock.

As April carried the dassie back towards the road, the dangling head stared at Smous again, but now the smashed eye and mouth were smirking. Smous stuck out his tongue at it and looked away.

It was about three days since he'd eaten. Hunger tortured him in different ways, sometimes gripping his bowels so that he had to bend double as he walked, sometimes attacking him with violent nausea and headaches, at other times no worse than a light muzziness, reminding him of the annual fast on Yom Kippur. How much longer could he endure it? He cursed his ignorance of the food laws, his woeful concentration in cheder classes, and Pinchvinch's droning voice: 'Kosher is not just a custom, it is a precise, divine law for a restrained, disciplined people. You may only transgress a Biblical law when your life is in danger.' *When your life is in danger?* How is a starving man expected to know when he's reached danger point? If only Pinchvinch had been more specific.

Naoksa had prepared a good fire. April shooed her away from it, then proceeded to skin and cook the dassie himself. Smous sprawled on the ground, chin on hands, watching the sun dip through the haze of their fire and plant itself in the flames. Around them the veld turned black.

'High tea is served,' said April with a little bow.

I must resist, prayed Smous, I must, the man is so well dressed we must be near civilisation and kosher food, I must hold out, God give me strength.

'A-a-ah!' he whimpered as a sizzling dassie thigh was handed to him. Then he tore at it with his teeth, gulping down the stringy lumps of meat without chewing. So, he thought, this is what Sin tastes like. He finished the thigh in an instant and plunged his hand through the flames, grabbing another chunk of meat. Sin, sin, he thought, who would have expected sin to taste so sweet? Then his guts buckled and saw the meat return to his lap still charred and steaming.

'Dear friend,' said April gently, squatting beside him, 'I think you have not consummated a meal for many a long day. Allow me please . . .' He began to divide the meat into small strips and handed these to Smous, holding back each piece until the previous one was thoroughly chewed and swallowed.

Smous sat eating with tears in his eyes, feeling as though he was an infant or old man being fed, feeling as though an enormous struggle – his whole life – had been lost. Through a blur of tears he watched Naoksa waddle over to the fire, crouched on her haunches, and reach for a piece of meat. 'Ag, what?' bellowed April in Afrikaans, 'go piss up your pussie, girlie, you go find your own food, you hear?' And he pelted her with a handful of burning twigs and ash.

'Oh, don't,' Smous started to say, but he couldn't speak; his shoulders shook with huge sobs, tears flowed down his cheeks, saliva spilled from his chewing mouth and dangled from his beard.

'What is it my friend?' asked April gently, but Smous could only shake his head dumbly, chewing and swallowing, chewing and swallowing, grasping for the next morsel with trembling fingers.

When at last he had done, he sat very still staring into the fire, slowly blinking his matted eyelashes. April drew a goatskin of water from his briefcase and set it down near Smous's hand.

'I don't know why that felt so important,' Smous said eventually. 'I left my faith years ago actually. As soon as I became a man I left my faith. Today you are a man, they said, and I fled. Oh, I still go to synagogue, but not, you know . . . with my heart. Still, it's just that we've always kept a kosher home . . .' He looked at April's face across the fire and sighed. 'You can't understand a word. There's no point in talking.'

April smiled. 'I understand you.' He pointed to the night sky. 'The moon shines bright. In such a night as this, in such a night . . . methinks . . . Oh dear Lord Christ, I don't know how the poet would put it, but my people would say –' he changed to Xhosa, 'Tonight the wonderful and the impossible can come into collision. So, talk.'

Smous shrugged. 'It is our custom when the boys are growing up   ' He gestured with his hand held boy-height above the ground.

'How old?' asked April.

'This high,' replied Smous.

'Twelve, thirteen,' said April and drew the numbers in the ash of the fire.

'Thirteen, thirteen exactly!' exclaimed Smous.

'Talk,' said April, smiling, 'talk.'

'When we turn thirteen it is the custom to be barmitzvahed in the synagogue, to sing the service.' He closed his eyes tight, then sang in a thin, shivery voice:

'Bless ye the Lord
Who is to be blessed
Blessed be the Lord
Who is to be blessed forever and ever . . .'

April winced.

'Exactly,' said Smous, 'I can't sing. Music goes into my head so very sweetly, but comes out sounding like a goose in pain. And I had the great misfortune to be born into a religion where the ritual is, unbelievably, to *sing* your way into manhood. And worse, where you have to practise this singing in a class full of your fellows. And worst of all, with a high-class torturer for a teacher. When I couldn't get the notes . . . oh God, I still can't think about it without going cold . . . he would drag me out in front of the whole class and pinch me like this –' He showed Pinchvinch's nip to the inner upper thigh.

April frowned at first, then nodded, 'Ah yes, circumcision. My people also.'

'I think he was trying to regulate the notes of my singing by tightening or loosening the pinch. All it did was turn it into one long screech.' Smous demonstrated and April's eyes popped from their sockets.

'In my bedroom at night I prayed to God, begging Him to help me, promising Him anything, a lifetime of devotion. I prayed to Satan too, and promised him a lifetime of sin, I think I once even promised to eat non-kosher food, anything – if only an exception could be made in my case, and I could be allowed to turn eleven on my coming birthday instead of thirteen, and then ten, nine, eight, and so on . . .' Now Smous told April about his childhood, producing from his shirt pocket the fragile illustration of Jonah and the Great Fish.

'What is it?' asked April in awe, 'what is this creature? Fear and wonder, fear and wonder!'

'If only you could really understand me,' said Smous, distressed by April's expression. 'I've actually seen one of these, from the deck of a ship. These miracles actually exist! I wish I could tell you . . .'

'Fear and wonder,' whispered April.

'Anyway,' said Smous, folding the illustration and returning it to his pocket, 'when the day of my barmitzvah dawned I woke with a fever. I was yellow and sweating. My best shirt was drenched as I staggered up to the reading desk in the synagogue. People were so shocked by how ill I was they hardly noticed my appalling singing. That was the whole idea. The fever had sprung to my aid. Not God, not Satan. Me. As I realised it I felt wonderful. Me making or breaking, creating, destroying – me, me, me. I even started to enjoy the singing. That was me too, that dreadful noise, that was my dreadful noise and so it was wonderful – wonderfully dreadful, only *I* could make a noise that was quite so wonderfully dreadful.' He sighed. 'If only I could have kept that feeling. But I panicked. I think it was seeing my mother's face sitting upstairs among the women, staring down at me. Well, I say staring – actually, her eyes were closed, but they were still staring, bulging through the eyelids. And I knew she had the same thought as I had, *me* doing it, me and only me, but in her mind it somehow turned into a curse: *only you . . . only you . . . only you . . .*

'I fell forward in a faint. I heard the great ends of the Torah rolling closed over me with a terrifying noise. Ear-splitting but soundless. I remember thinking – God has been winded. By me! They carried me home. Everyone got drunk. Even my mother who'd never touched alcohol before in her life. They filed past my bed, shook my hand, said the customary thing: "Today you are a man," then sniggered as they passed.'

Smous stopped speaking and turned his glazed eyes onto April, who rocked his head from side to side and whispered, 'Truly, we shall never see so much nor live so long.'

'So,' said Smous flatly, 'I don't know why it should have mattered so much eating your food. I have already failed as a Jew in so many ways.' He paused, then said, 'I'm a joke. Here I am, almost forty, I think, and I'm telling you about my barmitzvah. Trouble is, very little has happened since then. A Russian soldier spat in my face a few years later, well, on my beard, my first beard, but nothing much else. Sat in a doorway . . .' He put his head back and drank from the goat-skin, his eyes shut.

Now both men heard Naoksa shuffling her feet in the darkness behind them, cold and hungry. 'Hush!' commanded April. This troubled Smous, but he had already yielded to the stronger man's power and, for some reason, the girl was to be shunned. She was quickly forgotten as April leaned forward into the firelight now, commanding attention:

'Yours was an exceedingly rather startling and magnificent tale, my friend,' he declared, 'much of which I believe I understood clearly. Initiation as a young man, circumcision, tests of strength, the driving away of ghastly spirits who wail with frightful song and appear as gigantic fish apparitions, so on and so forth. Among my people there are similar customs and I too had to endure them, as I shall now relive to you. But sirrah, if you think your initiation was a shocking business, nothing can compare, no, no, oh goodness no, with mine. For it went so drattedly astray I fear my life will not be robbed of the curse till death it do part. Prepare yourself, sir, mine is a tale to pulverise a heart of millstone, for mine, sir, mine is the sorry tale of a vanished foreskin –'

'I'm sorry,' interrupted Smous, shrugging extravagantly, 'I think I'm lost already.'

'Foreskin . . . circumcision, like you,' said April and explained with a precise arrangement of his fingers.

Good God, thought Smous, I'm dealing with a Yid here, a Yid black as coal . . .

April's Story

' . . . As with your people,' said April, 'when a boy from my people comes of age there is initiation. This is the custom among my people, the Thembu people of the Mbashe Valley far, far from here – you see, in honourable ditto to yourself, I am not a native of these parts, but far from home, far from the banks of the Mbashe. My people have suffered much, persecuted like no other: a reign of terror from the east, from the Zulu King Shaka, from that bloody tyrant and homicide, from his bloody hordes and the bloody fugitives from those hordes – from these came a bloody business all round . . . but there's a story for another time. Our subject is the coming of age.

'We are growing towards manhood, I and my chums, and now we must prepare to depart from our youth with great occasioning, with dancing, sacrifice and feasting. I was fed personally by no less than the great warrior Mqhay, our own great Mars, our own great thing of blood, with – *ou!* – such great occasioning we left our homes and our youth behind and journeyed to the banks of the Mbashe where the initiation hut stood.

'When the moment of circumcision arrived I feared I would flinch, and this would bring great disgrace – calamitous disgrace, disturbance and dismay – you cannot imagine what size disgrace I'm hinting at. But I was blessed. When the moment came, when my man was laid on the sheepskin and when he was cut I flinched not a jot. Thus far all was well, wondrous well . . .

''Tis the custom next to dispose of the foreskin for it holds great magic. There is no toe of frog nor adder's fork more strong – believe this is true, my friend, to gasp at what beswamped my fortunes now.

'The custom is for each to bury his own skin, secretly, secretly, to bury it in an anthill where it may be consummated by a great host of different bellies, so that it cannot be pieced together, no, no, there is no witch's familiar clever enough to do this thing. Now, it was as I approached my secret anthill, carrying the skin, my own skin, my past youth, this magic, it was *then* that mishap did hap – Ahom! – men and horses, Zoop! I'm gone!

The skin fell into the river. I hoped it would drown. But it floated like a leaf, and flowed, flowed, there I see him go, there floats a brown leaf on the blue water, showing himself to all persons and spirits im-material, for any to fetch up and eat for his magic.' April stopped, clasped his palms over his head and rocked himself back and forth, humming softly.

Smous was enthralled. Not by the story – he had already lost the thread of it – but by the way the man spoke, by the way his white teeth bit deli-cately into thick and muscular vowels; by how his voice would soar high, shrill and gabbling, then suddenly dip into low dry murmurings; by the way he talked with his hands, his long fingers plucking at points in the air, as if snatching at spider webs, or else with one fist bunched, the little finger daintily crooked.

April cleared his throat. ''Twas not just I, but all of us, all my chums from the initiation school rounded up and carried away by these men – Englishmen by my troth! – drunk and sporting – carried to an English military garrison, much to our general startlement. The English, we had been told, had officially abominated slavery in all four corners of the great and glorious Empire twenty years before my birth. What is this then forsooth? No point dwelling, for we are theirs now, slaves, servants, or what you will, christenised January to December, and, personally speaking, April's fortunes are faring fine. I am given to one of the officers, the Englishman Quinn, a man of the greatest learning, a somewhat good sort and a jolly damn reprobate too, a man whose mind goes flying with both angels and vultures, a splendid all-rounder you might say! So often is he getting into one damned scrape after another he is forever confined to barracks with the time in his hands, and one day he says, "April, dammit, we're going to teach one another all we know. You will teach me Xhosa and I will teach you English – to read it, write it and speak it inside out."

'Oh, my friend, how can I begin to tell you how ignorant I was? You see before you now a person of ruddy outstanding learning and read-ing, but 'twas not always thus. When I first saw writing on a page I thought it was witchcraft, it's true. How could marks on a page whis-per a man's thoughts? I recall . . .' April bashfully put his head to one side. 'I recall one time sitting on a book to silence its whisperings and blind its sight so it should not see my ignorance and confound me no more.

'But as I start to learn – oh, my friend, dear friend and mooncalf –

what explosions, waterfalls and cathedrals, what heart-thumps galore did I learn in a twinkling of myself, and learn and learn and so forth, forever and ever amen. But the great, greater, greatest, was yet to come. I was to make the acquaintance of that other great Englishman, the one who has said all things to all men. Listen now how we met first.' April leaned across the fire; the flames flickered over his eyes, his teeth, the tiny bubbles on his lips.

'Among the many talents of my master, the Englishman Quinn, he is a past master exposer of the art of the rapier foil and fencing. So! They came to him for help, those ribalding, rollicksome, damn theatricals from Port Elizabeth – to help in their forthcoming portrayal of the Tragedy of Coriolanus by the great poet Shakespeare, to help portray the great contests of strength between the Roman and Volsci warriors with their fencing fights.

'When they are ready to portray this Tragedy I am allowed to go into their sacred hall and I am allowed to stand at the far end to watch their Tragedy unfold itself. I found it was these people's customs to paint the face and powder the hair, making themselves appear like ghosts, and then to sing their voices to a crowd who gathered for this exhibition. We are in the dark and these damn theatricals are in the light. On that night wisdom touched me. Oh dear me, on that night April's poor heart was a garden of blossoming and withering flowers, and all because of only one thing the warrior Coriolanus said to him across the dark. He spake thus: "There is a world elsewhere."' April slowly whispered these words across the fire again and again, until Smous believed some magic was being conjured from the flames, 'There is a world elsewhere . . . a world elsewhere . . .'

Now April grinned broadly and clapped his hands. 'War!' he boomed. 'War, the terrible bad war between Englishman and Boer – war, but I am happy. I am betrothed to a goodly woman, a cook in the camp, and she has borne me three fine issues, Caius Martius, Audrey and Ophelia, and we are on the move with a fine battalion of Her Majesty's Imperial Yeomanry, and I, I am riding alongside my master Quinn. They will not arm us blasted blacks, but all the same I am riding alongside him, because over the years I have learned not only the English, but many, many languages – this is my outstanding talent – and now I am my master's translator and scout, I am his disciple and know-all, I am a man's best friend, a paragon of comrades, I am the fellow's left bollock, goddammit!' April sighed nostalgically.

'From a distance a person seeing us could think he was beholding the warriors Coriolanus and Tulus Aufidius over there, riding side by side. Hommmmm . . .

'Nearby to where we now sit is the settlement called Middlepost where I will take you on the morn. Four years ago we attack and vanquish him. The Battle of Middlepost. A day of great glory and great, great sadness. Many, many Boers slain, eleven of our fine officers and men slain. Zoop! Zoop! The earth drinks blood, she's a pagan savage, not fussing, no, no, the drought's over for her. My noble wife and excellent two daughters slain also – Zoop! Zoop! Zoop! – burned alive in one of the wagons. It is a –' He suddenly stopped speaking, closed his eyes and bowed his head. All around the veld chimed with crickets, a ghostly pulse. Then he coughed and resumed.

'The ruler of Middlepost is the Boer Breedt. His loss was a fine male offspring this war-torn day, but he must go grieve in the prisoner-of-war-camp at the Green Point in Table Bay, this is where we send him, and his wife and daughter, they must go grieve in the concentration camp at Brandfort. So now Middlepost is ours.'

'Mil-poh,' repeated Smous slowly, taken with the sound of this word.

'Middlepost. So. I told you how my life was cursed by my vanished foreskin. Here now is the curse. The war is over, the Boers are returning and the English are leaving. All but this man Quinn. He has learned of great riches under the veld, riches greater than water, riches like in the north, on the Rand and at Kimberley where they dig sun and stars from under the ground. So he stays on in Middlepost, the Englishman Quinn, and gives two peace-offerings to his old foe the Boer Breedt. He gives first a fine and splendid grandfather clock made in America, oh gee! And then he gives next his most prized possession of all. What's that? Me. The servant that can speak with a hundred tongues, perfect for this trading-post, perfect for bartering and buying with all the peoples of the land.

'The Boers have a saying, "New masters, new men." So now I think I am a new man, but – beshrew me, yoh! – what a hopeless complexation, for the Boer Breedt, Baas Stoffel, he says to me . . .' Here April abruptly changed to Afrikaans, the switch into coarser sounds making Smous frown and lean forward. "Nay, April, you are not a servant of mine, no fear, man, I am but the humblest dust of the earth. Nay, you are the servant of a greater lord and master, you are the servant of the Lord God Jesus." And then he tells me, Baas Stoffel does, of how this God Jesus was crucified because of my sins. *My* sins and this good god dies? "Yea," he says, "yea, your evil, filthy, reeking sins, *siss*, man, *siss*, *siss!*" So I listen in big fear to Baas Stoffel and I make with my head so – ja, ja, ja – but secretly I think, because of *me*? It's not possible. No, I know better, I know the truth . . .' April's eyes widened as he whispered across the fire. 'It's that vanished foreskin. Someone has found it and eaten it for magic. This is why I am now the most cursed sinner the world has ever known, and this is why an innocent god has been crucified to death on my account.'

April wiped the sweat from his face and neck, rubbing it between his palms. 'But I can be saved from the curse, Baas Stoffel promises me this, I can know the Lord's mercy. All I have to do is believe in Him. That's easy. Believe in Him and renounce all my reeking sins and all the Englishman's teachings, and all his foul, hell-damned Shakespearing filth!'

He fixed Smous with a haunted gaze and now his voice roamed from one language to the other. 'So you see how sadly the circumcised dog was smote? Me living with both my two great masters. And oh, oh, the Englishman has only to whisper in my ear, he has only to whisper of his England and his Shakespeare, and I am a lost soul falling out of the God Jesus's marvellous light back into the reeking darkness again – still dreaming of travelling to these worlds elsewhere, travelling with dear Mister Quinn, as one day he has promised we shall do, of touching with my own two hands the magic snow there and the shivering calfspines in the great British Library, travelling – oh yes, i'faith – travelling to that royal throne of kings, that seat of Mars, that other Eden, demi-paradise . . .' April's eyes filled with heavy tears, and he held out both hands, weighing palmfuls of the night air, weighing the choices in his life.

Struggling to keep his eyelids from falling, Smous took hold of the man's hands and said, 'Dear fellow, I haven't understood a word you've said, but I have enjoyed listening to you all the same, and I'm sorry if your life has been hard.'

April answered, 'Thank you. I think you have heard me.' He reached out and dragged his briefcase across the ground towards them. 'Here lies some comfort,' he said, 'though I shame to show you.' He took out an old blue notebook, one which a child might use in school, and, flicking shyly through the pages with one thumb, showed Smous glimpses of his sketches and writings. 'These are the stories of my people, the Thembu people of the Mbashe Valley, who still reside there, so travellers tell me. These are the stories I remember.'

'Mh-hh . . .' murmured Smous, stretching out to be more comfortable. He was thinking of the dassie's face sailing through the air, its smashed grin mocking him, the sweet taste of its unclean flesh. Nothing had happened. The Lord had not wreaked vengeance, the land had not become burning pitch, a habitation of dragons, a court for vultures, every one with her mate. Instead, as far as he could ascertain, the melancholy man with the marvellous voice was taking him to Calvinia tomorrow, and his long journey would be over. He felt content. Behind them, he could hear Naoksa scratching the bushes as she had been doing for hours, hoping to be drawn closer to the fire. He ignored her, rolling his head on the earth, listening to the small crunching noise, looking at the stars which stretched from one horizon to the other, great white clouds of stars lighting up the veld.

'Perhaps in these stories of my people I will find the magic that will truly unlock my life,' April was saying. 'In all events, I come here to the bush now and then, I must come to write out these stories, even if they be just bloody stupid fairy tales.' He stopped speaking and gave a sigh, Smous was fast asleep. 'The ape of death,' April whispered, then sat motionless. Hearing Naoksa scratch the bushes again, he suddenly leaned towards her and said, 'Do that once again, girlie, and I'll butcher you.' She seemed to understand, for she went still and made no more noise that night.

April lowered his head onto his chest, fixed his gaze on the embers of the fire, and in a warm, dry voice, sang quietly:

> 'We call to the ancestors
> Come, smell, there's meat in the walls
> Will they hear?
> Will they hear?
> The dream tree rests in our cheeks
> The young moon rides – come – the beer is foaming
> Are they come?
> Are they come?
> Early the ants bite
> O, it was always so
> They are not here.
> They are not here.

Here is not home, they are not here
We wake, we sit, we disappear
So.'

3. MIDDLEPOST

Middlepost

A moment before Middlepost came into view there were tiny changes on the landscape: scraps of paper, thread and wool caught on the bushes, smashed glass gleaming among some rocks. Smous smiled and sighed with relief; he had crossed the wilderness and reached the other side.

When the settlement itself appeared he almost mistook it for another oasis, except that the trees were too full and dark to be palms. Then he began to detect the paler specks of roofs and windmills, and the smile returned to his lips. Kulvidya at last, he thought, who would ever have believed it. And indeed it was difficult to believe. Lazar's letter had spoken of a 'delightful little backwater not dissimilar to Plungyan', yet the settlement ahead looked so very small; it looked, in fact, as though it were no more than a single road, as though a single road had been plucked from a town elsewhere and placed in the middle of the veld. Smous frowned. Middlepost dropped from view and immediately the white road began to dip and curve, seeking it out again.

The three walked in silence, as they had done since the furious row which began the day. April had demanded that Naoksa cover her breasts before they set off; she, suddenly fearless, had refused. With Smous sitting bewildered in the middle, the two screamed at one another, each in their own language, until April lost patience and attacked Naoksa, clouting her head, whipping her breasts with his fingertips and pulling together the ends of the torn dress. She held these herself now as they walked, one fist on her chestbone, eyes fixed on the ground, jaw set. April walked ahead, the umbrella graciously held above Smous's head, but his step was heavy. Retelling his story the previous evening had summoned up a host of nightmares, leaving his features thick and grey, and a flutter in his belly.

Impatient with his gloomy companions, Smous filled his cheeks with air and, puffing silently at an imaginary trombone, prepared for his triumphant arrival. Then a gnat shot into the glowing shadow of the umbrella and passed his nose several times. The insect was too small and fast to see, and its noise hardly more than a sizzle on the hot air, yet for some reason it sent a shiver down his spine. He remembered the seagull giving its warning cry when he woke in Table Bay – 'Naa! Naa! Naa!' – as it perpetrated the first disaster of that long day.

Smous flicked his head. How absurd to imagine either the seagull or this minute insect had some foreknowledge of his destiny. He gave voice to his phantom trombone as they turned a bend in the road and Middlepost reappeared, now only a few hundred yards ahead.

The crunching sound of the group's footsteps remained clear, almost echoing, as they left the veld and entered the settlement. On the outskirts stood a group of wattle-and-daub huts, crudely whitewashed. There were women squatting outside the doorways, tending their young or cooking; a few raised their arms in lazy salutes as April led the group into Middlepost.

Smous's first impression had been correct; the place consisted of a single road, marked on the left by a long row of trees which led the eye swiftly through the settlement and out the other side. This half-avenue of trees was the immediate, dominant and attractive feature of Middlepost, promising water and shade. They were mostly pepper trees, large, shaggy, and unfamiliar to Smous; there were also, much to his surprise, two firs, and then, towering above the main house, a huge bluegum.

The house was low and sprawling, with roofs of corrugated iron and rough-cast walls, coated with a mixture of whitewash and pig's blood. Behind the building you could glimpse a large yard with outhouses, animal pens and windmills.

Across the road was a trading store, with goods displayed outside: buckets, brooms, untanned hides and animal horns, native trinkets for bartering, pumpkins spread on a sack, baskets of potatoes. The neighbouring building was long and had a blistered, red door, which now opened.

The first thing Smous noticed about the Boer who appeared and ambled towards them was that his feet were bare. He wore grey-green moleskin trousers and a beige flannel shirt with a paler sweatcloth tied round his neck. Squat and heavy, he reminded Smous of the tortoise he had raced in the Karoo, or something you might find underground, a rock or tuber; his muscles bulging like malformations, his skin hard and dry, and his wide beard, worn without a moustache, looking like a bush of roots. His hair was cropped close, a lighter red than the beard. His eyes were remarkable – blue, lazy and moist. They travelled slowly across Smous and Naoksa, then came to rest on April.

'Ah!' exclaimed April cheerfully, scenting trouble. 'Now, i'faith, la, permit me to affect an introduction 'twixt this, my good Master Stoffel Br–'

'April, where have you been, man?' interrupted Breedt.

'In the veld, Baas Stoffel,' replied April, immediately switching to Afrikaans, 'Baas Stoffel knows I sometimes spend the evening in the –'

'The evening? It was round four o'clock yesterday afternoon when we went looking for you.'

'Ja no, Baas Stoffel, perhaps I had already gone by then, I –'

'Perhaps you had, because we looked for you in every place we could think of.'

'Oh. No, then it sounds like I was gone by then, Baas Stoffel. For definite.' April hesitated, waiting to see if Breedt would interrupt again, then resumed, a little feebly, 'I always go on the veld Tuesday nights, Baas Stoffel, I –'

'Nights, ja *nights*,' said Breedt, stressing the word without raising his voice, which was an exceptionally deep one. 'And you know, April, the farmers mock and scorn me for granting you that free night. "A free night?" they laugh, "since when?" – and I answer them, no, look, he works hard for me, day and night, in the store, in the house, even on the sabbath when I must rest, he works, so to my way of thinking he deserves a free night. But they deem me a freethinker, April, or to be less polite, a fool. But maybe I am. Do you think I'm a fool, April?'

'Never, Baas. My Baas's a good Baas, a big wise Baas to us all,' said April, his mouth going dry. 'I just left a bit early yesterday because I was a bit . . . downcast. I –'

'Downcast? There's a feeling I recognise. Particularly this morning.' Breedt's lazy eyes drilled into April's skull.

'I just . . .' – April licked his lips – 'was thinking, there wouldn't be no traders coming through at that time of –'

'Traders? No, there weren't any traders, no.'

'Oh. That's good, Baas Stoffel, I thought maybe –'

'But there was a division of English soldiers.' Breedt waited for his servant to react.

'Oh,' said April eventually, and, when this didn't seem sufficient, added, 'Soldiers? Well, soldiers would not be wanting to do any buying, thanks be to Christ.'

Breedt sighed heavily and slowly between each of his next statements. 'These soldiers wanted to buy, April. These soldiers had been in the veld for days. These soldiers were hungry, thirsty, tired, you name it. These soldiers have stocked up here before. These soldiers had made a special detour to stock up here again, and you know why?'

'No, Baas Stoffel,' lied April, for he remembered the soldiers now.

'No? Then let me tell you. These soldiers like stocking up here because they like dealing with the native who speaks so beautiful and smart. They prefer to deal with him, and not with a Boer, if they can help it. You remember them now?'

'Baas,' mumbled April, trying to sound both affirmative and non-committal.

'And when the native who speaks smart couldn't be found, you know what they said?'

'No, Baas Stoffel, what did –?'

'They said, no what, we're only a day's ride from Calvinia, let's go there, stock up properly there, rest up properly there, we've detoured so far already, might as well go on to Calvinia now. And so they did, April, without buying a single thing.'

April shifted uneasily. What a pity to be humiliated in front of Mister Immerman before he'd had a chance to perform the splendid introduction he'd planned. Meanwhile Smous was transfixed by the Boer. Like his body, the man's voice seemed to have taken form under the earth, travelling on currents of its own, below all others, reaching up through your feet.

Breedt seemed oblivious to the strangers. He sighed heavily again, this time letting the expulsion of air carry him forward into a stroll around the road, staring all the time at his bare feet, while one hand plucked at the smocking on his shirt.

'Permit me to explain something to you, April. When I got back from the prisoner-of-war camp nine months ago and found all my livestock gone, either stolen by the English or used for target practice, it was like a hammer to my heart. I had worked hard on those flocks of sheep, herds of goats, they were my life, my wealth, my honest wealth. Why had the Lord spared some of the other livestock in the district, but not mine? Why was I now required to open this store' – he patted a stack of hides as he passed the doorway – 'to sell the other farmers' produce? Why was I now forced to open my home to overnight travellers, to gain revenue from them – strangers, foreigners, unbelievers – allow them into my home like it was some licentious lodging establishment? Why, why, why? That I couldn't answer, other than to say it was the Lord's Will and His Way is often written in tears and blood.' Breedt's path had taken him directly behind April, where he now stopped, talking softly into the man's back. 'But these things are not in my nature, April, running a lodging house for travellers, or trading, no, no. And trading with the English, the very people who destroyed my livelihood, that's a bitter herb to chew on. I will never learn to love trading, April, no. Never. No man nor no thing will ever make me. But I do it all the same. I do it out of humility to my Lord and to earn sufficient revenue that one day I may purchase new flocks and herds and return to a blessed existence on the land. But, but, *but* – do you understand, April? – when it comes to an incident like yesterday in the store with the soldiers, I tend to lose my sense of humour about it. Does that sound unreasonable to you?'

'No, my Baas,' whispered April tensely, wishing he could turn round to face Breedt. The latter nodded slowly, staring at his feet, then said quietly, 'A person would be entitled to be cross, April, nê?'

''s Baas.'

'A person would be entitled to be *very* cross.'

'Very cross, my Baas.'

'A person would be entitled to be buttock-thrashing cross.'

'A person would be entitled to the lot, my Baas,' agreed April unhappily.

'I've been a little bit like that all night, April.'

'Baas.'

'And all this morning.'

'Baas.'

'I thought of doing terrible things.'

'Oh Baas . . .' April muttered, wishing he'd slept better so he could think of something else to say.

'So do you know what I did, April?' Breedt asked with sudden urgency, scurrying around to face him.

'No, Baas, what did my Baas do, Baas?'

'I took my anger to God,' Breedt said with a vague gesture to the red blistered door through which he'd first appeared. 'I took it to Him and asked Him what I should do with it.' He stopped and waited.

'And . . . what did He suggest, Baas?' asked April.

Breedt rested his moist gaze on April until he was certain there had been no irony in the question, then said, 'The answer I received was thus: "Let your moderation be known to all men. The Lord is at hand."'

'Ahhh . . .' said April.

'So now I am at peace,' said Breedt, 'and my anger has gone.'

'Oh!' exclaimed April joyfully. 'That's good, my Baas, peace is good to feel, my Baas . . .'

Then it happened. Flushed with relief and sluggish from his bad night's sleep, April made his mistake – he turned his back on Breedt to beckon Smous, saying, 'Now, can I introduce –'

'Is that the end of the story, April?' interrupted Breedt, his voice thickening.

'Baas?' enquired April, swinging back cheerfully.

'Are we finished discussing the matter?'

'Ja, my Baas, I thought . . .' April stopped. Something was wrong, but what?

'*You've* decided we've finished discussing the matter?' asked the Boer slowly.

'No, I . . .'

'You just said we'd finished.'

'Ja, no, I just want Baas Stoffel to meet this gentleman here –' and again April turned his back on Breedt to beckon Smous.

The blow seemed to come from nowhere. One moment April was talking, the next his face was filled with Breedt's fist. It stunned them all, none more so than Breedt himself. He had struggled with his anger all night and was convinced he had overcome it. April's overwhelming feeling, apart from a ringing in his head, was of embarrassment. Naoksa stared at the ground, secretly pleased. Smous was appalled; again and again in his mind's eye, he saw Breedt's bunched fist slamming into April's face, the recurring image shuddering like the blow itself, until Smous felt it was he who had been struck.

To his surprise he found himself stepping forward and taking hold of Breedt's arm which was still raised in mid-air, hard and cold as metal. Grunting, the Boer swung towards Smous and snatched at his waistcoat, his fingers closing round the concealed sewing pins. April watched his master spring back exactly as he had done the previous evening. With a small laugh he stepped forward, intending to say, 'Oh my Baas, I did the same myself,' but never got further than 'Oh'. Breedt misread his laugh, and, with a roar, struck him again in the face, now with all his strength. April staggered backwards, lost his balance, struck his head against a stone pillar at the store's entrance, removing a patch of whitewash, and fell finally among the buckets and brooms with a crash.

Breedt stood hunched, panting, staring at the bearded stranger, flummoxed by the prickling current which had passed through his hand. Smous, meanwhile, was desperately searching for his English scroll, which did not seem to be in any of his pockets. He found instead the illustration from the Russian Bible, and, in confusion, thrust this towards Breedt.

As the page fell open, it undulated slightly and the sun caught the embossed gilt of the border; so the first thing presented to Breedt was a glowing square of light. Then, as the page went still, he saw Jonah and the Great Fish. He could instantly identify them from his knowledge of the Scriptures; less recognisable, though, was the Russian alphabet surrounding the picture. Stranger still, was the uncanny resemblance between the portrait of the prophet and the small man now trembling before him: the dark hair and beard, the long nose, the almond-shaped eyes, these were identical to the figure riding out of the fish's mouth on a column of vomit. Now Breedt's eyes flickered over Smous's clothes and he realised he had never seen a waistcoat like this one; the quilted maroon cloth patterned with an alien plant – tiny silver rūta. Was it this that had pricked his hand? He stared and stared.

The suspense was too much for Smous. He remembered Breedt's fist slamming into April's face, and feeling faint, staggered back. Then his stomach heaved and a watery soup, all that remained of the dassie, poured from his lips. Now it was Breedt's turn to stagger back. He glanced in amazement from Smous's vomiting mouth to that of the Great Fish – then uttered a small, strange sigh, turned and fled through the red door where he'd first appeared, slamming it behind him.

Smous straightened, spitting out threads of bile and wiping his beard. A woman appeared from the house across the road. She was a heavy, middle-aged figure, her skin lighter than April's. Wiping her hands on an apron stiff with grease and dried blood, she made her way across the road, taking no particular interest in the newcomers, but with eyes fixed on the unconscious April. She stood above him for a moment with a smile, then gave a few hard kicks. When he failed to respond, she shook her head scornfully and nodded at Smous and Naoksa to help lift him, the woman taking hold of his feet and directing the processions towards the wattle-and-daub huts on the outskirts. She led towards the largest hut which had no windows or door; a curtain of hessian covered the entrance, which she impatiently kicked aside. Inside, the air was hot, stuffy and black, but the woman, knowing where to aim, gave a high-pitched grunt and heaved April's feet into the air, leaving him to crash down onto the bed. Then, muttering in an odd, distorted way, she abandoned Smous and Naoksa and pushed her way back through the hessian curtain. From outside, another woman's voice was heard asking, 'Has the bastard had a hiding at last?'

The cook answered in her distorted voice, 'Heee haah, Baashh Sohho hi hi goooh.'

'So,' said the other woman, 'his brain was always too smart for his head, that one.'

As their eyes grew accustomed to the dark, Smous and Naoksa saw that April's hut was exceptionally tidy. The floor was the earth of the veld, but carefully cleared and brushed, and the walls freshly whitewashed. April's clothes were neatly draped over two hangers suspended from a nail in one wall. The bed on which he lay was wrought iron, army issue, but without a mattress. Next to it stood an overturned tea-chest with a clean stack of cooking utensils and cutlery, all army issue. Along the opposite wall was a surprising piece of furniture: a carved stinkwood bookcase, tilted awkwardly because of the uneven floor. It was bare except for a single volume: a small black Bible on the top shelf, its title engraved in High Dutch. Above the bookcase was a framed, embroidered motto written in Afrikaans: 'Earthly possessions are like a handful of flies.' From the ceiling hung whitish strips of dried meat and a cluster of mealie cobs. The only untidiness in the room was in one corner where a tangle of orange blankets on the floor suggested another bed. Above hung a canvas jacket – too small for an adult – with a ragged pair of khaki socks protruding from the breast pocket.

This reminded Smous to check his own clothes for the English scroll. It was definitely missing, presumably lost on the veld. 'Fool,' he whispered to himself. 'You're still going to need that.' Clearly this settlement was not Calvinia but some terrible place of violence from which he must flee. His searching fingers touched the pins in his waistcoat, and he decided to get rid of these before they caused any more trouble. Crouching, he pressed them into the ground. Naoksa squatted opposite, speculating whether this was some form of magic. For a long time they stayed like this, watching one another. Once or twice Smous moaned, 'Oh Golda, Golda . . .' and she stared back with that patient but despairing look, wondering when he was going to start taking control of events. Smous felt sick with fear, hunger and thirst. He buried his head in his hands and pulled at his beard in frustration; it was so caked with dust it felt more like cloth than hair.

Without warning April reared from his bed, the springs squeaking, and shouted, 'Get out of my castle!', hurling a tin mug at Naoksa. It clattered against her knuckles as she scurried through the hessian curtain. 'The south-frog rot him!' yelled April. His eyes were open but unseeing, his lips grey, his neck drenched with sweat. 'A common slave . . .' he croaked, 'a common slave, you know him well by sight, held up his left hand, which did flame and burn like twenty torches joined . . . or do I mean tortures, *tortures* . . . ?'

There was a giant, whitewashed lump behind April's ear from the stone pillar outside Breedt's store. Smous remembered Gommie, and the lump on his head after the carriage accident. 'It's happening again,' he muttered. Watching April loll on the bed, he began to feel giddy. The two men frowned at one another across the room, as if across a great distance, before both suddenly fell asleep.

'Are you a friend of my pa's?'

Smous opened his eyes to find a fourteen-year-old boy leaning over him, clutching a schoolbook. 'What's the matter with him?' asked the boy, speaking in Afrikaans, 'do you know what's happened?'

'Huhn?' murmured Smous, recognising April's features in the boy's open face.

'I'm Klippie,' said the youth and then, whispering confidentially, very like his father, told Smous, 'My real name is Caius Martius, a fine name, hey? From long, long ago, from when him here was full,' he tapped the bookcase. 'But I'm not allowed by the big Baas to use it any more – "No, never, Klips, you can't." ' He grinned. 'Still, Klippie is good too. Means stone. Because I'm so very, very strong. Feel,' he said, thrusting a clenched bicep towards Smous who cautiously tweaked it.

'Hmm,' said Smous. 'Perhaps you can tell me, is this Kulvidya? It isn't, is it? We're not in Kulvidya, are we?'

'What language is this?' retorted Klippie with fierce interest.

'Kulvidya? This – here – Kulvidya?'

'Feel,' said Klippie, now presenting his tightened stomach and punching it violently. 'Go on, hit it. It won't hurt, hit it! Go on.'

Frowning, Smous punched the boy's stomach lightly, then said, 'I think we must get a doctor for your father . . . Is this your father?'

'What language?'

'A doctor. *Doc-tor.*'

'German? American? Hit my leg, go on. Won't hurt, go on!'

With a sigh Smous rose to his feet, and pointed urgently to the whitewashed lump behind April's ear, the sweat pouring off him, the grey scum on his lips. Klippie nodded and shot from the room.

A few minutes later Smous heard the sound of heavy boots crossing the earth outside the hut and then a doctor's leather bag pushed through the hessian curtain. Hoping against hope, Smous thought Lazar might appear, but instead Breedt entered the hut, smiling gently.

'Hell, April, now what have you gone and done, man?' He nodded politely at Smous, who noticed that the Boer had worn his boots for the visit, though their laces were untied, trailing in the dust. 'Hold open that curtain, Klips,' he said to the boy following him. Light poured through the entrance as the Boer sat on the bed and began a careful examination of April's injury. 'Little bumpie, nothing to worry about, no, skin isn't even cut,' he said to no one in particular, then began to rummage in his bag, humming a little tune. April woke and, finding his master on his bed, attempted to sit up; but, as before, his head lolled over to one side as if it had grown too heavy for his neck, and he crashed back onto the springs.

'Take it easy, man,' said Breedt.

'It's my ear, Baas,' whispered April. 'Hurts like devil's nails, Baas . . .'

'Your ear?'

'This one, my Baas.' He pointed to the side with the whitewashed lump.

'Only the one? Then we must thank the Almighty for giving you another, nê?' and he winked at Klippie in the doorway. 'Oh, by the way,' he added to April, 'you dropped some things outside the store, which I've given back to your boy'. He nodded towards the briefcase and umbrella which Klippie was holding.

'Please, Baas,' groaned April, 'ear hurts, my Baas . . .'

'All right, April, all right,' said Breedt compassionately. 'You shall find comfort, you shall find mercy.' He crumbled a greyish tablet into a mug and added a measure of orange medicine. A smell of cloves filled the hut. 'Doctor Kiesow's Specific Nerve-Pain Remedy,' he informed Smous. 'Cape Dutch Remedies – best in the world.' Now he carefully supported April's head while he drank. 'There you are, my friend, earache will be gone in a couple of hours and you'll be back on your feet good as new by the evening. Anyhow, I'll leave the medicine here,' he said to Klippie. 'If he's still got a bit of pain in a few hours, you can give him another dose.'

''s Baas.'

'You watched how I did it?'

''s Baas.'

'You watched properly?'

''s Baas.'

'With both eyes God gave you?'

''s Baas.'

'Good boy.'

''s Baas.'

April groaned as Breedt heaved himself off the bed and whispered to Smous, 'Pardon me, but I wonder if I may be permitted a word alone with my old friend here?' When Smous shrugged nervously in reply, Klippie explained, 'He's a traveller from afar, Baas,' and led him through the doorway.

Outside, Smous was surprised to find the day almost over. The air was thick with smoke from cooking-fires all round the wattle-and-daub village. The men were back from work, squatting alongside their women. All raised hands or hats automatically as Smous surveyed them, and a little chorus of greetings – 'Baas ... Master ... Baas ... Master' – passed round. Smous nodded vaguely in return. On a cleared space nearby, a group of children were playing a stone-throwing game, their shadows long and blue, the late afternoon sun streaming through clouds of dust. A fight broke out and everyone suddenly surrounded one tiny girl, kicking and stoning her. Shocked, Smous turned to Klippie, who strolled closer but didn't intervene. The girl fled and the game continued. Still Klippie stayed on the outskirts, looking both aloof and lonely. Smous noticed how much darker his skin was; apart from him and his father, everyone else in the village was coloured more like Naoksa, a yellower brown. Yet these were clearly not her people; she was crouching against the wall of April's hut looking fearful and wretched.

Now Breedt arrived at Smous's side, saying, 'Forgive my rudeness, making you stand out here. Come with me please,' and led towards the main settlement. Naoksa scurried after them. The Boer spoke quietly. 'I've looked in my Bible and I think I understand.' He waited to see whether Smous wanted to comment, then added with a smile, 'April thinks you've dropped from the moon. He can't understand how else you could have walked through Karoo. But I think I do.'

'Is this Kulvidya?' asked Smous suddenly. Breedt kept his gaze steady, a slight smile on his lips, not wishing to show he couldn't understand the language.

'It isn't, is it? No, it isn't,' concluded Smous gloomily.

Breedt watched him carefully, then, pointing in an exact way, asked, 'Your name please?'

'Ah,' said Smous understanding. 'Smous.'

'You're a smous?'

'Smous – yes.'

Breedt gave a hearty chuckle to show that he didn't mind having his leg pulled, then said, 'All right, and your name?' Smous frowned at him.

Breedt hesitated. He had asked the man his name and the reply was 'smous'. Perhaps this was not the word smous as in Afrikaans, but a different word, a name in this man's language. 'Your name,' he asked again, 'your name is Smous?'

'Smous,' confirmed Smous.

Breedt bit his lip, embarrassed that he had laughed, and said quietly, 'Forgive me please, Meneer Smous.'

He led into a secluded yard behind the store, shaded by a sprawling pepper tree. In one corner a goat was burying its head in a rusted bucket, snuffling among the contents. Kicking the animal aside, Breedt lifted April's blue notebook from the bucket.

'I wish to request a favour please, Meneer Smous,' he said in a tone used for all serious matter, so laden with courtesy it was quite unnerving. 'I found this book in April's belongings and I wonder if it is not perhaps here that the root of his nonsense lies. He's a good man at heart, a devout Christian I think, and I'm a fair judge of human stock, yet there is still this stubborn pagan streak I can't bleed out of his heart. The other farmers mock me for trying to lead these people out of the darkness. The old saying is – if Adam was dark how could he have blushed? And so I'm mocked, and they call me a *missionary*, but I just can't help myself. I cannot and I will not live my life surrounded by raw savagery, no, no, *no*!' He sighed and flicked through the blue notebook, his head held well back, as though something might spring out at him. '*Siss* . . .' he whispered with disgust and showed Smous some of the drawings. In one a grotesquely ugly woman rode a baboon back to front, the tail held like reins. Another was of a gigantic bird with long legs and strange feet, which April had coloured red; forked lightning sprang from its beak while it laid eggs that tunnelled through the ground. The last drawing was oddest of all: a naked and hairy dwarf with such a long member he had to carry it slung over one shoulder, a smug grin on his face.

'Np!' squeaked Smous as he swallowed a giggle.

'Ah, good,' said Breedt, 'you're not frightened. I hoped it would be so. Their witchcraft can't reach you. Destroy it for me please,' he said suddenly, thrusting the book at Smous with a box of sulphur matches.

'You want me to burn this?' asked Smous.

Breedt stretched out a hand and cautiously pinched the silver rūta on the collar of Smous's waistcoat. They no longer pricked him. He gave a small gasp, then started to go. 'Oh . . . Meneer Smous, naturally enough, you are welcome in my home, welcome at my table. But I need hardly say that, no – hey?' He glanced at Naoksa who had squatted under the tree, but decided not to broach the subject, and hurried away.

For a moment Smous stood motionless in the yard. He closed his eyes and sniffed the air. It smelt clean. He listened. A cow was clearing its throat, a cockerel called, there were dogs barking, someone singing. He wondered why he had felt so frightened all day. Then he opened his eyes, cleared his throat like the cow, with a long, determined noise, and lit a match.

The edge of April's notebook had just caught alight when a lamb came bleating round the corner. It was followed almost immediately by two large dogs, German Shepherds, one jet black, the other with patches of gold. Round and round the yard they ran, the dogs easily catching up with the terrified lamb, nipping it lightly on the neck and belly. Now a man's voice was heard – 'Hellas? Mab?' – and an Englishman ran into the yard with a loping stride that was both urgent and graceful.

'Afternoon,' he said to Smous, who replied, 'How*areyou?*'

'Considerably better now I've caught up with this lot, thank you, yes.' The man took a moment to catch his breath, never lifting his eye off the chase which continued round the yard, weaving between the figures and circling the tree in which Naoksa now crouched fearfully.

Quinn was a large man – not exactly fat, but certainly large-boned. Smous noticed that his moustache and whiskers were identical in style to April's, and that his linen suit and khaki slouch hat were also similar, though in much better condition. And April did not have riding boots like these, or the lilac cravat in watered silk. Quinn adjusted the large canvas satchel that hung from one shoulder, lifted his hat and ran his fingers over thinning blond hair, pasting the strands into his sweating scalp, gathering them at the back and squeezing them into a little tail.

'They're playing, merely playing,' he assured Smous who was watching the chase in horror. 'Not so, Mab?' – now addressing the black German Shepherd as it careered past his leg, tongue lolling greedily. 'More sport in mischief than in murder, yes? One injudicious bite and what has one got? A pauper's picnic and all the fun's passed. Normally they kill the lambs, of course,' he said, raising his voice in Smous's direction again, 'but I'd say they were adapting agreeably, don't you think, after only . . . what is it? Oh, a fortnight maybe. All the sheep are abandoning their young this year. They do, you know, when the drought's severe, but he was one of the first –' He nodded towards the frantic lamb. 'No, one's true concern is that the little idiot doesn't grow up thinking he's a hound. Still, long before then he'll be off, I expect. Knackers'll drop, he'll scent his first ewe and then . . . abandon us all.'

This prophecy, though delivered flippantly, seemed to touch something in Quinn, for he suddenly snapped, 'Oh, do stop it, all of you – you're making me giddy,' and scooped the panting lamb into his arms. The dogs came to rest round his legs, where they leaned, reaching up now and then to nip at the lamb.

It was only now that Quinn noticed Smous was a stranger, and strolled closer to inspect him.

Viewed close to, the Englishman's face had clearly never been handsome, though perhaps it had once been leaner. Now it was as though he was pressing his features against glass; his flesh had grown smooth, shiny and red. Because he perspired constantly and sprinkled himself with perfumed toilet water several times a day, he gave off a damp, sweetish smell, which reminded Smous of mildew.

'Russian, I'd wager,' said Quinn, scrutinising Smous with his head to one side, ' . . . of Hebrew origins. Yes?' He waited for a moment before asking, 'Do you have *any* English?' – then, after one more pause, concluded, 'Ah! Then one must fatigue you no further.' He was about to turn away when he saw the notebook in Smous's hand, one corner charred where the flame had struggled and died. 'That's April's,' he observed, 'may I?' and took it from Smous's hand. He examined the book, then glanced suspiciously around the yard. After muttering, 'Good heavens, there's a girl in that tree,' he frowned at Smous and asked, 'Did Mister Breedt ask you to burn this? *Breedt?*'

Smous smiled and shrugged.

Quinn smiled also, parting his lips and revealing bad teeth. It was a charming smile though, giving his face a peculiar delicacy. The grey teeth were held together very neatly, as if he was carrying a flower petal there.

Then he closed his lips and kissed one finger, requesting secrecy, while he slipped April's notebook into his satchel.

When Smous saw Quinn next, the Englishman was very drunk, though no one else seemed to notice.

He staggered into the dining room at a stiff and alarming angle, and slowly made his way to his table with the floppy steps of an infant learning to walk. He had dressed for dinner, as always, in white tie and tails, and had oiled his hair to a gleam. Now he fell into his chair with a crash, but still the Breedts, sitting at an adjoining table, failed to look up or make any comment.

Smous was seated alone at a third table in the middle of the room, facing the Boers. Breedt had summoned him from the corridor after saying grace, and the three had sat in silence waiting for Quinn, the Boers staring at Smous. The room was gloomy, swimming with candlelight. The only sound came from the American grandfather clock which, after the war, Quinn had given to Breedt as a peace-offering, along with April.

Mevrou Breedt was a stocky, muscular woman, sufficiently like her husband to pass as his sister, sitting heavy and still in her chair, except when she would gently roll one buttock off the seat and release a fart of extraordinary resonance. The first time it happened Smous got a terrible fright, thinking that someone had snapped their chair in two. Then, as he grew familiar with the rolling movement which preceded each crepitation, his surprise turned into disbelief that, again, no one else seemed to notice or mind. If it didn't stop he would scream with laughter. Mevrou Breedt fixed her small, puffy eyes on his twitching nostrils and lips, as if daring him, which made it much worse.

When at last Quinn was slumped at his table, glaring at the water jug on it, the door from the kitchen was nudged open and April entered carrying a tray of soup bowls. He wore a bandage round his face as if suffering from toothache. Like Quinn, he walked at an extraordinary angle, but there the similarity ended – this was not routine, and it was impossible to ignore; the mutton soup was slopping out of the bowls and pouring off the right edge of the tray in a thick and continuous stream.

'April!' hissed Mevrou Breedt.

'Sorry, Ounôi Hannie,' said April, 'sorry, Baas Stoffel,' and attempted to straighten by jerking his head upright, but this only produced a violent lurch to the other side, so that the soup now drenched his left arm. Smous felt as though he was back on board the ship. Fighting his maimed balance, April passed all three tables – without unloading his tray – and headed into the shadows.

''s he drunk?' enquired Quinn censoriously.

The Breedts ignored the question, or indeed the possibility. Alcohol was forbidden at Middlepost. They were powerless to stop their English lodger drinking, but preferred not to notice it. Now they conferred in whispered Afrikaans. 'What's the matter with April?' asked Mevrou Breedt. 'I thought you said it was only a little bumpie.'

'Ag, he's just making like it isn't,' her husband said, while April crashed into a sideboard somewhere in the dark. 'He just wants attention. You know what they're like when they get the smallest affliction, how they want to be pitied. Ignore him.'

But this was difficult to do, as April careered backwards into the centre of the room, wrestling with the sides of the tray, the bowls empty. 'Sorry, Ounôi . . . sorry, my Baas,' he muttered, before slipping on the trail of soup and hurtling into the kitchen from where there came the noise of falling pots and breaking crockery.

A moment later the cook put her head round the door, and, in her distorted way, announced, 'Ihhh thii Ahihh's sihh, Baashh.'

'Ja, all right,' said Breedt, shooting an embarrassed glance at Smous, 'he's only shamming, but anyhow, Marie, take him back to his hut. We'll get our food ourselves.' Marie started to complain that she had already carried April home once today, but Breedt, now on his feet, shooed her into the kitchen.

'Serve ourselves?' said Quinn with an arrogant toss of his head which sent a strand of his carefully oiled hair swinging over his nose. Then, realising he had revealed that he understood Breedt's Afrikaans (a language of which he normally claimed ignorance), he sat back in his chair, breathing heavily.

Breedt reappeared with three fresh bowls of soup which he quickly distributed to Smous, Mevrou Breedt and himself. Then he took his seat and, his moist eyes resting on Smous, began to suck noisily from his spoon.

Quinn watched the others eating for a moment, before taking a deep breath and bellowing 'GARBETT!' – utterly shattering the pious atmosphere of the room. Mevrou Breedt shot him an angry glance, along with a small but noxious fart. 'GARBETT!' yelled Quinn again, and when still no one appeared, struggled to his feet, took the candle from his table and, weaving unsteadily as the liquid shadows, made his way into the corridor. His calls grew fainter as he searched through the sprawling thick-walled house and out into the yard.

When the others finished their soup, it was Breedt and not his wife who rose to clear the plates, an arrangement which Smous found novel. Now he was left alone with Mevrou Breedt. She stared at him directly, lifted one buttock and farted, lightly. Smous giggled, swallowed it, and hiccupped. As if in reply, the woman opened her mouth and gave a low, drawn-out burp. Smous chewed his moustache in torment. She waited, daring him, then burped and farted simultaneously. Smous clutched his chair. What was going on? Was this a greeting, a code, yet another unintelligible language for him to decipher? As if intrigued by the farmhouse architecture, he twisted round in his seat, following the line of the ceiling to the small sash window behind him, then only just stopped himself screaming as he found Naoksa's woeful face and hands glued to the panes.

Something will have to be done about that girl, he decided.

She had been an embarrassment ever since Smous entered the house, following him everywhere, even into the bedroom that Breedt provided for his use. This was a refreshing, sunlit room on the back of the house, with white walls and a large soft bed in which Smous buried his head to sniff the clean linen. She even followed to the bathing-shed, but was, at least, persuaded to wait in the yard while he went inside. The water was brown and heavy, making it difficult to lather the soap, but, after the journey through the Karoo, the hot bath was ecstasy, spoilt only by the feeling that a pair of eyes was spying on him through the wall. He was sure of this, and somehow knew it wasn't Naoksa. She was still waiting outside when he finished, and dutifully padded after him back to the bedroom where he discovered fresh clothes. These were Breedt's and much too large, but clean, and, like the bathwater, a pleasure next to the skin. Finally, the only reminder of his harsh journey was the dirty figure of Naoksa squatting in one corner of his beautiful room, her dark eyes burning into him – as they did now, through the dining-room window.

Something will have to be done, he thought grimly, something will have to be done about our Golda.

The Breedts and Smous were half way through their second course – massive platefuls of goat stew – when Quinn came swaying back into the room and fell into his chair. A moment later, the kitchen door opened and Garbett appeared, carrying a tray with a single bowl of soup.

'Be cold by now,' whispered Mevrou Breedt happily.

Her husband nodded and added scornfully, 'But at least it's the proper way, the proper form,' then began to gnaw on a chunk of goat, his lazy, moist eyes keeping watch, as always, on the bearded stranger.

Having served the soup, Garbett took up his position behind his master. Quinn's ex-batman was a youngish man, yet walked with a stooping, angular creep. Having been interrupted at his leisure, his braces had twisted when they were hastily pulled over his khaki shirt, and on his feet were open-toed sandals revealing sharp, yellow nails.

'I thought last night was April's let-off night, Tuesday yesterday, wasn't it? Could've sworn it,' he said in the narrow accent of his native Midlands. His mouth opened only at one corner when he spoke, like a looped piece of string. When he realised Quinn had either missed or ignored his sarcasm, he tried again. 'Could've sworn I was standing here last night serving at table, oh-ar, could've sworn that was only last night and not a week previous, mmm.'

'With you, Garbett, with you,' Quinn assured him, sipping listlessly at the tepid soup.

'Just so as it's known I won't be able to do this sort of thing every night of the week, sir,' insisted Garbett.

'Don't believe anyone's 'sking that of you,' replied the other.

''Cause my legs wouldn't be able to take the strain, sir, no-o-o, terrible gyp waiting at table, sir, terrible on the feet if they'm as flat as mine.'

'I'm sure.'

'I mean, sir, if I was capable of that sort of gyp I could have opened up some bostin' little lodging house along the coast as some of the other batmen did after the cease-fire, sir . . .'

'Yes.'

'My duty is waiting hand, foot, and finger on you sir, and there you'll never have no row nor bother – it's standing, *standing* that's blue murder on the flat feet, sir, mmm. Polishing shoes, buckles and belts, there again a man can be sitting down a lot of the time, the same for sewing, darning or picking the veld fleas from your digging gear, mm-ar. Even washing and ironing, I've fathomed ways of sitting alongside the task at hand, side-saddle like.'

'Really?'

'So just in case anyone's planning any changes around here, changes involving long-term *standing*, I just –'

'Nobody's planning any changes, Garbett,' explained Quinn patiently. 'It's simply tonight because April 'pears to be a little 'nebriated.'

This extraordinary news silenced Garbett for a moment. His drooping eyes flickered with curiosity, then he returned to his theme:

'But if there ever *was* to be changes, sir –'

'Lord 'lmighty!' murmured Quinn.

'I'll serve on a Tuesday when April's let off sir, but . . .'

'Not any other night, clearly understood and 'preciated.'

'Just so as it's known.'

'Which it is.'

'Just so as it is.'

'It *is*.'

'Fair do's, sir, just wanted to state my case. Soup all right, sir?' Before Quinn could reply, he leaned close and whispered, 'Pinched you an extra large bowlful, sir, and the bastards haven't even noticed!' Quinn gave a small nod of appreciation while cursing inwardly – no wonder he couldn't get through the stuff.

> 'And shall ye miss me
> When mh-hh-hhh . . . ?'

– Garbett crooned through his teeth, celebrating his cunning. He was forever singing this snatch from some forgotten ballad, a habit which drove his master to distraction.

Smous finished his stew down to the last morsel, as well as the melon segments served, oddly, with the meat. Mevrou Breedt remained a source of fascination; each of her courses had been accompanied by a plate of biscuits toasted to a cinder, while everyone else had enjoyed thick slices of fresh-baked bread. Glancing now to the English table, Smous noticed a fragment of crust had lodged in a deep crease at the side of Quinn's mouth. This was to recur at every meal over the months to come and, like a tilted painting on the wall, it would nag at Smous till he could look at nothing else.

'Sir?' said Garbett. 'Sir?' he repeated when Quinn ignored him, and then again, stretching the tiny syllable into a whine, 'Si-i-i-ir?'

Quinn put down his spoon, closed his eyes and, on a sigh, asked, 'Yes Garbett, wha's 't?'

'A new traveller, sir,' whispered Garbett – in case Quinn had failed to notice the small man sitting across from them. It was not unusual to see strangers in the dining-room, overnight travellers who were given bed and board for a small tariff, but they were normally farmers on livestock-drives, officials traversing the colony, European explorers, naturalists or newspaper correspondents, settlers heading north; normally more presentable characters than this unkempt and hairy figure.

'Yes,' said Quinn, growing more animated, 'but perhaps not a new traveller, Garbett, 'haps more of a guest. A guest of Mister and Mrs Breedt. You might have been und' the impression this God-forsaken spot was sufficiently festooned with tribal variety without the addition of his, might have thought life here was sufficiently vexing without a hook-nose on which to tangle our fortunes, might have thought 'se things, Garbett, but would have been wrong! We must check our Baedekers, entry under "Middlepost", but almost positive they give no warning of this. We shall have to write to the ed'tors, you and I, Garbett, we shall have to complain.'

'Sir?' enquired Garbett, his forehead creased with confusion.

'A Hebrew, Garbett, the fellow's a Hebrew.'

'A Hebrew, sir? A Hebrew, Hebrew, Hebrew, brew, brew, brew . . .' Garbett hesitated, then asked, 'How can you tell sir?'

'Ne' mind,' replied Quinn curtly – to have done otherwise would have been to speak of the bathing-shed peephole. He brought the subject to a close: 'The fellow's a Hebrew, you may take my word.'

A Hebrew – so it was true; Breedt's eyes slid across to Quinn and for a brief moment they engaged one another's stare. The Englishman smiled faintly, for the Boer had made the same mistake as he had earlier, revealing he understood more of the other's language than he normally admitted. Then they looked their separate ways again.

'A *Hebrew?*' ruminated Garbett. 'Well, swipe me!'

Billy Garbett

Smous accepted it was not Kulvidya he had reached, but somewhere called Mil-poh, yet what remained puzzling was the way the locals denied all knowledge of Kulvidya. He knew his pronunciation was less than perfect, but people elsewhere had understood what he meant. Here, everyone would shake their heads and ask one another if the word was a greeting in his language. All Thursday he trailed round the settlement, but no one could help him. Even April didn't know what he was talking about and that was very odd since he had understood Smous's pronunciation perfectly on their first encounter in the veld. Now when Smous visited his hut and found him, grey-skinned and feverish, trying to correct his tilting walk, balancing the black Bible on his head or, more often, retrieving it from the dust, April shrugged when Kulvidya was named and pointed to his damaged ear. But his son, Klippie, winked at Smous; and that wink, more than anything else, confirmed Smous's suspicion that someone had instructed all the locals to fake ignorance of Kulvidya. With one exception.

William Thomas Garbett, former private and batman in the 103rd Staffordshire Company of the 2nd Battalion of His Majesty's Imperial Yeomanry, was answerable only to his former officer, Major Giles Septimus Kavanagh Quinn, and, when asked about Kulvidya, immediately replied, 'Calvinia? You – go – Calvinia? Oh-ar, don't fret there, chap, I'll take you to Calvinia, chap, soon – I wi-i-ill!' Then, after giving a quick shrill laugh, added, 'You stick with Billy, chap, and you'll be happy as a dog with two knobs and plenty of trees!'

On Friday morning he arrived at Smous's room and swept him off for a tour of the settlement. He was carrying champagne kid gloves and a white straw boater, prized possessions from a shopping spree in Cape Town after the war, and which he liked to wear whenever Quinn was out of sight. As they set off now, Smous noticed the man exchange his stooping creep for a proud saunter, tilting the boater rakishly and flicking the air with his gloves as he indicated the sights of Middlepost. Although these were few, very few – really only two – Breedt's cluttered store at one end of the settlement and, at the other, a granite cross marking the mass grave of the British slain during the Battle of Middlepost – Garbett nevertheless managed to make the tour last three hours, and the moment's silence held in front of the granite cross was his only that morning. To a man like Garbett, who held the pleasure of speech over that of listening, Smous was the perfect companion.

'See her? Rammed her,' Garbett would say of almost every brown-skinned woman or girl they saw. 'You can an' all, dare say, anywhere, as and when. Only have to click your fingers and they'll come running like flies round horse-muck, running and stripping on the move. I've never – ooo wait! See that one? The milkers on her! Wouldn't get many of those in a wheelbarrow. No, between you and me, there's no bummer back in Tipton be claiming more tail from his debtors on the Friday afternoon round-up than as what I've had here, bet you a pound to a pinch of shit. The only drawback is the drain on your own juices and the awful gyp on your knees.' He winked and sang tunelessly:

> 'And shall ye miss me
> When mh-hh-hhh . . . ?'

'No, come to think on it there is another drawback I'm bound to reveal. The terrible, *terrible* niff of your average brown-back. You'd think they was hung with old rags inside, some of 'em. So if you fancy it you want to try my method. It's like swimming underwater – if you can hold your nose long enough you're home and dry! D'you savvy? Mind you, with the conk on you, probably take in a lungful to last a line of 'em. Ay? No offence, chap, Billy's only gaming – he's known for it, he's pulled the legs of officers and gentlemen, and tell you what, I find the higher the rank the better they can take a jest, they ca-a-an! All right, my lovely?' he said, suddenly rounding on Naoksa who was trailing after Smous. All morning Garbett's eyes had been exploring her body in the gaping turquoise dress while he made odd noises through his nose, more like snoring than breathing. Now, unable to resist any longer, he reached into the dress and gave one of her breasts a quick hard squeeze saying, 'How's that for a sweetener, my love?'

Smous watched with astonishment, horror and envy, then told himself again something would have to be done about the girl.

At twelve o'clock precisely, Garbett hitched up a pony cart, fetched a hamper from the kitchen, and invited Smous and Naoksa on the luncheon run to Quinn's current digging site.

Over the brow of the first hill they passed a lone white building under a group of trees and a windmill. 'The schoolhouse,' announced Garbett, and Smous, half-standing in the cart, was able to look through the large window and see Mevrou Breedt with her class of five children from the surrounding farms, of varying ages but the same golden pink colour. 'The brown-backs go in with them Tuesdays and Thursdays,' Garbett said, while Smous stretched his neck to gain a better view of the Boer woman. Sure enough, she was rolling her buttocks on the chair, then holding one cheek poised. Smous glanced to the children – surely *they* would laugh? But no, they remained solemn-faced, upright at their desks, left arms held behind their backs as though tied. Puzzled, Smous sat back as Garbett chattered on. 'You know what they say of the brown-backs? Unschooled and you've got yourself a savage, half-schooled and you've got yourself a servant, fully schooled and you've got yourself a headache. Now what I reckon . . .' He stopped as Smous suddenly filled his mouth with air and went, 'Phhhf!' jabbing one finger towards the schoolhouse. 'Oh-ar,' the Englishman laughed. 'The Farter! She claims she's been served that from the concentration camp, claims it's knackered her insides. Good, I say, good, it's judgement on her, I say. We should have starved 'em all, bleeding Boer bitches. Breaking wind is the only good use you could make of her holes, wouldn't touch 'em myself – be like ramming the rough end of a pineapple. Christ, it makes you choke to think on it, bleeding barbarian bitches. Swine 'em, I say!'

Something about the way the man's mouth set on these last words, like a string knotting tight, froze Smous's smile. Soon he would have to start learning English, and Afrikaans. It would be so easy, he'd heard them day in, day out for five months – so why didn't he? Staring at the landscape around him, the little grey bushes and broken stones, like rubble, he knew the answer.

He still wasn't sure he'd be staying.

Quinn's dig was a few miles further on, below the slope of a hill studded with vertical stakes, demarcations of the areas already searched. Hellas and Mab began to bark even before the cart came into view and bounded over to harass the pony. Quinn sat on a fold-out canvas stool, wearing a pair of yellowish-green sun spectacles, with a sifting tray on his knees, a bucket of earth before him, and the lamb sprawled, panting, in the cool of his shadow. Equipment was dotted round the site: picks, shovels, a dry-blowing machine caked with grit and rust, and a contraption which Quinn called his 'See-saw' – a tree trunk levered across a boulder, under which

smaller rocks could be crushed for examination. An assortment of human
bones were piled nearby, one or two skulls staring out darkly. The veld
was still littered with the war dead, picked clean by scavengers. 'Least
precious stuff here,' Quinn would comment, though he felt duty-bound
to collect and dispose of them, hoping he wasn't burying Englishmen with
Boers too often. A sullen young Hottentot, Quinn's helper, squatted
alongside the little mountain of bones, dozing in its shade, twitching now
and then to drive off the flies.

Emphasising the discomfort of treading across the stony ground,
Garbett crept over to where Quinn sat and peered into the sifting tray.
'Hit home yet, sir?' he asked, as he did every day, in the same whining,
gloomy voice. Quinn didn't reply. He seldom did, since Garbett knew
perfectly well that if he 'hit home' he wouldn't stay sitting in the boiling
sun, but would, more likely, be found cartwheeling through the centre of
Middlepost. 'Some wet, bird-haunted English lawn . . .' he murmured, a
distant look in his eyes, signalling he had things on his mind and didn't
wish to be disturbed. 'Wet, bird-haunted English lawn . . .'; this phrase
had been going round and round his head all morning. Opening the
luncheon hamper, he took out a chilled water bottle and drank with a
jerky, impatient noise; then, having displaced sufficient liquid, added the
contents of his hip flask. This was Bokswater – named after a Bushman
who was, single-handedly, responsible for all Quinn's present predica-
ments.

It was two years ago, during the army's occupation of Middlepost, that
Quinn first heard of Bok, famed in the district for his water-divining
powers, and notorious for the rot-gut he could concoct with this water –
fermenting fruit, grain, certain shrubs and various other substances which
his customers preferred not to know about. His former skill was exploited
by the farmers to locate new wells, and the latter by their servants,
secretly, after work-hours. 'Like that shepherdess in France, I hear you
can stroke water from the earth,' Quinn had said on first meeting the
ancient figure. Bok fixed him with a melting, honeyed look and from that
instant the unlikely pair became friends. One night, after they had drunk
two and a half bottles of Bokswater, the Bushman led out onto the veld
and showed Quinn where to dig. Two pieces of quartz were found, the
blue-and-white rock veined with another colour, an unmistaken waxen
yellow. Like everyone in recent years, Quinn had learnt some of the
simple tests for gold, and now, with some amusement, applied them:
light-reflection, scratch and heat tests. All were positive. A month later he

took the samples with him on leave to Johannesburg where an old school friend had settled, a geologist working for one of the mining companies. The man grew increasingly impressed as he analysed the pieces and spoke about the possibility of an exceptional reef just six feet below where they had been recovered. 'I'd dearly love to know where that was,' he said, 'but if you have any sense you'll no sooner tell me than anyone else.'

Taking a deep breath, Quinn resigned his commission after the war and, ignoring the general cries of astonishment, stayed on at Middlepost.

There had, so far, been no further finds.

The problem was simple but frustrating. Both Quinn and Bok were so drunk the night of the original discovery neither could remember where it was. Now Bok led Quinn from this bend in the dry river bed to that lip of rocks on the hill-face, but nothing jogged the memory and the earth yielded only grit, dust and human remains. Soon the Bushman grew bored and drifted back to the more profitable business of brewing rot-gut, leaving Quinn to search on alone, sifting through the veld, grain by grain.

'Some wet, bird-haunted English lawn,' he muttered again this Friday lunchtime, topping up the chilled water bottle with his Bokswater. 'Wet, bird haunted . . .' Whose words were they – Tennyson, Kipling? It was driving him insane.

'Brought you a little something to cheer you up,' whispered Garbett, slipping a gemsbok-tail fly-swat into Quinn's hand and chuckling. 'Filched it from the bleeding Boer's store, from right under his nose and the bastard never even noticed! Could filch his knackers if they weren't in a sack.' Quinn gave a muffled grunt of thanks – Garbett's endless gifts irritated and touched him equally – then set the fly-swat aside, discreetly wiping his hand on his trousers.

Now, as Garbett began a detailed account of his morning's tribulations, Quinn took advantage of an early intake of breath to say, 'Poor thing, sounds like you've had a wretched day already, we mustn't keep you *standing* more than absolutely necessary' – emphasising the word with a neat bite of his grey teeth – 'so that will be all, thank you so much.' He smiled to himself; he'd been looking for a chance to say that ever since Wednesday night's dinner.

Garbett's mouth hung open. He closed it briefly, then said, 'Appreciate your concern, sir, but there is one other thing –'

'That will be *all*, Garbett, thank you.'

'But sir –'

'Garbett!'

'Si-i-i-ir!' insisted Garbett. 'You asked me to remind you that the choker from Calvinia is expected this afternoon!'

'Ohhhhhh,' groaned Quinn, dropping his head into his hands as he remembered the letter brought by a traveller the previous week.

> To Major G. S. K. Quinn.
> Sir,
>   I shall be visiting your district of Middlepost on the afternoon of Friday the 16th March in pursuit of a matter of gravest importance, when it would be, I am confident, to our mutual advantage for you to receive me and remain in attendance during the proceedings. May the Lord bless you and keep you. I have the honour to subscribe myself
>   Your obedient and humble Servant
>   I. A. Buthlay, the Rev.
>   Minister, D.R. Church Calvinia.

'Yes, thank you, Garbett,' said Quinn now, 'I must own that the matter had slipped from mind.' He emptied the sifting tray back onto the veld without bothering to examine it. 'But who is this man and what does he want of me? "*My* district of Middlepost!" What does he mean, what is it about?'

Garbett sucked in his mouth to remind his superior that he had, only moments earlier, been told to shut up.

'All right, I'll ride back after lunch, thank you, Garbett,' sighed Quinn, corking the water bottle tetchily; it wouldn't do for his breath to smell this afternoon. Now, as Garbett retreated, smirking slightly, Quinn turned to Smous, his gaze just visible through the greenish-yellow lenses. He had not spoken a word to Smous since their first encounter, appreciating, as few others did, that it would be wasted breath. However, he had taken to staring at him with a peculiar brand of aggression: repelling the newcomer yet daring him closer. Smous would hold these stares as long as he could, then look away, blushing.

'Ooh!' squealed Garbett as they rode back into Middlepost. 'I know summat I haven't shown you, this is great, chap, mmm, you'll love this!' He stopped the cart a few yards past the granite cross, alongside a stretch of cultivated land which separated the grave from the main house; a stretch filled with trees, vegetable gardens, animal pens and chicken runs. Although the greenery was parched, there was a lush, slightly tropical atmosphere to this area of Middlepost. The gardens were fed by a circular stone water-tank, so here you might have the unusual experience of stepping into a puddle or listening to the sound of water dripping onto bricks. Turkeys strutted slowly through the bushes, adding to the lushness with their soft gurgling noises.

Garbett led across the gardens to a round whitewashed construction, shaped like an igloo. 'Ammunition dump during the war,' he explained, 'now the home of my mate – the Tipton Slasher.' Grinning, he picked up a handful of stones and hurled them against the stone wall. There was a commotion within, followed by the sound of a struggle against wire meshing. Garbett beckoned Smous and Naoksa to follow.

The Tipton Slasher, revealed in a makeshift cage built onto the other side of the igloo, was a large male ostrich thrashing around, further scratching its legs and neck, losing more feathers from its ragged body. Of all the strange beasts Smous had seen since arriving in Africa – the talking bird in the sugarhouse, the dog-monkeys loping around the toll-house on the mountain pass, the racing stone in the Karoo – of all these, this was the strangest. To look first at its tall powerful legs, you imagined they belonged to some fantastic bird of prey, but then, as your eyes travelled upwards, you discovered a peculiar front-heavy body with stunted drooping wings and a ridiculous neck weaving around in the air, leading finally to a tiny head wearing an expression of permanent fury. And no wonder, thought Smous – had God run out of ideas during its creation?

'Ugly sod, ay' he?' said Garbett poking a stick through the wire. 'This was another of our schemes to make we fortune,' he remarked, pairing himself with Quinn. 'Their feathers fetch the earth, they do-o-oo, but we never got the hang of it, awkward buggers to farm. This one, the Slasher, he's the only one left and he's mine, Mister Quinn give him me.' Garbett's eyes shone with pride. 'He told me a Roman emperor once served up six hundred of their brains at a banquet. Bostin', ay' it? You want to see them run – people ride them, they're fast as a horse, can kick like one an' all – but you're not so brave now, are you, my Slasher?' he asked, thrusting the stick at the bird's head. 'They hate this, hate anything near the eyes,' he said as the bird whipped its neck against the wire, dodging the stick, giving dry hissing coughs. 'But it's good for discipline, ay' it, Slasher, good for discipline?' With a sharp jab Garbett drove the stick against the ostrich's gullet and held it fast in a corner of the cage. 'See them claws?' he panted, nodding towards the bird's two-toed feet. 'I've seen them rip open a man with them claws, kicking and pummelling, horrible sight, young brown-back he was, poor sod never stood a cat in hell's. But you know what you should do if it ever happens to you? You fall flat on your face directly in front of the brute, that's the thing to do, flat on the ground, and then the bastard can't get enough purchase under you for a really decent kick, see, so he's forced to run straight on past. Hard to credit, I know, but it's the honest truth, told me by –'

Naoksa had suddenly sprung at the cage, clambered up one side, and now, gripping the meshing with fingers and toes, began to shake it with all her strength. Smous had never heard noises like the ones she was making, hoarse moans from the depth of her stomach. What was the matter with the girl now, he wondered, blushing. Perhaps she hadn't eaten since arriving at Middlepost?

'Here,' said Garbett, 'what's up with you, my lovely? No need to get so mithered,' and he wrenched her away from the wire, taking the opportunity to slip one hand deep into the turquoise dress. 'No need to be afeard of the beast, not with Billy Garbett so near.' Naoksa continued to moan and struggle, one hand restraining Garbett's violent squeezes, the other reaching towards the cage. 'She's been driven mad with lust by the length of muscle on that bird's neck,' grinned Garbett. Smous glanced around uneasily; there was no one else about, Naoksa's dress was half off, something terrible was about to happen.

'We must go back now,' he said, taking Naoksa's wrist. The sound of Smous's language distracted Garbett, who loosened his grip. Smous pulled Naoksa free and hurried with her across the gardens.

That's it, he decided, something has to be done about her – and *now*.

At that moment he noticed Breedt under a clump of trees, pacing in his bare feet. The Boer appeared at first to be marking out some obscure private territory, then it seemed as if he was awaiting someone or something. He walked around slowly in haphazard directions, arms at his sides straining against some invisible force, fingers stretching to their utmost. Now he would stop in front of a tree and carefully present his palms, as if gauging the temperature before touching it.

Frowning, Smous led Naoksa along the path. Breedt heard them, swung round, and, seeing who it was, broke into a radiant smile. 'Preparing for this man who's coming from Calvinia,' he said in vague explanation of his behaviour, before adding in a whisper, 'I'm glad it was you near.' He looked deep into Smous's eyes. 'You seem troubled.' At that moment Naoksa pulled away from Smous's grasp and Breedt saw him grimace irritably. 'Ah now ja,' said the Boer, 'I wondered when we would talk of her'. They strolled towards the house, passing a simple wooden cross under a young bluegum. Without stopping, Breedt reached out and stroked it. 'I wish you could have met my Dawie,' he said to Smous. 'He had the face of a saint. Those kind of eyes, you know, soft hair, but – oo hang! – you wouldn't want to tangle with him, no, no. What a warrior! Like his namesake. Your great King David . . .'

As they reached the house a maid emerged and began to sweep the yard. She was a scrawny girl with eyes deeply set under a jutting brow, and a baby tied to her back. Breedt saw Smous glance at the maid, then back to Naoksa. 'Would that help?' the Boer asked, 'if we took her into service?' and made the offer explicit with a gesture from girl to girl. Smous understood and nodded. 'Marie!' bawled Breedt towards the kitchen, and a shout of 'Hohmiihh . . .' was heard in reply.

'She's coming,' translated Breedt.

Smous shifted uneasily, for Naoksa had scented danger and was growing fearful. He suddenly realised he was in control of her fate and didn't wish to be. Flicking his head sharply to change the pattern of his thoughts, he studied the yard. It was a wide area of beaten red dirt flanked by two circular constructions. Near the kitchen door stood a cooling shed, the rough bricks interlocking with slabs of charcoal in a honeycomb pattern, while, at the other end, a stone water-tank stood in eternal readiness next to the tallest windmill. The yard was mostly used for milking or slaughtering the animals, so a distinctive smell, of milk and blood, hung in the air. Every evening since his arrival, Smous had made sure to be here when a sheep or goat was dragged in by Klippie and handed over to April (slaughtering was the one duty not impaired by his wounded balance, since it was done kneeling) and he would watch transfixed, feeding his secret appetite for these things. How wildly the animal kicked as April clamped his knees around it and stretched back the neck. How bright the blood was, springing into view like a mouth opening. How calm the butcher's face stayed. How quickly a sheep could change from animal to meat, as April sliced and nicked with his blade, or kneaded with one fist, pulling with the other, the skin tearing away with a rasping sound, while the air filled with that ghastly intimate smell, warm and fatty, like someone's spit meshed in your beard.

'You know,' said Breedt abruptly, startling Smous, 'may I just say – I love your silence. It moves me greatly.'

Marie pushed through the screen door and made her way towards the group, wearing her usual combative expression. 'Ja, Marie,' said Breedt, 'look here, we've got a new helper for you,' and nodded towards Naoksa.

'Ahh nhh neeh ha newwh hehhah, Baashhh,' Marie protested, but Breedt interrupted her swiftly. 'Don't do a whole dance round the fire please, hey, Marie, no, just take her away and clean her up nice for us, give her one of your nice little dresses and aprons and find her some nice work to do, nê?' With a sigh and a rolling of eyes, Marie took hold of Naoksa, who swung towards Smous in alarm.

Don't look at me like that, you stupid fool, he wished he could say, it's for your own good, it's to keep you out of trouble, and anyway it's not the end of the world.

'Happy now?' asked Breedt as they watched the retreating women. Smous was far from happy, yet not exactly sad. The feeling was unique, bewildering and extraordinary. It had been so very easy to get rid of the girl. He felt both ashamed and powerful. Yet they seemed like the same thing, or at least similar. Different, yet similar. How could that be? In trepidation, he filled his lungs and smelled the milk and blood hanging over the yard. There we are again, he thought, different things, yet really quite similar.

'Baashhh!' called Marie, reappearing at the doorway. 'Heeess hehh! Hh hihhihah ih hehh!'

'Is he?' asked Breedt, but he could see for himself, through a window: the minister from Calvinia was standing in the dining room, chatting to Quinn. Both men were dressed in khaki, both were British. The Boer stared hard. It was like a glimpse of his home during the army's occupation. Smous jumped again as Breedt's fingers suddenly flickered across his, like a child reaching for comfort. They stood holding hands for a moment, then the Boer gave a little whimper and led towards the house.

God's Tongue

'The sorriest countryside in all Creation, between Calvinia and here,' Buthlay was saying, each intake of breath producing a shrill whistle. 'You keep longing for some heather-bell to colour the scene, a braw ben or two to gird the skyline . . .'

'Ahhh,' purred Quinn, while thinking – No, no, give me instead 'some wet, bird-haunted English lawn'. The phrase was still lodged in his mind. Whose was it? Browning, Shelley? Didn't matter, it'd be wasted on this man anyway.

' . . . or even just a decent field of girse!'

'Mmm, ahh, yes.'

Neither of the Britishers looked round as Breedt and Smous entered the dining room and stood against one wall. If anything, the place was even gloomier now than at night, with the sunlight barely able to filter through the crusted insect screens, and the American clock ticking mournfully above an arrangement of small, bare tables. The Reverend I. A. Buthlay paced between these, fingernails tapping along the surfaces like scurrying mice. He was one of several Scottish Presbyterian preachers currently ministering the Dutch Reformed congregations up and down the country, his churchmanship acceptable to the ecclesiastical board in Amsterdam (where he had done part of his training) and his citizenship acceptable to the authorities in the Cape Colony. Today's twelve-hour ride from Calvinia had exhausted the gaunt figure; brown-and-purple blotches covered his bald head which was long and bony, like a sheep's, with the same glucy eyes.

'Ah. Dear me,' commented Quinn in response to another tirade about the local countryside, worried that the shrill panting showed no sign of abating, and wishing the man would loosen his twice-about white neck-cloth. Quinn gave a small laugh. 'Clearly the journey has shaken your sensibilities. May one assume you to be newly arrived in these parts?'

'Took over the Calvinia parish just after the war. Brought out of retirement. An early retirement too, though few can, I know, believe that to look on me. You may stand warned. This is how a few years spent in the missions of equatorial Africa can malafooster a man and ool his spirit. Might have thought my time there was sufficient penance for a lifetime's sins, but not so, alas. Instead I find myself roasting alive in a place called Calvinia. Still, mustn't wurp. Dree the dirdum, eee? Dree the dirdum.'

'Indeed, indeed,' agreed Quinn, turning away to direct a grimace of bewilderment into the nearest corner.

'But anyhow, never travelled this your way before, never had cause, till now.' This last statement finally took Buthlay's gaze onto Breedt, though he continued to ignore Smous. The room went silent except for the clock and the whistling of the minister's breath. Quinn shifted uncomfortably, still unclear why he had been summoned to the meeting. He watched Breedt freeze under Buthlay's stare, adopting the stance learned in the prisoner-of-war camp, arms hanging, head bowed, eyes glazed.

'Will you have some, ahh . . . tea?' asked Quinn eventually, unable to bear the tension.

'As long as it is the real thing and not yon redbush rubbish people hereabouts drink,' replied Buthlay without lifting his eyes from Breedt.

'Well, no, I'm afraid that's precisely what it is, that's all they keep,' said Quinn, emphasising the word *they* so that Buthlay should remain in no doubt whose home he was visiting. 'Will that be acceptable?' Without waiting for the reluctant grunt of consent, Quinn exclaimed, 'Right – tea!' rubbing his hands and turning in a circle. To his relief he spotted a familiar figure preparing to eavesdrop in the corridor. 'Ah, Garbett, good. Yes, tea, if you'll be so kind.'

Garbett wondered whether to point out it was not his duty to fetch tea for Breedt's guests, then decided the situation was so interesting he shouldn't disrupt it. He strode to the kitchen door, kicked it open and commanded, 'Here, they want tea.' Now it was Marie's turn to consider a protest, but the sight of her master standing with bowed head among the Britishers touched her. She nodded and filled the kettle.

'Tea. On it's way,' chirped Quinn. 'You'll be staying overnight I presume, Reverend?' – hoping now to escape with a statement like 'Then we shall meet at dinner no doubt', but halted by Buthlay snapping, 'Well now, I'd hardly be planning to turn on my heel and endure that grugous journey twice in one day, would I? Ooh, d'you mean my poor animal has not been relieved of its burden or watered yet?'

Quinn considered Buthlay. This uncouth man was clearly under the impression that he, Quinn, and not Breedt, was lord here, unable to imagine things any other way. Smiling broadly, Quinn turned to Garbett. 'See to the minister's horse and baggage, would you.'

This was too much for Garbett. 'Sir, it's not my –'

'Garbett!' cried Quinn, suddenly and loudly, still smiling, but clapping his hands rapidly, as if dispersing poultry.

Muttering sourly, Garbett scampered off while Quinn beamed graciously. 'Shall we be seated?' he suggested, sitting at his usual dinner place. Smous followed suit, but Buthlay moved towards Breedt and said, 'Mister Breedt, I am a shepherd in search of his flock.' This was a statement he had prepared during the long ride from Calvinia, saying it again and again to the open veld. It had as little effect on Breedt. Buthlay gave a quick smile – a frightening sight, as though someone had grasped the back of his scalp and tugged it. 'A shepherd in search of his flock,' he repeated, 'and no shepherd has ever been made to search so vast a distance as I today. Perhaps you might be persuaded to climb out of your dwaam and point me in the right direction?'

Breedt had prepared a statement as well. 'Can we speak in Afrikaans, please?' he asked, in that language.

As if nothing had been said, Buthlay now addressed Quinn. 'When I took charge of the Calvinia parish, Major Quinn, just after the war as I told you, I was delighted at first by the grand swelling of my congregation on the days of holy communion, a swelling from the outlying farms and nar district, particularly this your settlement. Then a few months later, coinciding I believe with Mister Breedt's return from his wartime confinement, there was a sudden falling-off of attendance over in Calvinia. The Middlepost lot were now being led in prayer, or so we heard, by none other than Mister Breedt himself. Despite the fact that he is not an ordained minister of his kirk, *our* kirk, and despite the fact that there is indeed no kirk here, no sacred house that God would call His own, the locals are encouraged to attend his makeshift prayer meetings rather than travel to Calvinia where our devotions are of a more conventional and convincing nature . . .'

Smous was sitting on the edge of his seat, unable to believe his luck; but it was true, he heard it over and over – 'Calvinia . . . Calvinia . . . Calvinia . . .' He chewed his moustache, waiting for a suitable break in the babble to make his move.

' . . . and with a day of holy communion due again this Sunday I thought the time had finally come for me to journey from Calvinia personally, and establish why this settlement should have fallen into a state of spiritual impoverishment. May I be so bold, Major Quinn, as to invite your comments on this matter?'

Quinn made an assortment of small noises, sighs and tuts, but his mind was elsewhere. *Some wet, bird-haunted English lawn.* A glorious phrase, but whose? Rossetti, Emily Brontë maybe, Blake – surely not, Macaulay? It was most infuriating. He must think of the answer or it would haunt him for months. Previous conundrums had, making him bellow with frustration alone in the veld.

Buthlay waited grimly, noting the faraway look in the Englishman's eye, and wondering why a man of his age held no higher rank than Major. Some scandal perhaps? And he looked like a Papist. Buthlay could normally spot them at a glance. Losing patience, he swung back to the Boer. 'A shepherd in search of his flock, if you please, Mister Breedt!'

'Please speak in Afrikaans.'

Buthlay sighed and moved closer, standing directly in front of the Boer, rocking back and forth on his heels. His shrill panting had ceased, but now he was pouring with sweat. It dripped off the end of his nose, his chin, his fingertips, spotting the cowhide rug on the floor. 'Aye, I've heard about you. All about you. I've heard a multitude of things. Things I . . .'

'Why won't you speak to me in Afrikaans?'

'Afrikaans,' repeated Buthlay slowly, for he had understood from the start, 'aye, there's one of the things I've heard. Your prayer meetings conducted not in the Holy language of High Dutch, but in Afrikaans.'

'Afrikaans is my Holy language,' retorted Breedt, 'given to my people by God. It is God's Tongue.'

'No, my friend, ooh no, no, no,' replied Buthlay, in English. 'Afrikaans is a language of the kitchens and kail-yards, and in whose creation the good Lord played no part whatsoever. You blaspheme to blight the Scriptures with it.'

'Afrikaans is my language. It is the language with which I shall speak to my God, and to any minister of my God. And there is no person nor no thing that can stop me. . .'

So the conversation proceeded, without pause yet in separate languages, each sticking doggedly to his own, while the other two men listened baffled; Quinn understanding only snatches of Breedt's Afrikaans and sometimes less of Buthlay's English, while Smous believed they were the same language, both burring and rasping in the throat.

' . . . auch, well, grunch away, grunch away,' Buthlay was saying, 'the subject is not, as it happens, ours to debate. The language of our church is decreed by wiser, more devout minds than yours or even mine, and the language of this country is decreed by its rulers. Had the outcome of the war been different, your opinion on these matters might well have been of some interest. But since it wasn't – and I remain entirely impartial on the subject of the war, I want that clearly understood – since it wasn't, one need gee one's ginger no further.'

'You think it's fair you don't talk the language of your followers?'

'I may not *speak* it, but I understand a fair bit – is this not apparent from our present discourse, eee? Certainly sufficient to deal with the day-to-day problems of my flock.'

'It's only their souls you cannot reach.'

'What? What did you say?'

'Oh I thought you just said you understand every . . .'

'Curb your impertinence, you scunner! Ooh, are you not a sweir and bare-faced bunch the lot of you, grunching away like a pack of beasts with thorns in their sides – you're in British South Africa, for God's sake!' Buthlay's voice was strange – dry and distorted – and a white scum had collected round his lips.

At that moment the kitchen door opened and Naoksa was pushed through with the tea tray. She was trembling so fiercely that the crockery rattled with a high, unbroken noise. Smous decided to take advantage of this eerie interruption to stand and address the minister:

'Kulvidya?'

Buthlay narrowed his eyes, as if noticing him for the first time, then demanded, 'And who's this here?' – his sudden turn sending a sprinkling of sweat onto Quinn's table.

'Oh ahh . . .' Quinn discreetly dropped his hands onto his lap to wipe them. 'A Hebrew guest of Mister Breedt's.'

'A *Hebrew*,' repeated Buthlay, staring at Breedt with renewed distrust.

'Kulvidya – yes, yes?' enquired Smous, waving his hands towards the road, then bunching his fists and jogging his knees, as though in the saddle. 'Kulvidya? Kulvidya?'

'What is the man saying?' asked Buthlay. Quinn smiled charmingly with arms raised in surrender, then gestured to Naoksa, instructing her to deposit the rattling tray on his table.

'And aye, there's another thing I've heard,' said Buthlay, arching his nostrils as Naoksa scurried past back to the kitchen, 'that at these prayer-meetings of Mister Breedt's, *savages* are encouraged to attend, despite the clear instructions of the Synod of fifty-seven calling for separate places of worship.'

Breedt shrugged. 'There's nowhere else for them to seek the Light.'

'Then leave them be.'

'I will not live my life surrounded by the infidel. And there is no person nor no –'

'Auch, will you not now?' cried Buthlay. 'So you take it upon yourself to convert them? To baptise and confirm them? In the name of God, who do you think you are? I've spent half a lifetime in the jungle trying to turn monkeys into men, and I assure you the battle is as writing with a blunted quill! Yon are beings with no order in Nature, no shame, no truth. And you take it upon yourself to convert them, without so much as the blessing of the church.'

'I have the blessing of the Lord.'

'Will you take your face out of here before I give you the thrashing of your life! The Lord's blessing fall on you? *You*! A maroonjous brute yourself, distinguishable from these savages only by the paler complexion! Beasts in the skin of men, drenched in Christ's blood, but still advancing with bent spines and cloven feet, eyes like milk and sores loose to the touch – the very air's like pus, man! – narring and gurring and wurping away in your various tongues, Chewa, Swahili, Afrikaans, which you call upon *me* to learn! Auch, Heavenly Father, does it not gar the flesh and fyle the stomach! And then you have the black effrontery to claim the Lord's blessing, on a barbarian such as you!'

'Sugar, Reverend?' enquired Quinn, bent over the tea tray.

Buthlay struggled to control himself. He reached for the cup and saucer, but his shaking hand sent these spinning away, breaking against the clock which at that instant struck four, startling everyone. Now there was no stopping Buthlay. He stood in front of Breedt, shouting in an odd, hoarse voice, lips foaming, disgorging curses, threats and visions of damnation. The Boer turned his gaze onto Smous, who was puzzled by the expression in his eyes, as though seeking guidance, or something else: courage, a dare. When at last Buthlay was finished, gasping and shivering, Breedt turned back to him and, speaking in broken English, said, 'Pardon me, but can you say that again please . . . it's hard for me if you talk so quick.'

The minister struck Breedt across the face. Smous blinked, remembering Breedt hitting April. The Boer took the blow without a sound, then, without pausing, smiled and presented his other cheek to Buthlay.

'Away with you, get out, take your filthy face out of here, you ramstougar barbarian scunner, you durk, you funker you, get out, OUT, OUT!' Breedt bowed his head obediently and left the room, directing a final look to Smous, a look of gratitude, again puzzling him. Buthlay was left roaming around, panting and clawing at the air.

'Reverend,' said Quinn, helping him into a chair, 'I insist you rest, you're in –'

'Well now and so be it,' interrupted Buthlay, pushing away Quinn's hands. 'Our problem is clear, the crossroad is reached, whither is our solution?'

'Our?' enquired the other courteously, ignoring the shove. 'I don't believe the problem is mine.'

'Of course it is, man!' snapped Buthlay. 'This is a renegade Boer we have on our hands, a grievous threat to both church and crown.'

'Then I must recommend you take the matter up with the appropriate authorities. Lieutenant-Colonel Molesworth, District Officer of Calvinia, will no doubt –'

'I'm taking the matter up with you! Don't fash yourself over Molesworth, you're the senior British officer here, the *only* British officer here they tell me – why d'you think I requested your presence today? I knew that with a little provocation yon grugous brute would fung in our faces and I wanted you to witness –'

'Actually, I believe the man behaved with notable restraint,' replied Quinn, keeping a polite smile. 'Oh, please don't misunderstand, one enjoys Boer-baiting as much as the next man, one is simply pointing out that the creature stood his ground admirably.'

'Major Quinn –'

'Reverend Buthlay, you labour under a misapprehension. I have retired from military service. I am a civilian here, a humble prospector of the land . . . "a land of sand and ruin and gold". You read much of this man Swinburne? Perhaps you'll permit me to recite a small selection after dinner?' He waited while Buthlay made a small, choking sound. 'Reverend, I am a guest here, a paying guest of Mister Breedt's, at this, his lodging house. I have no authority to implement any punitive action concerning my host's . . .' He suddenly stopped. *Swinburne.* Could it be his – the wet, bird-haunted lawn? It could, very possibly. Swinburne . . .

Meanwhile Buthlay had risen from the chair, his face bluish-white. 'Are you telling me you intend no action after what you have witnessed here today? Retired? Your duty to the crown is not something you may retire from, sir!'

Quinn paused, his smile remaining, but eyes clouding. 'I appreciate your counsel, Reverend, though I am astonished to hear it delivered by a . . .' He refrained from saying a *Scotsman*, holding the word on his tongue and rolling it about like a scrap of bad food, before continuing:

' . . . by a gentleman whose own greater duty should surely preoccupy him to the exclusion of my humble, earthly one.'

Buthlay stared at Quinn. That wide red face blasted open by drink and the climate. Such a face could only belong to a Papist, a lapsed and disgraced Papist.

'Have your man saddle my mare again, will you, and return my baggage to the road. I must return to Calvinia in order to report not only a renegade Boer, but –'

'My dear sir, I am more than happy for you to report who and what you wish,' sighed Quinn, wondering how on earth the situation had arisen where he and Breedt were lumped together. 'But you are in no condition to return to Calvinia this evening. To ride through the night would –'

'See to my mare and baggage.'

'Oh, see to your own frotting mare and baggage!' cried Quinn, and strode from the room, breaking into a run as soon as he was out of sight. His limbs were trembling, his mouth dry, his throat parched.

Buthlay charged to the kitchen door and, switching effortlessly to Afrikaans, bawled, 'My horse and my bags, come on now – quick, quick!' Marie bobbed and hurried into the yard.

Tearing back through the dining room, Buthlay came face to face with Smous. All anger had drained from the minister. Instead he wore a terrible look of panic.

'Kulvidya?' enquired Smous hopefully, but the man had already gone.

In the early hours of Saturday morning Quinn had cause to thank the Reverend I. A. Buthlay.

Sodden with drink, yet unable to sleep – *if only he hadn't lost his temper, if only the man hadn't achieved that* – he reached for a volume of Matthew Arnold's essays and verse, which always provided comfort from the philistinism of people like Buthlay, and was moved to tears when the book fell open on a favourite piece:

But on the stairs what voice is this I hear,
Buoyant as morning, and as morning clear?
Say, has some wet bird-haunted English lawn
Lent it the music of its trees at dawn?

The Sabbath

'Brethren,' said Breedt to the gathering before him on Sunday, 'over the last few days I have been reading and re-reading my Bible and I must tell you of the tremendous joy I have been granted – the words have come up off the page with such freshness – oh, my Brethren, it's been like a fragance, it's been like when the veld blooms after the rains. The chapters I've been reading are from the Old Testament . . .' Now he hesitated, a thoughtful expression on his face, before slowly heaving his Bible off the rough wooden lectern and holding it up for their inspection. He required both hands to do this, for it was a giant book with a binding in worn yellow leather, brass protectors on each corner, the lock hanging open. 'The Old Testament, Brethren, three-quarters of this Good Book. Three-quarters . . .' he repeated and then, to make the point clear, allowed the Bible to return to the lectern with a crash which, though carefully controlled, raised several eyebrows.

'Oh, my Brethren,' Breedt said slowly and quietly, in his deep, deep voice, 'what a fine, brave, warlike people you can read about in the Old Testament. The Israelites. A people who again and again are subjected to the most terrible persecution and torture, wars and captivity, famines and droughts, and great, *great* treks. And yet who, again and again – read it for yourselves in this Book – again and again they survive. They survive, Brethren, triumphant and proud, their identity intact. Not clever or fancy folk, no, but farmers and warriors, simple pious men, the very salt of the earth these people, a chosen people, one of God's chosen nations. It is truly inspiring to read of them.

'One of my favourite stories is the story here of Jonah.' The place was marked in his Bible with a sheaf of handwritten papers: the relevant chapters translated from High Dutch into Afrikaans, a painstaking task which he would do himself, sitting up late into the night. 'Permit me please to read it to you. It's not very long.' He cleared his throat with a low rumbling noise and began to read: '"Now the word of the Lord came unto Jonah, the son of Amittal . . ."'

Sitting at the back of the gathering, Smous was feeling uneasy. When

Breedt cautiously invited him to attend the Sunday morning service, Smous had not, of course, understood what was being said, so his nod of consent was as arbitrary as a shake of his head might have been. The Boer was dressed in his normal clothes with the unremarkable addition of boots and a khaki corduroy jacket, but no religious trappings. Even when Smous was led through the blistered red door into the building next to the trading store, he did not recognise the sunny interior as a place of worship.

The Hall, this is what Breedt called it, smelled of hessian and new metal. The walls were stacked with supplies for the settlement: blocks of salt for the cattle, sacks of grain and sugar, boxes of lime for making whitewash, rolls of wire fencing, the gleaming sections of a windmill not yet assembled. The far wall was hidden by a canvas curtain and it was only when Breedt pulled this open that Smous realised where he was.

A giant wooden crucifix was rooted in the red earth floor, its tip touching the corrugated iron roof. It was like a tree in the room. Smous gawped at the idol, letting his eyes roam over the act of torture it portrayed, remembering the terrifying wayside shrines in Litva with rough-hewn, mallet-faced Christs. Part of Breedt's crucifix was badly charred. The fire had consumed most of one leg and wasted an arm. But, despite the nails in his flesh and the burning of his limbs, the figure wore an expression of heroic defiance – for this was no delicate or ascetic Christ; this was a stocky, muscular Christ, a warrior Christ, a Boer Christ.

By the time Smous realised what was happening it was too late. The congregation was already arriving, nodding at him politely as they set down the various chairs and stools which each had brought: farmers from the district with their wives and children, as well as the other family who lived in Middlepost, that of Naude, the blacksmith and saddle-maker. The Boer women were a mysterious lot: their faces buried within deep, white sun-bonnets, like an order of nuns. Outside on the road the servant population gathered, dressed in their best clothes. They were herded into neat lines by April, bellowing like a sergeant major. His stance was still unbalanced and Klippie had to support one elbow. In the middle of the front row stood the unhappy figure of Naoksa dressed in the new clothes she had been given, a giant white cotton dress that swamped her and made her look like a child.

Since Quinn and Garbett were the only people missing, and since Smous suspected their absence was significant, he chose the easier way, and stayed, sitting on a box at the back of the Hall. Uncertain whether to cover his head, in the Jewish manner, he compromised by leaning his elbow on a window-sill so that his palm could casually rest on the curls of his hair. He was intrigued by Breedt. Who was this man? He seemed to be a storekeeper, an innkeeper, a dispenser of justice, the local doctor and, it would now appear, the local priest.

'" . . . right hand and their left hand, and also much cattle,"' read Breedt, concluding the Story of Jonah, and looked up. 'Brethren, Middelpos is not like this place Nineveh you've just been hearing about, a place where the Lord can scent the Beast on the wind or spot his spoor on the land – ag no, my people, Middelpos is a place of goodness and light, of devotion, abstinence and truth. So I was a little puzzled last Wednesday morning by the arrival of a stranger with a mysterious likeness to the Hebrew prophet Jonah.' Smous stiffened as, all around him, eyes began to glance in his direction. 'However, he issued no threat, no warning that the Lord was raising His Scourge. Thursday passed, nothing happened, so I thought – Oo hang, Stoffel, your mind was running away with you there. But then, *then*, Brethren, with Friday came another visitor, but of very different stock, a man claiming to be a minister from our church in Calvinia, but whom I recognised as a minister from Satan.'

The congregation leaned forward, twitching with curiosity. Buthlay had been seen arriving at the settlement and departing in fury half an hour later, but no one knew what had transpired. Now he told them. It was an astonishing story, all the more so because many of those present had fought Breedt over the same issues that so inflamed Buthlay: whether to attend communion in Calvinia, whether to allow their servants to pray alongside them (or, at any rate, out on the road where they shifted now, bored and hot, unable to hear the sermon and waiting for the next hymn), and whether to pray in Afrikaans rather than High Dutch. Even a crucifix was in defiance of Calvinist tradition. But Breedt was in persuasive mood today, his heavy brow glistening, his eyes closed, his voice trembling with passion.

'Brethren, in this little makeshift place of worship, the kind of place our forefathers might have used on the Trek, or like the places we ourselves used during the War of Freedom, in this humble place we gather to thank our Maker for the special Blessing He has bestowed on our people. For as He did to the children of Israel, Brethren, the Lord our Father has also given us a promised land, a land of milk and honey, and he has given us a language with the name of that land carved into it – Afrikaans, the language of Africa. Hear it, please. Afrikaans, the language of Africa! Now ja, all right, I have encouraged us, Brethren, to speak to God in this, His own blessed Tongue, and I ask you – IS THAT THE WORK OF A FREETHINKER?'

The sudden bellow caused Smous's elbow to slip from the window-sill and he almost fell off his box. Apart from his stifled yelp and a sprinkling of dust from the rafters, all else was still. Breedt's eyes were open, the moist pupils had turned to ice – while above and behind him, the dark eyes of the warrior Christ glared also, and higher still the roasting iron roof creaked slowly, once, twice . . . seven times, that holy number; Breedt listened, counting, then resumed in his quietest voice.

'A freethinker, Brethren, some of you call me this. Not to my face, no, but like jackals round the corner you go, yowling and whining – *free-thinker, missionary*! Well, I'll say back to you now, but to your faces, it is not me that has lost my way, it is our church. And I will say to you that here in Middelpos we can and we *must* sow new seeds of devotion to the Glory of God.

'Brethren, I sent the minister of Satan fleeing, I sent him fleeing with his forked tail between his legs, but he will return, of that I have no doubt – *oo gonna*! – and when he does it will be with an army riding under the crown of England. Ag, the crown of England's foot, man!' he suddenly cried. 'It's the crown on the horns of the Beast, the most feared, the most final – the Beast of Blasphemy! And when this abomination returns – to burn our farms again, to use our livestock for shooting practice, to torture our womenfolk in the concentration camps – then you will have to ask why is the Lord forsaking us? This is not a place of wickedness, this is not Nineveh – or, hang on a minute, *is it*? God smells wickedness here! What is this wickedness? Is it your doubt he smells, Brethren – your doubt that I am wrong and that *the minister of Satan is right?*'

People rose from their seats shouting, cheering, protesting. But Breedt was beyond their reach, standing hunched over his lectern, eyes blinking uncontrollably, beard speckled with saliva. His congregation turned to one another, arguing and squabbling, fingers stabbing the air – towards heaven, towards the earth of Middlepost, towards Calvinia.

Breedt's sermons often ended like this. It was one of the reasons they were so popular.

Among the gathering, a fair proportion believed Breedt to be a blessed visionary; how else could you explain, for example, his strange stillness ('like a rock just before you dynamite it')? Others took a more pragmatic view. You must remember, they would argue, that his was a terrible war;

incarcerated, lost all his livestock, grieving for a son. And there were those who simply thought him mad. But, however feelings might divide over Breedt himself, if Buthlay returned with a detachment of soldiers it would become a simple matter of Boer versus British, and everyone would stand together.

Glancing over the roaring crowd to the small bearded man sitting at the back, silent and bewildered, Breedt whispered his thanks.

First Journey to Kulvidya

'We must transport all womenfolk, children and livestock up into the koppies there beyond old Ampie's land –'

'No, no, we build fortifications right round Middelpos, we –'

'Fortifications? That's *their* way, skulking behind blockhouses and trenches and forts borrowed from the Americans, that's their way, man.'

'Where from? It's a kind of laager I've got in mind.'

'We'll hit them like we did before, on horseback and in commando.'

'Then how do we defend the settlement?'

'All right, people, people, please let us stop all this talk of fighting. Long before there's any fighting we're going to sit down and negotiate with –'

'Ja-a-a, you go and negotiate, my old friend, you'll find Satan's always very happy to negotiate . . .'

'What about the hell-blistered Rednecks already here? Quinn and his hyena Garbett. That's my main worry.'

'Ag, easy. I'm telling you, a person must just show them his bullwhip and he'll choke on the dust from their running feet. Now will you listen to what I propose. We transport the womenfolk . . .'

This was Swanepoel speaking, youngest of the farmers. He had shoulder-length black hair, smooth cheeks, full red lips and grey eyes so pale that in certain light they gave his face an almost sightless look, both drowsy and cruel. 'Pretty enough to be a little girlie,' the farmers used to say of him – until the war. Swanepoel had been a bitter-ender, fighting on long after the official surrender, committing legendary acts of bravery. It was he who was most often to be heard calling Breedt a freethinker and *missionary*; they disagreed over everything, except this latest business with Buthlay. Swanepoel was bored with farming and pined for the war as for a loved one.

The farmer wanting to build fortifications was Reukes, a nervy, long-eared man who had lost an arm in the war and jerked his stump as he spoke; while it was Naude, the blacksmith and saddle-maker, suggesting negotiation. He was a colossal, lumbering figure, his face glazed a blackish purple from his fires, gentle-natured, chewing always on the sticks of dried meat called biltong. The oldest farmer (he claimed to be one hundred and three, and to have travelled on the Great Trek and back) was van Jaarsveld, skin knotted like bark, and he offered a different view:

'Listen here. Nothing's going to happen at all, nay, huh-uh. It's Wednesday. If they were coming, they'd have come.'

The others wondered if he was right – life here was so isolated there was endless space for your imagination to run wild – but whether or not the soldiers were actually coming hardly mattered. At last there was something more exciting than the drought to talk about. Since Sunday the farmers had ridden into Middlepost each evening to discuss the situation, gathering in the Hall, whispering deep into the early hours, while moths fluttered around the circle of oil lamps, now and then hitting the glass with that tiny bump, like a tap on the window, making your spine prickle.

Sitting at the centre of the group, with Smous at his side, Breedt could not remember when last he felt happier.

Then on Thursday morning he woke to a surprise. Not the arrival of Buthlay with an English division, but a different emergency. Smous was leaving.

The previous evening, coming across Garbett packing a hamper, Smous had been amazed when the Englishman grinned and said, 'Calvinia, chap, *Calvinia*! Savvy? Told you I'd take you to Calvinia.' There was a tiny gleam in the man's eye which troubled Smous, but he thought no further of it. He could not sleep for excitement. As soon as it was light – the air still, poised before another burning day – he rose, dressed in his original clothes, all meticulously repaired and cleaned, and, feeling equally refreshed by the week's stay, mumbled farewells to the Breedts and clambered onto the mule-cart Garbett was packing on the road.

The Boer didn't know what to do. There were overnight travellers, a Dutch family, to be breakfasted and seen on their way. As soon as this was done, he went to the Hall where now he paced, glancing through the window at the cart where Smous sat, basking in the morning sunshine.

Breedt had always been suspicious of this journey Garbett made each month. Its purpose was supposedly an exchange of correspondence with the district officer in Calvinia, but why was there so much mail – bags and satchels of it every time? No, no, the Boer knew the real reason. To be spied on was bad enough. To have the current mission whisk away his new spiritual guide was unbearable. Smous couldn't go now, not with the threat of Buthlay's vengeance hanging over Middlepost. But to confront the situation would mean *talking* to the English and nothing would make

Breedt do that. 'Stop them,' he said to April whom he had summoned, and before his servant could protest, 'Don't ask how, man, just do it – stop them!'

Leaving the Boer praying before the crucifix, April stepped out onto the road wondering how best to deal with the problem. He saw it as an important test, for he was only recently back at work. Although the hearing in his right ear was lost forever, he was proud of the progress in his balance, and his umbrella now proved useful as a walking stick.

Sitting on the cart, Smous watched April cross the road towards them, and raised a cheerful hand in greeting. April lifted the umbrella to reply and immediately unbalanced himself, going into a little tumbling run, as though on a steep slope. 'Good morrow, my dear Mister Smous,' he said, crashing into one of the mules, and then, steadying himself and the animal, turned to the Englishman. 'Garbett,' he said (using a form of address which infuriated the Englishman), 'the gent Mister Smous is requisitioned humbly for duties here's truly and may not journey with you towards Calvinia please.'

'Come again?' asked Garbett, as he moved to the other side of the cart, securing the luggage.

'Mister Smous may not journey towards Calvinia.'

'Oh-ar, may he not now – and why's that?'

'He is requisitioned for duties in Middlepost.'

'Requisitioned? Duties? God's truth, I could have sworn he was a guest here, didn't realise the bloke was on active service.'

This remark had been directed, inadvertently, towards April's damaged ear. To disguise his deafness, he quickly repeated, 'Here, in Middlepost.'

Garbett noted the error with interest, then said, 'Well, we'd better ask him, hadn't we?' and turned to Smous. 'Mate, you – want – Calvinia? Or – you – stop – here – Middlepost?'

'Kulvidya! Kulvidya!' chirped Smous excitedly.

'*Kulvidya*,' mimicked Garbett out of the looped corner of his mouth, then swung back to April, who had repositioned himself so that he could hear. 'Seems like he knows bugger-all about any duties, seems like he's all set for some place called *Kulvidya*.'

'Regretfully, my dear Mister Smous, this is not being possible,' said April.

'Oh-ar?' said Garbett, 'and what duties would Mister Smous be "requisitioned" for, then?'

After a long pause April said, 'Ag – tsk!' unable to think of a single reason why Smous should be forced to remain in Middlepost. His mind often went blank with Garbett. It was a puzzle. Why should he be able to hold long and erudite conversations with Quinn, yet become tongue-tied with this illiterate wretch? It had something to do with the way each man wore his Englishness. On Quinn it was like a robe, rich and voluminous, with room for you to shelter, while Garbett's was like a thin scarf pulled tightly round him and guarded fiercely. 'Ag – tsk!' said April again, watching Garbett move round to his deaf side.

'April,' Garbett called, smiling gleefully. 'Your trouser flap is open and the filthiest great womb-brush is falling out!' And then, 'April – blah, blah, blah-bli-blah!' and now, 'April, quick, look sharp – there's a horse behind you!' – which there was. April went flying as the animal careered past, while the rider, the young farmer called Swanepoel, yelled, 'April, you helldamned dent-head – what you doing in the middle of the road, man?'

Using his umbrella, April clambered to his feet, and, ignoring the sniggering Garbett, took hold of Smous's arm. 'Accompany me please!'

Garbett was there in a single bound, grasping Smous's other arm – 'You stop here, chap!' The two faced each other across Smous's knees.

'Garbett,' cautioned April in a hoarse voice, 'don't cause me to bear my supplication to that man of honour who holds authority over your poor person and can dejobulate any orders in a twinkling of themselves.'

'Come again, mate?' grinned Garbett. 'Sorry, but I never did get the hang of heathen tongues. Would it be my employer you mean?'

'No. It would be my friend.' It was April's turn to smile. He knew no answer would goad the Englishman more.

'You flash stinking bloody blackbat,' cried Garbett. 'D'you want me to lamp you one? D'you want me to swine you? D'you want me stick a boot up your arse to the tenth lace-hole? D'you want –'

At that moment Quinn strolled out of the house with the dogs at his side and the lamb in his arms. Over a fine lawn nightshirt he wore a cobalt-blue djellaba embroidered with Nile lilies. He was never at his best in the mornings; he always felt he had woken with a fever. His skin was icy to the touch and alive with a minute, distressing shiver. It helped then to carry the lamb about; its small and nervous body served to disguise his own trembling. Smous noticed there was the customary fragment of food lodged at the corner of the Englishman's mouth, a remnant of his breakfast.

Quinn surveyed the extraordinary sight before him: a bewildered Smous on the cart, arms pulled out either side by April and Garbett. 'Is there a problem of some sort?' he enquired in a dull, irritable voice. They both started to explain, Garbett in a gush of indignation, April fixing his ex-master with supplicating eyes and saying, 'Sir, it is preferable please if the gent Smous remains here in Middlepost, please.'

'Why so?' asked Quinn, knowing perfectly well, and scanning the surrounding windows for a glance of Breedt, which he caught as the Boer ducked too slowly inside the Hall. Ignoring Garbett's gabble, Quinn looked back to April and asked again, 'Why? Hm?'

'Just . . . please,' said April, trying to smile.

'Oh, come along, April,' said Quinn, 'one is not best pleased to discover your splendid education has equipped you with no better argument than "just . . . please".' April dropped his head bashfully. 'I ask again,' said Quinn, tickling the lamb's throat, 'why is it preferable for – Garbett, will you please be silent, nobody can hear themselves think!' He waited till Garbett grudgingly obeyed, then resumed, 'Why is preferable for Mister Smous to remain here? What is he needed for?'

'O, reason not the *need*,' suggested April hopefully.

'Ah, Shakespeare,' purred Quinn, '"allow not nature more than nature needs, man's life is cheap as beast's." Well thought of, April, a fine sentiment, a fine argument.' He turned to the other and said, 'Off you go, Garbett.'

'Without Mister Smous?' whined Garbett incredulously. 'But he's panting to reach Calvinia –'

'Then perhaps he would do better to travel there with someone else,' said Quinn, trying to engage Garbett's eye privately; for the man was so incited by April, he was forgetting the true purpose of his trip. But Garbett was beyond all hints. 'Nobody else'll take him, sir, they'm all pretending they've never heard of Calvinia, mmm, no, and all the while your poor bugger here's hopping about, trying to –'

'Garbett!' protested Quinn in amazement, but in vain. Garbett's jaws looked capable of working free and flying through the air where they would continue to judder and chatter. Quinn thought fast. The issue was not worth pursuing, and dangerous in public. He swung towards Smous and said, '"To the elements be free and fare thou well,"' then, with a philosophical shrug to April, concluded, 'Ah, Shakespeare – yes?'

Wondering how Breedt would react, April gulped and gingerly touched his good ear, while Garbett sprang gleefully onto the cart, lashed his whip and set off.

Turning back to take a last look at the curious settlement, Smous saw what looked like a dumb-show performed for his departure:

The instant Quinn strolled back into the house, Breedt popped out of the Hall and stood shaking his fists at the retreating cart. Now suddenly the tiny figure of Naoksa tore out of another doorway and began to race down the road after Smous, screaming wildly, only to be intercepted by April who looped her neck with his umbrella, lifting her off the ground and over-balancing himself. Now they all disappeared in a white flash as Garbett's cart passed beyond the half-avenue of trees into the dazzling sunlight.

Smous wished Naoksa hadn't appeared, but dismissed the matter with a flick of his head and turned to the front, to the north, to Calvinia at last.

'Here we are,' said Garbett with a giggle. '*Kulvidya*!'

Smous didn't know what to think. After travelling for several hours, Garbett had slowed down the cart, combed the landscape with a pair of field binoculars and then turned onto a narrow dirt track which led across the veld for many miles, snaking between low hills and ending eventually at a group of broken stone buildings – an abandoned farm. The mules came to rest in the shadow of a windmill gouged and twisted with rust.

'Kulvidya?' whispered Smous in disbelief.

'Kulvidya!' confirmed Garbett, still giggling, then whistled a little signal, scanning the buildings. A moment later a tiny figure emerged from one, shading his eyes. This was Bok, the ancient Bushman, Quinn's gold-diviner. He was dressed in the tattered uniform of an English bandsman, the buttons of the tunic missing, showing his raw-boned frame inside. His jaw had once been knocked out of place in an encounter with a leopard, and when he spoke it was with a clicking sideways movement, like a buck chewing; the inspiration, long ago, for his nickname. 'The Garbett Master, welcome, welcome, the Master Garbett, come well, come well,' he chanted, in English.

'Bok, you old swine,' laughed Garbett, 'this is my mate, Mister Smous.'

'The Smous Master, welcome, welcome, the Master Smous, come well, come well.'

'Good, ay' it?' said Garbett to Smous, then nodded towards the luggage, 'now cop hold of some of this and lend a hand.' When they had unloaded everything, Smous and Bok doing the work, Garbett giving instructions and toying with his gloves, the Bushman led into one of the disused sheds, propped open a trapdoor and beckoned them down. After hours of squinting at the glare of the veld, Smous was blinded at first and aware only of a sharp, fetid odour. Now, as his eyes adjusted to the light from a small fire, he found himself in a place that was more like being underwater than underground. Through a permanent haze of smoke, the walls swam with liquid – Bokswater, the Bushman's notorious rot-gut – in dozens of vessels stacked one on the other. The stench came from a new supply brewing on the fire, and from bony goats and moulting chickens stalking the shadows. Garbett lounged against a table while Bok began a well-practised routine: unloading the luggage of empty bottles and refilling them from his supplies.

'We hear there is strangers, yessss,' said Bok in his sing-song way as he worked. 'Hear Middlepost has strangers, yessss, hear even there's a Bushman girlie new come, yessss. And now we hear there's holy doctor come on black horse, hear the Master Breedt is black too, black and blue with big, big troubles –'

'Oh-ar?' asked Garbett, 'how'd you hear all that then?'

'Nooo, the Master Garbett, nooo, there's nothing can go free when the old Bokkie's eyes is out and seeing . . .'

'You mean when those buggers are sober enough to go to their school-classes,' laughed Garbett, nodding towards two ten-year-old boys on the floor, snoring in a daze. They were identical twins, wrapped in one anothers arms, their naked bodies gleaming in the firelight. 'You want to see they go regular,' cautioned Garbett, 'or the Farter'll come looking for them.'

'Six-and-two-score smalling issues the Bokkie's bred,' sang Bok to Smous who was startled by a sudden grunt of confirmation from behind – an old, blonde half-caste woman was slumped in the corner, smoking a pipe and waving feebly.

When all the containers were refilled and repacked, Garbett deigned to assist in the next procedure: inserting paper, cardboard and straw between each vessel, so that they should not clink on the return to Middlepost. Now Garbett paid Bok with an assortment of coins, trinkets and cigarette cards, and then, flicking his gloves, signalled the return to the cart.

'Has the Master Lord Quinn now find his riches, riches, riches?' asked Bok when they were back in the frest air.

'Has he heck as like!' snapped Garbett, 'and he never bloody will!'

'O, but he will, will, will, so the Bokkie smells, he smells riches more than water, he smells true, the Bokkie smells.'

'Well, you're right *there*, son,' said Garbett with a wink to Smous, 'but for the rest you're a swining old twister and poor Mister Quinn's the only one who can't see it.'

'Noooo, the Master Gar –'

'Yeeeess, the Bokkie Bastard,' grinned Garbett.

'Then why the Master Lord Quinn already find riches, two pieces of riches, true and proper, why so?'

This stumped Garbett. Those two pieces of quartz. It was a mystery. He shrugged impatiently and changed the subject, pretending to threaten Bok with his fist. 'And where did you get that uniform from? Uniform of a Redcoat Bugler – took the Queen's shilling, did you, during the war?'

'Noooo, the Master Garbett, the Master knows –'

'The Master knows you've plundered the skeleton of some poor lad who died five thousand miles from home and hearth.'

'Noooo, the Master –'

'You stinking old crack – piss off,' laughed Garbett, whipping the mules, 'see you next month.'

'Farewell the Master Garbett, the Master Smous, farewell, farewell, the Masters go well,' intoned Bok as he disappeared in a cloud of dust.

Garbett drove towards the low hills, then turned into a concealed cleft, stopped and instructed his companion to set up camp. While Smous did so – puzzled, and beginning to sense something wrong – Garbett sprawled in the shadow of the cart, opening his food hamper and saying, 'Another job jibbed. Don't know about you, chap, but I'm sweating balls of string and could eat a scabby horse.' They remained at this camp for the afternoon, evening and following morning: to allow enough time for a journey to and from Calvinia. Then, after lunch, they set off again, soon reaching the main dust road, and, as Smous dreaded they might, turning south, back towards Middlepost.

Throughout the overnight stay Garbett had chattered away, telling Smous about his youth in Tipton, about the goodness Mister Quinn had shown him, how, in turn, he'd stood by Quinn during his 'troubles', about their plans for the future once they'd made their fortune, and about many matters on which he held opinions. Smous had listened with his usual glazed smile, but now as they turned back towards Middlepost, confirming his worst suspicions about being fooled, he swung away from Garbett with such uncharacteristic fury that the latter was startled into silence. The Englishman grimaced. It was often like this; people were so humourless, they could never take a joke. The Hebrew wasn't worth the trouble anyway, you might as well talk to the ostrich! Garbett hated silence. The fear of it had haunted him since childhood, but here in Africa it was so much worse; it was the one drawback of living here. He stared out across the endless veld and shuddered. Then he looked at the glowering figure sitting next to him and suddenly said, 'No good spitting feathers, mate, what's happened is your own look-out, your problem is clear, it's sticking out like a blackbat's knob in a blizzard! Learn some English and stop snitching yourself! Learn some English, you stupid bastard, you're not a bleeding monkey. Savvy? Savvy?' Smous remained still, his eyes glued on his boots. Using a softer tone, Garbett said, 'But I want you to promise me one thing, chap – you're not to go telling all and sundry about where we've been, you're not to go blabbing it all round the 'Post,' and when Smous looked up with his usual expression of incomprehension, Garbett burst out laughing and began to sing:

> 'And shall ye miss me
> When mh-hh-hhh . . .?'

He suddenly went silent and squinted along the road. In the distance their route was blocked by a hunched black shape. Neither man could say what it was; the striking thing was the sheen of its blackness, deeper than any shadow on the surrounding landscape. Now, as they drew closer, it abruptly changed position and its outline fell into place: a horse with its rider hanging from one twisted stirrup. They were still too far away to identify, but both Smous and Garbett stiffened and the mules slowed down, fearful of the way the animal ahead was prancing on the spot, tossing its head, as though preparing to attack. A putrid stench drifted towards them.

'WHAAA – BUR-R-R-H – GAAAN!' Garbett cried to the mules. They were on a downward slope, powerless to resist the man's vicious whipping, so broke into a panicky canter, heading straight for the horse. 'Jesus Christ Amen, it's the choker's mare!' whispered Garbett, 'the Jock choker from Calvinia.' At the last moment the horse gave way, rearing off the road, swinging its dangling rider into the bush. Through clouds of dust, the men caught a glimpse of the beast's inflamed eyes, its coat slimy with sweat and blood, the saddle wrenched to one side, Buthlay's foot trapped in that stirrup, his clothes in shreds, raw bone where the flesh of his hands and face had been.

* * *

'How was Calvinia?' asked Quinn, one watchful eye on the dog-and-lamb chase in progress round a nearby tree.

'It's still there, sir,' replied Garbett cheerfully as he clambered from the cart.

'Lieutenant-Colonel Molesworth well?'

'Sends his compliments, sir,' said Garbett, twinkling, unable to match the deadpan manner Quinn was assuming for the benefit of Breedt, who had come out of his store to gaze, astonished, at the bearded figure sitting on the cart.

'And I notice Mister Smous has returned with you.'

'Ar, didn't fancy Calvinia, sir, decided to come back, sir, he di-i-id, thought he'd pine for we.'

'Or perhaps you were the wrong guide after all,' observed Quinn, glancing briefly at Smous's face, grey with dust and shock, and then, before Garbett could register a protest – 'All right, good man, well done, convey the mail-bags to my room.' He was about to turn away when he noticed a gleam in his servant's eye, suggesting all was not yet revealed. Quinn's nostrils flared. There was a ghastly stench in the air, familiar from the war. Looking beyond the mule-cart, he now saw Buthlay's horse take form through the settling clouds of dust. Breedt saw it in the same instant and stumbled forward, eyes wide.

The black mare had followed the mules into Middlepost, sensing they would finally lead her to safety. Her ordeal had lasted for a week, for it was last Friday that Buthlay had galloped from the settlement in fury. A few miles out his left hand suddenly slackened on the reins, all sensation draining from that arm. Puzzled, he struck his shoulder with his right hand, trying to stop the numbness spreading, but now, without any grip on the reins, lost his balance and began to slip from the saddle. Calling to his Saviour – 'Jeeeeeee!' – he arched into the air, jerking and twirling, knotting one stirrup around his ankle before hitting the ground. The mare tried to shake free, but only further twisted the leathers round Buthlay's leg. Terrified, she now began to gallop, for many miles, until the lop-sided weight became too tiring to drag. As night fell the predators of the veld arrived, at different times and in different groups, sometimes driving one another off, sometimes surrounding the horse in unison: a family of Cape foxes giving their soft, long screams, a meerkat jerking onto its hind legs to survey the scene, a pair of genets arching their slim spotted bodies, spraying, hissing, calling to one another, 'Uff – uff – uff.' None were large enough to attack the stamping, whinnying giant that was attached, confusingly, to the sweet-smelling carrion, so they bided their time, waiting, one or two braver ones darting in whenever the mare went still, to tear and nibble. When a pack of black-backed jackals appeared out of the darkness, yowling and chattering, all others fled, even the horse, finding new strength.

So it continued, day after day, the small beasts tracking the mobile feast through the bush, while kites, buzzards and vultures circled it from above. As the mare grew weaker so the hunters ventured closer, some boarding Buthlay's corpse and travelling along as it slid and bumped over the surface of the veld, protesting at the ride, snarling and flapping, feeding and drinking.

Only insects gorged on the carcass now as it lay on the road at Middlepost, and, except for their frantic hum, the place was silent. Quinn took a long, steady look, trying to remember Buthlay's face – they had met so briefly, was he drunk or sober at the time? – then glanced at Breedt. The Boer had adopted that familiar stance, learned in the prisoner-of-war camp, head bowed, arms heavy, waiting. He had prepared himself for the arrival of a British force, eagerly anticipating it, but had never expected things to end like this. Police would arrive from Calvinia to investigate Buthlay's disappearance – it was surprising they hadn't already – and although he had not been killed by human hand, it could be argued that Breedt was responsible, provoking him beyond endurance, forcing the poor exhausted man to ride back to Calvinia before resting; it *could* be argued thus, by an Englishman, to English police. And Quinn was the only witness.

Quinn had told Buthlay that he held no authority over his Afrikaner host. This was not true. And it was at moments like this, with the two poised in the eerie humming stillness on the road, that both felt it, and Quinn revelled. To see the Boer like this was most satisfying; that great, hefty, ugly man timid as a child, that famous warrior weak as a slave. Quinn thought back to his first sight of Breedt, during the Battle of Middlepost, in hand to hand combat with three British soldiers. There was something terrible in the way he fought. His bulbous features seemed to draw in and close, so you couldn't see eyes, nostrils or mouth, but only the stump of a head. There were animals which looked like this when they charged, nothing could check them, or when they were cornered, thrashing around with the same horrifying, blind ferocity. And there was something else, something Quinn couldn't place, and was frightened to dwell on. But to observe Breedt now was quite a different matter: it was to be shown, clearly and irrefutably, the defeat of him and his violent, coarse people, and the total failure of their impertinent War of Freedom.

After a long, long pause, making Breedt wait, Quinn finally gave a little shrug, as if to say, this business never had anything to do with me, then strolled into the house, scooping up the lamb on his way. Hellas and Mab were sampling Buthlay's remains, but these proved too rotten for their palates.

Breedt didn't move. He felt the danger passing, and it was strangely frustrating, strangely humiliating. Quinn's power was so effortless and his mercy so benign it drove Breedt mad, it made him roam the house at night, grasping the walls, wanting to tear them down. How much better when your conquerors beat or tortured you. At least that was genuine, at least that fuelled your plans for the future.

Now he looked at the carcass hanging from the black mare. Even Buthlay's death was disappointing. Breedt would have preferred him to reach Calvinia first, to report their confrontation, so that people would hear of his new ideas and his defiance, his courage. The mare shivered and a tremor passed through Buthlay, throwing open the bony grin to show that his tongue was still intact, glistening with maggots. Breedt went cold. The man on the ground was not dead; he would not be finished with so easily; he had simply reverted to his true form, an unholy presence who would live at Breedt's side from now on, sent, like the Israelite, to test him. They were both here now, the spirits of good and evil, ready to battle for his soul. Breedt turned to Smous who was finally climbing down from the cart, brushing the dust from his hair and clothes, a numb look on his face, unable to believe he was back in Middlepost. 'You must please forgive me,' said Breedt. 'When you rode away yesterday morning I had no idea you would return, or that you would bring . . .' he gestured towards Buthlay. 'You must forgive my doubt. You must forgive my ingratitude, you must –' He broke off, weeping, and hurried into the Hall.

It was only now that Smous noticed Naoksa standing at the corner, shyly, on one leg, the other foot scratching her calf. She gave a little wave, a gentle flapping of both hands, and despite his regret at finding himself back in this place, he was touched by her welcome, touched in quite a new way.

An Englishwoman

I suppose . . . he thought, I suppose she's become my family. We've been through so much together she almost feels like family. She's a heathen, true, stunted and small, a midget almost, but at least she's called Golda, so that's a plus. Family? Strange thought. Like my sister, like the real Golda. That must be it. I suppose.

But it was difficult to leave the matter there. It was difficult, in fact, to think of anything other than Naoksa these days, and yet the subject was filled with contradictions. He would never forget the moment of handing her over to Breedt, of discovering he had control over her fate, of feeling his strength and shame side by side for an instant. And her golden breasts, impossible to forget them either, bared so shamelessly in the Karoo. How wonderful it was to see them, day in, day out; and yet – once again, a contradiction – he enjoyed them being covered now, so they might be uncovered again one day, and then perhaps covered once more – and perhaps even a look finally at those other breasts, those buttock-breasts. Why not? She was a slave in the house to be instructed however he chose. A slave. And yet also a friend. Almost like family, almost his sister. These contradictions went round and round, confusing yet rather pleasant, a contradiction in itself. An odd business, he would think, fingering the grey at his temples, for a grown man to fill his head with. But perhaps safer than anything else . . .

Garbett's prank had shaken him badly. He would wake in the middle of the night panicking, sometimes mistaking his bedroom for the one in Plungyan, sometimes wetting his bed. He had lost all confidence that he could find Calvinia, lost courage in the option always held in reserve: to walk there as he had done from Ceres. He was no longer sure the place existed. It wasn't *Calvinia* he heard people often mention – he convinced himself of this – even when the party of mounted policemen arrived in search of Buthlay, even then he told himself it wasn't *Calvinia, Calvinia, Calvinia* they were saying, it must be another word, he had been fooled before, he wouldn't be again.

The police found no trace of Buthlay. His remains had been fed to the other dogs of Middlepost, the starving mongrels, and the meat of his horse distributed among the servants. His bones, clothes, and riding tack were buried deep in the veld. Everyone told the police the same story: the minister had never arrived at the settlement in the first place. Mystified, they gave up and returned to Calvinia.

Buthlay's successor at the church there was a young, nervous man from Holland who made no effort to round up a congregation from the surrounding district. So the people of Middlepost continued to attend Breedt's sermons and, for the time being, stopped arguing with him. It was hard to deny what he told them (concealing his own terror, for he had begun to see the black mare with its fallen rider everywhere): 'Was not the minister of Satan struck down? Has not God shown us what *He* thinks?'

The moment Smous decided to banish thoughts of travelling onwards, he began to like Middlepost more. Because it was so small, and its environs so barren, when it yielded pleasures these were intense. Walking into the house at midday was one, escaping the heat, smelling the cool whitewashed walls, the scrubbed furniture, the meat roasting in the kitchen. And everywhere in Middlepost that smell of sheepswool, of the oil in the wool, everywhere that faint, reassuring animal smell. The half-hour before sunset was another pleasure, in the clean yellow light and long blue shadows, everyone growing alert to the night ahead when the surrounding darkness and silence would make you think Middlepost was the only place on earth. And those long evenings sitting on the porch or out on the road under the stars, the people rocking in their chairs, chatting or humming, now and then breaking into one of the old songs, bitter-sweet melodies from the Great Trek and the War of Freedom. Or someone might tell a ghost story, making the children gasp in the darkness and, later, wake shrieking in their beds, unable to say whether it was a headless phantom frightening them, or the memory of their forefathers' bloody battles and impossible journeys.

It was not that different to Plungyan.

Smous grinned when he came across a broken milking-stool in the backyard one day, and, having repaired it, claimed a spot next to the kitchen door as his own. He would sit there happily, close to where Naoksa worked, and be constantly fussed over by Breedt.

Smous felt he had earned a rest. The last few months had involved such upheavals: leaving Plungyan, the sea-trip, that haunting first day in the

Cape, his wretched life as a smous in Ceres, his heroic journey on foot through the wilderness; yes, he had earned a rest. These days he would lean back against the whitewashed wall, fill his lungs with the smell of milk and blood in the yard, tip his hat over his eyes and doze in the sun.

Winter came as a surprise. Had he been here long enough for the seasons to change? How long exactly? Difficult to say. His beard had grown longer, he could stretch it to his navel, and his fingernails had begun to curl under. Surprising also was the severity of the winter. Not that there was any rain (the drought was the worst and the longest anyone could remember) and the days remained warm, but the nights grew fiercely cold. An extra quilt and jackal-skin kaross were provided for his bed, and, on top of these, he would throw the ragged sheepskin coat Breedt gave him. He enjoyed sleeping under the enormous weight; buried alive was how he thought of it, this being a fate he often contemplated with a kind of joy.

The mornings too were icy, but bracing, and terribly reminiscent of home. He would snap off little icicles from the mouth of a water pipe and peer closely into them, remembering the Babrungas frozen over in winter; or he would stand under the fir tree and look up at the sky through its familiar branches, smelling the frosted bark and the cold air. As in Plungyan, little happened in Middlepost during the winter. European travellers came through infrequently and it was rare for them to stay overnight; a few Hottentot tribes drifted into the settlement to barter, but Breedt would have nothing to do with such activities, and April's manner was even more scornful, often frightening them off before any trans-actions were made. A Bushman band came through one day, which greatly excited Naoksa – until she discovered they didn't speak her dialect. Like everyone else, they were strangers.

Throughout the winter she became more and more preoccupied with the Tipton Slasher, Garbett's caged ostrich. She would mimic it perfetly, loping round the yard or posing on one leg with that curious, front-heavy stance, head weaving and dipping through the air. The others pointed and laughed, but Smous was troubled. He didn't like the way she could lose herself so utterly, pour away her human spirit and become a beast. And why this one? Others only ever provoked her to fear, cruelty or hunger. What was the difference here? Could it be the same thing that moved him – that the giant bird was barely able to take three paces in its prison?

Sometimes, observing from a distance, Smous would see it suddenly hurl itself against the meshing round the stone igloo. It seemed never to learn that the cage was the stronger, and to surrender. He would go closer and stare at the small furious head. If beasts had no reason, were their instincts nevertheless as vivid as thoughts? Was this creature able to summon up a picture, however vaguely, of open space and of itself there, flapping or gliding or whatever it did? Was there a scent of that drifting from the veld on gusty days, filling the reeking little cage and driving the bird mad with longing?

'Take my advice, sit down, relax,' Smous whispered through the wire meshing. 'Honestly, it hurts less.'

Now, as winter drew to a close, an incident occurred, unremarkable in itself, but it was to set off a chain of events and lead eventually to an episode which none would forget; though, by then, few could explain why it was happening.

It was a morning in September, seven months after Smous's arrival in Middlepost, when a wagon reached the settlement on its way to the interior. The traveller was an Englishwoman journeying to a family in Upington where she would become the children's governess. A tall, moon-faced woman, she had never been away from England before, never, indeed, beyond her home town of Bath, so the boat journey to Southern Africa, the four-day wagon ride from Cape Town through the Karoo with only her Mfengu driver as company, all this had taken its toll. She fainted upon arrival and a disgruntled Breedt carried her into the kitchen where he kept his medical bag. After reviving her with hartshorn he instructed Marie to brew a cup of redbush tea and, having wasted enough time on the despised foreigner, returned to his store.

Smous was in his usual place outside the kitchen door, leaning in to watch Naoksa crawling across the earthen floor, polishing it. The polish used was dung, which, when completely dry, would harden into a resilient umber glaze speckled with fragments of straw.

The Englishwoman sat sipping miserably at the redbush tea. She had never tasted anything more dreadful than this brew, red as earth and smelling of wet straw. Even the china was peculiar: such a thick and graceless cup, you had to open your lips wide to sip over the brim. She was aware of staring eyes and glanced at the figures around her: Marie, chopping a goat's carcass on the centre table; Fleurjie the maid, collecting fat to make soap; Naoksa, cross-legged on the floor, scrubbing out the stinking bucket, and Smous leaning in through the doorway, a small and hairy figure.

'What is this place called?' she asked to break the silence. The figures all frowned at her; none spoke English. 'What season is this?' she asked now. 'Someone in the place called Ceres said it was the end of your winter. Can that be? Is this your winter? In *September*? It was midsummer when I left England, yet so very much çooler than here. This uncongenial heat, can it possibly be winter?' The figures remained silent and staring. 'I'm told you have endured the most unrelenting drought for many years – is that true?' The silence began to feel like a conspiracy. She smiled at the staring faces and tried to lighten the atmosphere. 'If it is true – the drought – perhaps I will have been of some little help, for I have wept without pause since leaving Cape Town. Your desert is awash with my tears . . .' She hesitated, feeling faint again. 'Oh, silly,' she whispered with a little laugh and stood up. She paced to the door, took fright at Smous, then lingered at the window, staring in disbelief at the harsh landscape.

Naoksa meanwhile was gawping at the Englishwoman's silk muslin dress, coloured a shade of wood violet; she had wished to impress her future employers upon arrival and worn her best outfit. Naoksa began to snigger, sucking in her mouth and cheeks, and pointed towards the hem of the dress: the delicate cream lace was buffing the dung polish, turning wet and brown in the process. Marie shushed Naoksa and cautioned the visitor:

'Hahhah, hoorr hesss ihh hehhinnh dihheee.'

'I beg your pardon?' asked the woman, then listened again to Marie's mangled sounds.

Now Naoksa spoke in her strange clicking language, 'I laugh because it is only a little misfortune. It is good to laugh at little misfortunes.'

Watching the Englishwoman's incomprehending expression, and knowing exactly how she felt, Smous couldn't help but laugh. Then Naoksa and Fleurjie joined in, and finally Marie as well, throwing open her jaws and revealing to Smous, for the first time, why her speech was so distorted – her tongue was cut in half. But his shock was only momentary; he was too happy. Here he was, surrounded by people he knew well, laughing together at a stupid foreigner.

The Englishwoman had also seen Marie's tongue, and its forked shape confirmed her worst fears about this place she had reached. She fainted again, face first into the unhardened dung on the floor. Breedt was summoned, but his sympathy had come to an end. He instructed that she be carried back to her wagon and told the Mfengu driver to depart immediately. He needed no persuasion. He and April were from warring tribes and a fight had started in the store. Trying to leave as quickly as possible, he whipped his horses frantically and the wagon careered briefly into a ditch alongside the road, scraping the luggage against the bushes which grew there. The corner of a newspaper (used to wrap books) caught on one thorny branch and tore away. It remained there all day, flickering in a slight breeze, but unnoticed – until Quinn returned late that afternoon from another unsuccessful day's prospecting.

Quinn was the first in for dinner that evening, waiting at his table when the others arrived. This infuriated the Breedts. He inhibited the prayers with which they liked to precede each meal. In revenge, the Boers decided to extend grace that evening, Breedt reading aloud from his giant Bible for at least half an hour, while Smous grew increasingly bored and hungry. Quinn, however, behaved impeccably. He seemed less drunk than usual – although in fact he was more so, numb with it – and sat with hands devoutly clasped on the edge of the table, and head correctly bowed.

It was when April appeared to serve the pumpkin soup that Quinn first spoke, and his voice was full and warm. 'England,' he announced to the room, like an invited speaker declaring his theme. 'England . . . it is April's avowed desire to visit England –'

'Sir?' interrupted April, having half-heard his name, and constantly fearful these days he was missing instructions.

'England,' continued Quinn with only the briefest glance at the heckler, and held up one hand, delicately but firmly, demanding attention and silence. This was granted by Smous and April, both fascinated, but the Boers kept their eyes averted and continued their meal, Mevrou Breedt breaking wind and snapping biscuits more noisily than ever.

'England,' said Quinn slowly, more like a singer than a speaker now, a singer finally ready to launch into his aria. However, after another long, long pause, he simply said it again, 'England', but now with finality, as if completing the aria, and then whispered a last, quiet, spent 'England', as if drowned by an ovation, dropping his head suddenly and grandly, and taking a drink from the water jug at his table.

The Breedts exchanged a despairing glance and began to talk among themselves, while April returned to the kitchen frowning with trepidation, and Smous drank his soup.

'Oh no!' exclaimed Quinn a few moments later, as though in mid-conversation. 'Oh no, no, no, no, oh dear me no-o-o! No, no, Mister Arnold, I think you'll find it's some wet, bird-*splattered* English lawn!' He put his chin on his chest and gave a harsh private laugh, then said, 'No, no, I'll tell you of England, 'pril . . .' He looked round, realised April was not in the room and saw Smous instead. The latter shrunk away from that odd stare, aggressive yet beckoning, but when the Englishman spoke his tone was cheerful:

'Hello, my little neddy-nosed chatterbox – how are you?'

'Howare*you?*' mumbled Smous.

'Thank you, very well, 'es, 'nk you. You been to England, visited h' shores?'

Smous shrugged vaguely.

'You mustn't think the account has 'scaped my mind, oh no, no, no, very fresh indeed . . .' He held his water jug up to the candle, showing Smous the yellow reflection inside the glass. 'Here's England for you . . . the colour of Cotswold stone . . . S'ptember sunlight. Marvellous stone. Studded with sea-shells, y'know, from the time when all of Albion lay on the ocean bed. Watched some men build a dry-stone wall once, outside village 'f Snowshill. Empty field, barrows of rubble – this stone, chunks 'n slabs 'n slices 'n bits 'n pieces of it. How did they know what amount to bring, or that it would all fit together, one broken piece 'gainst the other, to make this long ragged thing of absolute beauty? To see it 'n th' late afternoon . . .' He shook his head slowly. 'Miss the light 'cause one used to take brush to pad, y'know, before one . . .' Now he laughed and clapped his hands. 'Oh, had I but followed the Arts! Behold the look of surprise on the artist's face as the world sweeps away fr'm his brief glimpse of it. Pitted himself 'gainst the universe and lost. Hoorah! That's the fate I should've chosen for self.' April had re-entered the room and now passed Quinn's field of vision. 'You afraid of death, 'pril, that something you've given much thought?'

'Sir?' enquired April, turning his good ear towards Quinn.

'Death . . . Death . . . Death,' boomed Quinn with a grin, then began to speak Xhosa, a language once learned from April (for a book then being planned, called 'Quinn's History of the Xhosa-Speaking Peoples') and which, when drunk, he still spoke fluently. 'Death – death, my friend, as in your proverb . . . what is it? "I rejoice that Kolomba's mother is dead!"'

April shied his head bashfully and steered the conversation back into English. 'Here is a finer one – "It is death alone that can suddenly make man to know himself."'

'Ah, Shakespeare.'

'Fie, fie – Walter Ralegh, sir.'

''oodness me.'

'In truth, a knight errant whose poetry doth leave a chap a trifle in the chill, wanting –'

'Int'r'sting what different people said at their deaths,' interrupted Quinn. 'Byron said "I must sleep now", Goethe said "Let the light enter", while Pitt the Younger is reported to have said – though accounts do differ – "I think I could eat one of Bellamy's veal pies."'

'Coriolanus said naught, sir, but the conspirators said, "Kill, kill, kill him!"'

'Well, they would, wouldn't they?'

'Perhaps so, but I would have preferred . . .' April saw the Breedts glaring at him, so hurried away to collect their soup bowls.

'Ancient Egyptians 'course,' continued Quinn as though April was still there, 'they didn't believe in death, arrogant buggers. Mind you, I knew a man out there wh'n one w's touring those parts with sketch-pad and journal making stupid, pompous notes for a tome that never transpired . . . pig of a journey, but ahh, why am I telling you this? Ah yes – knew a man in Cairo who died simply from touching a note of their currency. It is foul stuff, crumbles in the fingers like sand of the desert, pungent smell as well, 'f course it's been in the pockets of beggars, lepers, what have you. Anyhow, never believed it could kill one, but tha's what he claimed, this man, those were *his* famous last words – "It was the bloody wog money!" Intr's'ting thought though, yes? Diseased money. I mean, here one is, inflicted with that "cursed craving for gold" Virgil warns us against, "this yellow slave" which Shakespeare speaks of, "thou common whore of mankind"–' He suddenly stopped, frowning at the frayed cuff of his dinner jacket and charting the progress of three drops of sweat – one behind his ear, another through his whiskers, a third on his chest – each moving across his flesh like an insect. When he resumed it was in a clear voice.

'A search which does, at this moment of time, I must own, seem perfectly foolish, perfectly hopeless. Yet we know the stuff is down there somewhere, so actually is it not perfectly sensible to hunt for it? Unless my geologist friend was wrong, or inebriated, or secretly ill-disposed to my well-being. Or, then again, maybe it *is* down there, and maybe one has already passed it by, yesterday say, when one refrained from digging one foot deeper here or half an inch deeper there, but moved on – in the wrong direction. How are we ever to know? About anything. Is life –?'

At that moment Mevrou Breedt, who had caught a crumb of toasted biscuit in her throat and taken a large gulp of water, made a horrible choking noise and sat back in her chair heavily, farting with shock, long and loud, the sound growing less crisp towards its end. Now, clutching at both throat and rear, she fled the room with an awkward hobbling gait. Breedt took hold of the water jug at his table and sniffed it. Then he rose, shot a terrifying look at Quinn, and left the room without a word. Smous took a strong sniff at his own jug and was forced to jerk back his head, eyes stinging.

'Thought we should all have a drink together,' said Quinn to April who happened to re-enter the room now carrying the next course, 'settle our diff'rences, depart this temperance house for an evening and visit the suck-crib. All such a strain, all so absurd otherwise.'

April was staring at the Breedts' deserted table in consternation. Quinn noted this, snorted with contempt, then suddenly asked:

'D'you remember Bobby Barton, 'pril?'

'Sir?'

'Bobby Barton. Young officer in the medical corps. When we were stationed near Port Elizabeth.'

'Uhh . . .'

'Extraordinary hair. Burnished copper. Boyish face, but always a little haunted. Not a bad little pugilist. And played the piano like he was blessed. No?'

'Uhh . . .'

'Doesn't matter. Just that he's dead. Back in England, but nevertheless dead. It's in the *Morning Post*.' He reached in his pocket and brought out the torn piece of newspaper retrieved from the thorn bush earlier, laying it on the table. 'Only the death column, so it doesn' tell one much. And 'nfortunately the date is missing . . .' He fingered the fragment of paper. 'Surprised you don't remember. His looks really were out of the ordinary, particularly the hair . . . You *must* remember. Surely. No? How is it you can remember some of the most stupefying twaddle Shakespeare ever

wrote, bu' not a single thing 'f importance? They could set the cap
of liberty on your head, my friend, and it would fall straight through,
you ludicrous, stinking ape!' These latter observations had been
murmured in the direction of April's bad ear, deliberately, to spare
Quinn the reaction if he'd heard. Now, lifting his voice again, the
Englishman continued calmly, 'Anyhow, I think we must eschew the
Bard and reach 'nstead for our Rossetti to say farewell to Mister
Barton – "Behold him how Hell's reek has crisped his hair and singed
his cheek," or, as an invert at the R.M.A. used to put it instead –
"How Hell's reek has curled his hair and rouged his cheek." Dear
God,' he suddenly growled, 'one could be on the moon!' Rising to his
feet, he permitted himself a single muffled noise in his throat – the rest
he would confine to his bedroom – then exited as steadily as he could
manage.

Breedt's revenge was immediate. The following afternoon, as Quinn's
three pets preceded their master from the veld, entering Middlepost with
the usual hectic chase, Breedt took hold of the lamb and, once Quinn was
in view, slaughtered it. He did this by nicking open the jugular and
bleeding the animal slowly, holding its small, jerking body in mid-air. It
was so particular a method that Smous, watching from across the road,
wondered whether the Boer thought this was how kosher slaughtering
was done, and if it was in his honour?

That night the lamb was served for supper; every piece of it, offal
included, even the head which was, by pre-arrangement, presented to
Quinn. Breedt intended the moment to be as chilling as the arrival of the
Baptist's head in Herod's court, but the effect misfired because of April's
maimed balance; he stumbled over a fold in the rug, sending the lamb's
head shooting off the plate and skidding across the table towards Quinn, its
boiled eyes meeting his in equal surprise.

Apart from this ghoulish moment, Quinn bore it all with poise and
grace, eating the entire head, even the eyes, then sitting quietly, an
amiable smile on his lips, planning his next move.

Watching from the opposite table, Smous pitied him. He had noticed
the customary piece of food on Quinn's mouth, a last fragment of the
lamb, and finally realised why it so nagged him: it was proof of the man's
solitude, proof that he had no companion intimate enough to recommend
extra diligence when wiping his mouth. Quinn saw him staring and smiled
broadly, by chance dislodging the fragment. It was a frank smile; Smous

felt as though the other had noticed him properly for the first time, and this was gratifying. But he felt also that sense of encroachment – the smile induced it even more than Quinn's aggressive stares – and he had to look away, blushing scarlet.

The Tipton Slasher

The moment of realisation was absolutely precise.

Walking one day out of the sunlight into the house, Smous was blinded as usual by the black interior and had to pause for a moment in the hallway. Before his eyes adjusted to the dark, and before he spotted her washing the wooden floor, he scented Naoksa – an unmistakable, dry, peppery smell which reminded him of their journey through the Karoo, and made him briefly, and strangely, yearn for it. She slowly took form among the shadows, oblivious to him, chattering softly to herself, labouring above her reflection on the wet floor; two halves of herself cupped over each other – one drab, shadowy, domestic; the other gleaming, upside-down, supernatural. The rhythmical scrubbing of her arm drew his eyes to the folds of her dress under her shoulder and he found himself regretting that she had been given such a large and clumsy garment, one that invented lumps and dents where there were none, deforming her small and fascinating shape. He felt that sudden movement of blood to his face and loins, rocking his balance, and then experienced a new feeling: he wanted to help her up from the floor, hold her for a moment, speak to her so that she wouldn't have to keep chattering to herself. He almost did, but then fled to his room.

He stared at himself in the mirror, something he never enjoyed doing: having to look at that bewildered brow, those sleepy eyes, the unhappy little mouth – all so reminiscent of Kottler's donkey. He examined the grey in his hair and beard, thinking how old he was and how little he had experienced. In a dull, private voice he said, 'No, no, I'm not going to let this happen, I don't want this, it's for the rest of humanity, not me.'

But it was too late.

'No!' he said through clenched teeth, wandering around the room. 'No! No! No!' He sank onto the bed. For almost forty years he had succeeded in isolating himself from all intimacy, or, as he preferred to think of it, intrusion. What had gone wrong now? Different images of Naoksa were tumbling through his memory, making no sense to his reason, yet perfect sense to his instincts: the fear he might do her harm, the strength and shame he felt handing her over to Breedt, and those breasts! And those buttock- breasts! If only these breasts, all of them, were the sum total of the problem, but unfortunately this was no longer so. It still seemed unthinkable to touch them, but that could be overcome; Garbett did it without a second thought. No, the problem had become much more serious than breasts.

The problem had become her.

Whenever she could, Naoksa left the house and went into the gardens. Smous stealthily tracked her, but without skill, so she was always aware of his presence. From behind trees or through bushes he watched her visit the ostrich or sit for a while, holding a sheaf of dried grasses between her feet and strumming them with her fingers, singing to herself. He found these secret viewings of her thrilling. Her loneliness – that's what drew him, that's what he understood, that's what he wanted to reach. And change.

He began to stare at her in a new way, to try and engage her eye differently, and then suffered a small but horrible pain every time she failed to reciprocate. When she looked at him it was in a habitual way, perhaps giving him a listless smile, marginally more pleased to see him than the others, but no more than that. The man who had helped her escape that trap above the endless waters, the man she had always believed would lead her back to her people, now seemed to have settled down and to be roaming no further. And Middlepost itself was completely unfathomable to her. The people were like birds, always eating. Yet although this was a place of plenty, where the men didn't need to hunt or the women to forage, for some reason she was made to work constantly on exhausting, meaningless tasks. Here it was considered foolish and bad simply to sit in the shade and be. Here time was something to be filled, not experienced. Why did this man not lead them away? This man with the loose hair and beard, the tiny hands and feet, this man that was adult and child in one body. Look at him now, stupid thing! – pretending to ignore her, this was his latest trick – striding past her with chin held high, or looking straight through her as everyone else did. Well, it didn't matter, she would ignore him also.

'Ohhh!' cried Smous alone in his room, 'I can't even find a way of hurting her! I do her the honour of falling in love, I honour this . . . this midget, this heathen midget, this deformed dwarf with extra breasts to sit on, I honour this *thing*, and she doesn't even notice! Ohhh, if only we could *talk* to one another!'

He had tried staring at her. He had tried ignoring her. There was only one stance left.

As he trailed round the settlement now, shoulders slumped, head drooping, his singular view – of his own feet trailing through the dust – prevented him noticing a new relationship forming at Middlepost; a relationship which had its roots in the Englishwoman's brief visit a month earlier, the fragment of newspaper left behind on a bush, Quinn tampering with the water jugs at dinner that night, and the slaughter of his lamb – for Klippie now trotted in its place, following Quinn everywhere. The two were barely able to keep secret their smiles which, although smug, were tranquil, giving no warning of the eruptions to come.

The first centred round the Tipton Slasher.

Although still early spring, that morning was baking hot. Smous spent it in the usual way, propped on his milking-stool outside the kitchen doorway, leaning back against the wall, mournfully watching Naoksa as she collected poultry feathers for refilling quilts which had torn during the winter. He kept falling asleep, half-waking, debating whether to move out of the sun, difting into sleep again. Naoksa was somewhere different every time he opened his eyes, now bent over scouring the ground there – now here, upright, stretching her back. Now Klippie was in the yard, pacing angrily because Quinn, who had been drinking through the night, was still asleep. Now Klippie was gone and Naoksa was mimicking the ostrich preening, pecking at her body, then raising her head and giving a little splutter, coughing out bits of feathers. Exactly like the bird, thought Smous hazily, as his head nodded forward.

He woke. The backyard was deserted. Peering into the kitchen, he saw Marie and Fleurjie busy at their tasks, but no sign of Naoksa. His senses still thick with sleep and sweat, but prickling with an odd, inexplicable fear, he rose and began to run towards the ostrich cage. Bolting through the green light of the gardens he heard cries: her voice, and others, but her voice unmistakably, rising shrilly above a screeching, chanting crowd. Clouds of dust rose from behind the stone igloo. What could be happening – had Garbett lain in wait for her there, as Smous often feared? What unspeakable thing was he doing to her? Before Smous reached the igloo, a mob swarmed into view, a bizarre procession which tumbled down a gully gouged in the veld by the drought. Smous stood on a ridge above, an astonished spectator, feeling as though he was still adrift in sleep.

Garbett was riding the ostrich. A network of ropes were attached to its neck, legs, wings, tail, stretching it in every direction, stopping it from attacking the rider or galloping away with him. The creature staggered along, choking and hissing, the membranes flickering across its dark eyes, making its head seem to pulse. Pulling at the ropes were the Hottentot and half-caste children of Middlepost, from toddlers to hard wiry teenagers – though it was Klippie, taller and darker than the rest, leading them, inventing a strange dance, stamping or flipping himself in the air, and a wild song of gibberish. Some copied him or cried out to their own ancestors and spirits, half-remembered from stories the old people told: U-tixo and the evil Gaunab, the night walkers, the chameleon and the lion lady. The air rang with ululating tongues, clicking throats and hoarse shouts. Several carried tins which they beat, this one had a drum from the war, others shook rattles of dried cocoons, stones and bones, and one boy blew a ram's horn, like the rabbi at Rosh Ha-Shanah, which made Smous shake his head in disbelief.

'WHAAA – BUR-R-R-RH – GAAAN!' cried Garbett, driving his spurs into the ostrich. He was stripped to the waist, the bones arching out of his white shoulders and sides, thin sun-reddened arms raised in triumph, eyes shut tight. He saw himself riding this fantastical bird through the streets of his hometown where the bummers and their gangs tumbled out of the foundries whistling and cheering, beaters from the enamel works, cackling black-frocked, hunch-backed women abandoning their low benches in the nail factory to point and gawp, vagrants who slept round the brick kilns, and all the townspeople flocking out of their homes and limewashed brewhouses, heaving the family hog onto the front wall as the town band turned into their road.

'And shall ye miss me
WHEN-DA-DE-DAA, DA-DE-DAAAII!'

– bawled Garbett, turning the little melody into a marching song, opening his eyes wide and pounding his fists in the air.

Scurrying around the outskirts of the procession was a frenzied Naoksa, darting in and out to deliver blows or hurl stones: at the mob, at Garbett, at the bird. Now she disappeared in a cloud of dust as the ostrich collapsed, unable to move further or breathe, the ropes tearing it apart, while Garbett jumped up and down on its back demanding more glory and the children whipped it with their ropes. A high-pitched note started above the ululating tongues, a noise half way between song and anguish, and now the chanting turned into panting, a heart-beat rhythm, the stamping feet began to shuffle on the spot, thudding into the earth, and suddenly they were no longer beating the ostrich to make it rise, but to kill it. What devils drove these children, Smous had often wondered, these children with the jagged mouths and dim, puffy eyes of their parents? Even watching them play you saw how murderous their tempers were, hurling stones at one another in a way that made you flinch. They seemed to have no more regard for themselves than the farmers did, whose word for them was 'smear-rags'.

Klippie was different. April had taught him that their blood, their tribe, was superior, and normally he kept himself apart and remote. But not today. He was wildly urging the mob as they fell on the ostrich, his taller and darker body silhouetted against the clouds of dust which rose from the gully as from an underground explosion. Smous choked and rubbed his eyes. Part of the mob was surrounding Naoksa: the witch, so their elders told them, responsible for all hardships, their poverty, their hunger, the beatings with the farmers' sjamboks, and above all, the drought, the endless drought. Naoksa managed to fight off the small, grasping hands, and run. Now, like a heap of leaves blown suddenly by the wind, the whole crowd lifted off the ostrich to pursue her. Garbett shrieked as he found himself abandoned on top of the huge, bucking bird, its legs trapped in a tangle of ropes. Suddenly April was there, careering out of a billowing dust-cloud, trying to disperse the riot, striking and stabbing with his umbrella, his lop-sided balance making him spin like a top. Screeching children fled in every direction. Garbett was thrown off the ostrich and, pausing only to give it a vengeful kick, scampered off. April lunged after, hoping to wound him unnoticed in the chaos, but missed. Growling with frustration, he caught a tiny, crippled boy instead and impaled him on the umbrella's twisted tip.

'Go on, go on,' Smous heard himself whisper, teetering on the edge of the gully. There was on April's face that same calm expression as when he butchered animals. 'Go on, yes, go on!' Then the earth gave way under Smous's feet and the next moment he found himself among a clutter of smoking rocks alongside the ostrich. It boomed with fright, loud and hoarse as a lion, its neck trebling in size, freezing Smous's blood, and finally sprang up, with neck, wings, legs and ropes churning the air, an insane, monstrous force. 'Get him!' bawled April, releasing the crippled boy who was swept away by his weeping sister. 'And take the hell-damned thing back to its cage!' The children obeyed, grabbing the rope-ends and pulling until the giant was still again, bowed and choking, and could be dragged away. Klippie stayed with his father, facing him defiantly, waiting while both caught their breath.

'All right, what's going on here?' asked April, in Afrikaans, cocking his head sharply, aiming his good ear at Klippie's lips. 'Since when do you play with Hottnot smear-rags? You don't play with them. Look at the trouble they cause. Tell me what's going on!'

'Wasn't them.'

'What wasn't?'

'It was my idea.'

'Ag what, never! It was that devil Garbett's idea.'

'It was my idea.'

April shook his head slowly, unsure whether to believe him or not. Something was happening to Klippie. He'd noticed changes in the boy, small unimportant changes, but all out of character, and happening more and more.

'Man, your blood is pure,' April said in a gentler tone. 'Honour it. Keep it pure.'

'Pure what?' challenged Klippie. 'Pure Boer?'

'What?'

'That's what we talk. Their tongue. I want to know, does it make me one of them?'

April frowned and blinked, then, unable to think of anything else, said, 'Ag, rubbish!' and swotted the boy's arm with his umbrella. The blow was soft, but to his surprise Klippie burst into tears and, muttering something about how little his father understood, ran off. April was motionless for a long time, then began to talk to himself in different languages.

'Rubbish, rubbish, rubbish . . . Hottnot half-breed smear-rag rubbish,' weakest kind of fruit, murrion flock . . . rubbish, rubbish.' His wanderings took him to where Naoksa lay, barely conscious. 'Bushman rubbish!' he cursed, stabbing her leg with his umbrella.

'Oh, don't do that!' exclaimed Smous, jumping up. 'Please don't do that.'

There was something in the way April lifted his head – perhaps he had not noticed the other till then, but there was something about his head slowly lifting with dull, aggressive curiosity that jolted Smous. Someone had once looked at him like this, *exactly like this*. Where was it, when was it? He couldn't think straight, his mind reeling from the bewildering sequence of blows he had just watched, blows to the ostrich, to Naoksa, to the crippled boy, to Klippie, blows ricocheting one against the other, and him watching, enthralled. (He hated himself for that.) But who was it, who was it? A fire in the next street . . . a travelling sign-writer called Glown . . . Glown's body in the gutter . . . Smous watching, his first beard on his chin . . . a soldier with a cough.

'Huhhh . . .' Smous murmured, feeling giddy, an old familiar sensation, the world slipping from under his feet. He closed his eyes for an instant, and when he looked again was surprised to find April's cheek and nose covered with spittle. It showed clearly against his dark skin.

'Sorry, Master Smous,' the man said in a cowed voice, 'the Master must please forgive me.' Smous put his hand to his mouth, realising what he had done, and mumbled a vague apology, but April was already hobbling away, leaning on the umbrella.

Smous glanced at Naoksa and sighed with relief. She was facing the other way, examining her cuts and bruises – she had not witnessed the incident.

But a while later he began to wish she had. It was, after all, an act of chivalry. He had been forced to intervene, forced to stop that terrible sequence of blows. And if April wasn't to blame for them all, it didn't matter, Smous couldn't be bothered to remember the exact chain of events. The important thing was that he had stopped it.

He spent the afternoon guarding the wounded, crouched alongside Naoksa in the shade of an old, peeling bluegum that faced the ostrich cage. He squatted on his haunches, elbows on knees, one hand shading his eyes; this was her way of sitting, and copying it made him feel closer. She never took her gaze off the bird, watching it intently as it preened what remained of its damp, bedraggled plumage. God, thought Smous, name me something that looks worse than a sick bird, and here's one of giant proportions. Like Naoksa, the ostrich seemed more angry than hurt, plumping itself up with a rattle of quills, pecking restlessly here and there, then straightening its long neck to give that familiar spluttering cough, sending out a spray of feathery bits, or to return Naoksa's stare; both flicking their heads to drive the flies away from their wounds. Look at them, thought Smous, just look. A bird with the legs of a mule and the head of a snake. A yellow dwarf girl with extra breasts to sit on. These are creatures from another world, another time, from a story someone has made up.

'You're both so ugly,' he whispered. 'So, so ugly . . .' Naoksa turned in surprise as he took her hand. How dry and rough her skin was. Like a lizard. Blushing, he let go and began collecting grass for the bird, pushing it through the wire, and watching the ball of food collect below the beak before travelling all the way down and rippling away under the feathers on its mantle. One blade of grass remained sticking out of the side of its beak, giving it a contented, nonchalant air.

'This is my father, picking his teeth after a good meal,' chuckled Smous, turning back to Naoksa.

She pointed and said, 'Just like old Gashay about to tell one of his stories, always with a twig in the mouth going this way and that.'

Smous held his breath and waited. 'We almost talked to one another,' he said eventually. 'Did you . . .?' She smiled and shrugged.

All afternoon they imitated the bird, sticking blades of grass in their teeth, weaving their heads around and glaring imperiously at one another, then lying back under the tree, howling with laughter. It seemed only minutes before the light turned yellow, the shadows blue, growing longer as you watched. And now, as was the way in this strange southern continent, darkness came quickly and the veld started to ring with crickets. Normally he hated their monotonous racket, but tonight it was strangely thrilling. Any moment now, as soon as it was pitch black, he would reach across again, and touch that curious, wonderful, lizard skin, any moment now . . .

Then he had a brainwave. A gift. That was the proper way to do it, that was the way of quelling these other feelings, of shame and fear. A gift, that was it. Luckily his most valued possession was in his waistcoat pocket, and it was something he had often seen her admiring.

He went cold as he saw her frown. 'Why do you present me with a gift?' she asked, one finger skimming over the tiny portrait of Jonah riding out of the Great Fish's mouth. 'Why offer me a gift when there is no fight between us?'

'Oh no, don't!' he cried as he felt them slipping apart. 'What are you saying? Try to explain to me.'

'Why a gift?'

'What – what – *what?*'

Equally confused, she shook her head; but then, since it would be an act of hostility to refuse, accepted the page torn long ago from the Russian Bible, sighed, and disappeared into the night.

He felt ludicrous – a middle-aged man without any experience of life. Listening to the ostrich shuffle in its cage, he slowly lay back and stared at the stars which began to shiver and leap as his eyes filled.

* * *

'My friend, come and sit with me,' Breedt called to Smous. 'You look like the man who left his heart in the sun. Me too this morning.'

The Boer was sitting hunched on an empty crate outside his store. It was the first of October and the first day of the shearing season, a date which, before the war, before the slaughter of his livestock, he used to regard as his proudest moment in the year. This was a time when a man might stand at the main gate to the kraals watching the teams of shepherds driving the flocks down from the grazing lands; the sheep only just distinguishable from the mottled bush through which they hurried, making the veld itself appear to be on the move; and the specks growing in clarity and gathering in number until they poured into the kraals and filled their owners with a biblical sense of prosperity. How sweet the feeling would have been, Breedt thought, this of all years, with the Israelite at his side.

'Come sit by me, my friend,' he said again, brushing the dust from a stack of dried hides, as Smous crossed the road towards him.

A procession of farmers was riding through the settlement to the kraals lying on the southern outskirts; the young bitter-ender Swanepoel with long black hair and that odd, sightless gaze, the nervy, long-eared Reukes with only one arm, waving the stump of the other at Breedt as he passed.

'Morning, Oom Stoffie. How goes it?'

'No, not too bad. And you?'

'Man, with joy riding rings round me! Prayed all night for cooler weather.'

'Ja, nice breeze for you people today.'

So they went by, grinning leathery faces under buckskin hats, calling out to him. He returned their greetings cheerfully, but inside he was aching. Reukes's stock had been spared the vengeance of the British and their drunken games of target practice – so had Swanepoel's stock, van Jaarsveld's, everyone else's: Le Roux, 'Hardehand' Klopper, van Schaik, Willem 'Duiwel' Jonker, Meintjies and Oupa Kriel – everyone else's stock had been spared.

Now as Smous slumped dejectedly onto the stack of hides alongside, Breedt watched Quinn stroll out of the house, yawning and stretching, Hellas and Mab pushing roughly past, bounding onto the road, tongues lolling, sniffing the morning air.

'Why did he single me out?' Breedt whispered to Smous through clenched teeth. 'Why was it me, why only me?' He waited politely, as he always did, for Smous to answer, before continuing. 'And the funny thing is this. If that Englishman ever finds his hell-blistered minerals I'll be a prosperous man too. That was always the agreement and, if nothing else, he is a gentleman and he'll keep his word, I believe. Funny to think, hey? Of all people, *he* could make it possible for me to buy new stock and return to a blessed existence on the land. He, the man who robbed me of it in the first place. Ja, anyhow . . .' He bunched one fist and scratched it lazily. Now Klippie came running into view, briefly drawing Smous out of his gloom. How different the boy looked from yesterday. Delighted to find Quinn awake and ready, Klippie careered round the road with the dogs, copying their grinning, panting jaws.

'By the way, I heard about the business with the ostrich,' Breedt confided to Smous. 'April is deeply contrite about wounding your servant girlie. You must please try and find it in your heart to forgive him, hey? He only did it because he's troubled about what's going on with the Englishman and his son. I told him there was nothing to worry about. Was that the correct advice?' Again he waited for an answer, his eyes narrowing as Quinn's party set off for the day's dig, the man on horseback, the dogs and Klippie trotting after, passing the last few farmers travelling in the opposite direction towards the kraals. Now the road was deserted, a breeze whirling through the dust thrown up by the morning's traffic.

'Was that the correct advice?' repeated Breedt, glancing at the small figure alongside him and wondering how to interpret the distant look in his eyes. Smous jumped as he suddenly felt Breedt stroke his hair. *Why was the man always doing things like this?* 'Did I not advise him correctly?' asked Breedt, now unsettled by the frown on the Israelite's face. 'I think perhaps you must please find out for us.' Smous sighed. It was impossible to keep ignoring this jabbering fool at his side. He faced Breedt and raised his eyebrows. With a delicate but exact tilt of his head, the Boer indicated the tiny retreating figures of Quinn and Klippie. Smous understood immediately, thought for a moment, then nodded.

So now they're asking me to spy on one another, he thought, setting off across the veld – and so what, who cares? Away from the buildings, the wind grew stronger and the windmills rotated from left to right, right to left, left to right, with a noise like empty rolling tins. This is the ugliest place in all Creation, he decided, and so I live here: the ugliest man. All night he had lain awake under the tree reliving that moment of giving his precious illustration to Naoksa. What had he done wrong, what had he done wrong? Left to right went the tin windmills, right to left . . .

It was about an hour later when he reached Quinn's new digging site in the dry river bed. He froze. There was something extraordinary in the air. A smell of secrecy. The river bank lay directly ahead, and the sudden drop beyond made him rise on tiptoe and stretch his neck. Nothing to be seen. He listened hard, but the wind was flowing round his ears with a camouflaging sound of its own. He knelt and crawled towards the edge. For the second time in twenty-four hours he bore witness to a strange episode happening in a dip below the veld's surface.

At first he saw only Quinn's animals: the horse grazing listlessly, the German Shepherds sprawled on a sunny rock. Mab's ears twitched, but Smous was downwind, his scent blowing back across the landscape. Although dry, the river bed was a fresh orange colour which hinted at dampness, and one or two shaded spots glinted from the stagnant puddles where tiny frogs and crabs lived. Smous could see no sign of any prospecting work in progress, no sign either of the Hottentot youth who had been Quinn's helper before. Now Smous heard voices and, ducking his head lower, dodging the wind-flow, finally located Quinn and Klippie. They were seated across a fold-out table in a dark cleft of rocks, talking intently, and in a particular way: the man saying something then waiting, the boy replying then waiting, the man nodding or shaking his head. Smous's eye was immediately drawn to the single object on the table: April's blue notebook which Quinn had stopped Smous from burning on his first day in Middlepost. He could see clearly the one curled and blackened corner. How April had searched for this book after his recovery, and here it was. His son was learning it by heart. Quinn would read a section, then wait for Klippie to repeat it; the boy would do this, then wait for his teacher to comment. Smous frowned, intrigued by the language both were speaking; it sounded to him like Naoksa's, with clicks and clucks of the tongue, but was, in fact, Xhosa – the language April had once taught Quinn, but never his son.

> 'We call to the ancestors
> Come, smell, there's meat in the walls
> Will they hear?
> Will they hear . . .'

– sang Klippie in a strong and beautiful voice, while Smous wondered if, or when, he'd heard this melody. Before he could work it out, the wind dipped and snatched it away. Searching for more clues, his eyes combed the little area and came across another object underneath the table: a small animal skull. In the shadow the bones looked specially white, crisp and weightless, as though afloat. Smous wondered if this was the lamb's skull, Quinn's former companion and pet, kept there like a talisman to guide this new venture.

Glancing up again, Smous squeaked with fright. Quinn was staring directly at him, over the boy's shoulder. Smous's body arched, preparing to flee – then he froze, puzzled by the Englishman's calm expression. Quinn slowly raised one hand (Smous thought he was going to wave) and made the same gesture as when he first took April's notebook from Smous: pressing one finger to his smiling lips and kissing it lightly.

'Well?' asked Breedt when Smous returned to Middlepost, '*is* there anything going on? What are they up to?'

'I couldn't find them,' replied Smous, deliberately not explaining his words with any gesture. Breedt was puzzled, then gave a little soundless laugh. 'Well?' he asked again, arms spread wide, describing his question.

'I just told you,' said Smous. 'What's the matter, don't you understand plain Yiddish?' and strolled away, smiling gleefully to himself. He was growing bolder. It was the one good thing to come out of this terrible business with Naoksa: he cared less what people thought, cared less what happened to him. Turning the corner, he saw Naoksa in the yard, hanging out washing. The wind pulled her thin dress and the sunlight glowed through it, showing the outline of her legs, every inch of them, from ankle to buttock breast.

'Ohhh . . . !' he murmured. Who knows how bold I might yet become?

The Music

The first thing Smous heard early one morning was piano music drifting from the veld. It was completely out of tune, yet magical, hurting and pleasing at the same time, a feeling which was all too familiar these days. Then he witnessed a strange arrival. Two old mules were pulling a large wagon into the settlement. It was driven by a beautiful woman, enormously fat, with flowing black hair and sparkling with beads and jewellery. All her life's belongings seemed to be crammed onto the vehicle, including a piano severely warped by the heat. Playing it was a small man with a waxed moustache and a smile constructed entirely of gold teeth.

It was summer. The day promised to be bright and hot, and now, with this arrival, special.

Others had heard the music also, and drifted onto the road to meet the wagon. Quinn was there first, beaming broadly, giving a little bow to the piano player – 'Signore Scuteri' – and offering his hand to the woman – 'Signora Scuteri.' As she stood, a cloud of dust rose with her. 'Pfff!' she laughed, fanning her arms, as though she had been excessive with face powder, and then, gathering up her embroidered black shawl, stepped down onto the road. Quinn kissed her hand and she rolled her large eyes, giggling coyly.

'The Signora is well?' he asked, and she, having no English, twirled round to demonstrate her robust health. Although enormous, she thought of herself as much lighter, and tended to glide on the tips of her small feet, and hold her jewelled arms away from her body as if about to float away.

Signore Scuteri was a more crumpled figure in dark beret and jacket. His extravagance was a multi-coloured silk neckerchief which played tricks with the light like fish skin. He embraced Quinn warmly and, in English, exclaimed, 'O my friend, my friend, I thank the Blessed Mother who has spared me to see you again!' Quinn disengaged himself as soon as possible. It was still early morning and he didn't wish Scuteri to feel his cold, vibrating flesh. However, the Italian was far too overwhelmed and had already moved on to embrace April, saying, 'My favourite old devil himself – the Professor!'

April, attempting to show no sign of his tilted stance, said, 'A hundred thousand welcomes. I could weep and I could laugh, I am light and heavy. Welcome.'

Now Scuteri saw Klippie and shouted to April, 'Professor, this cannot be! Is it?'

'It is, O Signore, truly 'tis,' replied April proudly.

'How he has grown, in only . . . what can it be?'

'Almost a year, O Signore.'

'No! Is it?' Then Scuteri swung back towards Klippie, and, pronouncing the name beautifully, said, 'Caius . . . Caius Martius . . . you are already a man!' and made the boy's eyes shine with joy. 'And the Billy Garbett,' said Scuteri, progressing down the line, 'how is you?'

'Ooh,' whined Garbett, 'been a bit off the hooks, tell the truth, sir, it's these bastard plates of meat.' He gestured to his feet and took a deep breath, but Scuteri had already moved on with a cry of, 'And *this*?'

'A newcomer, Signore,' explained Quinn, moving forward to oversee the handshake. 'Mister Smous, please meet one of my oldest and very dearest friends, Signore Scuteri.'

'I am honoured,' said Scuteri.

'Howare*you*?' replied Smous, a little overawed, and surprised by how frail the Italian's hand felt. Close to, both Scuteris were a lot older than they first appeared. The Signore's face was hollow and worn, despite the rouge and lipstick, which shocked Smous, while grey roots showed through his bright orange hair. And now, as the Signora descended on Smous to kiss his cheeks, he was startled by how clearly her wrinkles showed, and he looked more closely at her mane of black hair with its bluish sheen.

'Excuse please,' said Signore Scuteri to the group, 'but I must go to salute His Holiness the Pope,' and crossed the road to greet Breedt outside the store. Their handshake was more formal, but still friendly, which puzzled Smous. He would have expected this extravagant couple to meet with Breedt's disapproval. However, the Boer seemed happy to see them and even helped unload the wagon. The piano, a large portmanteau and several smaller utility bags were carried into the Hall, while the personal cases were taken to a bedroom which had been prepared at the back of the house.

Once the Italians had breakfasted, filling the bleak dining room with a raucous and festive atmosphere, there occurred the first ritual of a Scuteri visit: haircuts.

They set up shop in the Hall, and throughout the morning the population of Middlepost and the surrounding district filed in one by one; April holding back the servants until their masters were done. The Signore cut hair, shaved chins and trimmed beards while the Signora busied herself picking out lice, applying sweet-smelling balms and oils, and, for those who could afford it, manicuring and whitening nails. Whenever either of them had a free moment, they would also try to interest their customers in trinkets and paste jewellery, as well as confectionery from gaudily decorated tins. Smous stared at their assorted goods. Could these people be superior smouses?

It was all most peculiar. The sight of the Breedts in the improvised barber's chair was extraordinary: Meneer Breedt exchanging a few pleasantries in English while Scuteri shaved his bulging head almost to the bone; Mevrou Breedt's bowels operating with a quietish hum rather than their usual thunderclaps. It was difficult to believe that just beyond the canvas curtain hung the charred and tortured Christ, and that Breedt had stood under it every Sunday delivering those blistering sermons.

When Smous's turn came, Quinn (who had taken the day off work) stood alongside telling stories and making the Scuteris laugh. But his trembling had not yet subsided and he was forced to clasp his hands or gesture excessively to disguise it. At one point he knelt and collected a lock of Smous's hair from the fluffy mounds heaped round the chair. Then, when only Smous was looking, he pressed it briefly to his lips. A little embarrassed, Smous nodded vaguely, assuming this to be a further sealing of the secrets they shared between them.

After lunch it was so hot that everyone retired to their rooms for a nap. The Scuteris were thoroughly exhausted after their morning's work and left the dining room with such fulsome farewells it was as though they were disappearing forever rather than for a few hours.

Smous went to his room and sprawled on his bed, his head propped against the wall so as not to mess his new hairstyle. He wondered if Naoksa would notice and like it? 'Oh damn her!' he said aloud, as he often did these days, then added, 'You seriously expect a savage to appreciate a civilised haircut?' He watched a column of ants progress across a patch of sunlight on the wall. The room was suffocatingly hot, and wisps of shorn hair itched on his back. He looked at his long fingernails and wished he could have afforded the Scuteris' manicure. He closed his eyes, then immediately reopened them. It was hopeless; he couldn't sleep at nights, what chance was there now? He rose and strolled out into the yard. The familiar smell of milk and blood was stronger than ever in the heat. Middlepost was deserted, and so silent that his lone, crunching steps reminded him of being in the middle of the Karoo. Gradually his wanderings took him round the house onto the road, and along the half-avenue of trees towards the British cross. Even the leafy shadows were hot today, redder than usual.

Then Smous saw Quinn walking his dogs. Or perhaps the reverse: the animals looked drained of energy while the man was frenetically active; and, as Smous came into earshot, even the Englishman's first utterance was canine.

'Whooffff!' he said. 'Hot, yes? Only foreigners like you and I are foolish enough to venture outdoors in these conditions. The locals are all . . .' He gestured vaguely towards the shuttered windows on the house, then lapsed into silence, gazing down the road through his greenish sun spectacles. There was the customary morsel from lunch lodged in the corner of his mouth, all the more evident with his moustache trimmed so meticulously by Scuteri. The cutting of his lank hair had left him looking younger, though his head was suddenly disproportionately small. As the silence continued, Smous began to rock from foot to foot, making an assortment of meaningless shapes with his lips. Being alone with Quinn was always awkward. At least when the others babbled at him he felt some sense of belonging among them, but Quinn's silence engendered a guilt about his failure to learn the local languages, and left him feeling like a child or half-wit, not worth addressing.

He was relieved now when the stillness was broken by a shot ringing out from one of the surrounding farms. Quinn reacted quite differently. 'Oh no, oh dear, oh God!' he groaned, turning to the blacker of the German Shepherds. 'Now Mab, let's pretend we didn't hear that –' but it was too late; the animal had begun to shiver and pant convulsively. 'Shell-shocked as a puppy during the war,' explained Quinn as he knelt down to massage her neck and spine. 'All right, girl, all right, Mabs, only someone shooting a hare or a jackal, far, far away . . . dear grief!' he cursed as the panic showed no sign of abating. 'Oh for Orpheus' lyre to calm the bitch's spirit. God! This will continue for an hour now, better kennel her,' he said, but made no move to rise. Then, as if the idea had only just occurred, he looked up at Smous and said quietly, 'Probably time you and I had a little chat. Would you come to my room?'

Since Quinn was pointing towards the house, Smous knew he was being invited to extend their chance encounter, rather than, thanks to the dog, curtail it. He gave a weak smile and nodded, then followed the Englishman who set off very briskly, as though not wishing to be seen.

Quinn's room was on the back of the house, at the opposite end to Smous's. After kennelling the hysterical Mab and tethering Hellas, he led through one of the back doors and down a pitch-black corridor. He unlocked his door and invited the visitor in with the words, 'Welcome to my sanctuary, my virginal bower.' The room was suffused with a sweet, almost sickly smell of toilet water, as though this had been used to disguise some other smell.

'Oh, bugger this!' snapped Quinn, and hurried over to close the shutters against the sun beating across paperwork on his davenport. Smous caught only a brief glimpse of the room before it was plunged into darkness. 'One has told that ghastly Garbett man again and again to close the shutters after cleaning,' complained Quinn, 'but he does not listen, insists it's "unnatural" to shut out the daylight, insists it's "not done". Bloody clot! This all right – not too dark for you?' he enquired. Then, as Smous stumbled against the bed, Quinn said, 'Perhaps I'd better . . .' and lit the oil lamp, which somehow made the atmosphere more nocturnal. The room was filled with furniture – a davenport and chair, a wash stand, a splendid brass bed, a tallboy with mirror, several campaign chests, three trunks brimming with books, and two mahogany wardrobes gleaming in the shadows, but no decorations on the walls, no framed pictures, no mementoes anywhere to be seen.

'Excuse me,' said Quinn, manoeuvring past Smous to the washbasin. Cleaning his hands was a ritual he would repeat fifteen, twenty times a day, always with a vague sense of embarrassment. 'You will note I take the precaution of visiting the river Pactolus *before* Dionysus bestows the golden touch,' he said with a little laugh, neatly folding the face-cloth and replacing it between two saucers. Because of the drought, water-rationing had become severe and you learned not to squeeze out a sponge or face-cloth after use. Now he sprinkled his hands and neck with perfumed toilet water, making the sweet smell of the room more piercing. 'Ah yes,' he said, noticing that Smous looked stranded, 'yes, please do ahh . . .' he gestured towards the bed, this being more comfortable than the one and only chair tucked into the davenport.

As soon as Smous clambered onto the bed he regretted this distribution of seating. Not only were his feet unable to touch the ground, but the bed squeaked and shifted every time he tried to improve his position. Eventually he crossed his legs, and, although far from comfortable, stayed like this, knuckles locked on knees.

'Shall we ahh . . . ?' asked Quinn who was pacing around in an unusually agitated way. 'Do you wish to ahh . . . ?' He came to a stop next to the smaller wardrobe and stood drumming his fingers on the wood. 'Drink?' he said now, adding quickly, 'I won't, but will you?' He mimed drinking and Smous, who had feared this would be on offer, hesitated. But only for a moment. Remembering Naoksa and his misery, he nodded eagerly.

There followed an extraordinary procedure. First Quinn unlocked the wardrobe with a key kept on a ribbon round his neck. The door was mirrored on the other side, so, as he pulled it open, a reflection of the oil lamp swung suddenly across the bed; and now an inner door was revealed with several more locks. One key was fetched from under the wash stand, another from the chamberpot beneath the bed, and the third from a secret pocket on the velvet curtains. When at last the second door was opened the luggage from the abortive journey to Calvinia was revealed. After searching in different containers here and there, Quinn found an unopened bottle and brought it across to the davenport.

'Only one glass . . .' he remarked, removing it from the neck of the water jug and laughing. 'Still . . . nothing strengthens the character like self-denial,' he said slowly, scrutinising the empty glass as though reading a minute inscription. With a sigh he poured out the Bokswater and handed it to Smous. 'They've done a splendid job trimming the beard,' he said from his position of closer proximity, and when Smous shrugged, stretched out a finger to explain, 'the beard.' Smous caught a brief smell of the man's fingers – a damp, metallic smell – and inadvertently jerked back his head. Then he sat with his glass on his knee waiting for the other to pour one for himself. 'No, no,' said Quinn, realising. 'Go ahead, do, I'm not ahh . . .' Smous tasted the Bokswater. It was like a blow to the head. He bounced his eyebrows in approval and trepidation, then drank some more.

'No, the thing is ahh . . .' Quinn began to pace again. 'Whenever the Signore and Signora visit, one has made it the practice to abstain from the grape – or *grain* in this case – to take a respite as 'twere, not that they'd disapprove, good heavens no, they'd happily join one, no, it's merely that one has found it preferable – pleasurable even – to be thoroughly compos mentis for the delights of the evening ahead. I mean, you know, one does hear oneself making a fool . . . d'you see? It's not as though one doesn't hear that. Anyhow, on every previous Scuteri visit, even the last time, one has always found the abstention effortless, and ahh . . . today it's less so. Which is a trifle worrying. However . . .' He went to stand at the window, hands behind his back, and his nose inches away from the shutters. 'So – there – we – are,' he said slowly, and stayed gazing at the shutters as though at a distant view.

'All right?' he asked after a while, turning to Smous and pointing to the drink. Smous nodded enthusiastically, feeling warm inside, and bold enough to change his position on the bed. After much squeaking, he ended up with his legs crossed again, but the other way round. 'Another?' asked Quinn, more as an excuse to hold the bottle than from any need to refill Smous's glass. 'Do you suppose it would matter if one took the tiniest daffy?' He stopped, clenched his teeth and eyes, set down the bottle and began to pace again.

'No, the thing is . . . one has had quite a trying time of late. The Dwarf, that was one's name for the lamb – well, one was very fond of him. I mean, one had to wean the bugger, you know. Milk on the finger. Oh yes. Brought to mind this man one knew in a remote village on the Nile, near Esna. English, this man, though a little odd, I'm afraid, and ahh . . . yes, this rather unusual practice he'd indulge in with a kid goat. Well, it follows, doesn't it? I mean, if it could suck milk off the finger, d'you see? Thought about trying it myself with the Dwarf once or twice. I know it sounds a little sordid, and one wouldn't dream of recounting this if you could comprehend a word one was saying, but, there you are, you know, what else is one expected to do in the middle of nowhere? I mean, there is the indigenous population –' He gave a little laugh. 'Meaning the natives of course, not the Boers. No, the native population, there is them, but ahh . . . not to one's taste. You know, one has the greatest possible regard for their culture, traditions, and so on, but draws the line at intimacy. As a friend at the R.M.A. used to say, "Only the coward takes his pleasure in the dark."'

His pacing had brought him back to the bottle which he contemplated. 'So, d'you see? What else is there? The Dwarf, I'm afraid. Anyhow, never plucked up the courage to try. Probably just as well. The little bugger's teeth were starting to come through just before its demise, so . . . there you are. Of course, Hellas and Mab miss him also . . .' He turned and considered Smous for a long time.

There was a knock on the door.

Quinn swiftly closed the wardrobe doors, without locking them, and propped a book round the bottle on the davenport, while coughing a little signal to Smous, indicating he should hide the glass. 'Yes?' he called finally.

'Sir?' came a familiar whine from beyond the door.

'Yes, Garbett, all right, come along in.'

Garbett's haircut had aged him, exposing sharp, silver hairs and exceptionally large ears. 'Pinched you this from the kitchen, sir,' he said, producing a small, dirt-caked melon from one pocket.

Quinn eyed it grimly. 'Thank you.'

'Bastards never even noticed. I –'

'Didn't they? Many thanks. That all?'

'No sir, no, come for your boots, belts and trunklements, sir.' He gave a little start as, creeping round the door, he found Smous on the bed.

'Very well, Garbett, quick as you can, thank you,' said Quinn who had gone to the window again, gently rocking back and forth, touching his nose on the shutters each time.

'Will you be wearing –?'

'You know perfectly well what I'll be wearing, Garbett, the Italians have visited often enough.'

'Sir,' muttered Garbett, immediately offended, and then, shooting accusatory glances at Smous, made his way slowly to the larger wardrobe. This did not require a single key. There was an awkward pause while he scrabbled around in the gloom, searching out the correct footwear. Quinn chose to break it by saying:

'One was not best pleased to discover you left the shutters open again, Garbett.'

'It's unnatural, sir, to shut off the daylight. Makes it so close, and the heat's summat awful, I'm a spot of grease already. It's not done, sir!'

Quinn turned a triumphant look towards Smous as if to say, See!, before replying, 'Well, perhaps not *done* if one be situate in the town of Tipton, Garbett, there may be little call for the closing of shutters in *Tipton*' – Quinn made the word sound like a tiny spit – 'but here, in far-from-darkest-Africa, your negligence has resulted, once again, in the ruination of my papers.'

'Sir,' mumbled Garbett sourly, approaching the davenport. Pretending to examine the curled edges of Quinn's paperwork, he took the opportunity to push aside the book and reveal the bottle. 'Oh-ar, and what have we here?' he asked with mock surprise, then took hold of the bottle and began a creeping walk towards the smaller wardrobe.

'May one ask what you're doing, Garbett?' said Quinn.

'You may, sir, mmmm, I'm doing what I was asked to do, sir, I a-a-a-am, asked by your good self, sir, helping you with your resolution, sir. "Whatever happens, Garbett" – I believe these were your very words, sir – "whatever happens you are to see to it that no drop of Bokswater passes my lips during –"'

'Yes, well, you'll be relieved to hear that Mister Smous is partaking of the Bokswater as a little light refreshment in this uncomfortable weather, and that I am not.'

'Si-i-ir,' said Garbett on a disbelieving chuckle.

'Mister Smous, kindly show Mister Garbett your glass,' said Quinn with an explicit gesture. Smous, however, was a little light-headed by now, and under the impression that a denial was required. With the glass propped on the covers behind his back, he held out both hands with a look of blissful innocence. Quinn closed his eyes and sighed. 'It is nevertheless the truth, Garbett,' he said.

'I believe you, sir, others wouldn't.'

'Garbett, good afternoon.'

'Sir, you begged me to –'

'Yes, Garbett, kindly put down that bottle, take the boots and whatever you need, and thank you so much, good afternoon.'

'Sir,' said Garbett dutifully, then put down the bottle in the middle of the floor and proceeded to the door with the boots and belts. 'I'll bring these back in half an hour, sir,' he said pointedly.

'Yes?' challenged Quinn.

'Just thought I'd mention it, sir,' he replied with a little glance at Smous.

'Oh yes, why so?'

''Cause that's when they'll be done, sir.'

'Garbett, hook it!'

'Sir,' he sang quietly, shot a last smiling glance at Smous, then departed.

'Lord almighty,' said Quinn, 'and they wonder why one drinks!' He collected the bottle from the floor, and, as one wreaking revenge, prepared to pour it. Then he remembered there was only one glass, sighed, returned the bottle to the davenport and mimicked Garbett: '"Back in half an hour, sir" – Lord almighty!' He strode over to the door, locked it, and, passing by the bed, reached behind Smous, causing him to jump, saying, 'May I?' as he collected the glass. He filled it and drank the contents down in one.

He gave a long sigh of relief and let forth:

'Can you possibly have any notion how much one despises that man? No, that's unfair, he's a good sort at heart, fiercely loyal, few others would have stood by one as he has, but then again – did one really wish him to? I mean, after the war, he somehow *stuck*. Terrified of returning to some wretched hovel in Tipton, I expect. "Oh sir, please sir, I'll work for nothing, sir . . ." You know, if there was anyone else one could let him go, but there isn't, except native staff, and can you imagine what this place would be like with only April to talk to? I mean, the poor thing's sweet but, you know . . . d'you see? So one's left with the ghastly, gabbling Garbett, smelling like a polecat and bringing me these endless, infernal offerings of rubbish –' He grabbed the melon Garbett had left and hurled it into a corner where it split with a rude noise. '"Brought you this, sir, brought you that, sir, mmm, I di-i-i-id, cheer you up, sir." You know, is one the poor relation in some raw-gas-tap-backstreet? And as for the mind . . . the *mind*?' He gulped down another glassful. 'I wish you could have seen them, the Garbetts of England, when they first came swarming out here for the Zulu War of seventy-nine, dear me, you should have seen them, those illiterate weavers, wool-spinners, beamers and millers taking the Queen's shilling and blooming into Redcoats. What a pitiful business all round. Their livelihoods have been destroyed by the new industries and they're coming out here to fight a nation trying to stop precisely the same thing happening to them. D'you see? Most of the other native nations had already succumbed: abandoned their lands, their customs, and trotted off to work the new mineral fields and mines. But not yet the Zulus. Arrogant buggers, but fine and noble with it, and such valour!' He gave a humourless laugh. 'The Garbetts called them savages. Oh, if only they could have seen themselves in the field, those Garbetts, with their little red eyes and gnashing little teeth, their grunts and squeals and squirts of pleasure as they rutted with bayonet and bullet. Here at last was the life of privilege so long denied them, industry and recreation rolled into one. And what rapture, what sport, oh how much finer than beak-hunting or ratting, or boxing the ears of their grey little wives – "When the drums begin to roll, my boys, when the drums begin to roll, oh it's thin red line of heroes when the drums begin to roll!"'

His outburst had sent several strands of hair tumbling over his brow.

He collected these in his fingers and carefully smoothed them back into the oil of his new haircut. Then, after downing another glass of Bokswater, he stared at the bottle and resumed in a quieter way: 'At least, some of us debated the morality of it, debated it every single night in the mess, some of us did, at least we knew what we were doing, but the Garbetts of this world were just ferrets down a hole, and I can't tell you what pleasure it would give me to bugger you now, sideways, inside out and upside down, you great walking piece of circumcised sausage, how I'd love to lower my naked nancy onto your oiled head and squirm about!'

Quinn had changed his theme without changing his tone, or looking up from the bottle. When he did so now, it was with a calm, matter-of-fact glance – to ensure that Smous was not, by some linguistic miracle, registering shock. Then he said quietly, 'Dear Mother of Jesus!'

He filled the glass. 'Will you have another?' he asked, passing it over. 'Apologies there's only the one glass, but still, I don't mind sharing if you don't.' He drew the chair closer to the bed and sat facing his guest with arms folded. Smous drank and smiled back happily, then changed his position on the bed again, feeling giddy as it swayed and squeaked beneath him.

'Ooooh . . .' laughed Smous woozily.

'All right?' asked Quinn.

'Goooood,' said Smous.

'You shameless sybarite!' whispered Quinn through a polite smile. 'Do you know Byron's poem "Mazeppa"? Mazeppa – that word mean anything to you? *Ma-zep-pa* – no? Probably Polish. Your part of the world, yes? Story of a Polish nobleman tied for his misdeeds to a wild Ukrainian stallion. Which is a little how I feel at the moment. You're a bit of a stallion, yes? Something of a wild Ukrainian beast, wouldn't you say? God, it would be rapturous to reach across now and rummage in your wild Ukrainian lap, don't you think?' Quinn was careful to keep all trace of lust from his voice and eyes, retaining an expression of detached, erudite pleasure, hands gesturing now and then with classical grace. 'It is heavenly, you know,' he informed Smous, 'to be able to sit here and say these things to your face. That hairy face with its glorious organ of flesh sticking out, catching the light just so, its sheen neither slack nor rigid, a face altogether so reminiscent of the lower visage, the lap visage, the loin visage, with its own little terrier's crop and oh such expressive featurettes . . . yes, fearfully thrilling to be able to say these things while you presume our theme to be literature or the climate. It's the separation, d'you see? Very like our everyday exchanges, except usually it is our words which deceive – today, my friend, it is your eyes. You look at my mouth and because it does not drool you mistake its employment. The mouth moves so quickly and so little, the word "primrose" looks to you the same as "arsehairs", while the expression "jiggle my danglers" could be me saying "Alfred Lord Tennyson" Ah yes, the mouth need move so very little, and yet the tongue is so very busy within, such a versatile organ, able to entertain and please in so many ways, please and tease, lick and flick, reach and search and . . .' He had to stop for he had almost gulped in ecstasy. He took a moment to steady himself, staring up at the ceiling as if pondering a philosophical question, then resumed: 'And so on. Now then . . . ahhh . . . what shall we do next? Hmm? You have first shot. What would you like to do now?'

Smous recognised the tune of a question, so leaned forward with an eager expression, feeling brave enough to parade his English vocabulary and wondering which of the five words to say first.

'I should close your mouth, my dear,' advised Quinn, 'or you may find yourself at the fairground swallowing swords.'

'Goooood,' said Smous, selecting his favourite English word.

'Mmm. Well, I'm game if you are, Ganymede.'

'No.' said Smous selecting another.

'No,' smiled Quinn, 'why not? Oh go on, try it.'

'Yes,' said Smous.

'Yes? Goodness, didn't take much persuasion.'

'No!' cried Smous with a grin.

'Oh, one of those are you? – hot and cold, hot and cold.'

'How*are*you?'

'Better and better with every passing moment, I do assure you.'

'Bye-bye.'

'That it, is it?' said Quinn with a gracious smile as Smous lolled back onto his elbows, a satisfied look on his face, for that was the longest conversation he had yet enjoyed in this country. 'Well, that was certainly diverting,' said Quinn, 'but not quite time for bye-bye, I –'

'Bye-bye,' echoed Smous, grinning.

'Yes, that's right, but be quiet now, you little chatterbox, you're as bad as the gabbling Garbett, can't get a word in edgeways. It's my shot now, I believe, and what I'd like to suggest is a touch more adventurous.' He undid one button of his shirt, as though the heat had become unbearable.

'How about it, hmm? How about me undoing a second button now? Hmm? And then you doing likewise? Until we are sitting here –'

Quinn hesitated momentarily as he saw Smous beginning to frown. 'Oh dear God,' he said, battling to keep his voice steady. 'Better stop, yet can't stop, oh sweet ambrosia, one shall swoon. Are you fond of frottage? No, control, control, Giles – *control*. Now then, may I?' and he took the glass from Smous's fingers, careful not to make contact, and emptied it. Now he fetched the bottle, employing the moment to take several deep breaths. As he leaned on the davenport, a fragment of newsprint slipped from between his papers, and fell to the floor.

'Ah yes,' he said, retrieving it, 'the Bobby Barton incident . . .' He glanced round at Smous. 'Oh, but you've seen this, you were there at dinner when I told April about – oh, but of course you will have gathered as little then as now, you stupid, bloody, delightful, hirsute, tool-nosed she-shirt whore . . .' He sat on the chair again to pass over the glass, then stared down at the newspaper fragment, the flesh on his face growing heavy. 'Don't know why one told April this was from the Death Column. It isn't. Announcement of Marriage. Why lie to April? Don't know. Don't care. The man has the brain of a parrot, of a magpie. Of a *slave*. "Either be wholly slaves or wholly free." April was, I fear, whom the poet had in mind. Don't suppose you know which poet it was by any chance? No? Driving me insane. *Memory's going*! But . . . April. So sad. Ev'ry opportunity. I put the brain in his head and it doesn't work.' He laughed harshly. 'No, but . . . what was I saying? Ah, yes – lying to April 'bout Bobby Barton's death . . . though is it a lie? Death, marriage – same thing. Loss of self. He was never comfortable with his nature, Bobby Barton, whereas I've always embraced my own. Perhaps therein lay the fateful attraction. Who can tell, how does one 'xplain why two strangers should join their hemispheres? Montaigne puts it well . . . at least I think it was Montaigne . . . "It was because he was he, and I was I."' He stared at Smous directly. 'Like you are you, an' I am I. God, you are beautiful . . .' He hesitated, studying the sleepy, lumpen features more closely. 'Beautiful? Well, perhaps only in a wilderness. Still, what d's it matter if I say so? You're beautiful, beautiful!' He laughed. 'Do you think lying is a lesser sin if it falls on deaf ears?'

Smous waved cheerfully and said, 'Gooood.'

'Is it? Perhaps. 'nteresting topic. Virtue and sin. Shifting sands. Barton and I were gooood, but deemed otherwise by the world, and –'

'Bye-bye,' chirped Smous.

'And he has indeed gone bye-bye now, that's correct. Goodness, how a few drinks helps conversation. Bye-bye Bobby Barton. Not for you the antinomian life. Too many protectors. Whisked back to Engl'nd where now we discover he was persuaded to plunge the shrieking cross into some bitch's bloody wound! Do forgive me if I put it less d'licately than you. What did you say? Gone bye-bye?'

'Bye-bye,' echoed Smous merrily.

'Yes. Thank you,' said Quinn coldly. 'Ah dear, one's rather ruined the rapture now, or rather the memory of Bobby Barton has. Never used to be the case with him, I do 'ssure you. So, how to restimulate oneself is now the dilemma? With somebody who one s'spects is not, as the friend at the R.M.A. used to say, of the Higher Faith. Yes, no?' He stared so directly now, that, despite a haze of contentment, Smous began to feel a familiar sense of encroachment, and had to look away. Now he tumbled back as Quinn suddenly rose, towering above the bed – but the Englishman simply snatched the glass from his hand and said, 'Off you go now, hook it!'

No translation was needed since Quinn had gone to the door, unlocked it, and was waiting there, eyes fixed on the floor, as one who wished no further argument. Smous had grown used to these sudden switches of mood from Quinn's behaviour at dinner, so, heaving himself off the bed and gratefully making contact with the floor again, he wove out of the room saying 'Bye-bye', and heard the door slam behind him.

The black of the corridor was impenetrable. With arms extended like a blind man he felt his way, turned several corners, then, seeing a patch of light high on the wall, stumbled towards it, pushed roughly at what he expected to be a stubborn door and, in the next instant, found himself reeling around the road blinded by sunlight. 'Sheeesh!' he cursed as he realised how very drunk he was.

Middlepost was as silent as before, but for a faint hum of insects and heat. A few berries fell from a pepper tree onto a tin roof nearby, sounding like a sprinkle of rain.

Then he heard music: a repetitive sequence of notes from the piano in the Hall. He staggered towards the half-open red door and peered inside. Signore Scuteri, dressed only in underclothes and trousers, was seated at his warped piano, face turned away, one ear inches from his tinkling fingers while the other hand reached into the instrument, tuning it. He was oblivious to all else, even the presence of Naoksa, sweeping the floor nearby, collecting the fluffy mounds of hair into a basket. She looked up and saw Smous in the doorway. The haircut she had been given during the morning was very severe, but enhanced the diamond shape of her head. She smiled slightly, bored with the work and a little sleepy, for the air in the Hall was hot and swimming with dust. Smous decided she had never looked more beautiful.

He stepped into the Hall. Still Scuteri didn't look up. Smous felt invisible, and powerful. He began to walk towards the canvas curtain at the other end. He didn't know why or what for; through the drunkenness he knew only that he felt such power his heart was thudding in his chest. Surely Scuteri would hear that? But no. Now Smous could hardly hear either, couldn't see or breathe properly. He reached the curtain and slipped through, directing the briefest glance back to Naoksa.

The colossal crucifix filled the small space between the curtain and the rear wall; the dark, varnished Christ glared at the glowing canvas hanging inches from its nose. The air here was even hotter, smelling of canvas and dust. Every breath made Smous giddy. The only sound came from the keys of Scuteri's piano, slow, isolated notes played again and again. Now Smous heard a different sound, a small rustling noise. He watched the edge of the glowing curtain. Her shadow fell on it. She hesitated. Now she touched the curtain, the shadow of her fingers growing darker as they met the canvas. The next moment her face appeared, wearing a puzzled frown. Incapable of any other movement, Smous beckoned her with a flick of his head. She slipped through and stood facing him, still frowning.

There was a small rolled carpet near the bottom of the crucifix, which Breedt would use for his sermons. With one foot, and almost losing his balance, Smous unrolled it, then sank to his knees, nodding at Naoksa to do the same. She obeyed, frowning more deeply now. They knelt, facing one another, Smous at a loss what to do next and confused by Naoksa's mixture of disapproval and complicity. 'If my husband learns of this,' she said quietly, 'if Kgototxe knows this he will have to beat me. And you – you, he will have to kill.'

'Yes, yes, shh, shh!' Smous whispered, glancing to where Scuteri was, and thinking, my God, what a time for her to start chattering!

Beyond the glowing curtain, the notes on the piano tinkled slowly, each one resonating in Smous's skull. He felt stupid beyond belief; a man of his age, about forty, or whatever it was, with a beautiful girl, yet not knowing what to do. There was nothing for it, he would have to make the first move. He began to unbutton his trousers, hoping this might encourage her to do something – lift her dress, or lie back on the carpet, or whatever the procedure was. He was uncertain which method they should use: 'Jewish copulation' or the other way, glimpsed once or twice, secretly, in the forest. And if they used that method, would her spit taste sweeter than the Russian soldier's? He doubted it. Didn't matter, he'd try anything now. Meanwhile Naoksa didn't seem to notice the unbuttoning, but continued to look into his eyes with a blank expression. He hesitated, wondering what he was doing wrong. Then he nodded towards the carpet, more harshly than he intended. She lay back, staring at the ceiling. It was most puzzling. With an expression now of, well, here goes, he dug inside his trousers. She glanced at this, then away again. He looked down – the purple grape just protruding from the trouser flap was not all that he had hoped for, but surely worth more than just a cursory glance. He caught her eye and implored her to look at the grape again. With a small sigh she did, fixing her eyes on it, and this seemed to do the job, for it gave a little jump and, like the object in some conjuring trick, slowly travelled towards her unaided. Naoksa reached up and took hold of what was more banana than grape now. Her gesture was listless, as if her only concern was to discourage the fruit from growing forever. Arching his head back, Smous found himself staring up the Christ's skirt, and murmured, 'Yishhh ...!' Suddenly there was a sharp scraping noise beyond the curtain. He gasped and swung towards it, expecting to see Scuteri's shadow reaching for the canvas. It billowed towards him. They would be discovered! The Bokswater swirled round his head, everything went grey. Then the piano started again. The scrape had been Scuteri shifting his chair, and the curtain had billowed in a breeze which had sprung up. The atmosphere settled once more. Smous looked down, eager to continue, but instead found the conjuring trick operating in reverse, banana reverting to grape, while in Naoksa's palm there lay a small white puddle, its colour heighted by her yellow skin. In utter confusion, Smous looked back towards the curtain, as if hoping Scuteri might step forward and explain. His head was turned away for only an instant, but by the time he looked down again, Naoksa's palm was empty.

What had happened to his seed?

Again and again in the months which followed Smous would relive these moments, trying to remember what had actually occurred, and cursing his ignorance of these things. He believed in that moment, glancing down the second time, discovering Naoksa's palm to be empty, he had also seen her licking her lips, as one who had just swallowed something. Had that really happened though, or was it his imagination, fired by the description of Jewish copulation by the Dolrogusky servants – the swallowing of seed – which of these was it? And if she had swallowed it, and if it was in her belly, his seed, did that mean what he feared?

As the piano continued to send its monotonous notes through the air, Naoksa rose and Smous buttoned himself, rolling the carpet with one foot. Then with a strange look at one another, almost of dislike, they slipped back into the Hall where Scuteri was still bent over the piano, face turned away, conscious only of his music. The mounds of hair shifted in a breeze from the open door, and a twist of curls wandered across the floor to Smous's feet, making him smile. Were these mine, he mused, from years ago? A boy aged three after his first hair-cut, nestling in a basin of sweets, waking into childhood. It's taken a long time, he thought, one finger checking his trouser buttons, to reach the next stage . . .

Outside, the breeze had done nothing to lessen the heat, but moved with a listless hissing sound, lifting dust off the land and drawing thin clouds across the sky. To Smous's surprise, Naoksa followed onto the road where she stood scenting the air. How ugly she suddenly looked, how hard it was to read her eyes, the whites filling with blood, how brutish. He shifted from foot to foot, worried he had caused her some pain or shame, but impatient also. She should have enjoyed it more, tried a bit harder, instead of just lying there staring at the ceiling.

He was about to move away when she let out a soft hoarse moan, from deep in her belly, and charged down the road. Smous struggled to concentrate. Was she leaving, for good? Should he let her go? Now he had a sudden image of Breedt springing from behind a tree and firing his shotgun at the escaping slave. Smous imagined her torso blasted away, his seed spraying in the air for all to see, imagined her running on, a hole in her middle showing a picture of the veld beyond. 'Oh God,' he groaned, and staggered after her. She left the road and turned into the gardens. Her movements were swift and silent as an animal's, springing and ducking, the shadows of the trees sweeping over her neck and shoulders in flashes of green and silver. Smous followed, stumbling through a vegetable patch, crashing into a dozing turkey which terrified him with its insane gurgle of fright. He reached the other side of the gardens and threw up his hands against the sunlight. The hot wind was stronger here, pushing across the veld unhindered. Naoksa had disappeared, though he could hear her somewhere close – peculiar, horrible shouts. It took a moment to locate where they were coming from, then he cried, 'Oh no, not again,' and lurched towards the stone igloo. As he tore round the side he was just in time to see her uproot the last corner of the cage. The ostrich burst from its prison among a shower of bloodied feathers. It stumbled, legs stiff and wasted, and for an instant looked as though it was bowing to Naoksa. Then it drew up, summoning its strength, neck hoisting and swelling. She rose too, lifting onto the tips of her toes and somehow further, determined to match the creature, stretching with it, face to face, rivalling its furious gaze and its wild force; then, although it was the bird that continued to grow, rearing above all else and booming in triumph, it was the girl who seemed to win, laughing as she fell back on her heels, becoming tiny again but human, and dismissing the beast with a stamp of her foot. After only a second's indecision, looking this way and that, neck weaving through the air like a rope, the ostrich turned towards the open veld and headed for freedom, lifting its wings and running with a loud thudding noise.

For the rest of his life Billy Garbett was always to regret that he had interrupted his duties that afternoon for a quick session with the kitchen maid Fleurjie.

They now appeared over a nearby rise.

All those present were to have different interpretations of what happened next. Someone believed Garbett ran towards the bird, someone else that he fled from it. But all were in accord about the most unusual aspect of the accident – the ostrich seemed to stop in mid-stride, as if recognising its tormentor, then deliberately changed its route to charge him. At the last moment, Garbett, recalling his own advice about what to do in these unique circumstances, threw himself directly in front of the giant bird, face first on the ground, his boater rolling away through the dust. However, instead of running straight over him, thwarted and impotent, as theory suggested it should, the ostrich performed an extraordinary leap, landing with all its weight on top of the shrieking man. Again and again it bounced on him, then stepped off, dignified and haughty, and, with a little backward kick, dismissed its victim with a scattering of dust. It surged forward again and disappeared over the brow of the hill.

Had Garbett or Fleurjie seen Naoksa release the bird? Smous thought probably not. And they mustn't see her now. He grasped her arm, trying to pull her back into the gardens, but she shook free and ran into the open. It didn't matter, Garbett was unconscious and Fleurjie nowhere to be seen. Staggering drunkenly, Smous followed Naoksa to the brow of the hill.

On the windy expanse below, the ostrich could be seen tearing through the bush, running for its life, neck whipping through the air, legs hardly touching the ground, coming as close to flying as it ever would.

'Yes! Yes! Yes!' cried Naoksa, her diamond-shaped face sharp and dangerous, jaws cutting through the air. 'Yes! Yes! Yes!' she cried again, then, turning to Smous, her words tumbling out hoarsely, explained, 'When the god Pisiboro found the hot coal hidden under the arm of the ostrich he stole it, on the third throw it remained in the sky. Look, how it became the sun! And some bits landed in the brandybush where our firesticks grow . . . So we have light, we have warmth, and every year the fire rises in the brandybush and we have ripe fruit . . . We have all these things, and it is good that way. So.' She turned back to look across the plains. They were empty now except for the rolling shadows of clouds; there was no moving speck to be seen, not even a small cloud of dust. The ostrich had vanished. But still she called to it – 'Yes! Yes! Yes!' – from deep in her belly, then stopped and scanned the veld, her face creased with pain. 'Which way?' she asked, 'there or there, which way?'

'It is gone,' Smous explained. 'Gone. Gone for good.' She looked at him puzzled. 'Gone,' he repeated, doing a vague impression of the galloping ostrich. 'Gone away.'

'No, no,' she snapped, 'not the ostrich. Me. Where I was born,' she explained, simulating a swollen belly. 'I don't know where it is' – now signing towards the ground – 'where our territory is.'

'Home?'

'Yes.' She knew he'd understood.

'Home,' he repeated thoughtfully.

'Where is it?' she demanded, tears of frustration in her eyes. 'There is every way here, which is a person to choose? There or there? Where? You tell me! Please tell me, where?'

'Never mind home, where's Kulvidya?' Smous asked mournfully, gazing across the landscape. It had so little character: bushes and rocks, a hill, more bushes and rock. Just to look at it was to feel lost. He took Naoksa in his arms and held her, trying not to sway or let her feel the swelling in his loins; so he stood with his chin on the crown of her head, and his feet some distance from hers. For a few minutes they stayed like this, she leaning into the clumsy embrace trustingly, while her eyes continued to scan the wilderness. 'Where?' she kept saying, spitting out the word. 'Which way must I go, there or there? Which way? *Where?*'

* * *

It must not spoil Mister Quinn's evening, of this Garbett was determined. The Tipton Slasher had broken several of his ribs (every breath burned), one foot looked like a swollen sponge, his neck and face were bruised, and a kick from those claws had opened the side of his nose, narrowly missing the eye. But none of this was reason enough to spoil the evening. Mister Quinn lived for these rare Scuteri visits, it was unthinkable that this ludicrous mishap should mar his pleasure. Throughout his military career, Garbett detested the scorn heaped on all batmen, the accusations of cowardice, and always boasted he would lay down his life for Quinn. If that day had come now he was ready for it. Particularly since, just three nights ago, Quinn had visited his room after dinner and said, 'G'bett, thank you.'

'What for, sir?' came the wary response.

''t for? For . . . your steadfastn'ss 'n charity . . . 'nt know what one would've done without you. S'mtimes one is so short with you, but . . . d'you see? One treasures you. J'st wanted to say that, it being Christmas in a few weeks, and . . . so, d'you see?'

With Fleurjie's help Garbett patched himself up, binding his aching sides, dousing his cuts with a sulphur balm, and rubbing his bruises with the last of his 'Pickle', an astringent spirit with which he loved to chafe his shins during the winter. From Breedt's medical bag, Fleurjie stole a bottle of Balsem Vita Wit; normally used for stomach cramps, but which she ground with tobacco and gave him to sniff, producing a pleasant numbing dizziness. Now she helped dress him in his ex-regiment's uniform, and wherever his wounds still showed, painted these with a mixture of flour and chicken blood, which gave his skin a startling pink glow. Struggling not to limp or wheeze, Garbett made his way towards Quinn's room with the polished boots and belts. Fortunately his master had continued to drink after throwing out Smous, and was unconscious, sprawled upside down across the bed.

> 'And shall ye miss me
> When mh-hh-hhh . . . ?'

– sang Garbett, staring down at the snoring figure, then slunk back to his room and waited for the night, when darkness and candlelight would provide the best disguise for his injuries.

At sunset, the others gathered in the yard for the next ritual of a Scuteri visit. An ox, purchased by Quinn, was led in among a small herd of cows –

this, so he should not grow alarmed too soon. The cows were then taken away while April lassoed the ox and tethered him to the fence. Both pairs of legs were roped together and now began the business of tripping him up, a feat not easily accomplished by a man whose balance tended to up-end him sooner than the beast. Eventually Breedt was forced to lend a hand, roaring, 'You're shamming, shamming!' at his servant. When at last the ox was horizontal, one eye staring with disbelief at the spectators, April stood above it with a machete and hacked open its throat. A lake of blood spread across the yard, turning gold in the setting sun. The hapless April now slipped in the middle, sending a fan of ripples out to the edges where Quinn's dogs crouched, lapping. It was then that Signora Scuteri fainted and had to be carried into the kitchen by a muttering Breedt. 'Blessed Mother,' chuckled the Signore, 'our Pope is angry.'

As April staggered back to the group, drenched in blood, Scuteri was the only one to applaud, grinning with golden teeth, and asking, 'My good old favourite Professor, what is become of you?'

Unable to hear the question, April laughed and answered quickly, 'Nay, nay, O Signore, 'tis not the demon drink, heaven forfend, good Lord, good grief and never, never whatsoever. Nay, 'tis just the old-age carry-on. A foolish fond old man, what? Comes to us all now and then, not so, O dear Signore – old age?'

Quinn sprang to the rescue, leading away the puzzled Scuteri. As they passed Smous, the Englishman beamed warmly, apologising for his earlier behaviour. 'My dear Mister Smous,' he said, 'believe it or not, but tonight you are going to the Opera!'

The recital took place in the hall after the roast-beef supper. The Scuteris slipped away from the meal before the end in order to change, as did Quinn. Smous already wore the evening dress which Garbett had delivered to his room with compliments from his employer. It hung on Smous awkwardly, but made him feel very grand. Although exhausted by his exceptional day, head aching from the Bokswater, he remained captivated by the Scuteris and the strange atmosphere they had brought to Middlepost. Now he followed the Breedts out onto the warm dark road, and stood with them admiring the stars. They were dressed in a way Smous had not seen before: Mevrou Breedt in a frilled bonnet and with a crocheted woollen shawl over her black dress; her husband in a mustard corduroy suit, gleaming riding boots, a gold chain spanning his waistcoat, and his neckerchief tied round a closed collar like a bow-tie. As they led across to the Hall, Smous was surprised to discover it laid out as for a Sunday service. The servant population was gathered outside in a square of yellow light falling through the doorway from dozens of candles, while families from the district were grouped around within, dressed in their Sunday best, everyone looking freshened by a new haircut. They had set out their usual chairs and stools, and in the first row there was a massive armchair, clearly a seat of honour, while the piano had been positioned in front of the canvas curtain. The Breedts took their place among the buzzing crowd and Smous began to drift towards his usual seat at the back, when Garbett, hovering round the entrance and gritting his teeth against the pain of his injuries, redirected him to a seat alongside the armchair, saying, 'Mister Quinn requests your person at his side,' and just managed a little smirk.

When all were seated, Garbett gave a signal through the doorway, then limped to his seat against one wall, where he huddled for the rest of the evening, praying for it to end. Now Quinn entered, in full dress uniform, deep blue, the jacket alight with medals and braid in gold and silver. It was a magnificent arrival, unfortunately ignored by the assembled Boers and spoiled further by Quinn's listing, floppy steps. Nevertheless, after only one serious stumble, he took his place in the centre armchair, straightened his back and lifted his chin.

As the audience went silent, small aggressive noises were heard from behind the curtain, scuffling and whispering, before a corner lifted. Smous froze, fully expecting to see himself kneeling on the floor, purple grape protruding from his trousers, and Naoksa lying on the floor passing her tongue across her lips. Instead, the Scuteris stepped out carrying music sheets, and were greeted with enthusiastic applause.

The Signora had collected her hair into a glittering black turret high above her head, and whitened her face, adding dark splashes of mascara, rouge and carmine lipstick. She wore a dress of reddish-gold taffeta with a georgette veil, like a gigantic goldfish caught in a stocking, the candlelight shivering over her festoons of jewellery and beads. Smous wondered if he had ever seen anything more glamorous. The Signore's gilded costume was as impressive: a Spanish matador, complete with pink-lined cape which clashed loudly with the orange of his hair, revealed now as he whipped off his beret with a cry of 'On with the spectacle!' and tossed it over his shoulder. The pink cape followed next, narrowly missing his wife's turret of hair, then he swept onto the piano stool and began to play.

'The primadonna begins with one of her oh-so-great roles,' announced Scuteri, twisting his head round. 'The role of Violetta, the consumptive courtesan in the masterwork *La Traviata*, by our beloved Giuseppe Verdi – this role she make in all our great houses in the blessed motherland and now all over the world she make this role . . .' As the introduction continued the Signora prepared herself, fluttering her hands over hair and face, brushing fingers to and fro across her neck, as if trying to erase the double chin, and then warming her voice with a quiet 'pa-pa-pa-pup!' As the piano led swiftly to the opening phrase she became more and more nervous; more nervous still as her husband showed no sign of concluding his speech – then, after a brief muddle, during which he extended the musical introduction in order to complete his own, utterly confounding her breathing, at last she began to sing, in Italian:

> 'How strange it is!
> Those words are carved on my heart
> Would a serious love affair be a mistake for me?'

Signore Scuteri conducted the singing while he played: he would snatch suddenly at the air, or jerk his palm upwards, trying to boost her higher notes. She ignored him; except when required to turn his music sheets. Then she was forced, often in mid-note, to lick her forefinger, smiling apologetically, and lean over the piano, her shadow briefly engulfing him. But for most of the time she was possessed with a new stillness. She held one fist clenched to her massive stomach, the knuckles white, while her other hand reached towards the gathering. She gazed at them very directly, but with a far-away look, both romantic and haughty, pitying them for being without her magic.

> ' . . . a poor lonely woman abandoned in this crowded desert
>   they call Paris.
> What can I expect? What can I do?
> Enjoy myself, and die in a whirlwind of pleasure!'

– she sang, Scuteri's jerking palm encouraging her voice higher and higher. She battled valiantly, clutching at the jet crucifix round her throat, but at the very top note she lost courage and resorted to a voiceless sucking, greatly flattering Smous, who mistook her grimace for a smile. The piece finished with Signore Scuteri's hands springing off the keys as if they had become white-hot from his impassioned playing, while the Signora gave a little curtsey and broke into modest giggles.

'Too slow, too slow, you fat Neapolitan bitch!' the man said in their native tongue as they bowed.

'It's you, ah? Too fast!' replied his wife, smiling sweetly at the audience, 'You play the same as you sleep – much noise, but dead to the world.'

'*Eh* – turd of the Madonna!'

'You play sloppier than a dog's dong!'

'And now, my dear friends,' announced Scuteri, reverting to English and flashing his golden smile, 'now our most dear primadonna will sing to you . . .'

And so it continued, song following song in the candlelit Hall, enchanting the audience and filling all with a particular yearning, impossible to locate or explain. Leather-faced farmers sat like enraptured children, with large, knobbly hands folded on their laps, while their wives dabbed at bony cheeks and whispered, 'Oo, but that was lovely, hey?' Smous kept glancing at Breedt, intrigued by a new expression in those eyes; moistened tonight not by his struggle, but something else, something frightening him. Quinn noticed as well and thought he knew what it was – such a pitiful creature, he mused, an ape with a haircut and fine clothes, bewildered by this beauty.

'And now,' announced Scuteri, 'I will humbly join our primadonna in the exquisite love duet from *Lucia di Lammermoor* by our beloved Gaetano Donizetti. My dear, please!' he commanded, and the Signora began to sing:

> 'Oh my ardent sighs
> Will reach you on the breeze,
> In the murmur of the waves
> You'll hear the echo of my weeping . . .'

When her husband joined in, his small body dilated with song. He abandoned the piano and, with swelling throat and heaving breast, unleashed his passion. The Signora quivered and made little gestures of restraint, then gave herself also to the ecstatic misery of the song.

'Farewell!' she sang.

'Remember! Heaven joined us!' he sang.

'Farewell!' they sang together, clutching at one another's hands in the last moment, heads thrown back and eyes shut tight. Then they flew into one another's arms, kissing and weeping, while the audience clapped and screamed like children.

'Peasants!' cursed the Italians as they took their bows. The Signore nodded towards Breedt:

'Just look at the Pope's brainless face!'

'And look at the Pope's wife,' chuckled the Signora. 'Any moment now, yes, here one comes – poffff! – a cheer from the rear.'

'And even the Emperor, alas,' said Scuteri, turning his gold smile towards the bravo-ing Quinn, 'has thoughts only for his new catamite tonight.'

'The Hebrew? Never.'

'Closer than shirt and arse, believe me.'

From his seat in the front row, Smous could hear the Italians talking as they bowed, and he marvelled at the raw melodies of their language, thinking it little surprise that it lent itself so well to song. He wondered when last he had felt so happy.

To let her voice rest, the Signora produced a violin and began to play, her husband accompanying on the piano. Smous frowned. Why was his mood suddenly changing? Perhaps it was the sad tune, perhaps because the Signora was losing her glamour: the violin pushed her chin into her mouth, and the scowl of concentration was cracking her make-up, sending little showers of powder onto the dark red-gold dress. But there was something else. 'Now listen,' he heard a voice saying, 'this is the second movement of Mozart's Sonata for Violin and Piano in C Major. You'll just have to imagine the piano . . .'

His head whipped round to the doorway, expecting to find Elie there, twelve years old, sitting cross-legged, hunched over his illicit violin, a blob of coal dust on his nose. The memory was like a pain shooting through him, and now there were others; random corners of his parents' house lit with patches of sunlight, lime-coloured; Elie at the railway station on the day of the departure, the only one who wept, his blind eye burning, the only one who hugged Smous; their father standing by, grinning, wanting to hug him also, but squeezing his shoulder instead, saying, 'Go well, hm?'; memories of the kitchen where smoke always hung in the corners like mist, and of his mother, leaning close, touching him and smiling – how could that be?, she never smiled – memories so clear he could smell the dough on her fingers; and again and again Elie, cross-legged, learning his Mozart. Smous blinked. Naoksa was sitting cross-legged in the doorway holding her sheaf of dried grasses, trying to follow the melody. Her dark eyes were fixed on the musicians, and now, as Smous watched, her tongue slowly moved across her lips. It was exactly the same gesture that he remembered, or thought he remembered, from this afternoon. Was his seed, the seed of his family, the Immerman seed, inside her? Could that really be possible? Damn my ignorance, he thought, damn it, damn it, damn it.

Feeling cold, he turned back to the musicians.

The Italians brought the tune to an end; the Signora gently removing the bow from the strings as though stretching a thread till it broke, while her husband slowly took his fingers from the keys and continued to play for a moment in the air.

'How charming,' said Quinn when this subtle ending had failed to inspire applause from the Boers. 'Wha's that piece?'

'Ah, no, there the memory fails, your Excellency,' replied Scuteri, mopping his brow on one brocaded sleeve. 'It is an old tune some of the musicians do play now and then between themselves.' He consulted his wife in Italian, but she shrugged and began to prepare for the finale.

'Mozart,' said Smous suddenly.

Despite the unusual pronunciation the name had registered. Quinn looked to Smous with surprise, then back to Scuteri for confirmation.

'Mozart perhaps,' shrugged Scuteri, adding contemptuously. 'Or perhaps not, he's not Italian, not of the chosen people!'

'Mozart,' insisted Smous.

'You know of Mozart then?' asked Quinn, giving the other's arm a little squeeze.

'Mozart,' repeated Smous mournfully, 'goooood.'

'Good, yes, very good. Ah, music, the universal language, yes?'

'It is God's gift,' said Scuteri. 'To hear it is to weigh out life ounce for ounce. You will find me and the Signora singing ten hours after our death, this I promise you.'

'Universal language,' murmured Quinn, 'like love.'

'So!' cried Scuteri, sweeping away. 'The Finale! And tonight, a little surprise.'

While the men were talking the Signora had moved through the audience distributing half a dozen songsheets, which she and her husband had copied out during the afternoon. The audience rearranged itself into little groups, frowning at the Italian scripts, while the Signore made his final announcement:

'So, my dear, dear friends, so now we must end our humble performance, and if you have enjoy it, we can take no merit – our gifts are from the Blessed Father, so if you wish to grant the thanks it must be in the prayers, ah? And the donations we collect as you leave, these we merely send home to Padua for the poor sisters of St Anthony. So, to end we do now honour the new resident of Middlepost by all to sing please the Hebrew Chorus from the great work of *Nabucco* by once more our most beloved maestro Giuseppe Verdi.'

Quinn glanced over to Breedt and gave a small smile to establish ownership of the idea, then beamed at Smous who was oblivious, staring down at the floor, lost in memories of home.

> 'Fly, thoughts, on wings of gold,
> Go settle upon the slopes and the hills . . .'

Smous was surprised to suddenly hear everyone join with the Scuteris; Quinn was the only one who attempted the Italian, the others hummed or sang 'Aaaa.'

> ' . . . the sweet airs
> Of our native land smell fragrant.'

Smous glanced round the Hall and at the group gathered in the square of light on the road: there was Naoksa strumming her dried grasses, staring up at the sky; next to her Marie, her jaws hanging open, the half-tongue roaming around her mouth.

> ' . . . the banks of Jordan
> And Zion's toppled towers.'

There was April too, singing his heart out, conducting with his umbrella; next to him Klippie who grinned at Smous, winked and held up the blue notebook from which he was singing instead of the songsheet. Horrified, Smous swung towards Breedt, but the Boer's heavy head was bowed over the sheet of paper, ears scarlet, lips twitching now and then, as he pretended to sing.

All around him, though, the others lent their different noises to the chorus, and, with the impassioned voices of the Scuteris soaring above all, the tiny settlement rang with song:

> 'Oh, my country so lovely and lost!
> Oh, remembrance so dear and so fraught with despair!'

Babel

It was extraordinary to be back in Plungyan after all this time, his mission a failure. The town was changed, burned by fire beyond recognition. Smous could not tell whether the catastrophe was man-made or not, for even the cobbled road to his front door was in ruins, collapsed on either side with only a narrow walkway down the middle. He followed his father towards the house, saddened by the gaunt neck in front of him. The house ahead was in darkness, the windows cold, charred holes, but he could glimpse figures moving around within, trying to keep warm. He didn't want to meet them, didn't want to admit his heroic mission had failed. His attention was taken by a house on the left which had not been burned, but where everything looked normal, with a warm glow from the windows. 'We should go here instead,' he said, turning back to his father, only to discover him gone. Smous remembered the old saying, 'Who comes to greet a pauper? A cold wind and wild dogs.' Voices whispered to him from the deep gullies on either side of the walkway. He knew he was in a nightmare and said, 'No, get me out of this now,' leaping over the gully towards the normal house. The light in the windows had turned blue and he realised, too late, here was greater danger than anywhere else, for a two-headed mutant was attacking him. 'Get me out of this, I've already said so,' he moaned.

'Meneer Smous, Meneer Smous,' whispered the mutant. 'Meneer Smous, Meneer Smous, Meneer Smous . . .'

Smous writhed and gasped. He believed he was awake, believed he was in his bedroom at Middlepost, believed it was only a few hours after the Scuteri concert, and yet standing above his bed, clearly defined in the moonlight that flooded the room, was the two-headed mutant from his nightmare. A dark covering fell from its shoulders, showing a mass of blue, deformed nudity with many limbs and no front to the torso.

'Meneer Smous,' it whispered, 'please Meneer Smous, please someone, please, oh loving Jesus, please help me.'

Smous recognised the deep voice, and saw now that one of the faces was Breedt's, but the other was lowered and he could not identify the short grey hair.

'Please man, I'll give you anything, do anything you want, please man, please before her husband wakes up, please!'

Smous sprang from his bed as Signora Scuteri suddenly swung her terrified gaze towards him. What had happened to her mane of black hair?

'Please, you're the only one I can turn to, please, this woman is sent from Satan's minister, she learned to fornicate with his black mare, and with his skeleton hanging from the stirrup, and now they've got me, my sin caught tight – *oo gonna*! – it's like a jackal trap, please God help me . . .' Breedt grasped the Italian's gargantuan buttocks and pulled, showing how little they budged. Smous gave his most heartfelt shrug of incomprehension ever. 'Ag, by the God Jesus!' whimpered Breedt, and, grabbing Smous's neck, dragged the bearded face between his body and the Signora's, so that he might look directly at the predicament. Smous saw two globes of white marble veined with blue, pressed against the rough hair on the man's pectorals, but nothing else was visible below these massive chests.

Breedt growled in desperation, and, collapsing onto the bed, pushed at the woman with all his might. She reciprocated as they struggled into an upright sitting position. Smous stared. These figures were from a dream: their faces and arms battling with such hatred, their thighs entwined so intimately. Now as the shoving subsided and the two looked at one another with dumb, hopeless expressions, Smous suddenly recalled seeing two dogs locked like this, and remembered how they were separated. He grabbed the water jug from his table and emptied it between the Italian's breasts and the Boer's chest.

'Aaaiiii!' exclaimed Breedt, as silently as he could, for the icy cold had contracted the vice. With pupils rolling into his skull, he placed one hand under the water jug and, wriggling his fingers like flames, whispered 'Hot, hot water, oh my Christ save me! Hot water, hot water . . .'

Smous understood and nodded. He rushed out into the pitch-black corridor, then sprang back. The Boer stifled another scream. 'Sorry,' whispered Smous, striking a match, 'but if I don't have a candle I get scared.' He hurried out again and rushed down corridors swimming with shadows and corners that suddenly leapt to and from his candle. At last he understood the Boer's gentleness all day, the fear in his eyes; and at last he could thank the Dolrogusky servants for revealing the method of Jewish copulation, which was clearly much safer than any other.

There was a light ahead, under the kitchen door. Charging in, he saw April bent over the stove; his first morning duty was to boil drinking water for the day. The man gasped as Smous grabbed his shoulder – his deaf ear had been turned to the door – then found himself being dragged out of the kitchen, along with a heated kettle.

Smous was panting with relief; thank God it was April and not Mevrou Breedt, who sometimes woke early, racked with indigestion, and fetched her toasted biscuits. He also felt sure that, for a reason he couldn't explain, it would be best if the bizarre coupling in his bedroom was seen by a servant rather than anyone else.

He was wrong.

When Breedt saw April's astonished eyes, he hit them with all his might, and then, as the man's dazed stagger brought him back within reach, he hit them again, and again, restraining him with one hand, striking and gougeing with the other. Long before the attack was over, Signora Scuteri had fainted, flopping backwards onto the bed, all tension flooding from her body, releasing her partner at last.

Grabbing a blanket from the floor, Breedt was gone in an instant.

Now Smous was left with two unconscious bodies in his bedroom: the naked Signora on the bed, April on the floor, blood trickling from under bruised eyelids. Smous decided he would have to transfer these people from his room before someone else arrived and misinterpreted the situation. He would have preferred to start with the Signora, but after one glance at her vast nakedness he knew there was no possibility of transporting it. He couldn't lift April either, but was able to drag him into the corridor, and out through a back door. Marie was making her way across the moonlit yard to start work, so Smous abandoned April at her feet saying, 'Help him, help him.' She began to ask, 'Whahh hhe – ?' but he had already gone, scurrying back to his room.

There he found Signore Scuteri, wrapped in a dressing gown, staring down at his naked wife.

'And I thought you were Quinn's catamite!' he roared in Italian, flying at Smous's neck. 'God's beast, God's pig!' Their struggle took them onto the bed where the Signora groaned and opened her eyes.

'No, no,' she cried, and, being stronger than her husband, wrenched him off with a single pull. 'It's not what you think, ah you fool!' she told him. 'I got up for the piss, turned the wrong corner, came in here, fainted with shame.'

'Lies, lies!' cried her husband. 'You lying gypsy goatwhore!'

'Ask him then, ask him!' she insisted, pointing at Smous.

'How can I ask him?' screamed Scuteri. 'He speaks less English than you, slit of the Virgin!'

Now Quinn appeared in the doorway, holding a candle. He was still dressed in his splendid dress uniform, having stayed up for a few nightcaps. He stared with disbelief at the naked woman in the middle of the room, and then at Smous's sheepish smile. Quinn's face was yellow with drink, now it turned white. 'Wh's th' H'll 's g'n on?' he demanded.

'Your Excellency, your Excellency,' pleaded Scuteri, 'it is the primadonna – she has betrayed me!'

'Sh's b'trayed us all!' snapped Quinn. 'Sh's no bl'dd' prim'donna, sh's from th' bl'dd' chorus, th's wha' sh' is!'

Signora Scuteri saw Quinn's contemptuous sneer and demanded a translation from her husband. She listened in horror, then bellowed:

'Tell him – tell him the chorus is the rock on which the Opera stands! Tell him the pigging soloists are capable of singing a ballad, but not a whole opera! Tell him that to get in the chorus you have to be pigging good!'

'Why should I tell him all that?' asked Scuteri.

'Because it is the truth!'

'It may be the truth, but what's it to do with you? You believe your own lies, like the thief of false paintings. You were never in the chorus. YOU CLEANED THE THEATRE!'

'Aaaaaaah!' wailed Signora Scuteri and buried her head in her hands, sobbing. 'But I *could* have been. Mother Mary has heard my gifts when I sing. She knows I could have been, I could have been . . .' She heard more voices coming down the corridor, and, grasping a sheet from Smous's bed, threw it like a shawl over her head; more concerned that no one should see her thin grey hair than any other details of her nudity.

Garbett's swollen face had appeared round the side of Quinn's body, now Marie's appeared, then Naoksa, who looked from the Italian woman to Smous with the same surprise as Quinn. Smous gave a little shrug, unable even to begin an explanation.

Finally the Breedts arrived. The Boer pushed his way into the middle of the room, dressed in a long nightshirt. He pretended to assess the situation in a glance, and then, as if too angry to look the Scuteris in the face, whispered, 'Go, now, go!'

Before sunrise they were gone.

* * *

That Sunday Breedt delivered his most terrifying sermon ever, without ever raising his voice, but with eyes glittering like ice. His theme was the imperative necessity for the Boer people to keep separate from the other, depraved nations of the world, excluding only 'the blessed Israelites' from his embargo.

'Different nations were created to be apart and separate,' he explained to the hushed congregation, 'and the Lord hath willed it thus. He looked down when the whole earth was of one language, He looked down at the builders of the Tower of Babel, the blasphemers building a tower to reach unto Heaven itself, and He said, 'Behold, the people is one, and they have all one language, and this they begin to do: and now nothing will be restrained from them, which they have imagined to do. Go to, let us go down and there confound their language, that they may not understand one another's speech.' So the Lord scattered them abroad from thence upon the face of all the earth . . .

'The Lord willed it thus, Brethren, and thus it must be.'

A few evenings later the Breedts sat down to decide April's fate. The woman couldn't see any point of keeping him at Middlepost now that he couldn't see, could hardly hear and was simply an extra mouth to feed. Tortured with guilt and fearful of the revenge his servant might take if banished, Breedt argued that the man could still act as translator at the store. He argued with such passion that his wife surrendered. As far as she was concerned the incident remained a mystery. Her husband claimed he had caught April with the Italian woman, but if that was true why had it taken place in Smous's bedroom? No, she feared her husband was lying; she feared he was covering up for the Hebrew; and she had only one thing to say. 'I mustn't hear anything more about it. I don't want to know.'

Three weeks after the incident, Klippie led his father to the store for his first day back at work. Breedt was not present, but had supplied a chair for April outside on the road. When he was seated, Smous went to greet him. He had not been to visit April during his recuperation, wishing he hadn't fetched him from the kitchen that terrible night. Now as he saw the slack, bruised eyelids, he thought of Elie after his beating by the Dolrogusky gate-keepers and felt faint, the earth tilting under his feet.

'My most dearest Mister Smous,' said April once he had identified the other's hair and beard. 'I have oft wished to converse with yours truly over the bygone weeks, for I am most sure you must feel drattedly bad about the whole rotten affair, and I wish to assure you of no malice aforethought

by me, no, no. Your mission that fateful night was to aid the Master
Stoffel, and the Lord alone knows we don't always bethink us clearest in
moments of stress. So, please dear friend and mooncalf, no tears on my
account. Remember it is out of our hands.' He drew Smous closer, and
whispered, 'The curse of the vanished foreskin,' then resumed in his
normal voice, 'and as far as the world goes, why tush, I shall, as the poet
says, I shall see it feelingly. The Master Stoffel I have assurified him also I
bear no malice for I know he did not mean to strike. His burden is a heavy
one, bringing light to us blasted heathens, yet keeping himself pure, he
hath told me this himself, weeping all the while – I know for I felt his tears
fall on my hand –'

'April, you old scapegrace!' called Quinn into his good ear as he arrived
to fetch Klippie for the day. 'Back at work at last? Quite right too, you lazy
bugger,' and he gave April's shoulder a tight squeeze, deliberately cutting
Smous, as he had done since the discovery of Signora Scuteri in his
bedroom.

'Took a little holiday, sir,' said April with a smile.

'We noticed. Indolent thing! Wait here, I have something for you, a
belated Christmas gift . . .'

'I don't believe I'm off anywhere, sir,' laughed April, not realising
Quinn had already gone, 'and is it Christmas already, b'God?'

When Quinn returned he was carrying a small book. 'Had it sent out
years ago and been saving it for self actually, for a day when one simply
had to have . . . some new . . . well, you know.'

'For a rainy day, sir.'

'For a rainy day, April – the very words I was searching for.' He passed
over the book. 'You have it. See, feel, the pages haven't been cut yet.
Brand new. Feel the binding – real morocco,' he lied, for it was ordinary
red leather. 'Isn't that grand?'

'Oh sir,' said April quietly. 'Sir, you mustn't make me weep, it hurts the
eyes.'

'Weep? Certainly not, nobody's going to weep.'

'Then why mock me by giving me a gift I cannot be using?'

'April,' reprimanded Quinn, squatting on his haunches and leaning on
the man's knees, 'you are an idiot. Despite a splendid education you
remain a hopeless idiot. I'm sorry one has to choose this of all mornings to
tell you, but honestly! Hasn't one always taught you that the *reading* of
books is the very least of their pleasures? Good heavens, man, Klippie can
read it to you, it's merely a volume of Donne's verses, no great rarity,' he

lied again, for the edition was early and precious. 'No, the true joy of a book, April, the fleeting, transitory, once-only joy is to cut the pages, each and every one, and then to hold it to your nose and slowly, slowly prise it open for the first time. Then, my old friend, then you catch a scent of its soul. And that is something you could do this very morning, is it not?'

'Sir,' replied April, grinning broadly.

'There you are then. Mock you indeed! You are an idiot, you are a bloody idiot.' Quinn lowered his head and blew his cheeks. He was so, so tired of humouring his man. Such a ludicrous, woebegone figure, no fight, a buffoon with the mind of a magpie and the tongue of a parrot. So like himself.

He spluttered suddenly, stifling a laugh, then stood and, speaking in Xhosa, turned to Klippie. 'Come, Ilitye, we have a day's work to do.'

For days after the Scuteri concert, Naoksa could think of nothing else. She had fallen among strange people, she was sure of this now she had heard their music. How restless it was. No sooner did it light upon something beautiful than it moved on, hunting for more. How greedy these people were in all things. Why did they not hold these beautiful notes and sing them again and again, to praise, to soothe, to heal? And why did they not sit in a circle to sing? How could you find harmony unless you copied the line of day and night? Instead they sat facing a wall. And, until the end, only two were permitted to sing. The rest had to keep silent and observe, like outcasts. It was terrible. Some wept – she watched this.

As time passed her confusion changed into pain, an ache in her chest and belly that made her hug herself, and she began to wonder if the concert was not, as she first thought, a ritual of bad magic.

All the people at Middlepost were to reflect on the Scuteris' visit and their music, and wonder about its powers, for everyone felt changed; happier or lonelier, restored or wounded. The two rivals, April and Garbett, had suffered most, but what specially hurt was that both had missed their moment of triumph. If only April could have watched the ostrich crush Garbett's ribs, it would almost be worth going blind after a sight like that! And if only Garbett could have seen Breedt gouge out April's eyes, he would have broken all his other ribs laughing.

Since Breedt refused to treat Garbett's injuries, Quinn took him to Calvinia, but no one thought to include Smous, who never learned where the injured Englishman spent that month after the Scuteris' visit.

While Garbett was in the Calvinia hospital, one of the doctors he noticed was an imposing Semitic figure with a huge beard and a gleaming top hat worn always, indoors and out; but Garbett didn't speak to this man and no connection was ever made.

Bokswater

''Twill be a storm,' so April kept saying these days, sitting on his chair outside the store. ''Twill be a storm.'

It was hard to believe. The drought had lasted so long now, it would surely last forever. Everyone had stopped talking about it and life at Middlepost had become quieter and slower than ever. When words were spoken they were usually in anger: someone had wasted water cleaning clothes or washing dishes, someone else had let their goats graze on neighbouring land. An outbreak of scab wiped out one farmer's sheep, and now people were terrified of their livestock mixing. The beasts were preyed upon by not only emaciated jackals from the veld, but the farmers' own trusted dogs, maddened by hunger. No cow had calved in twenty months and recently they stopped producing milk. In place of butter you melted down animal fat; a taste which only Smous relished, remembering it from home. As food became scarcer it had to be found elsewhere. In Calvinia the earth was too arid to sow and they were selling bags of wheat-seed cheap. But the ghastly dry paste you made by grinding this down was like eating sand; it made you angrier than ever. You turned to the veld, learning from the older Hottentots which of the shrubs and tubers were edible, which held moisture, which were poisonous; yet these things proved bitter, unpalatable also. Staring closely at the veld your anger changed to fear. The whole crust was loosening, splitting into pieces, curling its corners to the sky, and crumbling. The world was turning to dust.

Still April insisted, ''Twill be a storm.'

And then at midsummer, just after the arrival of the new year, nineteen hundred and four, it gradually became clear that the blind man had scented changes in the air before anyone else: a new sweltering humidity which left your clothes and bedsheets drenched, and warped the bark on the bluegums. The heat was worse than ever, but the foreigners at Middlepost were the only ones to complain. The rest turned their sweating faces to the heavens, sniffing and grinning. April was right, the rains were coming at last.

''Twill be a storm,' was how he put it each and every day, and Quinn would briskly add, 'Blow winds and crack your cheeks!' The Englishman was in buoyant mood. Within hours of moving to a new digging site he had discovered some promising fragments in the dry-blowing machine; fragments coloured that distinctive waxen yellow.

Garbett was sent to fetch the Bushman Bok, and after a lengthy performance, during which the wizened figure in bandsman's uniform examined the earth, listened to it, and threw the bones, he declared, 'Certain, certain, the Master Lord Quinn, riches are *here*, riches, riches, more than water, certain, certain, the Bokkie has smelled this and the Bokkie smells true.'

Quinn asked, 'How deep?' but the Bushman would only smile in reply, as one who did not wish to spoil all the surprises which the future held. This appealed to Quinn. He arranged for a drilling rig to be set up on the site and began to search deeper into the earth. A gang of workers was assembled and now Klippie began to spend less time with Quinn and more back in Middlepost.

In the late afternoon each day it was Smous's habit to visit the patch of beaten dirt behind the wattle-and-daub huts and watch the children's games; the children who had rioted on the ostrich and Naoksa, the chidren called 'smear-rags', a few Hottentots but mostly half-breeds, their poor mixture of blood showing as pink and grey blotches on their skin, like burn-marks. They had suffered badly from the drought, their small shapes growing tense and bony, jagged as the stones they played with. Smous would watch these games, waiting for fights to flare up, flinching and grimacing when they did, but unable to stop staring, noting every detail, studying it, remembering it.

But since Klippie's return the games had stopped and nowadays Smous often discovered the children huddled round April's son, whispering urgently, and, on one occasion, singing quietly:

> 'Will they hear?
> Will they hear?'

Smous frowned. That strange melody again, those questions lifting into the air, one after the other, like beckoning fingers. He saw an argument begin and went cold as the group swung towards him with dull, swollen eyes and toothless mouths, but they were quickly calmed by Klippie. 'It's all right, he can't understand. He's not their spy, he's their pet, their idiot,' and he laughed harshly.

At all other times though, the fifteen-year-old boy's presence was tranquil, almost angelic. Even when he watched the other servants abuse his father, tormenting the helpless blind man that had once governed them so mercilessly, even then Klippie never intervened, but stood with hands folded behind him, gently flexing his thick proud neck, almost nodding.

Smous was used to a constant thirst these days, a burning in his throat which he couldn't shift, however many times he swallowed or coughed; and blisters on his lips which he checked constantly with his tongue, growing almost to like the changing, broken shapes. But now a new thirst began to preoccupy him. The feeling was different. It arrived as a prickle deep in your guts, a prickle of disgust, creeping upwards, slowly changing into something else, a particular kind of excitement. 'Boks-wa-ter.' It was the first new word he had learned in their language since those months in Ceres, 'Boks-water.'

In his new buoyant mood, Quinn had decided to forgive Smous's indiscretion with the Italian woman and invited him again to his room, and then again. They requisitioned a second glass from the dining room and would sit drinking late into the night, Smous on the bed, Quinn on the chair, arms folded, an expression of repose on his face while he described his secret appetites, growing more detailed, more inventive each time. But always it ended the same way, with him abruptly losing his temper and throwing the other out. Sometimes Smous would stay in the corridor, ear pressed to the door, when he would hear odd sounds – muffled groans and splashing – and the next time he was allowed in the room he felt sure that one wall had been recently whitewashed and that the familiar scent of camouflage was stronger than ever.

One night, half way through their drinking bout, Quinn suddenly put back his head, closed his eyes as though in pain and, in a voice which didn't sound like his, sang:

> 'A handsome lad is Paudeen
> On fair-day or market-day
> But not more handsome than in March
> Aboard his curragh in the bay
> Oro Mór, O Moreen,
> O golden-haired one, will you come?'

His explosion that night was more violent than before and as Smous hurried from the room, a three-quarters-full bottle came flying after him.

Having succeeded in catching it, Smous found the Bokswater comforting to keep in his room. With water-rationing getting worse by the day, it was helpful having *some* liquid to sip at, even this oily ferment, and it helped calm him also, helped drive away those ridiculous ideas of setting up home with Naoksa and of a baby with her yellow skin and his thick hair. And he loved the feeling which the Bokswater brought, of giddiness, of the world spinning within him; and of becoming unwell, vaguely wonderfully unwell.

'Bokswater . . . Bokswater . . .' he said to himself all the time, practising the word until he could pronounce it perfectly. Soon the bottle was finished and he could try out his new word on Quinn. Quinn whispered, 'Dear Mother of Jesus, a fellow antinomian after all! Quite right, quite right, some of us were born to fly free,' before furnishing another bottle. Then Smous accompanied Garbett on the next 'postal run' to Calvinia (a trip he never imagined repeating) and, although without funds to buy his own supplies, it was exciting merely to stand in Bok's fetid underground cavern and inhale deeply, clicking his curling fingernails against one another, sending tiny shivers through his hand. He felt a peculiar power and wisdom, felt he was finally shedding his unformed, puerile nature and becoming someone else, someone he had always wanted to be. 'Elie, you damn old drunkard,' he whispered affectionately when he next looked in the mirror, 'welcome to Southern Africa!'

Ilitye

When Mevrou Breedt failed to return from the schoolhouse one Tuesday afternoon, nobody took much notice until dusk began to fall, and then, with still no sign of her or the Hottentot driver, Breedt nodded Smous towards the pony cart and together they rode up the hill to the school. They discovered her driver waiting at his usual place under the pepper tree, looking confused and anxious.

Without waiting for the explanation which began to tumble from the man's lips, Breedt approached the school. Then, halfway down the path, he stopped abruptly, folded his hands behind his back, hunched his shoulders, and stood facing the large window. Inside the classroom Klippie was standing next to Mevrou Breedt, who was bound to a chair. He was holding a machete under her chin. Although Klippie's words were inaudible through the glass, the message was clear and Breedt advanced no further, but let his moist gaze roam round the classroom, taking in the other children dancing round the tables, waving assorted weapons. All smear-rags. The farmers' children had been allowed home.

'Legs!' commanded the little blond boy who was keeping watch, and the men sitting round the Hall raised their feet off the floor. 'Hell, that's a big one,', someone remarked as the scorpion moved slowly across the earthen floor, 'the hotter it gets, the bigger they grow.'

'Looks quite tame,' said a second farmer, 'you could train him to do tricks.'

Another aimed a broom at the insect. 'I'm going to train him to lie down and make like he's dead.'

'Don't, man, you'll just annoy him. And even if you get him, his wife'll be around somewhere, and, like with us, it's the females you've really got to watch.'

The farmers chuckled and nodded agreement, watching the scorpion disappear under the mealie bags stacked against the wall. For a while all sat in silence listening to the moths bumping against the oil lamp. The heat of the night was exceptional.

'Well,' said the young farmer called Swanepoel, yawning and stretching. 'Very sorry, my friends, but I just don't see the problem, no I don't. I could go up to the schoolhouse now with my shotgun, they wouldn't even see me out there in the dark, no. One moment young Klippie would be chatting nicely to his friends, the next he'll be chatting to the angels.'

'Ag Jesus, they've got fires and guards up there,' said Reukes, the farmer who had lost an arm in the war, 'they're not stupid.'

'Guards?' laughed Swanepoel. 'No, *them* I think I could probably get past.'

'We're not slaughtering smear-rags, nay,' said the ancient van Jaarsveld, 'they're all offsprings from the district, all offspring our labourers have bred, we're not all of a sudden going to start slaughtering smear-rags, nay what, huh-uh, there must be other ways round this.'

'Anyhow, they could go and slaughter us first,' said Reukes with a nervous laugh. 'Oom Stoffie says there might be a firearm in there.' This news silenced everyone and they turned to Breedt sitting next to Smous in the shadows. He said nothing, so Reukes continued, 'He says Hannie's always kept one hidden in there since the war.' Again all eyes turned to Breedt for confirmation, but again he remained silent and brooding, and again Reukes had to deputise. 'Says he's not sure whether the smear-rags will have found it yet. He says –'

'What he'd also like to say,' interrupted Breedt suddenly, using his quietest and least predictable tone, 'is that he'd hate to see his wife harmed by one of the others once we've despatched Klippie off to the angels.'

'Never!' said Swanepoel, who always enjoyed contradicting Breedt. 'The rest are good smear-rags, I know them.'

'Bok's twins are in there,' said Naude, the blacksmith and saddle-maker, his massive bulk hunched over a little machine on his knees, like a miniature guillotine, slicing a stick of dried meat. 'Anyhow, who wants a piece of biltong?'

'Bok's twins? *Oo gonna!*' said Reukes. 'They'll be good and slammed for a start, they'll –'

'That I wouldn't have thought was likely,' interrupted Breedt, 'since we have no intoxicating liquors in Middelpos, and –'

'Maybe that's why Bok lives somewhere there on the veld,' said Swanepoel.

'We have no intoxicating liquors in Middelpos,' repeated Breedt teadily, 'not in Middelpos nor in the vicinity of Middelpos.'

'Ag man!' said Swanepoel impatiently, 'all my labourers get their rot-gut from Bok.'

'I think that isn't true, Gertjie,' said Breedt with a patient smile, 'because if it was, a person must start asking why you're permitting such transgression of God's will.'

Swanepoel was about to reply that it was common practice on all the farms, when he noticed the other men in the Hall glancing at him with pleading eyes, so instead sat back sulking, and took out his chewing tobacco. 'Hey, Sampie,' he said to the blacksmith, 'lend us your cutting thingie.'

'Not mine, it's Stoffie's.'

'He won't mind,' said Swanepoel, grinning at Breedt. 'Give it here.'

'No, *siss*, man,' replied Naude. 'You'll make my biltong smell of tobacco.'

'Ag don't make like an old woman, man, give here.'

Breedt observed the friendly scuffle, thinking how flippantly the other farmers were treating the schoolhouse siege. They had all hurried to the emergency meeting when summoned, arriving with noisy declarations of support, but he wondered what their true feelings were. Hannie Breedt was not popular among the farmers' wives; her condition made her reclusive, and her shyness was often called arrogance.

'Feet!' said the little blond boy watching for scorpions, and again the men raised their legs off the ground, Swanepoel taking the opportunity to snatch the biltong-cutter off Naude. Before the blacksmith could protest, the younger man pointed urgently to the insect:

'Look, man, hell, that's the mate of the male that went across before, hell, what a beauty – look!'

'How do you know that's the female?' asked Naude unhappily, watching Swanepoel press the sticky tobacco roll into the biltong-cutter. 'How do you know it isn't the other way round?'

'Tell by the swagger of her arse,' replied Swanepoel with a quick provocative smile at Breedt, and then turned to the little blond boy, who was his son. 'All right, Frikkie, now come on, now you tell us what the hell is going on up at your school.'

'Dunno,' replied the seven-year-old, who had the same grey, unsentimental eyes as his father. 'Klippie used to try and make us all learn a song of his, after classes.'

'You as well?' asked Swanepoel, his smile fading.

'All of us. But we lot told him to go walk! It made my mouth feel dirty, his song. I came home and washed it with soap.'

'What was the song?' asked Breedt. The other farmers had gone quiet.

'Dunno. A native song,' replied the boy.

'Hottentot?'

'No, native . . .'

'What the hell does "native" mean?' growled Breedt.

'How must he know?' interrupted Swanepoel hotly. 'How must he know what hellish language it was, Zulu, Xhosa, Matabele, how must he know?'

'What tribe's Klippie?' asked Reukes.

'Klippie was born in a Redneck garrison!' snapped Breedt.

'Ja, but you know what I mean, what's April?'

'Thembu,' muttered Breedt.

'So then April must have obviously –'

'Ag, by the God Jesus,' said Breedt, 'April has spent his whole life making like he's a hell-blistered Redneck. Now why should he all of a sudden start teaching his son Thembu songs?'

'No, there I haven't got an answer for you, no,' said Reukes, laughing nervously and shrugging his stump. 'But anyhow why don't we get April in here and –'

'I've already talked to him. He knows nothing about what's going on.'

'And you believe him?' asked Swanepoel.

'He gave me his Bible oath.'

'Ja-a-a!'

'Anyhow,' mused the ancient van Jaarsveld, 'as the old people say, the blind still can't lead a person through the night,' then fell silent as Breedt glared at him.

'What else would Klippie try and get you to do?' Swanepoel asked his son.

'Dunno,' replied the boy. 'Used to sometimes laugh at my baby Jesus dollie, and say that I was like a little girlie and that I fed it and changed it and everything. I told him to go walk! Told him I didn't, told him I crucify it sometimes as well –'

'You do *what*?' asked Breedt.

'Will someone please explain to me,' interrupted Swanepoel, climbing to his feet and pacing the Hall furiously, 'please explain to me why we ever decided to let smear-rags into the school with our offspring twice a week, so that my son here – my son, brought up as a Christian – he now goes to classes where he doesn't learn ordinary lessons, no, no, he learns Thembu songs hot from Satan's arse! Can someone please explain this for me?'

'Ja, I can do that for you, Gertjie,' said Breedt quietly, then paused to show disapproval of Swanepoel's vulgarity. 'Have you ever tried giving orders to a wild servant who can't speak Afrikaans? We've got one in the house at the moment, the girl who arrived with Meneer Smous. Please go and have a few words with her, please go and try and communicate an order to her. Or maybe you'd prefer to go to the school and learn *their* different tongues?'

'Ja well,' said Swanepoel, collecting his son, 'the foot's not on my neck, nê? Not my wife in there,' and strode into the night.

'All right, people, people,' said Naude, finally able to retrieve the biltong-cutter and cautiously sniffing it, 'everyone's getting over-excited. The smear-rags are having a little game, that's all it is. By the morning they'll have had their fun, a wild old time away from their homes, and then they'll get bored and come out. We must all just relax, hey.'

'And if they don't?' asked Reukes with an uneasy laugh.

'If they don't get bored they'll get hungry. Already they haven't eaten since midday. And then what? In these dry days. Half a cup of wheat-seed paste? I think we must all go to bed and stop making ourselves worried. At breakfast-time we're going to find a crowd of tear-stained rascals trailing down the old hill there, rubbing their little bellies and giving us their little backsides to thrash,' and he popped a slice of biltong into his mouth and began to chew contentedly. The men considered this advice, which sounded sensible, then looked towards Breedt to wrap up the meeting, but he remained silent and motionless. They glanced at one another, wondering if any was brave enough to leave. Since none were, there was a general shifting of positions on the creaking chairs and stools, a blowing of cheeks, a daubing at sweaty foreheads, and one or two nervously checked the ground now their look-out was gone.

Naude was wrong. The children did not emerge from the schoolhouse the following morning, nor by the afternoon, but barricaded themselves in further, nailing planks across the windows and doors so that nothing could be seen from outside. With Swanepoel a noticeable absentee, the other farmers spent the day at the school, several carrying shotguns, to demonstrate support. But Breedt kept apart, pacing the veld nearby in his particular fashion, fingers stretching like a cat, raising his forearms against an invisible resistance, dropping to his haunches and holding his palms out towards a bush or rock, as though testing its temperature.

In the middle of the sweltering afternoon something was thrown out through a crack in the schoolhouse door. A stone with a note wrapped round it, written by Mevrou Breedt. Her message was: 'They'll let the Israelite bring in some food. We are starving. Don't make me go through this again.'

Food supplies were hastily gathered: whitish sticks of biltong, a loaf of bread, a supply of crisply toasted biscuits for Mevrou Breedt, two jars of wheat-seed paste, one of grape syrup, and a large flagon of precious water. Carrying the hamper, Smous made his way to the door of the school, feeling both thrilled and embarrassed, aware that all attention was fixed on him: from behind, the Boers, from ahead, a glimmer of eyes through the barricaded windows. He reached the door and, uncertain how to proceed, knocked politely. After much shifting of furniture and squeaking of nails, it opened and he was beckoned in.

The schoolhouse consisted of one large room, the darkness criss-crossed with pencils of sunlight. The atmosphere was hot and thick, though there was also a strange energy in the air, carried in the sweetish smell of urine and children's sweat. All the tables and chairs had been smashed to make the barricades, and the children were ranged among the debris, squatting on the floor or perched on the window-sills and shelves. Smous remembered their games, their stone-throwing games, how they would attack one another so viciously, and how they had attacked the ostrich and Naoksa that day. He had always watched them, horrified and fascinated. Now he was in their midst, them watching him. He bit his moustache. In the middle of the room sat Mevrou Breedt, stern-faced, her arms and ankles tied to the only undamaged chair.

'Warriors!' shouted someone in Xhosa, and immediately all began to sing:

> 'We call to the ancestors
> Come, smell, there's meat in the walls
> Will they hear?
> Will they hear?'

Outside in the sunlight, all the Boers, even Breedt, lifted their chins and listened in silence to the Xhosa song.

As Smous's eyes grew accustomed to the criss-crossed light in the room, he located Klippie squatting on the floor, stripped to the waist like most of the children, and busily writing on a sheet of paper.

'Welcome,' said the youth in Xhosa, without looking up.

'Howare*you*?' mumbled Smous.

The other children had fallen on the hampers and were already feasting – grabbing, shoving, choking – they had never seen so much food. The only ones, apart from Klippie, who remained alert to the siege were Bok's twin sons, one at each window, clutching improvised spears and bottles of their father's rot-gut. They stared at Smous with puffy, red eyes. It occurred to him that several of the children were perhaps drunk, particularly one small half-caste girl who kept falling backwards as she attempted to swig from the flagon of water, spilling it everywhere.

'So,' said Klippie, signing the piece of paper and handing it to Smous. 'Take this for them to read please,' he commanded, pointing one finger, then collected the burnt biscuits from the food hampers, pushing screeching children out of the way, and began to feed Mevrou Breedt. She chewed slowly, mustering all her restraint, but her whole body quivered and Smous heard a familiar noise, abrupt and wet. The look of humiliation in her eyes was terrible. He felt giddy, and lurched. Klippie muttered an order to one of Bok's twins and in an instant Smous found himself back in the dazzling sunlight.

He made his way back to the waiting group with short, deliberate steps, trying to give himself thinking time. He could have virtually overpowered the children on his own. Should he attempt to communicate that to the Boers? He blessed and cursed his ignorance of their language. However, when he reached the group, no one sought his opinion. They gently pushed him to one side as they gathered round Klippie's note.

We ask only to be taught Thembu folklore along with our other studies.
Your servant
Ilitye.

'Since when's he called Ilitye, and what in the name of all damnation does it mean?' asked Breedt, but the others were laughing too loudly to hear. Then another Xhosa song was heard from the schoolhouse, all the voices united within, and the Boers' jeering subsided.

'What's going on, Oom Stoffie?' asked Reukes. 'Those smear-rags in there are all Khoi or mongrel, what do they want to learn Thembu folklore for, what satanic hold has that boy got over them?'

'Ja, maybe some sort of witchcraft, some sort of bloodsucking business,' mused van Jaarsveld, gazing round at the scorched landscape. '*And shall ye dare – to look down there – in Satan's lair – where men walk bare –*'

Breedt smiled calmly. 'Brethren, Brethren, please. It's as Sampie said last night, it's a game. Klippie's a bright, popular boy. He's thought up a game for them that's a bit more exciting than hunting dassies or pebble-catch. It's a game – a game that's going on a bit too long, but still a game, make no mistake please. Now come with me back into Middelpos where we shall pray together for a gentle outcome to this foolishness.'

But riding back in the pony cart, Breedt was trembling. 'What *is* going on?' he whispered again and again, half to Smous, half to himself. 'What *is* going on?'

The road dipped into the dry river bed, and as it rose over the opposite bank, Breedt nodded towards a movement in the white dust. Smous saw a yellow snake slipping along the road. 'Sure sign that the big rains are on their way,' said the Boer. 'The snakes start moving away from the river beds so they're not washed away in the flooding. It'll be the frogs next.' And he drove the cart towards the reptile, carefully aiming one wheel at its rippling back.

The following day none of the other farmers visited the schoolhouse. Smous spent it sitting under the pepper tree, daydreaming, enjoying two fantasies: in one, he led the Boers in a heroic charge on the schoolhouse; in the other, he was inside, fighting on long after everyone else had perished. Meanwhile Breedt paced slowly to and fro, confronting the building as if it were human: with his eyebrows raised, waiting for an answer.

That night at supper Breedt addressed Quinn directly for the first time that either could remember:

'I would like . . . to please ask your counsel,' he said slowly, and with difficulty, in English. 'Your counsel about the . . . thing that . . . is now happen.'

Quinn had been holding forth that evening on a variety of subjects, including the satirical works of Juvenal, the voluptuous flowers of an English summer and his travels in Egypt. This latter topic was inspired by the presence in the dining room of two explorers and naturalists, a pair of elderly German brothers, staying overnight on route from German South West Africa to Cape Town. Despite the fact they had no English, Quinn directed his non-stop discourse at them all evening, though its true purpose was to stop Garbett complaining any further about his new duties: since April's blinding he was forced to wait upon Quinn at every mealtime.

Breedt meanwhile had to serve the guests, a duty he detested. You slaved for yourself, your family and God, and for no one else; this ethos was deeply embedded in his people. To appear less servile he attempted some small talk with the Germans, finding a few common words in Afrikaans. Hearing the brothers reply and recognising traces of his own language in theirs, Smous sat forward in his chair, feeling a momentary link, through them, to Breedt. But for most of the time the Germans were silent, the candlelight glittering on their spiky white hair and on the pince-nez through which they peered suspiciously at the meagre helpings on their plates, or at the drunk jabbering Englishman at the next table. There was a way they scowled at things, jerking their chins into stiff, wrinkled necks which made Smous think of cockerels. The evening was intolerably hot again. Despite the cool aspect of the shadowy room, all six men were pouring with sweat.

'I would like to please ask your counsel, Mister Quinn.'

When Breedt spoke directly to the English table, every feature on Garbett's face sprang apart, but Quinn showed no such surprise, never lifted his gaze off the Germans, and indeed hardly took breath. '. . . Now departing the Nile, and fetching up in the city of Keneh with her great temple nearby, built to the cow-headed goddess Hathor, goddess 'f love and joy . . . Ah! Egypt! What a –'

'Mister Quinn . . .' said Breedt

'What a marv'llous country. Filled with Englishmen such as I, dreamers, digging for treasure 't one kind or 'nother beneath the ground. Ah, the variety of human 'magination and 'ndeavour –'

'Mister Quinn, I would humbly –'

'I mean, take the Chinese f' example. Explored China, have you? Self neither. Anyhow, they see the human ear as an inverted foetus! Isn't that 'xtraordinary! Practice medicine as other cultures practice needlework. Extraordinary!'

'Mister Quinn –'

'Now, we had a man injure his ear here a few months ago. And wha' I'm saying is if he'd suffered this injury while holidayin' in China say, well, they'd've j'st pin-cushioned the dear little foetus, and all would've been sweet 's a jujube.'

Breedt's eyes flickered and he went silent.

'Or take 'nother 'nfortunate mischief – actually happened to the same

chap, but this time it was his eyes – walked into a door cl'msily left ajar . . .'
He stopped, sighed, blew his lips. 'H'ever, who is one to decry the local
med'cal practices of Middlepost? Who is to say that th' sugar and water
panacea 'ministered after the accident won't eventually result in the full 'n
joyous restoration of the man's sight? Shakespeare wasn't above recom-
mending a binding of flax 'n eggs for the same condition – didn't help the
character in question, but he was a bloody good writer all the same. Still,
s'pose you'll prefer Goethe. *Goethe* – yes?'

'Goethe?' repeated the brothers, furrowing their brows.

'Oh, couldn't agree more, a lugubrious wordsmith! But a great favourite
'f two friends of mine, countrymen 'f yours as it happens, whom I hope you
shall meet, Hellas 'n Mab are their names.' He winked at Smous, then
sighed again, watching a drop of sweat fall from the end of his nose onto the
plate of fried pumpkin. Now he sat still, listening to the ticking of the
American grandfather clock.

'Is this why . . . this . . . happen?' asked Breedt. 'Is this why Klippie is . . .
mad? His pa's accidents?'

Quinn closed his eyes. A moment earlier a vague memory had come to
mind. A picnic when he was a boy, a patchwork of green and gold fields –
perhaps it wasn't a picnic, perhaps he was in a drawing room staring at the
fields through a window that reached to the ceiling, or was it a huge
painting? A feeling of emptiness, of having lost something beautiful. He
opened his eyes and was surprised to find himself in Middlepost, with
Breedt addressing him.

'Is Klippie mad over April?'

The Boer's bulbous head swam in and out of view, its baked colours
melting. God, Breedt and his vulgar people! How Quinn pitied them.
There was something so bleak and lonely in their souls, even in their
pride, even in their strength, so ferocious it was suicidal. He thought
back to that first terrible sight of Breedt during the Battle of Middlepost,
head like a stump, without mouth, ears or eyes, blind animal violence.
And something else, something worse, something he couldn't place.
Their war was an act of suicide, their whole history was. You could hear
it in their language, a language of diminutives and negatives, everything
getting smaller, going backwards; 'no, no, no' – they said it all the time,
squandering the word! You could see it in their faces: in Breedt's eyes,
in that moist, hurt, brutal gaze. Here was a man capable of anything,
except gratification.

I loathe you, thought Breedt at the same moment, staring back at Quinn,

I loathe your little smiles and the way your eyes don't open properly because you're English and you've seen everything before, I loathe your red neck and your pink face and your long thin woman's hands, I loathe the way you smell like piss and perfume mixed together, I loathe your coldness – embarrassment, that's your only feeling – so you talk, talk, talk, and you quote from your poetry and your past, I loathe your past, I loathe your poetry, your music and your paintings of wet lands and small skies, I loathe your opera-houses and your libraries and your museums. Your museums most of all.

Your people are doomed, thought Quinn.

Your people are dead, thought Breedt.

And now he realised how much he wanted to see Quinn dead. Quinn and Garbett. Like the Scottish minister they could vanish off the face of the earth. Everyone would keep the secret, the whole of Middlepost would shut tight over it. He glanced at the Germans. Them too, he'd like to see them vanish too. His head was buzzing, spinning, burning. The room was pulsing with heat, it seemed to be keeping time with the American clock, the clock Quinn had once given him as a peace offering, along with April.

'Is it because of . . . April's accident?' he asked again, but hoarsely now. 'Is that why Klippie is now . . . go and do this?'

Quinn considered the question. What had started it, this business at the schoolhouse? He had been trying to remember for days now. He recalled his long lessons in the veld with Klippie, such a beautiful boy, such a fine proud neck, such a pity he was dark-skinned. But there was something before the lessons, something that started it all. What was it? He clicked his tongue impatiently. His memory was going. 'Tell you one thing, Garbett,' he said suddenly, "f one had any inkling how accident prone dear April was, one would never 've 'mployed the fellow in a military capacity, you may take my word.'

'No sir, dare say, sir,' agreed Garbett, relishing Breedt's discomfort, 'dare say, dare say . . .'

'Lost my appetite,' said Quinn rising to his feet. '"Boys, close now the fountains, the meadows have drunk enough,"' he murmured as he departed. This was the current phrase going round in his head, whose authorship he couldn't place.

Smous rose to follow, practising 'Bokswater, Bokswater' under his breath, but was checked by a sound like water dripping into the room. Had the rains started? He turned to find Breedt drumming his fingers on the

Germans' table, his mind elsewhere, the brothers scowling like cockerels. Breedt took Smous's arm and whispered, 'Be at my side for
now, please.' He lit an oil lamp and led Smous out, abandoning his
guests.

The night was sweltering. Breedt headed for the wattle-and-daub huts
on the outskirts of the settlement. Because of the weather the people had
let their fires die when their meals were cooked, so the small buildings lay
in darkness, their whitewashed walls shining in the gloom. An eerie
silence hung over the place. Shadowy figures were squatting at the
doorways as usual, but no one spoke. Most had children or relatives inside
the schoolhouse and were fearful of what the Boers would do to them. A
quiet chorus of greetings, 'Baas . . . Baas . . . Baas . . .', followed Breedt's
progress to April's hut.

The blind man was sitting on his bed in the dark, eating a supper of
mealie porridge heaped with sugar. The room had lost all trace of tidiness
since Smous had seen it last. Clothes had fallen from the hangers,
unwashed cutlery and pieces of food were scattered across the earthen
floor. Having heard no one enter, April gasped as Breedt sat on his bed,
and the porridge spilled over his hands.

'April,' Breedt said, 'you must help me quickly now. No argument
please, hey, no! – before something terrible happens.'

'Baas . . . Baas Stoffel?' enquired April, trying to feel Breedt's face.

'Ag man!' said Breedt impatiently, brushing aside the sticky fingers.
'You hear what I say?'

'Baas Stoffel?' wondered April, trying to turn his good ear towards the
figure next to him.

'By the God Jesus, April, will you please stop making like you're deaf!
I've seen you and the Englishman talk and you hear him perfectly well.'

'Ja no, I'm also well, thank you, Baas,' declared April, on his feet and
leaning towards Breedt with his good ear.

'April!'

'Baas?'

'What is going on?'

'No, I'm only having my supper, Ba –'

'Up the hill, at the school!'

April sighed heavily. 'If only I knew, Baas. It makes the heart so sore,
Baas.'

'April.'

'Baas?'

'What does the word "Ilitye" mean?'

'Ilitye? Means the same as my son's name, Baas – means stone.'

'Stone.'

''s Baas.'

'In what language, April?'

'In my language, Baas, the language of the Thembu people of the –'

'April.'

'Baas?'

'April, I believe that I have been successful in putting the Name and the Blood and the Work of Jesus into your very mouth.'

'Ja, no, definitely, my Baas, I am feeling them there, my Baas . . .'

'Yet there remains this little stubborn streak of paganism in you I just cannot stamp out, no. Help me, April. Help me to understand why you have encouraged your son to do these terrible things.'

'No, my Baas, I haven't, Baas, I swear by the Father, the Son and the Holy Ghost, I swear I –'

'Who then, April? Who else could teach him his name in Xhosa?' Breedt rose and began to pace round the small room, waiting for the reply.

'That's the terrible bad mystery, my big Baas,' lied April, for he knew and suspected Breedt knew also, but was frightened of the confrontation. 'I don't know where this bad thing has come from,' continued April, 'perhaps it is the story I've told you, my Baas, the curse of the vanished foreskin, Baas.'

'Curse of the vanished foreskin,' repeated Breedt quietly, staring into space.

'You still there, Baas?' asked April after a while. 'Ha-a-ah!' he cried now as his groping hands touched Smous who had not yet made his presence known.

'April,' said Breedt on a long sigh, and stepped forward.

'Baas?'

The Boer took his servant's face into his hands and stared into it closely. April's half-closed lids flickered nervously, showing glimpses of silver eyeballs shot with pink. 'April,' said Breedt again quietly.

'Baas?'

'I think . . . No, no, you *can*. You *can* . . . sort of . . . see me. You *can*, can't you?'

'Well, in my head I can, Baas.'

'Then why do you lie to me?'

'No Ba –'

'Listen to me.'

'Baas.'

'You lie about your hearing. You lie about your sight. And now you lie about your son. Your tongue is roasting in your jaws.'

'Baas –'

'I *know*, April, because I understand the temptation of lying.' April gulped, astonished by the admission. 'It is . . .' continued Breedt, 'it is the fearful burden you and I will carry to our Maker on Judgement Day.' Breedt remained there for a long while, shaking April's head slowly in his hands, resisting the impulse to embrace him fully.

The following morning, after the Germans had departed (refusing to pay their full tariff because they were only given half their supper), April was taken to the schoolhouse with Breedt and Smous, and was propelled towards the front door. He stumbled forward, arms outstretched, calling, 'Klippie? Klippie?'

'My name's not Klippie,' came the hoarse reply, but April didn't hear. He stopped though, waiting for a response, then said, 'Klippie, you must come home with me now.'

'Is that what they made you say?'

'Klippie. Can you hear me?'

'Come no further.'

April decided to try a different tack. 'Caius . . .' he called, feeling a ripple of pride, 'Caius Martius –'

The shot blasted a hole in the ground near April's feet. He faltered, then turned to where he thought Breedt was and shouted, 'Don't think he's in there, my Baas, but there's someone with a big gun, Baas.'

But Breedt had already turned and walked into the veld, so that Smous should not see his shock. He stood staring at the ground, blowing silently through his lips, while April stumbled back to Smous cowering behind the pepper tree.

An hour later, Swanepoel rode up the hill and found the group sitting in silence under the tree, April and Smous asleep, Breedt with both palms held an inch away from the bark, his fingers vibrating slightly. 'Still sitting around loafing?' asked Swanepoel from his horse.

'Ja, well,' said Breedt, settling back with a smile. 'It's too hot for work, nê?'

Swanepoel was jigging in the saddle. 'Lost another ox this morning. The grey one with the hanging neck. Choked on a dry mealie cob. They'll eat anything now, they're gnawing the fence-posts.' He sniffed the air. 'How long would you say?'

'For the rains? Oo, soon, soon. Bloke came through from Clanwilliam yesterday afternoon, tells me they've already had some their way.'

'That a fact?' Swanepoel surveyed the distant settlement from his vantage point. 'You should start preparing. She'll wash away a few buildings again.'

'That's for sure.'

'Man, when she starts coming –'

'Hell!'

They grinned at one another like boys.

'But this one'll be safe,' said Swanepoel, nodding towards the school.

'Oo ja,' laughed Breedt, 'that's why we built it so high. You won't remember the old school, no.'

'Never, Oom Stoffie, no, no, I came to this one here.'

'That's right.'

'Look,' said Swanepoel as his horse shifted impatiently. 'Groenie says he saw three smear-rags running across his land early this morning, heading for the open veld.'

'Three from in here? Then there's only fourteen left,' concluded Breedt, without much comfort. 'Plus Klippie. Plus Bok's –'

'Anyhow, thought you'd like to know.'

'Thanks, Gertjie.'

'And I've cross-questioned my little Frikkie and he thinks that all they've got in there is a couple of spears he saw them making, and the slaughtering knife.'

'And a fire-arm.'

'No, he doesn't think –'

'They have. They've found it.' Breedt rocked forward on his chair and drew patterns in the dust with his bare toes. Swanepoel went silent for a few moments and stared across the veld, then resumed. 'All the same, those are cubs in there. You know and I know we could finish this in five minutes and Hannie wouldn't get harmed in the process, never! So what are we waiting for?' He held the older man's gaze, his heart thudding; furious about the dead ox, he needed to release some energy.

'Nothing to do with us,' replied Breedt eventually, smiling calmly. 'We must take our orders from the Almighty's Throne of Grace, and His wishes are still for restraint.'

'Ja, but I'm asking what you really think. In your heart of hearts. What you think in the middle of the night.' Breedt's calm smile remained steady, his gaze resting upon Swanepoel's face, trying to measure the degree of blasphemy or threat from the younger man, but the pale eyes were unfathomable as his own.

'Ja well,' said Swanepoel, steering his horse away, 'you know where to find me, hey.'

'Thanks, Gertjie,' Breedt called after him.

'Who was that, my Baas?' asked April, waking.

'That was the Baas Gertjie Swanepoel,' said Breedt, watching the distant horseman with a mixture of feelings. 'A brave man. What he did in the war, nê?'

'Ahh,' agreed April and, forgetting himself, spoke in English, 'we thank the gods our Rome hath such a soldier.'

'Ja,' sighed Breedt grimly, 'Rome's foot, man!'

Next to them, Smous slept on, enjoying one of his happiest dreams: he was on the train racing away from the station at Mazheik into the forest of spruce, rushing through dark green shadows, smoke lingering on the branches, gathering speed as he was propelled on his heroic mission to Southern Africa, breaking into the sunlight, onto the field of his childhood games, plummeting down the marshy banks, onto the Babrungas, sailing over monsters which rose from the deep, and finally onto beautiful sunny plains, the fabled plains of Litvak legend where great herds of ancient bison roamed, but where no man had ever set foot . . .

That lunchtime when Smous took the food supplies to the schoolhouse door, he was not allowed in as usual, but had to pass the hampers through a gap in the barricade. A few moments later smoke began to curl from the chimney. There was no breeze, so it hung in the air, dark and heavy, slowly laying a shadow across the building, as though branding it. Breedt broke the silence to say, 'Must be hot as all hell in there,' and Smous nodded as though he had understood, feeling the glamour of the siege diminishing, or rather twisting into something else. There would be violence – real, bloody violence. He feared it, and longed for it. A violence that would exclude him, a violence that he could witness, recoil from, yet feast off, secretly. As he watched the smoke rise from the chimney, a huge shiver passed through him.

There was a surprising visitor in the middle of the afternoon: Quinn, in exceptionally high spirits. The moment he dismounted, the children began the Xhosa song inside the schoolhouse. Breedt looked away in disgust, so failed to notice the glimmer of pride behind the Englishman's sun spectacles.

What started this business, wondered Quinn as he listened, smiling, to the song. Wish I could remember.

'Calls for a celebration,' he suddenly declared, quickly adding, 'today's dig! Particularly successful. A celebration of Marie's finest redbush tea!' He winked at Smous. 'You don't really wish to sit around in this appalling heat, do you? Let me offer you a lift back to the "homestead", as I believe the Americans say.' Now, as Breedt looked away again, he mouthed 'Bokswater', and Smous nodded eagerly.

Breedt was left alone, watching mournfully as the two galloped down the hill, together on Quinn's horse, Smous's arms clasped round the Englishman's waist.

It was sunset by the time Smous staggered from Quinn's room. Feeling bold, he decided to seek out Naoksa, but on the way to the kitchen, he found Breedt pacing bare-footed in the dining room. The candles and oil-lamps had not yet been lit for the evening, so the room had a peculiar gloom, as though underwater, the man no more than a shadow against one wall. 'You must help me,' Breedt whimpered, 'because I'm going mad. O look, *look* how close it's come!' He pointed to a small window behind Smous, who turned and almost screamed. A huge animal's flank was pressed against the panes, its black coat squashed and shining. Now it shifted and moved away. Smous hurried to the window. It was only an ox that had been rubbing its hump against the window frame. But this revelation did nothing to calm Breedt. 'Satan's steed,' he said quietly, 'you remember, the black steed, the skeleton hanging from the stirrup smiling at me. Oo God! You must, must help me!'

Ei! Here we go, thought Smous as Breedt took his arm and led him out of the house. The glowing sky was lilac, the distant hills purple. In the Hall the light was grey. Breedt pulled open the canvas curtain and the great crucifix loomed from the shadows like a tree. Breedt knelt, gently pulling Smous down alongside.

'The Saviour will smell the fumes of intoxication on you,' whispered Breedt, nodding towards the Christ's nostrils arched in torment, 'but you mustn't worry. I shall convey to Him what I know to be true. I shall assure Him that the fumes descended when you visited the Englishman's room to guide him to a path of enlightenment, but that no drop has ever passed your own lips. Thus we can help one another. I can plead for mercy from the Son and you can ask the Father to lend aid in our hour of need. Look!' said Breedt suddenly, startling Smous, and nodded towards the face on the cross. 'See how He sees.' Breedt widened his blue eyes, again frightening Smous, and rolled them towards the statue's varnished stare. Smous noticed for the first time that the Christ had no pupils. 'Ja, He looks blind,' agreed Breedt, sensing his thoughts, 'but sees everything. Whatever we do He is there, somewhere in a corner, watching. And blushing. So it is indeed fortunate that His perception goes beyond the sight and stink of our sick flesh and that He can root out the goodness in us, wherever it is, to fill us with light . . .' He stretched up and touched the statue, stroking the charred stump of one leg, where a fire had once raged.

'When they came back from the concentration camp after the war, my womenfolk, my wife and daughter, my Hannie and my Antjie, when they stood in the doorway here, I thought it was something from, you know, one of the ghost stories. There they stood in their big sunbonnets, but there were skulls inside. Ja, they were in a very, very bad state. The doctors in Calvinia told Hannie it would help her insides to eat burnt bread and biscuits, they say the charcoal helps, but she was in such fearful anguish, she believed the only relief could come from Our Lord . . . and from the body of Our Lord.' He lowered his hand and examined the traces of carbon on his fingers. 'Shame, hey, it was meant as an act of devotion, but because she was upset I fear she went a little too far. Hell, but we had a terrible fight in here that day.' He looked round the dim Hall, then rested his eyes on Smous. 'Is that why this is happening, up on the hill, because she set fire to Our Lord and chewed on His foot? If it is, I want to assure you that she is a good person and a saint actually.'

He smiled up at the Christ. 'Notice how Our Lord never stops staring? That's because He smells my roasting tongue. It's not Hannie's sin causing all this present business, it's mine. I've done such loathsome things. Well, you've seen. Christ has seen. April saw. Poor April. He's lost his sight. His sight, not his tongue, yet he's cast no slander. Marie, in the kitchen, she's the one who lost her tongue. Shame, she's so cross and old now, but she was so pretty before her tongue had to be cut. That was a while ago. And yet, now we all understand when she speaks, but she's also cast no slander. About what she and I did together. I hated spilling the blood of her tongue, but what choice has a person got? How must he know beforehand others aren't going to cast slander? Sin spreads. And we just cannot have this place running with sins like an open sore. And the sores sticking together, each of us sticking to the next one, *siss, man, siss*! Drought? You think that's why the ground burns under our feet?' He fell silent.

'So, good,' he said finally, smiling gently at Smous. 'Thank you. You have helped me, as always, helped me to work it all out, face the truth, face the facts. Your silence is so deep. There is so much to be gained from your peace and calm. The rest of us run around jabbering and screaming like monkeys. So, mine are the sins, but because I am still needed, the rod of wrath must fall on Hannie and hers is the blood to be shed. It will happen any day now, when I suddenly get up from my chair under the tree and run into that school, with my brain boiling in my skull like it sometimes does – I can feel this abomination happening and there's nothing I can do to control it – that's when her blood will be shed, I know it, I can see it happening already.' He gave Smous's arm a little squeeze, as though it was he who needed consoling, then whispered a short prayer, crossed himself, and rose to go.

'Oh, by the way, I've already sent for Antjie to come home. It's only right she be here for her mommie's funeral. Perhaps I will let you meet her. She's a good girlie.'

Smous was left alone in front of the Christ. He felt happy, savouring the comforting feeling which the Bokswater always brought, a feeling of being vaguely unwell, a feeling of being absolved from all responsibility.

I'm living my life peacefully here, he told himself, I cause no one any trouble, so I don't see why anyone should cause me any in return. It's their troubles, let them sort it out, damn them all, I don't care, I'll watch if I want, I'll do what I want.

He drew one of Quinn's hip-flasks from his pocket and threw back his head, peering up the Christ's skirt as he drank, reliving that glorious, carefree day when the Scuteris were in Middlepost. 'Yi-i-iy!' he suddenly squealed as he heard a small movement near his foot and remembered the scorpions, but, swinging round, he saw a frog, a tiny brown frog hopping across the Hall.

'This one's had it good and proper,' said Breedt, pointing down to a dead frog near the school gate. 'They're leaving the river beds just that bit too soon. The sun dries them out. Must feel like the flames of Hell to them, hey? There goes another.' He pointed to a frog jumping through the bush nearby. 'Man, just think how far they've climbed to get up here.'

Smous was sitting under the pepper tree, watching the Boer pace around the school yard. Breedt was in high spirits this afternoon, while Smous felt irritable. The major event of the day, depositing the lunch hamper outside the school door, had come and gone without incident. Now there was nothing ahead, except a long, baking afternoon. And he was dying for a drink. If only Breedt's pacing would take him further off it would be worth risking a swig from the hip-flask. But the man's random wanderings only ever went as far as the road, where he would stop, hands on hips, and stare to the north.

This time Breedt saw what he had been waiting for: a tiny cloud of dust moving towards them. 'She's here,' he whispered, running to his horse. 'Isn't it funny?' he called to Smous. 'I'm a nervous as a new-born calf. She's here, she's here!' He dug in his heels and galloped off to meet the approaching party. Smous took a long drink. Then two more swigs. And then a quick last one, before the group on the road reached the school.

It was a strange sight: Breedt riding alongside a mule-cart and chatting to a canvas tent erected on the back. At first Smous thought the Boer was talking to the Hottentot driver, but no, it was the tent. Smous leaned forward and squinted. The tent was tightly fastened and probably stifling inside.

'Listen here,' called Breedt without reining his horse. 'I'm going to see them in to Middelpos. You'll be all right here, nothing's going to happen this afternoon.'

Smous watched the group progress down the hill and sighed with relief. He tilted back his chair, leaned his head against the tree, pulled his hat over his eyes, and settled down for at least an hour's undisturbed peace, sipping at the flask. However, the moment Breedt had vanished from sight, a stone came flying through the air and hit Smous's feet. Leaning round the tree, he was surprised to see the school door open with an arm beckoning him urgently.

As soon as he reached the door, he was dragged inside. He blinked in the gloom. 'Quick, quick,' a figure whispered hoarsely, and he felt small hands patting his clothes. 'C'mon! We saw it! Where? C'mon, where?' The patting hand found his flask, whipped it out, and disappeared into the shadows.

The dark room stank. As Smous stepped forward, he slipped wildly, then saw the floor was glinting with puddles and maggots. His next surprise was that the place was almost deserted. Apart from a naked half-

caste girl asleep in one corner, there were only Bok's twins gulping down
the contents of the hip flask, and a figure – presumably Klippie – sitting
cross-legged on the floor, wearing a strange head-dress of wool and
feathers, his face in shadow, a blanket draped over him. The rifle and
machete were propped nearby. Mevrou Breedt was still tied to the chair,
its seat and legs dripping with her excrement. She looked up at Smous
with sleepless, bulging eyes, but said nothing. A fire crackled in one
corner. The walls were blackened, and the smoke had painted a
thundercloud on the ceiling. But why a fire, wondered Smous, the room
was already stifling, and food supplies were always pre-cooked. Many of
these were scattered among the refuse, untouched and rotting. The air
was thick with swarms of gnats.

Smous hovered. Had he been summoned purely for his flask? Then the
figure under the blanket beckoned to him, and Smous approached,
crouching down.

Klippie had not slept at all during the four-day siege. His eyes were
like open wounds, looking even redder because of the whitewash that
had been ritualistically caked over his swollen face. His whole being
seemed to have thickened and distorted; the light in those red eyes was
alert, yet cold; and his voice had gone, it was the sound of someone
suffocating, dry and hissing: 'Take . . . take . . .' A sprinkling of whitewash fell from round his mouth. 'Take . . . take this.' He passed a tiny
bundle to Smous. 'Take it to my father, he will know what to do.' When
Smous gave his customary frown and shrug, the red-eyed apparition
shivered with such rage Smous was sure his last moments had come.
Klippie tried to rise, but stopped, gasping, in pain. Smous lowered his
gaze in case the blanket fell open to reveal some terrible wound. Both
waited till Klippie caught his breath, then faced one another again.
Bristling with impatience, Klippie pointed to the bundle, pointed to the
door, pointed to his eyes, making the lids droop, and groped around like
a blind man. Finally he turned his terrible gaze on Smous, his expression demanding, *Now* do you understand?

Smous nodded and rose.

'Wait!' commanded the creature in his voiceless rasp, and clicked his
fingers. The twins kicked the naked girl awake, and suddenly Smous
found himself surrounded by the three children, who, he now noticed,
were all coated with whitewash. It made their wasted limbs look like
the salted sticks of biltong the farmers were forever chewing. They
began to dance with clenched fists and thudding, shuffling steps,

splashing through the refuse. In hoarse voices, they chanted:

> 'We called to the ancestors
> They came – smelt the meat in the walls
> They *did* hear!
> They *did* hear!'

Klippie joined in, the veins on his neck bursting with the effort to produce some sound. Smous noticed the youth had attempted to sharpen his teeth, smashing several in the process.

> 'They *are* come!
> They *are* come!'

– sang the group, reminding Smous of the stamping, panting, ululating mob surround the ostrich, falling on it, trying to murder it.

> 'They *are* here!
> They *are* here!'

As soon as the song was over, the twins rushed Smous to the door and pushed him out.

He stood dithering in the sunlight, automatically reached for his flask, then remembered the twins had taken it and whimpered, 'Bokswater, Bokswater!' He examined the knotted cloth Klippie had given him. There was a patch of blood seeping through, yet the tiny bundle felt weightless. He slipped it into his trouser pocket. Walking towards his chair under the tree, he was acutely aware of eyes watching through the barricaded window. He didn't know what to do, unwilling to leave his post, yet certain that any hesitation would provoke a gunshot from the school. He felt sick. It was happening – they were forcing him to participate, they wouldn't leave him on the sidelines to watch, to recoil, to revel secretly. He passed the chair, reached the gate, turned down the hill towards Middlepost. He desperately wanted to wipe his smeared boots on the bushes, but even so brief a halt felt dangerous. Klippie's whitewashed face suddenly came to mind, with its smashed teeth, and he shivered. Why was it so familiar?

As he reached the river bed, he saw Breedt galloping towards him, returning to the schoolhouse. Before the Boer had a chance to say anything, Smous began pointing at different parts of his body, describing every ailment he could think of – sunstroke, chest pains, the most urgent diarrhoea – then hurried past, not looking back, despite Breedt's shout of

'What? Is everything all right up there?' – now breaking into a little trot and, as he saw the outskirts of Middlepost, a final dash.

April was seated at his usual place outside the store, head on his chest, dozing in the heat. He was woken by someone leaning over him, puffing with exhaustion and terror. Having identified the features and beard, he said, 'Greetings, oh mine friend, great Smous of that name, greetings on this balmy scorcher of a day, 'twill be a storm, 'twill be a –' then the tiny bundle was pressed into his palm and he went silent. With chin raised and slack eyelids flickering, he untied the cloth, pressing his knees together to prevent any portion spilling to the ground. At the last moment of unfolding, a corner of the material stuck on the deepening patch of blood, but, prising this off carefully, he spread open the bundle.

Smous was unable to identify the item now revealed. It was clearly a tiny section of flesh, brown-coloured flesh, a deep, purplish brown, but he found it impossible to say which part of the body it came from. If anything, it looked like a slice from some internal organ. The edge had been roughly hacked, and, as April's fingers now examined this minutely, Smous began to feel faint.

The blind man had no difficulty identifying the fragment; as soon as his fingers made contact he knew what it was. His confusion was caused only by Smous's inability to say it was Klippie who had sent the bundle, and, lacking this information, April reached a different conclusion:

'Oh great praise and honour,' he whispered in Xhosa. 'My life is restored. Ahom! Rejoice! All is restored.' He turned towards Smous, and, reverting to English, asked, 'Where on earth did you find it after all this time?' Now a frown of doubt crossed his brow. 'Nay, it cannot be, it cannot . . . Yoh! But it can, yes it can, it must, it damn well *must*! For there's more things in heaven and earth, and worlds elsewhere, and surfeits of sweetness, and so on and so forth, and *eyyyyyyyy*! I have it back, and that's all that is mattering. I have it back!' Springing to his feet, he exclaimed, 'An anthill, point me to an anthill and follow me not!' When Smous was slow to react April swore briefly, then, speaking in a jumble of languages, directed thanks to an assortment of deities – his ancestors, Jove, King Edward VII, William Shakespeare, the Holy Trinity – and made his own way towards the veld, one hand groping ahead, the other clutching the precious bundle.

For a long while Smous stood in the middle of the road watching the man wander further and further into the bush, stumbling, tripping, groping for an anthill. Now he would cut his hand on the thornbushes, spring back and put it to his mouth; now he would raise the other hand, the hand holding the little bundle, and kiss it, and dance in a circle, throwing back his head, singing to the sky. The sounds drifted back to Smous and warmed his heart. Although confused as ever by the exact details of the event, he felt sure he had accomplished some supreme act of charity.

It was only now that Smous became aware of several new features in Middlepost. Floodboards had been nailed across every doorway since his departure that morning, and, far more astonishingly, everywhere he looked, there were frogs. Turning in a slow circle, eyes narrowing in disbelief, he saw the creatures in every hollow and shadow on the ground, hopping, slithering or pausing, little pulsating bodies on the road, on the porch of the house, outside the store, sudden flicking jumps catching the light and disappearing in puffs of dust.

'The plagues of Egypt,' he whispered, remembering, in the same instant, Pinchvinch's blood-curdling descriptions and the games with Issy on the banks of the Babrungas. He was almost levitating with revulsion when he was distracted by a figure running out of the house.

Naoksa saw the frogs at once, but wasted no more than a glance as she hurried to the edge of the settlement, face raised to the sky, scenting the air. As though dancing across hot sand, Smous picked his way over the frogs and joined her.

'Golda, hello.'

She kept her gaze on the sky and said quietly, 'I fear.'

'Are you well? We hardly ever see one ano–'

'The rains that are coming are big rains, the male rains, the black bull searching for women.'

'I'm well. Very well in fact. Very happy . . .'

'My fear is that he comes searching for me.'

Smous pointed to the distant, stumbling figure of April. 'And I just made someone else very, very happy.'

'Will you help me?' Her last words had been a question. Smous raised his eyebrows, encouraging her to continue, while he made every effort to concentrate. 'I've spoken to the woman in the house,' Naoksa said, 'the woman with no tongue. I think her ears are cut also, for she never hears me. I have told her I must not go in the open when the rains come. Sometimes she makes me gather eggs. If she makes me do this during the rains, then I fear the thing that will happen.'

Smous frowned. Naoksa seemed troubled, that much was clear,

perhaps he should comfort her? But his hands stayed in his pockets, twitching.

'If the bull takes me, it will be far away. To the heavens where his flashing light makes the women like the stars, or to the waters where he makes them the wives there, like the flowers in the pool. These things must not happen before I reach my people and greet them again, and hold Kgototxe and Bo again.'

'Yishhh . . .' sighed Smous. What was the stupid girl chattering about?

Naoksa looked at him closely. 'I *will* get back to my people,' she told him. 'I *will*, whether you take me there or not.' She saw him shrug and shake his head, so now she made the one sign they had both understood before, the sign for home, with fingers tracing a birth into the land. But Smous had forgotten and thought she meant something else.

'Look,' he snapped, 'if you're with child that can't be helped, we'll have to deal with that at a later date, all right?' He glanced nervously at the confusing folds of her oversized dress, trying to detect the true shape of her stomach. 'For the present, the damage is done, so we might as well do it again. So, do you want to come to my room, come have a drink – yes or no?'

Now it was Naoksa's turn to lose patience. 'We shout into the sandface, you and I!'

'Sorry,' said Smous seeing her frown, 'sorry, I don't really mean . . . It's just, I think, you know, when it comes to you and me, and I've never actually told you this before, but –' He stopped. Even though she didn't understand his language he couldn't bring himself to say it. 'Good God!' he exploded. 'Just listen to me, stuttering like a boy and I'm old enough to be . . .' He grabbed her. 'Who are you? What are you? You come and go like something in a dream. One moment you make sense, the next not. Who are you? Speak to me!' She let him shake her, offering no resistance, but looking down with that calm, sullen face which was worse than anything. 'Oh . . . you!' he cursed, unable to think of anything else to say, and released her. She turned and hurried back to the house, glancing towards the heavens.

Smous snorted in frustration and roamed around, stamping on frogs. His route took him to the mule-cart which had brought the Breedts' daughter. The tent on the back was folded now, giving off a strong medicinal smell, a peppermint smell. He was momentarily drawn to this scent, then turned away and looked at the sky. It was most peculiar, lighter than usual, as if whitened by the heat. The horizon seemed almost to bulge.

'Oh come on, if you're coming,' he whispered to the rains, 'come on, *come on.*'

When Breedt failed to return for dinner, Smous thought back to their brief meeting near the river bed, hurrying in different directions, and now remembered that the Boer's horse was laden with new supplies for the schoolhouse vigil: a blanket, oil lamp, the giant Bible, and something which had not previously made an appearance, his shotgun. Apparently he was planning to spend the night there.

Both Smous and Quinn were expecting the Breedts' daughter to join them for dinner, but there was no sign of her either. Instead they watched the kitchen maid Fleurjie cross the dining room with a tray of food, and disappear into the dark corridor on the front of the house.

When it was clear there was only the two of them for dinner, Quinn made a few changes to the normal routine. He went into the kitchen, and, distributing a few trinkets, allowed Marie and the maids to depart early. Next he dismissed a smirking Garbett, saying, 'We'll serve ourselves, Garbett, thank you so much. We feel like roughing it tonight.' Then Quinn went to his room, returning with a bottle of Bokswater. He pulled Smous's chair over to his table, blew out the other candles in the room, and invited him to supper.

Quinn enjoyed that evening more than any other in Middlepost. He fussed over Smous, filling his glass, fanning him with a napkin as the night grew hotter, fetching each course from the kitchen, humming waltzes and marches, and then, when the meal was over, brought another bottle from his room along with 'something special' he wished to show Smous. It was a pane of glass with a small heap of yellowish grit. Quinn was convinced he had finally located the place where the pieces of quartz were recovered before. That afternoon, as he watched his labourers sinking another borehole, he imagined standing on the lip of the mine that would be dug next and felt himself gently leaning forward, and falling. Deeper and deeper. He saw inside the earth and it was filled with a strange fluid, red as blood, sometimes luscious, dark and burning, sometimes threaded with beautiful light; and he fell and fell, boulders tumbling through the fluid also, hissing and steaming, exploding, releasing blinding white ore, and the fall was marvellous, and it never ended. 'Goooood, yes?' he prompted Smous, pushing the pane of glass under his nose. 'Hmm, gooooood?' Smous peered down and echoed the word encouragingly while thinking the grit looked exactly like grit. A drop of his sweat fell into one cluster, turning it to mud, but Quinn didn't notice. He was staring past, to the reflection of the yellow candlelight.

'So like the colour of Cotswold stone,' he murmured. 'We had this place near Snowshill. And that is where . . . that is where, one summer, I learned a fact about self which ruined my life. Was a boy at the time.' He laughed and clapped his hands. 'Up 'ntil then I had enjoyed every luxury, every privilege due to a child of the ruling orders. But then I w's sent away to school, and here a particular master took a particular interest in my name, a particular, savage interest. He thought there w's a touch of Irish in the name, a touch of the peasant, a touch 'f the bogs. *Bog boy* became his name f' me, *bog boy*, and the other boys were quick to join the chase. That summer, my first summer back fr'm school, I asked Father . . . certain that he would deny it and become outraged, certain that the master would be ch'stised for making my first term so hellish. But Father laughed and, assuming an Irish brogue no less, I'll never forget the sound 'f it, assuming this brogue, he said, No sure, we're the fortunate heirs of the Lord So-and-So of County So-and-So . . . we can trace our ancestry right back to So-and-So. Couldn't hear what he w's saying, couldn't understand his words in that dreadful Shelta brogue, like some famine-driven lurker! But it was true. My veins were running with the bogs of Ireland. Bog blood for a bog boy. I remember standing at a window staring out at the fields, the Cotswold fields, the fields of England, realising they were no longer mine. *Bog boy, bog boy*. So it went on, at Marlborough, at the R.M.A., so it went on, till here. The Boers will nev' know how much they flatter me every time they curse, *Englishman, Englishman*!' He laughed and whispered into the glass, 'Englishman, Englishman,' tracing the outline of his lips with one finger.

'That summer I made the acquaintance 'f th' vilest of our flaws, the easiest to fall prey to, the most pernicious. Disappointment. There and then I promised self never to entertain its sickly presence again, and am proud to say I have kept to my word. As far as disappointment and self are c'ncerned, I am utterly beyond its reach!' He smiled broadly at Smous, holding the tip of his tongue between grey teeth, then sang softly:

> 'Oro Mór, O Moreen
> O golden-haired one, will you come?'

Smous looked at Quinn. He shone with a new childish spirit this evening. Touched by this, he decided to do something he'd been wanting to do for months. He reached out and gently removed the customary fragment of food lodged on the corner of the Englishman's mouth.

Quinn was greatly moved.

'Tonight,' he said quietly and stretched across the table. Smous was surprised to suddenly find the man's hand in his, then shook it cheerfully and released it. Quinn frowned. 'Are you truly as dim-witted as you seem?' he asked. Smous's nostrils twitched. The Englishman's sweetish, damp odour was becoming stronger, squeezed out by his darkening skin. These signs were all too familiar. With a sigh Smous sat forward in his chair and waited for the inevitable dismissal.

It was hopeless, Quinn decided, watching him through half-closed eyes, this man has not understood a single word I have ever said to him, and yet knows me too well. Like everyone before him, he's grown bored, he reads me as easily as the time . . .

Smous couldn't say what happened next. The moment slipped out of sequence, blurring, in his drunkenness, with some which followed and one from long before. His first thought was that something had fallen on him – the clock, a wall – for the candle-lit space in front of his eyes was suddenly invaded by a dark looming shape, before something bumped against his nose, crushing his cheek. It took several seconds to realise this was Quinn's face and that the man's tongue was wrapping round his own. The sensation was not altogether unpleasant. There was even a moment of relief, tenderness, yielding. It was the taste Smous couldn't bear; it was that which sent his mind spinning back over the years to a moment on the other side of the world, a soldier kissing him, spilling yellowish-white juice in his beard, his first proud beard, meshed there, filling his head with that stench, warm and fatty, impossible to remove. It was this which made him giddy now and, fearing his stomach would heave, he brought his jaws together with a click that flayed part of Quinn's upper lip.

The Englishman rocked back on his heels, only momentarily stunned. 'You are a flirt, my friend,' he said coldly, trying not to splutter on the bubbles of blood, 'that most d'plor'ble of all carnal creatures, the flirt. Know them well, army's full of them. One shouldn't be surprised. Is not your tribe renowned for it, slipping through the fingers? How shabby, how very sad that tonight you should earn one's deepest and most 'nutterable contempt!' Lifting his pane of glass and gripping it carefully with one hand, he took hold of the American grandfather clock with his other and dragged it onto the floor with a splintery, chiming crash and a roar of his own. Steadying the glass with both hands, he left the room.

Smous scrambled off the floor where he had fallen in surprise and stuck out his tongue at the retreating figure, puzzled that his kindly gesture, removing the fragment of food, should have led to such violence. A patch of wall caught his eye, where the clock had been, alive with candlelight and shadow. The shapes formed themselves into Klippie's whitewashed face, mouth open, smashed teeth showing. Smous gasped and flicked his head, then grabbed the candle and stumbled into the corridor. He turned towards the front of the house, his flame softening the corners and melting the walls. It glistened across the backs of several frogs on the floor, but he was too drunk to care. He saw light under a door ahead, blew out the candle and dropped to his knees, inching towards the keyhole, the sharp smell of newly polished brass greeting his nostrils as he drew close.

Within the room, a slim fair-haired girl, aged about twenty, sat at a table, a book lowered on her lap and her neck stiff, alerted by the crash of the clock. Her supper tray was pushed to one side, the bowls meticulously emptied, no crumb on the plates, the napkin neatly folded. She was dressed in a delicate lavender shift. Her skin was unnaturally white, as if never exposed to the sun. Here and there on her neck and bony hands were large, strange freckles. Her face was turned away from Smous, so all he could see of her features was one jawbone. Despite the smell of brass from the keyhole, he could detect within the room that same medicinal, pepperminty scent which had lingered on the mule-cart.

He stayed at the keyhole for almost an hour, excited by the silence in the hot dark house. The girl never shifted, except to turn the pages of her book, which was a Bible, and to move her jaw slightly as she murmured her prayers.

Smous had imagined many different ends to the siege, but never this one. Cossacks with drawn sabres charged the schoolhouse, hacked off Klippie's whitewashed head and threw it to Smous. At last he recognised it: Gommie, the man knocked over by the carriage on Smous's first day in this country; Gommie, his face coated with sand, even his open eyes, and his grinning mouth showing teeth shaped like the mountains of Table Bay. Now the Cossacks emerged from the schoolhouse, triumphantly carrying Mevrou Breedt, still tied to the chair dripping with her dung. 'Oh, cover her,' Smous whispered, appalled, as he noticed the woman was no longer the Boer, but his own mother, and that her breasts had been carefully eased out of her blouse, 'cover her for pity's sake, she's not like the damned savage!' But the Cossacks simply offered the rejoinder, 'There's no pleasing a Yid,' and bore her grandly into Middlepost. In anguish Smous clawed at his beard and a little puddle gathered in his palm, which had yellow skin. He put his tongue to it. The puddle grew and began to gush.

He woke to find his bed drenched in blood, except it wasn't blood, it was sweat. Or perhaps he had wet the bed. He couldn't be bothered to examine the sheets. The nightmares were getting worse. Waking was getting worse. He searched round the room for a drink, unable to remember where he had hidden it this time. Behind the wardrobe. No, it wasn't there. 'Bokswater, Bokswater,' he muttered, starting to panic, before discovering the bottle had slipped off the cross-bar and was lodged further down.

Once he had drunk a glassful, he realised there was a different silence outside. He pulled on his clothes and walked into the yard. Despite the hour, about six o'clock, there was no ringing of insects, no birds, no cockerels calling, no noise from any of the animals, and the windmills had never been stiller. The sky was bright and the heat fierce as midday, yet the rising sun itself looked dulled, its outline strangely defined, its colour brownish.

Smous hitched up a pony cart – the animal was quivering with unease – and rode out to the school. On either side of the road, the vast silence of the bush made him hesitate to draw breath.

Nearing the school he saw Breedt sitting under the tree. His position was odd: head fallen backwards against the bark, mouth hanging open, eyes closed. The shotgun was supported between his knees, barrel pointed towards his face. Grimacing, Smous stepped closer. There was no blood. Breedt was simply fast asleep, and the noise of Smous's arrival did not wake him.

The door of the schoolhouse was hanging open. It creaked. Smous stiffened, expecting someone suddenly to appear, but when no one did, and the door creaked again, he realised there was a current of air up on the hill; it could hardly be called a breeze, more a draught from a shifting on the earth somewhere else.

Smous walked to the door and peered round. There were only two figures left inside the class-room: Mevrou Breedt on her chair, Klippie on the floor, and both were fast asleep. The boy was curled in his blanket, knees pulled up, one hand lying open near his face, the way an infant's hand falls in sleep. The thickness and distortion had left him and now he looked so like a child again, a very young child, that Smous couldn't bear the thought of what was going to happen next – particularly since, for the moment, it was up to him.

He toyed with the idea of waking Klippie and quietly leading him away. He toyed with the idea of climbing back onto the pony cart alone and returning to Middlepost, leaving these people to sort out their own affairs. Or there was always his original plan. He could hide in the veld nearby and watch, just watch. He considered these options, then sighed and went to wake Breedt.

The Boer came into the schoolhouse without his shotgun for he could sense all danger had passed. He knelt alongside Klippie and picked him up carefully, not wishing to wake him, though the boy's exhaustion was so deep there was little danger of this. Carrying him gently in one arm, Breedt collected the machete from the floor and cut away the bindings round his wife.

'Have you brought the strawberries?' she asked, suddenly waking.

'Strawberries?'

'Ag, you've forgotten. Trust you.' She turned to Smous, her voice quiet and matter-of-fact. 'He's forgotten. Trust him.' She sighed. 'The patch is dead now, it's a hang of a difficult job to keep them going through the drought, but that summer, they came out of the earth so beautifully. And this one time, this one evening – oh, how could he forget? – we took the children out there, sun had just gone down, and we sat there, the four of us, eating strawberries. The children were in their nightclothes, and we'd brought along some fresh cream and a bowl of sugar. So you could just keep pulling the fruit straight out of the earth, dip it in the cream, dip it in the sugar, and then feast till you could feast no more. This was before the war, oh, long before the war, well, our Dawie was killed in the war, of course. But anyhow, that's what Middelpos was like, and that's what we were like. So tell your friends that. And I honestly don't think it's asking a lot to expect one of those strawberries now.'

The two men stood frowning down at her, Smous because she reminded him of his mother, Breedt because he couldn't think what to do. 'Uhh, I think . . .' he said, 'ja, if you could please just take the boy.' He passed Klippie into Smous's arms. 'Then I could uhh . . .' He extended both arms to his wife, but as she attempted to rise, the chair came with her, and she sank back with a small scowl.

'Ja . . .' said Breedt slowly, 'all right, uhh . . .' He guided Smous back into the sunlight. 'If you could wait here my friend. Don't worry, he isn't going to wake. Oh, I'll need that –' He fetched the blanket from his supplies at the tree and went back into the schoolhouse, shutting the door.

Smous leaned against the wall holding the boy. The sleeping head was resting on his shoulder and the body felt surprisingly light. Smous stared at the pony cart at the end of the path, thinking how easy it would be to walk to it, carrying the boy, and to ride away. It was so easy; it was almost easier than staying. But perhaps the boy deserves to be punished, he thought, I don't know, I don't want to know, I just want to be left out of this. It's the heat – you can't breathe. It's the silence – you can't hear. So how are you expected to think straight? 'Bokswater . . .' he murmured. 'Bokswater . . . Bokswater.'

He stood motionless, the boy in his arms, waiting.

When the Breedts emerged, the woman had removed her dress and was wrapped in the blanket. She walked with difficulty, but had gathered her resources and there was nothing pitiful in the way she held her head. Smous found it more upsetting than if she had wept. Her husband walked at her side, arms ready should she stumble, and Smous followed, carrying Klippie. The pony cart was too small for all of them. Breedt asked Smous to look away, then helped his wife onto it. 'Uhh . . . I'd better take the boy now,' he said, lifting Klippie from Smous's arms. Breedt's voice had remained calm and respectful throughout, as one whispering in church. 'You go with Hannie, perhaps you can drive, hey, please? and I'll come on the horse.'

People were going about their morning duties when the group arrived in Middlepost. All stopped in their tracks to stare at the woman in the blanket and the boy slung across Breedt's horse. In a soft courteous tone, the Boer asked someone to fetch the female servants and when they arrived, weeping for their mistress, she was covered with more blankets and helped from the cart. Breedt issued a few instructions, and then, as his wife was led into the house, called, 'I'll be with you in a minute, my dear love.' Now he dismounted and carried Klippie into the Hall, signalling Smous to follow. He hesitated, glancing towards April seated at his usual place, oblivious to what was going on, beaming joyfully – he had found an anthill the previous afternoon and buried the bundle.

What had been the tiniest current of air on the hill was growing into a breeze, suddenly shifting the open door of the Hall, beckoning Smous in. He shrugged and entered. Breedt had laid the boy on the floor and was kneeling above him, his lips moving rapidly, praying. Smous went cold. It was going to happen exactly as he had hoped, he was invited to watch their violence.

'I'm not going to stay,' he said, but Breedt had already strolled past, turned the key in the door and placed it in his pocket.

Now he returned to Klippie, and nudged him with one foot, less and less gently, saying, 'Klippie . . . Klippie . . . you have to wake up now. We must have a talk, then you can sleep.' The boy did not stir. Breedt looked at Smous. 'Fast asleep,' he said. 'I understand how he feels. I've lain awake all week too. It's a terrible thing not to sleep.' He tried nudging the boy again, but without success. 'No,' he concluded, 'dead to the world. And . . . and . . .' he sighed heavily, 'there are very few ways you can wake the dead.' Now he put his head in his hands and Smous wondered if he was crying. 'Ohhh,' groaned Breedt, 'I'm so tired, so very, very tired . . . I don't feel like work now, I just want to sit down and have a little rest, tsk, ag, tsk, so tired, so tired . . .' He continued to complain quietly as he roamed around the Hall, selecting items from the goods stacked against the wall, then brought these over to Klippie. Now he flipped the sleeping figure onto his back, making the blanket fall open and reveal the thin, naked body, whitewashed all over, except for trails of dried blood where he had circumcised himself. Smous shut his eyes tight and sank to the ground, spine against the locked door.

He listened to the sound of rope being looped, followed by the sizzle of knots drawn fast. Now the sound of hessian being slit and a whispering noise as the contents spilled out; now the sound of some wooden object being pushed along the ground. It was only when Smous heard the boy begin to moan that he could no longer stop himself, and opened his eyes.

Klippie was still lying on the ground, but with wrists and ankles tied. Breedt was crouched over the soles of the boy's feet, occupied in some task which Smous could not see. Then he caught a glimpse of a small machine in the Boer's hands, the machine which the farmers used to slice biltong. Smous looked away quickly, looked instead to the faces of the man and the boy. Both expressions were extraordinary. The Boer worked with a tired look, eyes moist and lazy, as if bored by some domestic chore; the boy's face was gripped with pain but he made no effort to raise his head and locate it. He was still half-lost in a sleep of exhaustion, still convinced he was enclosed in the safety of a nightmare. But his eyes finally shot open when, setting aside the slicing-machine, Breedt took a handful of salt from the split sack and rubbed it across the sole of the boy's foot.

'It's all right, Klippie, it's all right,' Breedt said quietly, reassuringly, while he restrained the writhing body. 'It's all right . . . just tell me the whole story, explain this whole business to me, and then you can have a sleep and I can have a sleep, because we've both had a hard week, both had the foot on the neck, so let's just have a talk now and then sleep.' The boy had no voice with which to scream. Stretching his mouth wide, he made a noise like wind across sand. 'All right, Klips, you take your time . . . it's all right,' Breedt said gently, setting to work on the other foot. 'It's all right, everything's all right . . .'

Smous had been scrabbling at the bottom of the door, trying to tunnel his way out. Now he rose, took several steps back, intending to throw his weight against it – but instead, to his own amazement, swung towards the figures on the floor, and, in a voice that came up from his stomach, shouted, 'BREEDT! NO! BREEDT! NO! BREEDT –'

The two men faced one another across the boy in equal astonishment. Breedt felt he had been struck: the Israelite had never used his name before; until that moment Smous himself wasn't conscious that he knew it. And the other word he had used – *no* – he had said that in Afrikaans. Breedt sank back onto the floor, looking like someone woken from sleepwalking. Smous felt that same strength he had known several times with Naoksa, and once with April. It was so easy to exert his strength, his choice, his judgement. It was so easy, why did he always resist it? Why did he fear it?

Klippie was unaware the torture had stopped; he felt only the crystals of salt dissolving, one by one, in the torn flesh of his foot. 'Wasn't me, my Baas,' he whispered now, to try and stop the pain. 'Wasn't me . . .' and then told a jumbled story of his education by Quinn. Breedt registered no special surprise at this information. His stunned gaze remained on Smous. There was a furious knocking on the door. Breedt slowly rose, slowly walked round Smous, eyes fixed on him, and slowly unlocked the door. The two Englishmen were standing on the road, Garbett in a crumpled blue-and-grey striped nightshirt, Quinn in his cobalt blue Egyptian djellaba; both men clutching their garments in the hot strong wind that had sprung up.

'Mister Breedt,' said Quinn, with some difficulty, his lip swollen from Smous's bite the night before. 'Kindly inform me what is –'

'Yes, but of course,' replied the Boer in English and stepped aside so the men might look into the Hall.

'Oh dear God,' whispered Quinn, 'oh, Mister Breedt, why have you done this to the child?'

'No, no,' said Breedt, 'why have *you*? The fight is you and me. Why the boy? You now know he must get hurt. This way or that way. And why? A lamb. A dead lamb.'

Quinn's mouth fell open. That was it. The lamb. That's what started this business. An Englishwoman, a scrap of newspaper left on a bush, Bokswater at dinner, Breedt killing the lamb, and then Quinn adopting Klippie as a new companion. That's what he'd been trying to remember for days. The lamb, he'd even kept its skull for a while. The lamb, that was it!

His grin tore the scab on his lip and blood trickled over his grey teeth. Now he began to shake with peculiar laughter, a dry knocking noise in his chest. As Breedt recoiled from the reek of Bokswater on his breath, it made the Boer look so prissy, wrinkling his nose and going '*Sissl*', that Quinn laughed harder. The shape of Breedt's neck abruptly changed, doubling in size, and his eyes, nose, mouth seemed to withdraw into the thickening, blackening muscles of his face.

'Ah, yes,' said Quinn, his laughter dying. He put his head on one side, viewing the Boer as he might a painting. Everything was becoming clear this morning. Now he understood why his first-ever sight of Breedt had been so shocking: that creature raging during the Battle of Middlepost, a stump for a head, barely human, wilder than a beast, a force without reason; it was a nightmare from his youth – Atropos about to cut the thread of human life, not with shears, but claws and teeth, not with poise but chaos.

'Ah, yes,' he sighed, smiling.

Garbett stepped back as he felt a shock go through the air, tightening like a cord around the two men.

'Yes, yes, yes,' murmured Quinn, eyeing Breedt, 'yes, yes, o golden-haired one, will you come? Come, yes, come, you mustn't be frightened.'

Breedt's head was burning. A sudden gust of wind pushed him an inch closer to Quinn. He must let himself go, he must fall on this man, close over him, God wanted it, God was blowing him forward.

'Come, come, yes, it's all right, I forgive you.'

Breedt wavered. Quinn forgiving him? Quinn showing him mercy? No, no, it was the other way round. For once. Surely it was. He was going to fall on Quinn, rip him apart. But still, even now, the Englishman wanted to be in control. Oh no – no, no. Mercy was not his to show this morning. And now Breedt remembered what a terrible thing it was, mercy, how much worse than violence. It made a man weep alone in his room and beat his brains against the wall. He stared at Quinn's flirtatious, smiling mouth, the blood like lipstick, then smiled also.

Quinn was puzzled. 'Mister Breedt . . . you realise I shall, of course, have to report –'

'No, I don't think so,' interrupted Breedt, his tone laden with courtesy. 'I think you and this man must go pack your bags hey, and . . .' he searched for the correct word, ' . . . depart, quiet and good, hey. Like gentleman.' And he strolled past them towards the house.

'Depart? Nobody's departing!' It was Garbett speaking now, hopping alongside Breedt as he crossed the road. 'You'll depart sooner than us, mate. We live here. Or have you forgotten the bleeding war – who gave who a lamping, who gave who a thrayping, who swined who?!' Breedt had disappeared into the house, but Garbett continued to shout, 'You'll be the one to depart, mate, straight back to a bleeding camp, mate! Depart? *You*, mate! From this life, mate – that's the only departing'll get done round here. Bleeding savage, bleeding swine. Swining barbarian!' He turned to the people gathered on the road. 'British!' he cried. 'British South Africa. D'you savvy? Not some half-soaked bleeding Boer swining republic, but British South Africa! King Edward VII, monarch of England, he owns this place, here, where we stand, here, Middle-swining-post – it is owned not by some bleeding Boer barbarian, but by no less than the King of swining England, my mates! Depart?! This is my home, I live here!' He stopped as suddenly as he had begun, noticing Quinn with head bowed, shaking with laughter again, blood spotting the Nile lilies on his djellaba. Garbett had a sudden vision of his return to England, and saw his family, thin cold people, white as corpses, and a shiver passed through him. A curtain of dust slid across the road, turning in on itself, then vanished. The onlookers were gone. Glancing down, Garbett saw that he'd lost one of his carpet slippers, and, clutching his nightshirt from the hot, tugging wind, limped across to the slipper, then jumped as the door of the house banged open and Breedt reappeared, his face set.

The Boer walked straight past both Englishmen, collected Smous and headed for the open veld. They passed April who, still oblivious of the morning's events, heard footsteps and called cheerfully, 'Greetings, greetings, 'twill be a storm today. Feel it, by Christ, feel it i'faith!'

The wind was blowing from the south, the direction Breedt now led Smous, urgently, as though needing to show him something. The landscape had began to darken strangely, the sky filling with foaming white and purple masses. It was difficult to keep upright. The wind grew stronger and stronger, drawing a sheet of red dust, almost a glow, across the land. Dry, low bushes began to twist and bend, rub together with a rasping sound, break off and take flight. Pebbles and small stones also, clicking and clattering, shooting, dancing and springing, advancing like living things. Now Smous could see the rain ahead: an immense black cloud melting to the ground, closing the gap between sky and earth, travelling towards the two men with a huge, rushing noise. The whole veld was enveloped in the bleakest light now, Breedt no more than a bustling, hunched silhouette dragging Smous forward. Suddenly the Boer stopped, changed direction, and hurried towards three other shadows bulging from the bush. Smous groaned. They were corpses of children from the schoolhouses, scorched black by the sun, their stretched skin gleaming, ready to explode. Untouched by predators (who, like the snakes and the frogs, had fled to higher ground), their only wounds were from a shotgun.

'Is this what you wanted me to see?' whimpered Smous, but Breedt had already charged on, muttering, 'Gertjie Swanepoel's work. Tsk. Man's got no restraint in him.'

'What do you want?' cried Smous. 'Where are we going? Ever since I arrived you've wanted something from me. Leave me alone. What do you want?' But the Boer's grip was unyielding and the only sound he made was a hoarse, insistent panting. Forks of lightning ruptured the dark sky and the thunder began, rolling backward, across the whole world, an empty world it sounded, and rolling forward, to flatten the last, tiny, scurrying humans. When at last the rain hit them it was with the force of water breaking from a dam, and now they could see nothing, hear nothing, could hardly feel the ground under their feet. Smous screamed. It was happening, it was happening again. 'And the waters prevailed upon the earth . . . and all the high hills were covered . . . and the mountains were covered . . . and all flesh died that moved upon the earth.' He fought to breathe. Suddenly Breedt's dark shape swam out of the chaos, only to vanish instantly. 'Help me!' cried Smous, lashing his arms through the pouring water. 'Where are you, where are you? Help me, oh help me please!'

'Smous, Smous!' he heard Breedt call.

'I'm here, I'm here! Where are you?'

'MENEER SMOUS!' roared Breedt, his deep voice reaching out of the ground like the thunder.

'I'm here!' Smous shrieked with all his might, but scarcely able to hear himself. 'I'm here!'

'SMOUS, SMOUS, SMOUS!'
'Oh God. HERE, HERE!'
'MENEEEER SMOUS?'
'YES – ME – SMOUS – YES – HERE!'
'STRETCH OUT YOUR HANDS!'
'WHAT?' screamed Smous in anguish. 'SPEAK YIDDISH, YOU FOOL!'
'TAKE MY HAND!'
'WHAT? SPEAK YIDDISH! HELP ME!'

Suddenly the veld was revealed in a flash of lightning, but, instead of one another, the men saw a twist in the sheets of rain, and both sprang away gasping – Smous thought it was an ostrich galloping to freedom, Breedt that it was a shivering black mare with a skeleton dangling from one stirrup. Then the light went, and they staggered past one another, Breedt calling 'MENEEEER SMOUS!' while the other began to giggle hysterically, answering, 'NEVER MIND ME, IT'S YOU – YOU'RE THE PROBLEM – WHERE ARE YOU?' He was crying with laughter – he couldn't grab hold of another human being inches away from him!

'MENEEEEER SMOUS!'

Now a roll of thunder drowned even Breedt's powerful voice; a slow, echoing noise from the centre of the earth, first grating, then cracking, growing louder and louder, impossibly loud, with no sign of softening or ending. Smous covered his ears, but it was no good; the thunder was no longer a madness happening somewhere else, *it was inside him*. His body would break apart. He tried to run, striking himself, striking the rain, but now his feet couldn't find the ground. 'Oh God!' he wailed. 'It's true!' – the story they once told him, that the world was not fixed, but twisting, flashing with terrible light and terrible darkness, roaring and churning, turning over and tipping its mighty oceans over the face of the land. 'And the waters prevailed . . . and all flesh died . . .' Now, through the deafening, tearing din, he heard laughter and glimpsed Breedt's head thrown back, biting at the rain. Huge white teeth snapped past Smous's disbelieving eyes.

'GO ON, GO ON!' he heard and, in the next flash of lightning, found the Boer towering over him, tall as the hill behind, his gleaming bulk shredded by white spears of light, the flesh running off his skull, the clothes dissolving on his limbs. 'GO ON, JA, GO ON,' Breedt bellowed to the heavens, 'I'LL NEVER, NEVER GET ENOUGH

OF YOU – FILL ME, FILL ME WITH YOU!'

A side of the hill broke away and an avalanche of mud hurtled down, reared for a moment in the air, glowing with red light, then crashed over them. Breedt boomed with joy, shook himself down, then noticed the other man crouched at his feet. Watching the monster loom out of the water, Smous cried out with relief, 'Oh, thank God, it's you. I'm drowning. Save me, like you did . . . on the banks of the Babrungas!' Despite the pandemonium around him, and despite the Israelite's foreign tongue, Breedt nodded, for it made sense to him also.

'Oh, my prophet,' he whispered, then knelt and folded Smous in his arms. The hot, wet blackness was exactly as Smous had always imagined the belly of the Great Fish, and he wept, saying, 'I knew you'd save me, I knew you'd come and save me.' Even after the vision passed, and even when he knew it was only Breedt holding him, he continued to weep, for a hundred different reasons he couldn't explain.

When at last the deluge passed, Smous disengaged himself from Breedt's arms, blinked, stretched, and watched the landscape slowly emerge from the blue mist. For a long time the two sat together in silence. The sky and earth remained dark and wet and reeking. Then one corner of the clouds lifted, a wave of sunlight broke across the veld and, like the rain earlier, came rushing towards them, spreading into every hollow, over every mound and bush, finally hitting them full in the face.

'Look, my friend,' Breedt whispered, pointing to where the clouds had lifted. 'Look, God is parting His hands and showing us His secrets. Look.' He held out both arms to the glistening, sparkling veld. 'You want gold and diamonds? Here it is. A person doesn't have to dig for it, here it is, this land. It looks so ugly and dry and sore most of the time. But look at it now. And in the next few days you are going to see a great miracle, exactly like in the Scriptures.' He skimmed his fingers through the film of water which had not yet soaked through the hard crust, creating a beautiful transparency and a sense of floating, then closed his eyes and held an expectant smile. Smous listened. Water. Water dripping from bushes, water gushing down nearby hills, water still falling from the great black cloud somewhere else.

Breedt was grinning. 'Just wait till you see the miracle that's going to happen in the next few days. And then you're going to ask, how many men have been lucky enough to see a miracle like I'm seeing?' He gave a little laugh and splashed his hands on either side, like a child in a stream. 'But then again, how many men have been lucky enough to be us, you and me, to belong to our special peoples – yours and mine? Now –' He climbed onto his knees and waddled through the water to face Smous.

'Now, this country is full of strangers at the moment. Travellers and strangers going this way and that, all wanting some milk and honey from the new promised land. But when we have driven out all the travellers and strangers – oh, just think – here we are at the dawn of a new century with this new country in our hands. How many men have known that?'

Breedt remembered Smous shouting his name in the Hall and his eyes suddenly widened, filling with the stark yellow light on the veld. 'Now you can fight us,' he said quietly, 'you can fight us like the others, and lose, and leave. Or you can stay here and help make history.'

4. CALVINIA

Hellas and Mab

For a week the rains fell and then, as Breedt had prophesied, there was a miracle. The desert bloomed. Every shrub and grass flowered, new buds rose from the softened earth and patches of colour began to seep into view; green, orange, blue, scarlet, white, gold. The people abandoned their routines to stand on the edge of the settlement and stare, frowning, at the great drifts. In this part of the world the only flowers you saw were carved on your furniture, painted on your crockery, embroidered around the mottoes on your walls; they didn't catch the sunlight in a way that made it seem, for once, a merciful force; they didn't summon hosts of unfamiliar birds and insects to come skimming over the edges of the veld, blurring those hard lines and drowning, finally, the maddening chime of the crickets.

The people ventured into the pastures of blossom, carving paths with their legs, crouching to smooth their palms across the petals, kneeling or crawling, grinning and waggling their wrists, for who had ever seen such things? Plants shaped like hearts, bells, arrows, some with wings, hair, beards, tongues, rude blushing folds and dangling lobes, waving and beckoning, casting a million different scents into the air, making your head spin. Traveller's Joy and Bird's Brandy — the children listened to these new words and laughed – Mouse Bush, Hare-bell, Grapple Thorn, Kaffir-cabbage and the Hottnot Fig. They leapt and tumbled through the whorls and clusters of colour, while their parents stood silent, shaking their heads. They had witnessed this miracle before, three or four years ago, when the rains came last, but many had forgotten how astonishing it was, or had come to mistrust their own memories. To think that throughout those blistering days, when everything seemed to die, all the time there were seeds buried under the ground, another plane of life, hidden yet indestructible. Looking at the world now, you would imagine it had needed an earthquake to tear away the lifeless veld and heave these magnificent gardens into its place – not just rain, not just water.

What else was possible?

On the first Sunday after the downpour, the population of Middlepost climbed onto their carts and wagons, and travelled the eighteen miles to the top of Ganaga Pass, which Smous and Naoksa had climbed a year earlier after crossing the Little Karoo. And, like Smous that day, the people now stood along the summit gazing down at the view.

'Brethren,' said Breedt. 'Here are not church walls surrounding us, no man-made roof closing us in, but, like our forefathers on the Trek and our brothers in the War, it is here we can best give thanks – here, under the empire of Heaven. Come, Brethren, let us pray.' The congregation obeyed, filling their lungs with the intoxicating air, and a whisper passed along the line, but many found it difficult to concentrate. *Under* the empire of Heaven? Surely it was the other way round. Surely these were the lands of Heaven spread out below them.

As it reached the bottom of the pass, the white road was lost in coloured pastures. The bright yellows took the eye first, rolling away under a breeze, turning red and white, glowing and softening, as though the land was shedding its skin, layer by layer, showing you deeper and deeper into its centre. The swathes of green made the Karoo seem carpeted with lawns and forests; and, most wonderfully, the blues brought it alive with a network of rivers, lagoons and great lakes where flat-topped hills rose like islands, or came adrift and floated away in the shimmering light.

Now the people began to sing an old hymn praising the glories of life. Slowly the mood changed, becoming more sombre, as the landscape below fell into a different shape. Compared to the rest of Creation, these undulating, multi-coloured plains were no more than a sleight-of-hand, the smallest proof of the Almighty's Power, a tiny warning perhaps. The flowers would grow more and more beautiful until the moment of absolute perfection when they would begin to die, and then you would have to watch the land slowly revert to the dry, scarred place you knew and feared, and you would have to fight it again, battling to keep every little thing alive. This way you would come to weigh the greatness of God against the insignificance of your life, of all human life, and so finally understand something about the universe.

Glancing down the line of blond and red-haired heads, their mouths and necks straining as they sang, loud and harsh now, it occurred to Smous that everyone was going to leap over the edge of Ganaga. They looked like a race of people without hope, gazing down at some fabled paradise beyond reach, able only to howl at it. How much happier the men and women singing behind them were, their servants, how much more comfortable they seemed with their homeland.

For his own part, Smous had never felt so like a stranger. When he stared at the view beneath him, his frown of wonder was deepened by the most vivid memories of home he had yet known. Summers in Litva when the meadows and forests would dazzle the eye like this, and the heat would be tempered, as now, with a blissful, wet, almost rotting smell. To close his eyes for an instant was to be back there. The pain took his breath away.

There was one group who didn't journey to Ganaga that Sunday, but stayed in Middlepost, their eyes combing the surrounding veld, waiting, as they had done since the end of the schoolhouse siege. These were the families of the children who had been in the school. Except for Klippie, the others were missing. It was presumed they had fled, but actually they were closer to Middlepost than anyone realised. Like the three corpses Smous and Breedt had seen before the deluge, all the children lay scattered across the veld. Invisible to human eye within the rainbow gardens, they were discovered by the host of predators, the jackals and foxes, genets and meerkats, who returned to the flat lands after the rains and feasted wildly below the surface of the blossoms.

Klippie and Mevrou Breedt made good recoveries. Both slept almost continuously through the week of the rains, and then woke to find the physical world so changed it held no memories of their ordeal. The patch of land behind the wattle-and-daub huts where Klippie had taught the children his songs and hatched their plans: that was gone, submerged in white flowers. The barren road to the school: that had become an unfamiliar narrow path crowded by long-stalked orange blooms, and no longer leading through a dry river bed, but blocked completely by a marvellous, rushing body of water. As for the school itself, you couldn't reach that at all for a while; it lay somewhere beyond the river, somewhere beyond that radiant lilac hill in the distance.

Breedt had tended to Klippie's feet while the boy slept, repairing, as best he could, the damage he had been forced to inflict. On waking, Klippie fashioned himself a pair of crutches and began to follow the Boer everywhere, overwhelmed by the man's spirit of forgiveness and eager to adopt him as a new master. But others were less charitable. Klippie had proved a true son of April's: a vicious savage with ideas above his station, and people threw stones when he came near, or spat and cursed. The boy's initial joy on waking to find himself in a new beautiful world was quickly soured and he retreated into his father's home, imprisoning himself.

'Shame, hey?' said Breedt to Smous as they passed the hut one day and he noticed the boy dart behind the hessian curtain. 'That satanic Redneck has a lot to answer for.'

On the morning after the first rains, the people of Middlepost were woken by the howling of Quinn's dogs, Hellas and Mab, locked in his room. When Breedt broke down the door, the German Shepherds shot out, all matted fur, wet tongues and teeth. Mab, shell-shocked during the war, had been driven mad by the thunder and ran in circles, shivering and panting convulsively, her head flat and tight, tail clenched between her haunches, while Hellas tore onto the road trying to locate Quinn's scent on the soaking earth, but without luck. The Englishmen had vanished.

Bewildered, Smous followed Hellas to the road and ran around like the dog, splashing through puddles, looking this way and that, then hurried back to Quinn's room, where he found Breedt standing in the centre, stunned. The walls were covered with scribblings and doodles, dates and names; names of places, real and mythological, in England, Egypt and Greece, names of loved ones – Bobby, the Dwarf, and others – names of poets, snatches of their verse; while a huge fresco covered most of the ceiling. It showed the hill at Golgotha with an extraordinary crucifixion: Christ and the thieves facing into their crosses, made not of wood but twisting human flesh, and penetrating them, spines buckling with ecstasy, naked buttocks squeezing tight. The place stank like the schoolhouse, for the fresco had been painted with Quinn's excrement, vomit and blood. Smous remembered the muffled noises he had heard coming from this room in the past, and how he'd often thought the walls looked newly whitewashed. The floor was littered with half-empty bottles, as if Quinn had set out to consume every drop of Bokswater he possessed. Some time in the early hours he must have passed out and been dragged by Garbett to a pony cart with as many hastily packed chests as would fit. The rest had been abandoned with the dogs.

Breedt wandered around in a daze, nudging things with his foot, pulling open drawers and wardrobes – where he found the mail-bags and satchels (finally explaining those trips to Calvinia), and now, behind them, a heap of cardboard boxes. One held all Garbett's gifts, those trinkets and pieces of food, dried or rotting, which Quinn couldn't bring himself either to use or to throw away. Another was filled with mounds of finger- and toenail clippings, hundreds of dates scrawled on the lid. In a third were Quinn's two pieces of quartz veined with gold; in yet another, his family Bible and Missal, both coated in dust, his pearl rosary and a folded gilt triptych. This was the box which most incensed Breedt and the first to be hurled onto the bonfire he now built in the centre of Middlepost. Everything from the room followed, every piece of furniture, even the splendid brass bed with squeaking springs on which Smous had so often perched; and from Garbett's room also; everything the Englishmen had owned.

Still delirious from the rains, the people gathered round the fire, singing, jeering, screeching with laughter. From one window Naoksa watched, quaking, like Mab, from the storm, while, from another, Breedt's daughter spied through the slats, then withdrew to her small table and sat reading her Bible, enclosed in the peppermint-scented shadows from which she never ventured.

When Quinn's room was bare, a team of servants scrubbed clean the walls and ceiling and repainted them, but still Breedt couldn't bear it. So he grabbed an axe and sledge-hammer, and hacked the room off the side of his house. The adjoining guest rooms were ruined and part of the roof collapsed, but now at last, with a splintery, gaping hole in the building, red stones and earth showing through the torn patches of whitewash, now at last Breedt felt he had cleansed his home, ripped out the evil sore that had been poisoning it for years, and now at last he found some peace.

Smous meanwhile was in agony. What remained of Quinn's Bokswater had been thrown onto the fire with everything else and, watching the bottles explode, giving off curious vapours and hues, he began to shiver. A drink would have calmed him, yet where was he to find one now?

Over the following days the shivering grew worse and he could find no relief. He would sit next to April outside the store where the sun beat down in a great blinding patch, but still couldn't get warm. It was comforting to be near a friend; specially one who could not see his shuddering limbs, his cold sweats, his swollen, red eyes. And a friend who said nothing, that was also a comfort, but kept very still, breathing deeply at the fragrance from the surrounding land, encouraging Smous to do the same.

After the storm April had learned of the damage to his son, all caused, as Breedt explained, by the Englishman's deviousness; a man whom April had trusted so deeply. He had also to acknowledge that the fragment of skin buried so joyously before the rains was not his. Fortunately Breedt was at hand to explain once and for all that any curse April might feel on his life had nothing to do with vanished foreskins and pagan superstition, but was, yet again, the result of his education by a depraved Englishman. At first April refused to accept this, but as the days passed he was left with little choice. After all, had Quinn not always promised a trip one day to the great House of England and that world elsewhere? And yet now he was gone, disappeared without trace, fled like a criminal. Surely an honourable man would at least have bid farewell? As April faced the clear facts and realised how much, and for how long, he had been deceived, his anger was such that he was unable to speak or move, but sat containing it within his blind head, while the days whipped past like seconds.

He enjoyed only one moment of revenge: when Breedt asked him to take care of Quinn's dogs.

They were killed in two separate locations, so that the second should not smell the first's blood. The precaution proved unnecessary. Hellas and Mab came to the slaughter joyfully, for they adored April and sensed no danger when he stood behind them and fastened his knees around their ribs. Instead they threw back their grinning jaws to lick his face, presenting their throats so tautly that even a blind man had no difficulty aiming his blade.

Now Breedt uprooted the granite cross, the monument to the English fallen, opened the mass grave and buried it among the skeletons. Next he visited all Quinn's digging sites, tearing down the boring rigs, sealing all the holes. Finally there was only one thing left.

'My friend, you must please forgive me,' the Boer said to Smous one day, as if noticing his shivering for the first time. 'That you required the Englishman's supplies so very much is something I didn't realise, no. We must furnish you with more.' When the other frowned and shrugged, he said, 'Bokswater', and Smous nodded eagerly. Breedt hitched up a mule-cart and together they set off from Middlepost, across the makeshift bridge now spanning the river, up the hill, past the schoolhouse, its whitewashed walls shining peacefully among the lilac blossoms, and then took the road to the north.

Anyone else might have failed to locate the turn-off among the confusion of flowers, but Smous could scent a different, tantalising odour beneath their fragrance. Without hesitation, he showed Breedt where to turn, leading him across the veld, between the low hills, and eventually to the abandoned farm.

The Boer had brought along his shotgun, but, as at the end of the schoolhouse siege, it proved unnecessary. When he hauled open the trap door and called the Bushman and his blonde, half-caste woman, they surrendered without a struggle.

'I mustn't see you in the district again, Bok,' Breedt said quietly, 'you hear?'

'Hear, o Baas, hear well,' replied the drunk Bushman, dancing to and fro. 'The old Bokkie hear and see well, he hear and see how for years he is kakking onto the great Englishman, the great O Lord Master Quinn, who is not pleased with this my land, he's wanting there to be riches greater than water under this my land, sun and stars under this my land. So, I sow some for him to find.' He took from his pocket a chunk of quartz veined with gold, like those which Quinn had dug out of the earth. Years earlier in the north Bok had looted these from the corpse of a prospector. Despite his anger, Breedt couldn't help smiling. He thought back to Quinn's ramblings in the dining room, pondering over his search in the veld, likening it to life, wondering whether it was worth the effort, wondering how complicated or straightforward the outcome would be. Well, my English friend, thought Breedt looking at the quartz in Bok's hand, it was this simple.

'But I also's think, think, think,' said the Bushman, watching him smile, 'I also's think the old Bokkie is kakking onto you also, the great big Boer Baas, because it is the Bokkie who is making the Englishman live in your house for a long, long time –'

'No, no,' protested the woman, staggering also, and having to throw back her lolling head to squint at Breedt. 'You mustn't listen, my Baas, we go now, the Baas never sees us no more. Just one thing, please my Baas, please can my Baas give back our twin smallings so we can take them away too, and Baas never sees them no more again. Please, my Baas, ja?'

'For years, years, the Bokkie is kakking onto the big masters,' sang Bok meanwhile, 'for years, years before you come here, the Bokkie is living on this my land, so he know where to kak –'

'No, no!' shouted his woman at the same time. 'No, Baas mustn't listen, just give us the twins back, hey?'

'You can chase the Bokkie far, far, far into the desert, he'll live there, jaaa, he needs no food or water but still he kaks, he's kakking wherever you chase him . . .'

'All right, Baas, just *one*, hey? Just give us one twin back, hey? You keep one, you give us one, hey? Please Baas, I loves them with all my heart, my Baas, please . . .'

'The Bokkie goes,' said the old man, dragging his woman along, 'but the Bokkie also stays, goes and stays, jaaa, farewell the Baas Breedt, farewell and welcome, the Bokkie goes, the Bokkie stays . . .'

When the two lurching figures had disappeared into the surrounding drift of purple flowers, Breedt lit a torch, threw it into their cellar and ran for cover. The explosion opened the earth and the old farm buildings gently toppled into a huge pit of flames, smoke and dust.

Smous watched, hugging himself and shivering.

At last all trace of Quinn and Garbett was gone. It was as though, like the Scottish minister a year before, they had never been in Middlepost.

'I'm sure you meant well, Oom Stoffie,' said Swanepoel, 'but nevertheless I think it was maybe a misguided act. And I think I speak for us all.'

Breedt's eyes flickered over the gathering in the Hall. All the farmers looked away. Now he glanced at Smous to share his surprise with someone, but found the small man hunched in his seat battling to control his trembling for the duration of the meeting. Swanepoel was on his feet now, strolling around the Hall, running his fingers through his long black hair.

'You see, I always felt it was not such a bad thing for old Bokkie to supply our labourers with rot-gut, no. More than that, I always felt it was perhaps how things were meant to be. I must hardly have to tell you, Oom Stoffie, how we can read in the Bible of Noah's drunkenness, and how one of his sons made fun of it, and how the offspring of that son was then cursed by the Lord thus – "A servant of servants shall be he unto his brethren." Well now, I'm not so great a scholar of the Scriptures as you are, Oom Stoffie, no, but it does seem to me that the Lord is perfectly clear here. He's putting servant-stock and drunkenness side by side. Perhaps the Lord in His wisdom understood that the life of a servant is a hard one and needs to be washed in rot-gut before he can endure it, nê? I've certainly always felt my labourers work in a much happier way when they're slammed. So anyhow, what I'd like to suggest is that when a new shebeen starts up – as it will – by someone else, somewhere else, well, a person doesn't have to go give it his blessing, but at the same time he need do nothing to discourage it neither.'

The other farmers murmured their approval, while Breedt wondered how best to demonstrate his anger: should he argue or simply storm out? Before he could decide, Swanepoel started speaking again:

'And while we're all here together, Oom Stoffie, I hope you won't mind if we mention one or two other things . . .' Breedt tensed. *We?* Had the farmers been meeting without him?

'We must all face the fact,' Swanepoel was saying, 'that our scheme to school our labourers' offspring alongside our own has been a mistake. Luckily not a tragic mistake, no, but nevertheless a grave one. *That* I don't think anyone could argue with,' he said, coaxing another murmur of approval from the gathering. 'However, it is a mistake born of good intentions, namely the difficulty of giving orders to wild servants. I'm sure that must have been a severe problem to those folk who were the early settlers in these parts, but anyway now we have a first generation of servants who can speak enough Afrikaans to teach it to their smear-rags, so there shouldn't be the need to keep schooling any further generations hereafter.'

Breedt found his voice at last. 'It isn't just the language. We're teaching them Faith as well.'

'Good. I'm glad you've brought that up, Oom Stoffie,' retorted Swanepoel, 'because the other thing we feel is that it's a bit of a joke having these people praying alongside us. It's a bit insulting in fact. In fact, a person can even call it a bit of a blasphemy. You know, they come along to the services, they stand on the road there, they make as if they're singing, but their hearts aren't in it, ag, what, never! Their hearts are still dancing around their witch-fires in the veld.'

'That's their religion,' contributed Reukes, 'and we must leave them to it.'

'And I often wonder,' mused Naude, chewing on a stick of dried meat, 'often wonder if they're not happier in their innocence than a lot of us civilised folk.'

'That's possibly true,' said Swanepoel with little enthusiasm, 'but anyhow, Oom Stoffie, isn't it you who has always reminded us of the old Tower of Babel there in the Bible? Of the difference between the peoples of the earth. The Divine difference.'

'I –' said Breedt.

'And – sorry to butt in, Oom Stoffie, but just let me finish – the other thing we also feel is that we're cutting ourselves off too much here from our fellow countrymen, and that it wouldn't be such a bad thing to take communion in Calvinia once in a while, now they've got that new minister there, the man from Holland who arrived after –'

'Who'll pray in High Dutch?'

'Who'll pray in our sacred language, ja.'

'Which half of you don't understand.'

'It is our sacred language, Oom Stoffie, and –'

'You'd –'

'Sorry, just let me finish. The important thing is that we unite with the congregation there. I know a lot of good men among them, men I fought alongside in the war, men we might have to fight alongside again before we can truly call this country our own. And I'm telling you – *that* is the only Divine Mission we must all unite on! Now, sorry, Oom Stoffie, you were going to say something?'

Breedt hesitated. He had suddenly become aware of how often the younger man had addressed him as 'Oom Stoffie' – a term of respect which had begun to sound like one of abuse. It painted a picture of an old man in a rocking chair, drifting through his days on the gentle intoxication of chewing tobacco.

'Oom Stoffie?' enquired Swanepoel.

Breedt coughed, then said in a quiet, steady voice, 'All the things you're throwing away today, these are things . . . these are paths I have been inspired, *commanded* to tread . . .' He hesitated, for everyone had immediately looked away again and there was a sudden silence in the Hall, a silence warning him not to continue. He sat with eyes unblinking, mouth half open. From beyond the open door came the song of birds over the drifts of flowers, but within the Hall the silence was complete.

Swanepoel broke it at last, saying, 'All right, I think that's every-thing. Unless anyone else has any –?' But the farmers were already on their feet, stretching and stamping the numbness from their limbs.

Breedt was on the verge of shouting, *I* called this meeting, *I'll* dismiss it, but caught himself in time, and clapped his hands instead, saying, 'Ja good, I think we've cleared up a lot of things today, good, always a good thing to do, clear the air.'

Swanepoel watched him, smiling compassionately, then lingered while the other farmers filed onto the road. 'You know, Oom Stoffie,' he said, once there was only Smous remaining with them, 'whenever I think about it I always reckon you had such a very hard war, one of the hardest wars of any I know, and I speak as one who saw some helldamned, bloodsucking stuff. But for a man to lose his son, his livestock, to have his womenfolk lose their health, and then for him to have to change his whole way of life, these have been a terrible burden.'

'And?' asked Breedt who was standing hunched, hands behind his back.

'No, I just want to say I understand how heavy your burden has been, and that if there had been any misjudgements . . . Anyhow, Oom Stoffie, as I said at the meeting, the important thing is for there to be a united Folk, for there to be no fight among brothers –'

'And for there to be no leaders, Gertjie?' taunted Breedt.

'Leaders? Oo God-juruh-ja, just no dreamers. There's the real harm done to you during the war. You've started to become like your conquerors, to think like them. An Englishman sees a red sunset and he's got to paint me a picture of it. When I see it, all I know is that a few more of my new-born lambs are going to perish in the heat tomorrow. Who's ever heard of a Boer painting pictures? Not even our women do that, never! Uprooting life and planting it somewhere else? Never. That's God's business, not ours, no. But that's how you've become – dreaming up this and that, not content to let things be. It's too long since you've farmed the land. You've forgotten how simple it all is. The sun rises, the sun sets, things live, things die, there are creatures with souls and creatures without, light and dark, like day and night. It's all laid out very clearly for a person, as long as he doesn't start dreaming. And that's the end of the story, finished forever.'

Breedt considered this, then asked 'How old are you, Gertjie?'

'Oom Stoffie? I'm twenty-two this winter.'

'Hell, and you sound like my grandpa.'

'You mean that as an insult. But I'm telling you something now –' For a moment Swanepoel's grey eyes darkened and shone. 'I'd've given anything to have lived then. To have gone on the Trek with those people. Strong as oxen, but the souls of angels. Man, there were mountains those people flew over –'

'Ja well,' interrupted Breedt, smiling, 'they were dreaming of a better world. Dreamers one and all.'

Swanepoel checked himself, held the other's gaze for a moment, then turned and went. Breedt felt calm and empty. Now they were alone, Smous could stop disguising his shivers, and sat hugging himself, rocking back and forth, clicking his fingernails busily. 'Bokswater? Bokswater?' he said, nodding at Breedt, trying to make him nod in return. 'Bokswater? Bokswater? Hm? . . . Bokswater?' He saw it was hopeless. 'Oh please,' – now he spoke in Yiddish – 'I'll do anything, I wish I could tell you . . . I wish you could hear me . . . Oh please . . .

Bokswater? *Bokswater?*'

'My friend,' said Breedt, 'you must get better soon. I'm going to need you at my side more than ever. Get better. I say that without anger or judgement. Born sinners, so what chance have we got? Our little Antjie is so eager to meet you –' He had taken hold of Smous's outstretched hand and felt how cold the trembling flesh was. 'But anyhow, first get better. The Englishman did so much harm to so many people here. I must pray. Go into the sun.' He propelled Smous to the doorway. 'You're cold. Get warm. Get better.'

But the road felt icy, the long blue shadows from the trees were glacial, and, as Smous's eye followed the distant figure of Swanepoel galloping through drifts of blue flowers, he imagined the man was rowing across the cold-water ocean towards Table Bay. Smous sighed and struggled to concentrate. How was it he had not noticed this before? The range of bluish hills in the distance were very like the three mountains of Table Bay – but melted down, melted together, like lumps of snow melted by the rain. He shook his head in disgust and slowly made his way to his room to pile his bed with winter covers and bury himself.

He could not say how long he stayed there, for how many days, weeks, or months. The oddest things began to occur. The patches of sunlight in the room were somewhere different every time he opened his eyes. Not only on the walls, floor or ceiling, but places the sun couldn't possibly reach: below the bed, inside his pillowcase, within the wardrobe. And he had a weird succession of visitors: his family, all badly wounded or maimed, seeking his medical advice; Breedt with a struggling cat, which he slaughtered and skinned in the middle of the room, then pressed the hot, wet skin against Smous's chest, saying, 'This will help draw out the poisons and fever. It's a remedy from the old people.' And Naoksa visited also, carrying an eggshell filled with liquid. 'Drink this,' she said, 'it will help. I am reminded of our happy journey together before we reached this place. You were happy, I think, though you would not eat . . .'

'Thrf-f-f,' spluttered Smous as he drank from the shell. 'What is it?'

'It is good. It will help. It is juice from the *bi* mixed with my own water.'

'Your words,' he said dreamily, 'your words are so sweet I don't want ever to understand them,' and let his trembling, sweating hand fall onto her stomach where he felt an unmistakable swelling. 'Is this real?' he asked in a hushed tone, then watched, horrified, as she nodded.

'So. I am with child.'

'Your words . . . your words are so sweet,' he murmured before fainting with shock.

Antjie

The girl had spoken in Yiddish, so he assumed he was still hallucinating.

'Good morning,' she said again. Smous turned his puzzled expression to Breedt in the doorway. The Boer beamed back.

'My name – Anna – Antjie,' said the girl. 'Excuse, no can . . .' she indicated the large, haphazard, brown markings on her skin and that it wasn't possible to shake hands. Smous frowned; if this was a dream, surely she'd speak Yiddish better? He flicked his head in disbelief, then gave a few heavy sighs, feeling close to tears.

'Sit?' she said.

He ignored the invitation, remaining marooned in the middle of her shuttered, peppermint-scented room. 'You speak Yiddish,' he said after a while.

'Little,' Antjie replied with an embarrassed laugh.

'How is that possible?'

'People where I now am . . . Yiddish people. They teach me little Yiddish. Me teach they little Afrikaans.'

'What is he asking?' asked Breedt in Afrikaans.

'Where I learned his language.'

'And what are you telling him?'

'What do you think? I just said "people". Now why don't you leave us alone?' Breedt chuckled approvingly at his daughter's spirit, and withdrew from the room. Now Antjie gestured Smous towards the thong-seated bench under the window while she sat at the table, smiling at him. 'You now sick?' she asked.

'Uh . . . yes,' he said, instantly ashamed, 'a fever. Very bad . . . uh . . . don't know how long it's lasted, don't know how long I've uh . . . Today, this morning, is my first morning up, so –'

'Talk slow,' she said, hands raised in surrender.

'Sorry?'

'Talk slow, for me.'

'Oh, I see, yes, sorry. This morning – yes? – you understand?'

'Ja.'

'This morning – my first morning – out of bed.'

'Ah.'

'So, it's . . . quite a surprise to meet you.'

'You sick. Me sick.'

'You're sick also, really?' said Smous, who had tried not to stare at the markings on her skin. 'And when will you be up and about? Well, no, you are up, but when will you be . . . about?'

'Talk slow,' she reminded him.

'Ah, yes, sorry. You – sick?'

'Ja,' she replied with a composed smile. 'The war – ja?'

'The war, yes.'

'Me and her mother – ja?'

'You and *your* mother?' Smous verified, nodding at the same time.

'In camp.'

'Camp. Ah-hah. English camp, prisoners and so forth?'

'Many, many sun.'

'Sorry? Oh, too much sun?'

'Many, many and . . . what's mean? And no –? And no –?' She patted her stomach.

'No food?'

'Food, ja, but no . . . many, many.'

'Not sufficient food?'

'Not . . . suf-fi-cient . . . food,' she repeated, then smiled at him. 'You teach me Yiddish. Me teach you Afrikaans. Ja? Yiddish, Afrikaans, kitchen tongues. Ja?'

He shrugged and went silent. There were traces of her parents' heavy features in her brow and jaw, but because she was thin, almost emaciated, the large shining bones and deep hollows made her face strikingly beautiful. She had inherited her father's watchful blue eyes, but these were softened by long, whitish lashes. Her hair, so blonde it was almost white, had been washed for the visit and caught into a bun. A plain, corn-coloured dress had been worn specially, with high collar and long cuffs to show as little of the disease as possible.

'Not sufficient food and too much sun?' concluded Smous. 'So now you have to . . .' He gestured round the shuttered room.

'Now, no sun.'

'Yes. Good Lord, that must be uh . . . yes. What a shame you're missing the flowers.' She raised her eyebrows enquiringly. 'Flowers?' he repeated. 'Flowers – everywhere.'

'No,' she corrected him, 'no more.'

Puzzled, he knelt on the bench and peered through the shutters. The veld had reverted to a mottled grey. 'Good Heavens,' he whispered, and sat back, dazed, wondering how long he'd been in bed. 'So anyway,' he said in a dull voice, 'uh . . . so, you have to stay in here all the time.'

'Ja,' she replied cheerfully.

'Why can't you come out at night?' She shrugged bashfully and indicated her markings. 'Yes, I understand,' said Smous quickly, 'and sometimes there are strangers in the house.'

'Excuse?'

'Strangers. Travellers. People you don't know. *Strangers.*'

'Strangers,' she repeated thoughtfully, then said, 'When this –' she indicated her markings, 'no more, ja?'

'Yes.'

'Then me . . . what's mean? Me. . . ?'

'Then you'll feel happier about coming out at night.'

'So.'

'Well, in the meantime, it's uh . . . well, I'm extremely honoured. It's very nice to meet you at long last.'

'It's very nice . . . to meet you,' she echoed, 'at long last.'

'Thank you. Yes.' He felt close to tears again, so gave a little laugh. 'Extraordinary to be talking Yiddish to someone after all this time. Really quite extraordinary. I'm surprised my voicebox still works.' He saw her frown of incomprehension, so said slowly, 'Yiddish. How come you speak it so well?' She shrugged, half-modestly, half-pretending she hadn't understood the question. He smiled, for he had used these tactics himself. 'Where did you learn it so well?' he persisted.

'No . . .' she said evasively. 'A place. You no, no . . . her place.'

'Extraordinary, all the same.'

They fell into silence. At the wash stand there were dozens of ointment jars – the source, presumably, of the peppermint smell – and a stack of spotless, folded towels. His eyes strayed to the small bed, barely visible through a heavy insect net. Blushing, he suddenly remembered her father fornicating with the Italian woman. And now he remembered her mother tied to the dripping chair in the schoolhouse. He longed to tell her, shock her. Her parents had bamboozled him for so long, gabbling or farting at him, how satisfying to sit now with their invalided daughter, and for her to be struggling with *his* language.

They will have told you, he thought, how soft I am, what a weak little man. Greying hair, but the mind of a child. Well, that was before the illness. What they don't know yet is how changed I am. The Englishman's Bokswater and the illness it brought – that was it, the end, that's as much as I'm going to take. So, you might think you're dealing with a weak little man, but take care. Take great care.

'I have no red book,' said Antjie suddenly. 'Have you red book?'

'Sorry?' asked Smous.

'I have no red book. Have you red book?'

'Uh . . . ?' He wondered if this was some rhyme she had used in learning the language.

'Red book', said Antjie smiling shyly. 'Red book. For –' She picked up her black Bible, licked her finger, rubbed it across the cover, then put it to her lips and cheeks as though applying make-up. 'I have no red book. Her mother, her father, say – no, no. But . . . red, pretty.'

'You want red to . . . put on your . . . ?'

'Red, red.' She nodded, then showed him how pale her skin was between the markings, pulling her face in disgust. He looked closely. Her skin was white, not pink or yellow, but pure white. 'What's mean?' she asked. 'Pretty, no –? What's mean?'

'Sorry?'

'Uhm . . . tsk! . . . Good-and-bad, day-and-night. So. Pretty-and –?'

'Ah. Ugly. Pretty-and-ugly.'

'Ugly!' She smiled. 'This, ugly. Red, pretty.'

'Yes, I see. Well, I don't have any red books, or any books actually, but uh . . . well, if I ever see one I'll bring it to you.'

'Thank you,' she said, then suddenly grinned broadly and clapped her hands with excitement.

Take care, he cautioned himself, take care, this is how they charm you before they hurt you. They all do this.

He had no intention of searching for a red book, so was all the more surprised when, a few hours later, strolling through the veld, he saw one lying in a patch of withered blue petals. It was the book of Donne's verses which Quinn had given April on his first day back at work, and which had been hurled into the veld after the Englishman's departure, falling among the flowers, and revealed now they had died.

'Take care,' he whispered, but retrieved it all the same, and, on his next visit, took it to Antjie. She huddled in front of a mirror, licking her finger, rubbing it over the dyed leather binding and carefully applying the stain to her face. When she was done, she turned to him and presented herself.

The red blobs made her markings pale by comparison, and her skin even whiter. She looked like a doll.

'Ugly?' she asked.

'Uh . . . no,' he mumbled, intimidated by her boldness and having to look away, 'no, no. Pretty, very pretty.'

Naoksa was pregnant. It had not been a hallucination – she was clearly, visibly pregnant. Smous watched her waddling around Middlepost, her tiny body unbalanced by the enormous bulge of her stomach, and wondered if perhaps the child might not be Garbett's? Or Miller's, the carriage driver who fornicated with her in the sugarhouse. How long ago was that? It seemed so unlikely the child could be Smous's own, so unlikely it could have been conceived in those few brief minutes below the crucifix. Yet, on the other hand, those minutes had been ecstatic. If only he could remember the details. Did she swallow his seed? And did people come into being that easily? Maybe, maybe not. Probably wrong, he thought, I am about most things. I'm the fool, don't you know, the one on the road watching life dance away in the distance.

'Oh God,' he whispered into the mirror.

And Naoksa had begun to smile at him again, ever since those visits during his illness; a smile that was perhaps compassionate, perhaps renewing their friendship, perhaps acknowledging the father of her unborn child, and husband-to-be.

'Oh God,' he whined. 'Oh God, oh God.'

He began to find her repulsive. Not only the swollen belly, but those preposterous buttocks – the girl was deformed. And that short, boyish hairstyle – the girl was a freak. And the way her face would wrinkle when she grinned, and that ludicrous chewing, clicking noise she called a language.

You think I want a son with your arse, he would imagine demanding of her, a son with the skin of a lizard, a son who's going to talk as if he's got knots in his voice? You think that's my idea of an heir? An Immerman heir? Or a Zali . . . or a Smous . . . or whatever I am.

'God help me!' he whimpered. Then he caught himself, stared calmly at his reflection and thought: wait a minute, that business was the folly of a weak little man, the man I was before. I don't have to be like that any more, or take the blame for what did or didn't happen then. What's done is done, fine. It might be done, but I'm not.

During his recovery he had spent many hours reviewing his life, and realised that his greatest talent so far had been an ability to summon illness whenever the going was tough. That fever on the day of his barmitzvah, the frostbite and pneumonia he nurtured during the Plungyan winters, his hot and bubbling belly, ever-restless, ever-surprising, and, of course, the Bokswater. What he had loved most was the feeling of becoming unwell – vaguely, wonderfully unwell. Now he felt strong again, but disgusted with himself and angry with the others for taking advantage of him. He longed to wield his strength, perhaps inflicting pain if need be, and almost immediately found the way forward; a new talent revealed itself, or rather a talent he had discounted before. A talent for trading.

Breedt's store was in chaos. The Boer wandered in and out of the dusty, cluttered place with little enthusiasm, while April had retreated to a small, windowless room at the back, where he would sit in the dark, plaiting the lengths of chewing tobacco for sale to the farmers. Smous quickly made the store his territory and discovered he was not nearly as incompetent as he thought. That was another fault of the old Smous, he decided, always imagining others knew better, had more talent, more experience. When it came to trading he felt inferior to his father or brother, or Kottler in Ceres, or the other smouses. But here in Middlepost nobody knew about his failings, so if he pretended to know what he was doing, people were convinced. And pretence, he now discovered, was the key to good trading. He had always believed it to be a dull and uninspiring occupation, but how wrong he was.

His first big sale happened almost by accident. A young Khoi tribesman arrived one day wanting to sell a beautiful tortoise shell filled with powdered bone and decorated with tassels of plant-string. With rude, squashing gestures, the naked savage demonstrated the trinket's aphrodisiac powers. Blushing and tutting, Smous offered a stick of dried meat in exchange, and the youth, being hungry, accepted. Smous thought no more about it until a few days later when an elderly American traveller noticed the tortoise shell lying on the counter and stopped to admire it. Without thinking, Smous found himself not only repeating the vulgar pantomime, but embellishing it. The old man was captivated and promptly offered half-a-crown for the item. Overjoyed, Smous was on the verge of accepting when some instinct told him to glower instead. The American immediately doubled his offer and, with a reluctant sigh, Smous accepted.

Now there was no stopping him. How easy it was to bully the tribespeople, and how easy to play a humbler role with European travellers, sheltering behind his ignorance of their languages to appear slightly backward and allay suspicion. April's great linguistic skills, Smous now realised, had never been an asset. Bartering was much better done in a fog of confusion. The small moments of authority he had felt over Naoksa and April was nothing compared to what he began to enjoy at the store. He made only one rule for himself: he would always set out to make a profit, even if it was only a halfpenny, in any transaction.

Within two months the store's income doubled, and this during the winter, normally the quietest period. Breedt was heartened by this, though by little else that life had to offer at present. Since the schoolhouse siege, attendance at his Sunday services was low, he was discouraged from preaching long sermons, and once a month the congregation would vanish altogether to take communion in Calvinia. The servant population no longer attended the services, and their children no longer attended the school. Their free time was spent in the shebeen which one of Swanepoel's labourers had started up in the veld, a discreet distance from the settlement.

These days Breedt found himself yearning for the period when the Englishmen were at Middlepost. That was the height of his power; fate had played him a cruel trick. Now he took to sitting on his porch, the days drifting by, assuring himself he was not surrendering, but merely waiting. Waiting for the Israelite to complete his miracle in the store and make it possible for him to purchase new flocks of sheep and finish his days in a blessed existence on the land.

It was a bright Saturday morning in October, seven months after the rains, when Swanepoel chose to make his move.

Smous's latest activity at the store involved sorting the goods which had lain for years in the corners, gathering dust. With Breedt's help he was carrying everything onto the road, while a team of servants swept and washed the interior. Already there had been valuable discoveries: a stack of springbok hides in excellent condition, kudu and eland horns which, when mounted, would fetch handsome prices from European travellers, beautiful fat-and-lye soaps carved one winter by Mevrou Breedt, several boxes of home-made candles, and much else. Smous and Breedt had been working since six o'clock that morning and had stopped for a rest, sitting in the sun, eating a late breakfast of bread and tomato jam, when Swanepoel stopped his cart alongside them. He smiled down at Smous, and then spoke a few words which sent a shock through the atmosphere:

'Meneer Immerman – Calvinia?'

Breedt was the first to react. 'His name's Meneer Smous.'

'Pardon me, Oom Stoffie,' said Swanepoel, 'but I think I'm talking to this gentleman here. Meneer Immerman – I – convey – you – to – Calvinia – ja?'

'*Immerman*,' repeated Smous in a hushed voice.

'Isn't that your name? You – Immerman?'

Smous nodded.

'Sorry, Oom Stoffie,' said Swanepoel, turning to Breedt, 'but there's been, I think, a misunderstanding here. Meneer Immerman only arrived in Middelpos, like all the other Europeans we see, on his way somewhere else. To join his family in Calvinia. How do I know? I made a few enquiries among the Jewish families there and I've learned of an uncle and cousin who've been waiting for him, ooo, for over a year now. So anyhow, me and Johanna and little Frikkie are on our way to Calvinia for communion tomorrow, and I wondered if I could be of help. Reunite this family torn asunder.'

Smous had risen to his feet. 'Kulvidya?' he asked Swanepoel, unable to believe this was happening.

'Calvinia. That's what I said. Hop in.'

Now Breedt stood, the colour draining from his face. 'Wait,' he said quietly, directing his plea to both men, 'please wait.'

'Can't, I'm afraid, Oom Stoffie,' replied Swanepoel, stretching lazily. 'We want to do as much of the journey in daylight as we can.'

'Just give me five minutes, please.'

'Ag, Oom Stoffie, five minutes. No, of course you can have five minutes, man, you can have ten, half an hour.' Swanepoel grinned. 'I must go up to the farm anyhow and pick up the family. Then I'll stop by here on the way back to collect him. That long enough, that sound reasonable?'

As soon as Swanepoel had gone, Breedt propelled Smous across the road, into the house, down the warren of black corridors, and finally into Antjie's room. She was washing her arms in a bowl; always a painful business, for the scabs would sting. Seeing Smous, she hastily covered her arms with a towel, and was about to protest when she noticed the look in her father's face. He whispered to her, then stood back, eyeing the situation nervously.

'What's happening?' Smous asked. 'Is that man really going to take me to Kulvidya?' Antjie nodded. 'How soon?'

'Now.'

'God. I must get ready. How did he know my name, that man?'

'You – uncle in Calvinia?'

'Yes. Oh, I see. What, he bumped into him there, or something?'

'Me and uncle, also.'

'What?'

'Ja.'

'*You*? How?'

'Calvinia is where her sick many, many . . . Dokter Lazar Immerman and Dokter Issy Immerman, ja?' Smous nodded, dumbfounded. 'Nava Immerman. Dokter Issy, wife, ja?'

'Yes.'

'Esther Immerman . . .'

'That's the daughter they had.'

'David Immerman, ja?'

'David Immerman? Who's David Immerman?'

'Little, ja?'

'Oh, I see, another one, God, they've –' He suddenly stopped, and glared at Antjie. 'But why didn't you tell me before?' Antjie lowered her eyes.

'What's he asking?' demanded Breedt.

'Shush!' she said. 'I'm going to explain it all to him.' Before her father could object she looked at Smous and said, 'Her father . . . what's mean? . . . you, here.'

'Your father wanted me to stay here?'

'Ja.'

'Why?'

She grimaced at the difficulty of explaining in Yiddish, then indicated Breedt, indicated Smous, and made a pious gesture with cupped hands.

Smous hesitated. Those cupped praying hands. He remembered them in brass, rusting brass, hanging from the hood of Miller's carriage that first day in Southern Africa; a tiny ringing to herald his arrival in Cape Town; and he remembered a sense of magnificence, of loneliness, a sense of his special destiny – like the old prophets – all his dreams on the banks of the Babrungas, all his great plans. How extraordinary that Breedt should have recognised these things in him. At last it made sense: the way the Boer looked at him, touched him. The man believed in him. How extraordinary. But it was too late.

'Well anyway,' he said to Antjie, shrugging. 'I must go and get ready.'

'Her Immerman,' she said, 'her father – say – no – please.'

'Sorry, but tell him I must go, it's ridiculous, I should have been there months ago, you see, it's uh . . . and I've got responsibilities. There's all my family still back in Plungyan . . . and they're waiting, you see, uh . . . for me, and uh . . .'

'Talk slow,' she requested.

'No!' he snapped. 'No, I won't talk slow. That's why I have to go and join with my people, everything has got so slow, people talking slow to me, and me always three slow steps behind. Slow, you want slow? It's like a dream, that's how slow it's become. And I'm almost *forty*!' he shouted suddenly, as though this were her fault, '. . . I think. Anyway, a man with huge responsibilities! All these poor people back in Plungyan waiting to hear from me, and here I am going slowly, slowly, slowly! You know it's terrible if you stop to think about it –' which he now did himself, for the first time in months.

'What's he saying, what's he saying?' cried Breedt in agony.

'I don't know, he's talking too fast.' Antjie turned back to Smous. 'Please, Her Immerman – her father, ja?'

'Yes, yes,' said Smous, inching towards the door.

'He say – store – good, ja?'

'Yes, well, I've enjoyed these last few months in the store, but there we are, I still have to go, I'm –'

'Please, Her Immerman!'

'Yes. What?'

'Her father, he say – me – you.'

'Sorry?'

'Her wife. Her hand . . . what's mean? He give her hand . . .' She demonstrated with a gesture, and immediately regretted it; the scabs on that hand were lifting and weeping.

'Np!' squeaked Smous, stifling his giggle.

'Ja,' she said, lowering her head. 'Ugly, ja?'

'No, I'm sorry, I didn't mean . . . it's just, you know, giving someone's hand in marriage is such a silly way of . . . Look, I'm sorry, thank you, thank him, I'm very uh . . . it's very kind of you both, that sounds silly as well, but I must –'

'WAIT!' roared Breedt suddenly, and charged out of the room.

'What did he say?' asked Smous.

'Wait,' translated Antjie quietly.

'Well, for a minute,' said Smous, pacing round the room, resolving to fight his way out if need be, to throw himself against the shutters if need be, flooding the room with sunlight, burning her skin, anything, if need be. Marry this girl, with the horrible scabs on her dead-white body? What a ridiculous idea. Almost as ridiculous as marrying the pregnant dwarf. Now was the time to leave, now, this instant, while the dwarf was working in the kitchen on the other side of the house. He wanted no frantic dash after the cart this time. He wanted to leave without her knowing.

Breedt rushed back into the room, holding a mass of bluish pulp in his hands. 'Tell him,' he instructed his daughter angrily, 'tell him I found this book, April's book of witchcraft, in the schoolhouse after the rains. Tell him this was the book he was supposed to have burned months before. But he didn't. He gave it to the Redneck, who gave it to the boy. So tell him *he* is responsible for all of my troubles! Tell him he can't just –'

But Antjie was given no chance to translate, for Smous had recognised the remnants of the book, and exploded also:

'Tell him,' cried Smous, 'tell him it was never my business. Tell him it wasn't my business if the book got burned or if the book didn't get burned. Tell him it was never anything to do with me! But tell him also I thank him for everything he's given me and everything he's done for me, but tell him that I'm . . . no, I can tell him myself, he'll understand . . .' He turned to the Boer and spoke in English:

'Breedt – bye-bye!'

Calvinia

Because it stayed out of reach for so long, he had come to picture Calvinia as a huge and fantastic town sprawling across hillsides, the roads rising and dipping, with buildings five, six floors high, domes and flags on the roofs – like Cape Town or maybe Telz – so his first surprise this Sunday was how small it was, more like Ceres, and how flat, with only a few dusty trees and windmills lifting into the sky. The streets were deserted, everyone either asleep or at church. It was strange to see shops again, though these were all closed, and some sealed with the same rough, splintery planks as the board-walks that flanked each wide dirt road. How different it had looked when, so often in the last year, he imagined himself arriving here and visiting Lazar's house.

Now he stood staring at it from the end of the path as Swanepoel drove away behind him. He could hear church bells. The gentile Sabbath, the same day of the week when he first woke in Table Bay. He wondered if, by some miracle, that had been exactly a year ago. But surely it would have to be a much longer time than that? Or else, no time at all.

I woke under the Table Rock, he imagined telling people, and I walked to Lazar's house. Yes, they said it was in a different town, but it took no time, and the church bells were still ringing when I arrived.

He fingered the edge of his quilted maroon waistcoat, which he had been wearing that first day. His boots were the same too, but the shirt and trousers were Breedt's. He tidied a few creases, then put out his hand to open the gate. This was made of timber, as it would be in Plungyan, as was the slanting-stake fence surrounding Lazar's small plot of land. But the architecture of the house was local: roughcast whitewashed walls, corrugated iron roof, raised porch, though it lay in so much shade from two large trees, Smous could half-believe it was in Plungyan. He narrowed his eyes as he walked down the path, listening to the chickens that scurried angrily from his feet, and thought, I woke under the Table Rock and walked back into Plungyan.

He pulled open the screen door and knocked on the inner one. It will be answered, he thought, by Froi Katzeff, the Russian widow, the housekeeper who Lazar wrote about in his letter, or maybe he'll have married her by now . . .

Nobody answered the door, so he knocked again, then opened it. A smell of cinnamon. A woman's voice humming in another room. A clatter of baking tins. The front door had led straight into the dining room; the curtains were still drawn, and thin, dusty shafts of morning sunlight fell here and there, on the plum-coloured chenille over the table, on a brass fruit-bowl, on the glass in a framed picture on the wall.

Now he heard shuffling in the next room and a man wearing a nightshirt appeared in the doorway. Could this be Lazar? What had happened to God Almighty, that powerful, all-knowing figure lumbering through the streets of Plungyan? Apart from the fact that Smous had never seen him without his top hat or a turban of bath-house towels, he seemed so much smaller in every way, deflated, walking with dragging steps, his ankles swollen and yellow. His head shook, slightly, incessantly; so did his hands; and apart from his face, where the colour was crimson, his skin reminded Smous of moulding dough, grey veined with blue. Yet the massive silver beard was unmistakable, the black eyebrows, heavy ears, and the voice, rich and confident as a Russian's:

'I thought I heard someone. Why didn't the damned girl answer the door? What am I paying her for?' Lazar had spoken in Yiddish. Now he hesitated, squinted at the silhouette in his dining room, and changed to Afrikaans. 'Meneer . . . can I help . . . ha?' The way the beard swung at you as he spoke; Smous remembered flinching from it as a child, remembered touching it once and discovering how coarse and dry the hair was despite its silver sheen. This man *was* Lazar. Incredible. Lazar – standing in the same room as him.

Smous wondered what to say. When at last he decided no sound came out.

He cleared his throat several times, then said, 'It's me.'

'Is that Her Yankelow?' asked Lazar, reverting to Yiddish. 'Sorry, I can't see a thing, hold your horses, hold on . . .' He pulled open the curtains, and, shading his eyes from the flood of light, looked again. Still he shook his head. 'I'm sorry.'

'It's me,' Smous repeated. 'It's . . .' He paused, trying to remember which name Lazar knew him by.

'Zeev?' asked Lazar.

'Hello, yes, good morning.'

'Zeev. Good God. Yes, I heard from someone . . . who was it? I don't know, a friend of a friend of one of the Boers. Anyhow, this character tells me you're somewhere in the district. But how can that be? Where have you been?'

Smous stared and stared. He saw Lazar visiting their house in Plungyan, negotiating Smous in the doorway without greeting him, saw his bulk filling the kitchen, how grand he was, how frightening, saw past his mighty profile to the sweating stove and the sweating walls beyond, drops of resin oozing through the splinters. He saw Lazar leaning over his bed once when he was ill, saw past the top hat to the patch of mould on the ceiling, shaped like a beautiful cloud. Smous blinked. Lazar had asked him something and was waiting. Smous couldn't remember the question, but decided to hazard a guess. 'It's a long story,' he said slowly.

'Zeev!' murmured Lazar. 'Good God, good Lord, my God. Hm! I must . . .' He walked closer and peered at his nephew through flickering lids, while Smous balked at the coarse smell of sleep on the old man's breath. He suddenly wanted to embrace Lazar – then remembered this was not done in the family and shook hands instead. 'How have you been?' asked Lazar.

'Oh, I've . . .'

'Hold on, hold your horses, I must send for Issy, he won't believe this. Debora!' he called.

'Baas?' came the reply, and a half-caste woman arrived at another doorway, a thin naked boy clinging to her skirt. His belly was swollen, the navel like a wart, his eyelids blue and crusted. 'Debora,' said Lazar, changing to broken Afrikaans. 'Man at door. Why no go?'

'Baas, I was now cooking, making Baas's breakfast.'

'Yah, and no listen, ha? You must listen, ha?'

''s Baas.'

'This – here – Baas Zeev.'

'Baas Zeev,' said the woman to Smous, bobbing in a little curtsey.

'From far . . . from home . . . from Plungyan,' explained Lazar.

'Plungyan,' repeated the woman, grinning, and showing a large gap in her front teeth.

'Go fetch Baas Issy.'

'But – Baas's breakfast –'

'Never mind my breakfast!' said Lazar in Yiddish. 'You can eat breakfast any day of the week, but how often do you meet long-lost family? Go to Baas Issy's house, tell him to drop everything, I don't care if he's in the middle of an amputation, or a delivery, or whatever, tell him to come *now*. Go, go on – go!' he commanded, shooing her out.

'Baas,' said the woman, grinning and bobbing as she scooped up her child and hurried out of the front door.

'The girl's a troublemaker,' Lazar informed Smous. 'Why I keep her on is a mystery of Talmudic proportions. And she robs me blind. Brings all the neighbourhood urchins to feed off me. Every time I look round there's another one. Terrible diseases, of course. And who's right in the firing line? The doctors, who else? We're falling like flies, you wouldn't believe the . . .' He trailed off, absently wiping his hands on his nightshirt.

'What happened to Froi Katzeff?'

'Who?'

'Froi Katzeff. A Russian widow, I think. You wrote –'

'Oh, that one. Don't mention that name please. Another robber, a money-grubber, a bawd, a disgrace, absolutely shocking, I kicked her out. Sit down, by the way.' Smous obliged, perching nervously at the dining table. It was so long since he had talked (those slow faltering conversations with Antjie hardly counted) he couldn't think fast enough, couldn't find the right words. Or maybe he had always felt like this with Lazar's side of the family.

'Zeev, good God!' marvelled Lazar, sitting opposite him. 'You want a glass of tea or –?'

'Uh . . .'

'No, we'll wait till the troublemaker comes back, she'll organise all that. Zeev – my God, to see you again.' He took in the dusty figure with overlarge trousers, long curled fingernails, sunbaked face framed by a tangle of hair. 'You're looking well, but you could do with a beard trim and a haircut. When last did you have the pleasure?'

'Oh, uh . . .' Smous thought back to the Scuteris' visit, 'about, I don't know, nine months maybe.'

'Well, I've got a very good man, a gentleman from Riteve, matter of fact, knows Plungyan well, he'll fix you up. God, I can't get over it. We've been so mystified. Where have you been?'

'It's a long story.'

'And near Calvinia, they said, not that far away. All this time? Was there a synagogue where you were? What have you done for the Sabbath, for the festivals?'

'Uh . . .'

The old man waited, but Smous said no more, lowering his gaze and scratching tracks in the chenille. Lazar decided his nephew was still the same, still odd, so he changed the subject:

'Isn't the heat dreadful for this time of year? It's going to be another impossible summer. Were you in the area when we had those thunderstorms a few months back?'

'Yes. Wasn't it incredible?'

'Incredible's the word. A lot of families around here had their homes washed away. Who would ever have expected such calamities in the middle of the desert?'

'The desert?' Smous gave a small nervous laugh. 'That's how you described it in your letter home. You made it sound so fascinating.'

Lazar grunted. 'In letters home you can make things sound fascinating –' He stopped and frowned. 'Which letter home?'

'There was only one before I left.'

Lazar sat back and thought for a long time; then, using his professional voice, a cautious, detached tone saved for circumstances of grave illness, asked, 'Zeev – have you heard from home?'

'No . . .' replied Smous, feeling a shiver travel up his spine. 'I was going to ask you.'

'But you've written?'

'A lot,' lied Smous.

'Me too. And no replies. It's a little worrying.' He left the thought in the air and rested a compassionate but expert gaze on the other, his palsy vanishing for a moment.

'Oh, I don't know . . . is it?' said Smous eventually, shifting on his chair. 'I mean, you know what the postal service is like in Plungyan.'

'Perhaps. It's just that we've heard such terrible reports of what's going on in that part of the world – well, you must've as well. The general opinion is that we got out just in time.'

Smous wondered whether to bluff through this one, then decided it was too important. 'No, I haven't heard. What reports?'

'Oh, don't ask – unspeakable things. Things to make my own terrible tragedy all those years ago, the burning of my house, the loss of my dear wife and daughters, your dear aunt and cousins, may they rest in peace, things to put that in the shade – a dreadful utterance, please God forgive me, but it's true. Now we hear of whole towns set on fire.'

'Not in Litva!'

'In Litva, of course Litva, where would I be talking of – China?'

Smous felt his cheeks redden, and he stared down at the table covering.

Lazar hasn't changed, he decided, he's still got to blow everything out of proportion. How could you set a *whole town* on fire?

'We get sent this Yiddish newspaper,' said Lazar, gesturing towards a pile next to the armchair under the window. 'You can have a look for yourself.'

I should have guessed, thought Smous, he's got it from newspapers – fiction and politics.

'The worst thing we read,' continued Lazar slowly, 'was of this town where the authorities – the *authorities*, mind you, not just drunken peasants – they rounded up some Jews in the market square, tied their hands, then set loose some patients from a madhouse who they'd supplied with iron bars and clubs. Unbelievable. Terrible tragedy.'

Smous tried to imagine the scene. He felt sick, yet wanted to know more details, wanted to see it. 'Not in Litva,' he said eventually, in a hushed voice.

'In Litva! Why d'you keep telling me not in Litva? Why do you think we left? Why did *you* leave? "Not in Litva" – where then?'

'But not in Plungyan,' insisted Smous.

'Not in Plungyan, maybe, who knows, I haven't seen Plungyan mentioned exactly. How can we know? Why aren't your parents answering our letters?'

'The postal service?'

'Anyway,' said Lazar, feeling he'd been too brusque, 'anyway, now that you've arrived, we can investigate the matter more fully. At least you're here, thank God for that, we thought we'd lost you as well –' He hesitated, realising he was making it worse, but unable to stop, frightened of the conversation lapsing into silence. 'Anyhow, I just thought, I was just hoping, maybe you'd heard. You know, at one time I thought maybe it was me. Your father and I were never the closest of brothers. Although, you know, it's still one's blood. But if they haven't even answered *your* letters –'

'Have you got a drink?' asked Smous suddenly.

'A drink? I told you before, when the troublemaker comes back she'll –'

'No, I mean something stronger.'

'Something stronger? It's eight o'clock in the morning!' He laughed. 'Have you become a drunkard like your brother?'

'No, no,' Smous laughed also, 'doesn't matter, I just felt a bit faint when you were describing –'

'Faint? Faint I can help you with, I'll get you the hartshorn.'

'No, I'm all right now.'

'If I had some drink in the house I'd happily give it to you, but I don't keep the stuff any more.' He stroked his chest slowly and said, 'Ox heart.'

'Ah,' replied Smous, mystified.

'You want to lie down?'

'No, I'm fine.'

'You want to put your head between your knees?'

'No, thank you.'

'It's the excitement.'

'Yes.'

'After all this time.'

'Yes.'

'I'm sure they're all right, your parents,' Lazar said, glancing away, his palsy quickening.

'Yes, I'm sure.' Smous rose quickly and walked to the mantelpiece, pretending to admire a Chanukah candelabrum in silver. 'I remember this from your house in Plungyan.'

'Ha?' Lazar twisted round in his chair. 'No, I don't think so. I think a patient gave me that here.'

'It's beautiful all the same.'

Lazar grunted, then tinkled his fingernails on the brass fruit bowl. 'This is from the old house.'

'Ah yes, I remember,' lied Smous.

'And there's your late aunt and cousins, may they rest in peace . . .' Lazar pointed to a framed photograph above the mantelpiece.

'God yes,' said Smous. 'I never knew you had one.'

'Of course you did. You must've. It was the first daguerreotype made in the district,' boasted Lazar, 'and thank God. Cost a fortune, but what a way to keep a memory alive.'

'Yes,' whispered Smous, staring past the stiff figures to a glimpse of countryside beyond. He could almost smell the rūta. 'Those fields . . .'

'Ha?'

'No, I'm just thinking how much it looks like Tante Selma and –'

'Well, it's a wonderful new science, art, whatever you want to call it. And here's Issy –'

Smous scanned the wall looking for another photograph, then realised Lazar was pointing through the window to a tall figure hurrying down the path. Smous braced himself, Issy had never liked him. He wished he could escape.

Now Issy arrived in the doorway and stood beaming down at his cousin, the sunlight flashing on his pebble-glass spectacles before those huge eyes loomed into view. It was difficult to recognise Issy. He had developed jowls, a paunch, hefty thighs, and his hair was receding. Could this large, balding man once have been the plump child in greasy spectacles whom Smous had governed so mercilessly on the banks of the Babrungas? 'Zeev, where have you been, man?' Issy asked, grinning. 'How goes it?'

Smous gave a little start. Issy had spoken in Afrikaans.

'You haven't learned the language yet?' asked Issy, reverting to Yiddish as they shook hands.

'No. Not yet.'

'It's not that hard. It's not that different from German. Which is not that different from Yiddish.'

'Well, I'm sure I'll –'

'How've you been?'

'Uh . . .'

'You look a bit wild,' laughed Issy. Smous remembered that booming laugh from the Plungyan bath-house; the men lounging against the warped walls, tipping endless pails of water over the heated stones, dozing and scratching, telling their dirty stories.

'Wild is the right word,' said Lazar. 'Apparently he hasn't had a haircut for nine months. Debora!' he called into the kitchen. 'Did she come back with you? Girl's impossible.'

'Baas?' said Debora, appearing at the doorway.

'Debora,' said Lazar in Afrikaans, 'come on. Tea. Breakfast. What you make?'

'Spicy buns, Baas.'

'Come on. Hungry Baas. Baas Zeev from far.'

'Plungyan,' she grinned, to remind him she had already been told.

'Yah, come on – *come on*.'

''s Baas.' She bobbed and left.

'Plungyan,' scoffed Lazar, 'what does she know about Plungyan?'

'She pronounces it very well,' ventured Smous.

'Watch out for her. Smiles too much, she'll strangle me in my sleep one night, I'm telling you . . .' He turned and bellowed into the kitchen, 'AND – CHILD – OUT!' This caused a fit of wheezing, his face turning black. 'Who does she think I am? I'm feeding half of Calvinia here.'

'So where have you been all of this time?' Issy asked Smous.

'It's a long story,' interrupted Lazar, 'which he's saving for another occasion.' Smous blushed and stared at his boots.

'Anyway, you're looking well,' said Issy, grabbing his neck and shaking it.

'So are you,' spluttered Smous.

'Who – Issy?' said Lazar. 'Issy's looking terrible – he's looking like an old man, and what is he? He's your age, and what are you?'

'Uh . . .' Smous quickly changed the subject. 'Yes, I remember, when I first arrived here, I mean in the Cape of Good Hope, one of the first things I noticed was how well everyone looked. I couldn't work it out.'

'And then you realised it was the sun on everyone's skin,' grinned Issy. 'It was the same for us. You remember, Tatteh?'

Lazar grunted. 'I had other matters on my mind.'

'And that first sight of Table Bay,' said Issy.

'Extraordinary,' agreed Smous.

'Did you stay up all night to see it?'

'Sort of I –'

'And at the dockyards, were you met by the people from the Landmanschaft?'

'Uh, no . . .'

'No?'

'No, I was uh . . . I was met privately.'

'Privately?'

'Yes, a carriage. We'd arranged from home . . . uh . . .' He saw the disbelief on their faces, so changed the subject again, addressing his cousin: 'Anyway, so you've got a new baby, I hear.'

Issy gave a shout of laughter, 'New? The little monster turned three last week. We gave him his first haircut, put him in a basin, showered him with sweets, all the old songs, the full works. What a pity you weren't here.'

'Mmmm . . .' murmured Smous, feeling a distant yearning and covering it with a chuckle. 'Basin of sweets. Now he'll think he owns the universe.'

'How did you know about him?' demanded Lazar suddenly. 'I haven't mentioned David yet.'

'Oh, uh . . .' Smous wondered whether to talk about Antjie. He couldn't think fast enough, so said, 'Who told me? Oh, someone here, in Kulvidya.'

'Kulvidya?' echoed both men.

'Mm.'

'*Calvinia?*'

'Mm.'

'When did you arrive?' asked Issy.

'Oh, uh . . . just this morning. Anyway, congratulations.'

'Thank you. You must come and meet them all.'

'Yes, I –'

'Where are you staying? Where's all your luggage? You staying here?'

'Uh . . .'

'We'll decide, we'll decide,' said Lazar. 'Stop interrogating the poor fellow – he thinks he's been pulled in by the Russian police.'

'Oh, don't be ridiculous,' snapped Issy. 'I'm delighted to see him, he knows that.'

'All right, all right, we're all delighted, specially since here comes Debora with our tea at long last, God only knows where she's been, growing the lemons while we wait, but anyway – Debora, come, quick, give Baas Zeev tea. He's from far –'

'Plungyan,' she chirped from behind her loaded tray.

'Where's the samovar?'

'Baas?'

'Ha? Samovar! *Sa-mo-var*! Tsssssh, I've only told her a million times,' he complained to the others, 'but she will not get it into her head you bring the samovar. Look at this, can you believe it? She's poured out three glasses, so every time we want a refill we've got to fetch from . . . *Where you go now?*' he demanded, as Debora started to turn, the tray still in her hands.

'Baas? To get the thing, how you call it, the Sammie's-vase.'

'But put down what you've brought *first* for God's sake!' cried Lazar, forgetting to speak Afrikaans. 'There's a man here who's travelled all the way from Plungyan and you won't give him a glass of tea! Put it down, *down* – then go fetch the samovar!' He turned to Smous. 'Can you believe this?'

'It's all right,' he started to say, 'I'm not really –'

'No!' shouted Lazar suddenly, noticing the little naked boy behind Debora. 'No, child, no! Child out!'

'But Baas, Baas,' protested Debora, setting the tray on the table. 'Sorry, my Baas, but he's sick today, Baas, I must look after him today, Baas. This is my youngest, Baas. Other days I can leave him, Baas, my daughter can look after him. She's a good girl to me, Baas, but today she's –'

'I don't care!' snapped Lazar in Yiddish. 'I'm not interested. I am not, not, *not* running a home here for your whole family, if this *is* your family. I've told you this before.' Lazar caught sight of the boy's dazed, starving face and hesitated, then lifted his arms angrily and shielded his eyes. 'Get him out. Out!'

'Go!' Debora shouted hoarsely at her son, clapping her hands. 'Shoo!

V'ts'k!' The boy turned and with slow faltering steps retreated to the hallway where he waited, propping himself against one wall.

'Every malady and contagion you can imagine,' muttered Lazar, wiping his hands on his nightshirt with a hard urgent rhythm, 'typhoid fever, malignant cholera, every kind of enteric infection, smallpox, you wouldn't believe what we're seeing here, Zeev, what with the war and . . . I hope you're careful, I hope you're sterilising everything, terrible pestilence.' Smous frowned, puzzled, remembering Lazar's dirty, cluttered bag and stained frock-coat. Now all were silent as Debora served the tea, warm cinnamon buns and fresh butter. Grateful for the break in conversation, Smous sat with downcast eyes, pretending not to notice Lazar's difficulty in drinking. The palsy was so bad he had to lower his face to the glass, making it clatter against the table, tea splashing over his beard and hands. Smous glanced at Issy. He paid no attention; he had seen it too often, at every mealtime.

How extraordinary, Smous thought, to be back among the family. The colour of their lips, the shape of their fingernails, the hair on their wrists, their smell, everything so familiar. And yet not. Like in dreams. And how extraordinary they should greet him so warmly, show him so much hospitality when they'd always disliked him, always thought him a fool. Yet nevertheless he was the family fool, and so welcomed. Extraordinary. Family. What did it mean?

'And get samovar!' commanded Lazar as Debora hurried from the room.

Now Issy turned to Smous and, adopting the same detached, professional tone his father had used earlier, asked, 'Have you heard from home?'

'No, he hasn't,' answered Lazar quickly.

'I'm asking him.'

'Well, he hasn't.'

'So, I'm asking.'

'Look,' growled Lazar, crumbs and butter flying from his shuddering hands, 'he hasn't heard. He's written like we have and hasn't heard a thing.'

'So what are you jumping down my throat for?'

'You keep interrogating him.'

'Of course I keep interrogating him. I'm delighted to see him again after, what is it – three, four years? I'm sorry you haven't heard from home,' he said, turning back to Smous. 'When did you last write?'

'Again with the interrogation,' complained Lazar.

'What *is* the matter with you this morning?'

'He doesn't want to talk about it. Stop it. You're upsetting him, you're banging in his head, you're making him weep.'

'No, no,' said Smous, through a mouthful of cinnamon bun. 'It's just the taste of this. I haven't . . . since . . .' He lowered his head, so that the others shouldn't see his tears.

'Have you got any drink in your house?' Lazar asked his son quietly.

'Drink?' said Issy.

'No, it's all right . . .' mumbled Smous.

'I may have some brandy.'

'No, thank you, it's all right.'

'Drink?' repeated Issy in amazement.

'It's all right, he doesn't want,' said Lazar.

'Drink – at eight o'clock in the morning?'

'He doesn't want!'

'So, who mentioned it? Did I mention it? Who mentioned drink?'

'You see what I have to put up with,' said Lazar, leaning across the table to Smous.

'Oh please!' protested Issy, 'you think he wants to hear you moaning? You think that's a cheerful noise to welcome a man back to his family? Believe me, he'd rather be interrogated by me.' He turned to Smous, 'So, how're you enjoying the country?'

'It's . . . it's quite strange.'

'Strange is the word,' agreed Lazar. 'I'm not staying.'

'He's not staying!' scoffed Issy.

'I've applied for America again.'

'He's applied for America!'

'You've applied for America?' asked Smous in astonishment.

'Certainly. This place is a madhouse. Worse than home. It's like jumping from the pan into the fire. Not me, I'm getting out, I'm going to America.'

'You'd move? You'd go through it all again?'

'What's there to go through? You stand up, you climb on a boat, you float across the world, you climb off the boat, you sit down again. What's the big fuss?'

'It wasn't quite like that for me,' said Smous, then looked away as both men raised their eyebrows, eager to hear his story.

'So anyway,' said Lazar, when it was clear that Smous was retreating into silence again, 'so, don't you agree this place is a madhouse?'

'It's a fine country,' interrupted Issy, 'there are changes to be made, things to be done, but the basics are fine. More than fine. A land of milk and honey. A beautiful young country. A chance for us to take responsibility for once. Shape it our way.'

'A madhouse,' said Lazar. 'Zeev agrees with me.'

'I . . .' said Smous.

'You called it strange,' said Lazar, warning him not to side with Issy, 'and strange it is. What's the point of going from one country full of violence to another? Now I want to be some place where there's no fight. America – the new world, the place where they respect the human species.'

Smous sighed. He couldn't believe it. Here he was, listening to another of those tedious political discussions Lazar's side of the family has always enjoyed. They might be on the other side of the world, but nothing had changed. He noticed Lazar looking in his direction as he talked and struggled to concentrate, fearing they might question him.

'And when you grow up in places like this,' Lazar was saying, 'like here and Litva, you're growing up with a diseased brain. Our fire, our own fire. For years I couldn't tell the story of our fire without changing it from an accident to murder, may God forgive me . . .'

Smous glanced away, remembering that famous row: 'Cossacks! Goose-fat! Cossacks! Goose-fat!' So, the great mystery solved at last.

'What does it matter?' Issy asked his father, smiling coldly. 'One day I had a mother and two sisters, the next day – *Zetz!* – all gone. Accident or murder, who cares? I didn't at the time. I –' He shrugged and stopped speaking. There was an expression on his face which Smous recognised from childhood, the expression he used to call 'Issy's Face', with half-open mouth, a small popping noise in his throat, and his enormous eyes disappearing behind the pebble-glass. Suddenly he seemed a weaker, gentler man. You could even glimpse the plump boy in bigger, clumsy, greasy spectacles; the boy who had watched his mother and sisters burn to death, the boy who had seen visions of their world ending. 'Anyway,' Issy said, his eyes huge and flashing again, 'it's old history. The point is we, all three of us in this room, we escaped without a scratch, but –'

'That's what you think!' exclaimed Lazar and, in an instant, they were shouting at one another.

Escaped without a scratch? Smous wondered whether to tell them

about the Russian soldier spitting on his beard. No. He wouldn't be able
to explain how shocking it was; he didn't understand it himself, why he felt
ashamed whenever he thought of it, ashamed that it haunted him. It was
so insignificant compared to what they were describing: people burning to
death, whole towns burning, lunatics beating out your brains in the
market place. He shifted in his seat, wishing he could leave.

'. . . and not just the pogroms, my God!' Lazar was saying. 'You
would see it coming in a hundred different ways. It was coming like
that storm here last summer, you could see this great black cloud
coming, and would they believe me, my own brother, would he
believe me?'

'Yes,' interrupted Smous, despite himself, 'that's why he sent me.'

'Well, he sent you to the wrong place,' snapped Lazar. 'He sent you to a
place where it's going to happen all over again. Where it already has, and
it's not going to go away, believe me, it's going to get worse. A madhouse,
isn't that what you called it?'

'No . . . I called it strange.'

'And you think a madhouse isn't a bit strange? You've been in a
madhouse?'

'No.'

'No, I'm a doctor, so don't tell me about madhouses.'

'If you could hear yourself arguing,' interrupted Issy. 'You argue like a
child. Or an old woman.'

'He agrees with me,' said Lazar, sitting back heavily and pointing to
Smous.

'He just disagreed with you.'

'He didn't.'

'He did!'

'No.'

'Good God,' cried Issy, and swung towards Smous, 'will you please tell
him?'

'Tell him what?' asked Smous cautiously.

'Whose side you're on. Where you stand on this issue.'

'Uh . . . Which uh . . . ?'

'That this country has got the same problems as home. What have your
experiences been?'

'Uh . . .' Smous felt like screaming. 'Well . . . I suppose, yes, I have
seen some persecution. But then again, they're only savages.'

'Thank you. Point proved,' said Lazar. 'Only savages – that's what the

Russians say about us. We burn their babies, eat their children, drink their blood at Pesach, nail up their prophets . . .'

'Well, I wouldn't call these people savages,' said Issy hotly, 'just because they're not as civilised as we are. Good God, it's their country – they were here first!'

'You don't have to persuade me,' said Lazar, 'I think they're a wonderful people. I just don't want to be around when they get their heads knocked in.'

'Why d'you call them savages?' demanded Issy, rounding on Smous, 'it seems such a cruel word to use.'

'But . . .' Smous spluttered, 'but they *are* . . .'

'Well, I'm sorry if that's been your experience, but I know some of them personally. Do you know any of them personally?'

'Well, yes . . .' replied Smous, his mind filling with the sight of Naoksa's pregnant belly.

'And do you find them savage when you get to know them?'

'Uh . . . no, not really. A bit primitive sometimes –' He hesitated as Issy's huge glare darkened. 'I was . . . uh . . . I was only using the word "savages" like everybody uses it.'

'But everybody doesn't use it! Their persecutors use it. I won't use it. Good God, we're talking about a people who have a covenant with the Lord not dissimilar to our own.'

'A covenant?' Smous paused for a long time, frowning, then summoned his courage and asked, 'Who are you talking about?'

'What do you mean who am I talking about? Who have we all been talking about for the last half hour? We're talking about the people persecuted and subjugated in their own country. We're talking about the Boers. Why, who are you talking about?'

'Uh . . .' Smous felt himself turning red. 'I was talking about the savages.'

'The savages?' said Lazar.

'The savages?' said Issy and then exploded into laughter. 'Oh, the *savages*!'

'What a mix-up,' said Lazar, laughing also, 'here we're talking about the persecution of Boers, and he's talking about the persecution of savages!'

'Good God!' said Issy, his grin suddenly vanishing, 'you mean you thought I was praising the savages? How can you even use a word like persecution about them? Do we not say to the Lord at Pesach – "Pour out Thy Wrath upon the nations that know Thee not?"'

At this moment Debora reappeared carrying a small brass samovar. 'Oh, *that's* from home, surely!' exclaimed Smous, eager for a change of subject, then bit his lip. Once again the naked child was staggering into the room after its mother.

'Debora!' Lazar cautioned in a low growl.

'Sammie's-vase, my Baas, yah?' grinned Debora, unaware of the child behind her.

'Debora, what I tell you?'

She swung round. 'Ai! Ag, my Baas, I tell him to go, he won't listen, my Baas. *V'ts'k*! *Go*! *Shoo*!' The boy remained where he was, gazing at the men with clouded eyes. Wailing in frustration, Debora swung the samovar at him. It narrowly missed, catching only a brief reflection of his staring face in the pinkish gleam – then, as the weight rocked back, the lid fell open, slopping scalding tea over his shoulder. Except for an instant, when his eyes focused strangely, almost in anger, the child didn't react, but stood wavering listlessly as before. Smous felt a familiar hateful relish pass through him, while Debora froze with shock and Lazar put his head in his hands.

'Or,' said Issy eventually in a measured tone, 'if you prefer to take a more scientific view of these things, I would suggest that you can't use a word like persecution about the savages because they don't feel pain like we do. When it does not contain a soul, living flesh is not as susceptible to feeling. As we can see –' He pointed to the child. The skin on his shoulder was lifting into a huge bubble, but the boy remained placid and staring.

'But . . . isn't that because he's sick?' asked Smous, flushed and confused, wishing someone would take the child away. 'Isn't he starving or –?'

'Not at all!' snapped Issy, his harsh tone reminding Smous he was talking to experts, 'their natural build makes them look –'

'Of course he's starving,' said Lazar, lowering his shaking hands. 'Half the savages in Calvinia are starving. And not just the savages. Where have you been? We've had a war, a terrible drought, people are poor. So? What am *I* supposed to do about it?' Lazar rested his flickering gaze on Smous until he was forced to look away, and sat fingering the tassels of the table covering. 'Yes, my boy, my boy . . .' muttered Lazar, then turned to Debora. 'Go fetch the carded cotton and chalk ointment from my –'

'Oh, don't give her –' Issy began to say and Lazar nodded immediately, remembering supplies were difficult to get.

'Here,' he said, pushing the butter dish towards Debora. 'Go put this on boy.'

'Tatteh!' whispered Issy. 'That's gorgeous fresh butter.'

Lazar sighed impatiently but retrieved the butter dish. 'Debora – potato. Ha? *Potato*. Take potato –' he mimed scraping a potato onto the boy's shoulder, 'and then a little flour, so –' he mimed sprinkling flour over the wound. 'He'll be all right. Go, go – go!'

Debora scooped up the boy and hurried out, while Issy gave a despairing laugh and told the ceiling, 'Now they'll steal half his potatoes and flour.' Lazar sat silently, staring round the sunny room, a faraway look in his eyes, his head moving from side to side as if saying no, as he wiped his palms on his nightshirt again and again. Issy turned to Smous, who tensed.

'Persecution?' said Issy. 'What the Boers have endured. You weren't in the country during the war. We were. Atrocities you wouldn't believe. The English are, I think, the most refined barbarians on God's earth. And still it goes on. Until recently, here, in Calvinia, in the Boers' own church, they were being forced to pray under a Scottish minister! Can you imagine? It would be like going to the synagogue back home and finding one of the Dolroguskys with the Torah on his shoulder and a sneer on his face, singing the Blessing. The insult! So –'

'Oh, what does it matter?' asked Lazar quietly. 'You think it matters what we sit here saying? This and that, so on and so forth. Men think and God laughs. Plungyan, Litva, it was all contaminated, the air was. You can tell, it's dying now. And we say we escaped it. Without a scratch. Where from? The lunatics never smashed in our heads, so what? They didn't need to. Our brains were damaged already. At birth. Not just us neither, persecution contaminates both sides. The Russians too, they're contaminated too, the lot of them, right to the top, the Tsar of all the Russias. It's very sad. Very, very sad. We don't need to say any more. No point. The ramblings of sick brains. We must just go to America, all of us, as soon as possible, see if maybe they can cure us there . . '

He trailed off and the room went quiet. Smous was staring at the floor while Issy glared at his father. The silence seemed as though it would continue forever, when Issy suddenly cleared his throat and touched Smous's arm. 'You know,' he said cheerfully, 'I was thinking when I was running over here this morning – our games. You remember?'

'What?' muttered Smous.

'When we were children, those games we played.' Smous managed a nostalgic grunt. 'You do remember!' cried Issy, then turned to his father, ignoring the small puffing, sniffing noises he was making. 'When we played these games he always had to be the hero. I had to be the no-gooders, the wicked Pharaoh and so on, or the victims, Isaac about to be slaughtered and so on. But *you* . . .' He gave his booming laugh and grabbed Smous's neck again, shaking it. 'You had to be the hero. Except in one game – the Story of Jonah.'

'Why, what were you in that one?' Lazar asked, trying to join in, 'the whale?'

'Ah, no. That was my favourite game, because there I was God. So I made him play it again and again.'

'No,' said Smous, wishing Issy would let go of his neck and that Lazar would clean the slime hanging from his nose, 'no, no, we only played it once.'

'He's forgotten,' laughed Issy, 'because I was God, the hero's forgotten. We played it many times.'

'No. We couldn't have. The water-mill had collapsed next time we got there.'

'The what?'

'The water-mill. Don't you remember? An old water-mill . . . We made it into the Great Fish, but by the time we came back the next day –'

'We played it *many* times,' said Issy emphatically.

'Well. Maybe,' conceded Smous, disengaging his neck from Issy's clutch, and rising. 'Excuse me, must go to your uh . . .'

'Through the kitchen,' said Lazar. 'Ask the girl to show you.'

Smous made his way into the kitchen where Debora was leaning on the window-sill, humming, her face pressed to the sunlit glass. She jumped with fright as he entered, then began to bob and grin, saying, 'Baas – Plungyan – Baas – Plungyan.'

'Plungyan,' confirmed Smous, glancing round. There was a hefty steam autoclave in one corner, used for sterilising instruments, and, for a moment, he wondered if she had hidden her child in it, for the boy was nowhere to be seen. Spotting the outhouse in the backyard, Smous hurried down the steps, sniffing the hot morning air and the smell of eucalyptus from the bluegums. He chased a chicken out of the small shack and stood above the bucket listening to his tinkling sound, while his eyes roamed around cobwebs in the corners, and a pile of Yiddish newspapers on a wooden box.

Newspapers, root of all evil, he thought, echoing his father. Then he closed his eyes, trying not to think what might have happened to his family back in Plungyan. Did Lazar and Issy know more than they were telling him? They seemed so very pessimistic. And mad. Both of them. Completely mad. As soon as Mama and Papa arrive here, he thought, I must tell them how . . . 'Ah!' he said aloud, *would* they be arriving here now? He clucked his tongue in fear and anger. The problem was huge, real, deadly serious. It was going to intrude, change everything, fill his life. 'Don't even think,' he whispered.

Smous went back into the dining room. 'All well?' asked Issy, rising. Lazar was weeping again.

'Look,' said Issy, 'my father wants to get washed and dressed, why don't we go round to my house, meet Nava and the children, and then later we'll all meet up for lunch and you can tell us your news.'

'Fine,' said Smous, 'but don't you have to work? I don't want to be any –'

'It's Sunday.'

'Oh yes.'

'They take Sundays very seriously around here,' said Issy, tugging Smous's arm, 'come.'

'I'll stroll round when I'm –' Lazar started to say, but his voice broke and Issy quickly dragged Smous out through the door.

On the road, Smous closed one eye against the glare and squinted at his surroundings. In the house it felt like being back in Plungyan, in the yard the smell of the bluegums reminded him of Middlepost; now he didn't know where he was. The street was deserted, wide and dusty, each of the surrounding houses isolated on its own plot of land, with other vacant plots in between, giving the town an empty, almost transparent look. You could see straight through to the slopes of hills beyond, where there were small orchards and dry yellow grassfields.

'You mustn't take any notice of my father,' said Issy as they walked. 'He's been very ill recently.' He stroked his chest. 'Ox heart.'

'Ah,' said Smous, frowning.

'How did you think he was looking?'

'Well –'

'He's lost some weight of course.'

'Yes, I –'

'It's a shame. He still looks good when he puts on the hat and the frock-coat, you know, but he gets these depressions, starts talking nonsense. America! He'll never go to America.'

'No, I don't –'

'Still, who knows? If someone had told us thirty years ago we'd be walking down this street now, would we have believed them?'

'No. God, no.'

'It is good to see you again,' said Issy, stopping and beaming down at Smous.

'Thank you. It's good to see you.'

'All those years ago.'

'Yes.'

'Our childhood.'

'On the banks of the Babrungas.'

'You remember it all?'

'Do I remember!' laughed Smous, and, glancing up at the pebble-glass spectacles, felt a sudden warmth for Issy, almost pity. 'I saw a Great Fish, you know, a real one, and my first thought was: I must tell Issy. And here I am telling you. At last! Isn't it incredible? From the deck of the ship I saw it. The most –'

'You saw what?'

'A Great Fish.'

'A whale?'

'Yes. It was the most –'

'Funny you should forget how often we played that game.'

'No, we only played it once.'

'Never!' laughed Issy harshly. 'You've forgotten.'

'Anyway, it's not important. But to actually see a Great –'

'You know what I've always wanted to ask you,' interrupted Issy. 'Why Jonah?'

'Sorry?'

'Why was he such a hero? Of all the biblical figures.'

'He wasn't.'

'Then why did we play that game again and again?'

'We didn't.'

'You've forgotten. Why Jonah? Because, with due respect, he's so unlike you. He's such a rebel. He's telling God off, and he's carrying on all the time, and he's such an adventurer. One minute he's running here, the next minute he's sailing there, now he's in the belly of a whale, now he's burning to death in the sun. He's always so angry and fighting. And you've always been so easy-going, so content to let things be. Where was the connection?'

'There wasn't. There isn't.' Smous felt himself blushing and tried to smile. 'Why does there have to be a connection? Can't we leave it as a mystery? Like language sounds before you learn it. Like music. It makes no sense, yet it does. The Great Fish, not Jonah. I've met Jonahs, I know Jonahs.'

Issy gave a little despairing laugh and led down a tree-lined road. An English farmer passed in a mule cart. On the back, a Hottentot boy was propped on the mealie sacks like a guard dog.

'So . . .' said Issy lazily. 'What work have you been doing?'

'Storekeeper,' replied Smous proudly; at last a subject he could discuss.

'Business? Huh-uh – can't see you in business!'

'No, well, I've –'

'And a family?'

'No. Not yet.'

'Girlfriends?'

'Oh yes.'

'Jewish?'

'Uh –'

'Not always,' grinned Issy.

'Not always,' Smous laughed nervously, 'but always Jewish copulation.'

'What's Jewish copulation?'

Smous chewed his moustache. 'You must know,' he said after a while, 'you're a doctor.'

'Never heard of it. How's it done? Always keen to learn new methods. What is it?'

'You kno-o-ow,' said Smous, grimacing, 'you must know.'

'I don't! Tell me. We're grown men, for God's sake.'

'Jewish copulation, the Dolrogusky servants were always –'

'The Dolrogusky servants? God help us, it'll be something wicked, something depraved, something perverted, I dread to think.'

Smous gulped. If only he could talk openly to Issy.

'Still . . .' said Issy. 'Does it work?'

Smous wondered what he meant by 'work', but was determined to show no further stupidity. He gave his version of a vulgar laugh and said, 'Certainly it works.'

'Then who's complaining?'

'No one.' They walked in silence. Then Smous took a deep breath and said, 'Just as a matter of interest, how long is it between conception and birth?'

Issy stopped and stared down at Smous, studying the grey in his hair and beard. 'You don't know?'

'Yes, I do,' Smous retorted. 'Of course I do, I was just –' He couldn't think what to say, so put his head back and studied the bluegum they were under, trying to look knowledgeable about trees. Finally, unable to bear Issy's dumbfounded scrutiny, he muttered, 'It's a year.'

Issy sighed. 'Zeev, is there some girl you've got in trouble?'

'No! Good God, no,' he laughed, and then added quickly, 'That's the beauty of Jewish copulation!'

'It's nine months.'

'Nine months. That's what I said.'

'You said a year.'

'No, no, I meant nine months. Like my last haircut. Must be about nine months ago. Some Italians came . . .'

'Italians?'

'Mm.'

'Where?'

'When? Nine months ago. So that must have been, ohhhh . . . let's see, it's about March now, so let's say –'

'March?' Issy was frowning darkly. 'Zeev, you don't know what month we're in?'

''Course I do. Give or take a –'

'Zeev, it was Yom Kippur three days ago. Where have you been? It's October. The seventh of October, nineteen hundred and four.'

'October.' He laughed. 'No, no, can't be. You can feel spring's coming. The nights are –'

'Zeev, it is spring and it *is* October. You're in the Southern Hemisphere.'

Smous hesitated. He remembered someone explaining this to him on board the ship; that strange voyage when, in three weeks, the year turned from winter to summer, and the world upside down. October not March. So that explained it, why everything felt so slow. He'd lost a lot of time somewhere. Issy was staring at him again, waiting for an explanation.

'October, hm? Well, if you say so.' Smous gave a little laugh. 'I haven't been doing much talking, so you sort of lose track of –'

'You haven't been doing much talking?'

'Hardly a word. In about two years. At least I think it's two years. Give or take. Probably wrong about that as well. Maybe it's five, ten, one.'

Issy began to wonder if it was a good idea to take his cousin home.

'My God, look at this,' exclaimed Smous, 'nobody seems to live here at all.' They had turned into a road where the houses were either boarded up or in ruins, the gardens devastated by the storm the previous year and never repaired, now tangles of scorched grey-and-yellow grasses.

'Mmm . . .' said Issy, his mind elsewhere, 'this was a Boer district. Killed in the war, I suppose.'

Ahead, on the left, a man was lying in the gutter. As they drew closer, Smous began to frown. His trousers were half off, his buttocks sticking into the air, everything about him utterly still. The position was peculiar, as though he had fallen on all fours, then twisted his shoulders and neck round to gaze at the sky. His eyes, thick as syrup, with a dull bluish light, were still fixed there. Remembering what Lazar had said about diseases, Smous edged away, but Issy stopped over the body.

'It's a disgrace!' he said tutting and glaring round the road. 'There's a shebeen in one of these houses.'

'A what?'

'Drinking-place. Home-brew stuff, well, anything, they'd drink one another's urine if the alcohol wasn't so diluted. Just look at that –' He nudged one foot towards a huge shard of green glass which, Smous now realised, was holding the figure in his peculiar pose, lodged between his guts and the soaking road beneath.

'You seen one before?' asked Issy.

'A dead body? Well, yes, you remember in Plungyan a man called Glown, the travelling sign-wri –'

Issy laughed. 'No, I mean a Bushman. Have you seen a Bushman before?' Smous looked down at the man and recognised the yellowish complexion and diamond-shaped face. So that's what Golda was, a Bushman. 'From north of here,' Issy continued, 'near the Orange River. Bushmanland. Now you don't get more primitive than Bushman, you don't get more *savage* than them.' He winked at Smous, reminding him of their earlier discussion. 'Very stunted people, mentally and physically. Can always tell them by the huge arse –' He nodded towards the jutting globes of flesh where the man's trousers had slipped down. Suddenly Issy laughed. 'That was very funny, when I said "Have you seen one before?" and you answered, "A dead body?"'

'Yes, well, I thought you meant –'

'Matter of fact, you won't see one deader than this. They don't believe in an afterlife, the Bushman. Or resurrection. Something about a message that went wrong between a . . . hare and a tortoise, I don't know, I can't remember the details, a message from the moon or some such thing, can't remember, anyway they believe when you're dead, you're dead. So . . .' Smous glanced away, wondering why the story sounded familiar. 'So anyway, nothing to be done,' said Issy. 'We know he's dead, he knows he's dead, everyone's in agreement. Come.'

Smous didn't move. 'Do we?'

'Do we what?'

'Believe in resurrection.'

Issy sighed impatiently, as though Smous should know for himself, then hesitated, scratching his heavy stomach. 'The Talmud isn't exactly clear. Different scholars say different things at different times. Judah the Prince thinks yes, Chiyya thinks no, Maimonides is a little vague, and so on. There's never been any evidence of resurrection – if Jesus Christ will pardon me saying so – therefore, I suppose, we're waiting to see which way the wind blows. Ach, I'm not even sure I believe in an afterlife. Whenever I've tended the dying I've found it so straightforward. You see very clearly that people just become flesh, bones, dust. Difficult to believe anything else is going to happen. I mean, where is this afterlife? Where are my mother and my sisters?' He snatched at the air playfully. 'No, I don't believe anybody is there. Perhaps I'm a Bushman.'

Smous echoed Issy's chuckle, though he was puzzled. Hadn't his cousin condemned the savages because they didn't possess a soul? What was your soul if not that fraction of yourself which would survive death?

'In Litva . . . in heathen times,' said Smous slowly, 'when you died they burned the paw of a bear or a lynx with your body because there were going to be such hard fights ahead on the road to Paradise, and such steep mountains to climb. It still sort of goes on. When the old peasants feel death coming they start growing their fingernails.'

Issy inclined his head and considered Smous through narrowed lids, surprised he should know such things, yet unwilling to appear impressed. Smous folded his hands behind him, closing the palms over his overgrown, curled fingernails.

'It's funny,' he continued, 'Paradise was always out of reach for the ancient Litvaks. In another story they say it's beyond the forests. There's this beautiful sunny plain where animals live, an animal kingdom, where no man has ever reached. And you know what? When I first landed on these shores I straightaway realised it was Africa they were talking about. You know, the sun and the animals. It's Africa, that's all it is. They never found out because in the legends no one ever makes it through the forest to this wonderful Paradise. Yet here we are. And funniest of all, it's what today's Litvaks fear most. That the Jews will chop down all the trees and get to Paradise first. And we have. I think that's funny, don't you?'

Issy cleared his throat. 'How come you know such stories?'

'Hm? From my father. When he toured the villages, when you didn't have to have all the special permits. He speaks Litvak quite –'

'He taught you Litvak legends?'

'Why not? They're marvellous legends, perhaps better than the Bible. And anyway, we're Litvaks. It's where we were born.' He reddened as Issy began to laugh. 'Oh suddenly we were never Litvaks,' Smous cried, startled by his own temper, 'just because we had to leave? And now, when we're welcomed here with open arms, will we not become Southern Africans either?'

'Mm,' grunted Issy in a way that suggested the conversation was becoming tedious. 'Come, we must get on.'

'Uhm . . .' Smous gestured vaguely at the Bushman's trousers, 'shouldn't we at least –' but Issy was already out of earshot. Smous glanced round the deserted road with its ruined houses and dried gardens.

Kulvidya was very strange.

'Uhm, look –' he said, catching up with Issy, then did a little sideways dance on the road to avoid a trail of horse dung.

'This is our road,' announced Issy meanwhile, turning the next corner. 'Over there's our –'

Smous hung back. 'Uh . . . look, I just need to . . . I'll just take a little walk on my own first, if that's all right. It's all been a bit overwhelming this morning.'

'Right,' said Issy, too quickly.

Go on, thought Smous, go and run home and tell your family how pathetic I am, how I haven't changed, what a disaster your cousin is, the little family fool.

'Don't get lost,' said Issy with a chuckle, 'now that we've just found you again.'

'No, don't worry, I'll –'

'Let me write out our address for you. Then, when you've had your walk you'll know where to find us.' He drew a piece of paper and pencil from his pocket, and used Smous's back to write on, glancing again at the grey in his cousin's hair and the dust on his neck. 'It's really good to see you again,' he said cheerfully.

'And you,' said Smous, 'and you.' He took the paper. 'Thank you. I won't be long.'

'It's really, really good.'

'Yes. Thank you. I'll see you in a moment.'

Smous hurried away from Issy, turned into another hot, deserted street, and broke into a run, panting with anger.

The worst thing, he thought, the worst was when he asked me what I did, and I said storekeeper, and he went, Huh-uh, can't see you in business. Why didn't I tell him, why didn't I say I've become good at that? Instead I almost agreed with him, almost said, No, it's true, I'm a disaster in business as well. My God, what appalling people my family are.

He fixed his eyes on the ground. What had happened to his people in Plungyan? He remembered those dreams over the last few months: of the charred, cold town, and his maimed parents, then flicked his head to drive the thoughts away and glanced round. Where was he? All the roads looked the same. Rows of whitewashed houses, many with curled Dutch gables, and avenues of dusty trees. Can you believe it, he thought, Issy was even right about this – I'm lost already!

He began to run again, then, turning the next corner, came to a sudden halt. It was the street of ruined, empty houses. He must have run in a circle. The Bushman still lay twisted in the gutter, half-naked buttocks in the air, thick syrupy gaze fixed on the sky, exactly as they had left him, except that a skeletal dog had begun to feed on one bare foot. Smous walked closer. The dog swung round and snarled, snout black with blood, paws gripped on its precious meal. Smous stood still and the dog returned to the Bushman's leg, guzzling wildly, choking now and then from the excess of it. Smous watched, fascinated, and listened. How silent this town was. He could hear doves, a goat bleating, someone hammering in their backyard, but these were far in the distance, almost echoing. Here the only sounds came from the feasting dog and the insects collecting over the Bushman's body. A procession of ants had reached one open eye and swarmed over it, reminding Smous of the sand coating Gommie's eyeballs that first night in the Cape of Good Hope. Why was Gommie always coming to mind these days? Klippie's whitewashed face had looked like him also. Smous had a sudden, clear picture of Gommie dancing on the beach in the dimming evening light, showing teeth shaped like the mountains of Table Bay, dancing and laughing. Presumably *he* believed in resurrection, in a second chance. Smous blinked. A second chance, a new life – this is what he had set out to find for his family. Was it too late? Were they lying in a gutter somewhere, like this Bushman, their brains smashed in by lunatics?

He flicked his head sharply again and again, snorting and growling under his breath, 'No, please, I don't want to know – I don't want to.' But it was no good. I must go back to Plungyan, Smous decided, and then, I can't go back to Plungyan. Lazar and Issy will help sort it out. But I can't go back to them either, I don't want to see them again. They're mad. What was Lazar saying? God knows. That we mustn't stay here? Where else am I to go? America. But why? I can't go to America, I can't set off on *another* journey. I can't go back, I can't go forward, I can't stay here.

He gave a little laugh. This was Kulvidya, the place he had so wanted to reach, battled and suffered to reach – and now he didn't want to be here. He sank onto his haunches, leaning against a tree. The ground at his feet was littered with tiny, hard berries. It was a pepper tree, like those at Middlepost.

'Get up!' he suddenly said to the corpse in the gutter, frightening the dog who snarled viciously. 'Get up and make everything all right again.' Smous went cold as the Bushman responded with a nod, but it was only the dog returning to its meal.

Now Smous became aware of ringing bells, the noise of a crowd, wagons and carriages, animals puffing and stamping. He rose to his feet and walked to the corner. In the next road stood a church with the congregation pouring into the sunshine and clambering onto their vehicles. He recognised several figures from Middlepost. Knowing to avoid Swanepoel, Smous hurried instead towards the large, comfortable figure of Naude, the blacksmith and saddle-maker.

The Savage

Breedt was amazed to see him again. Peeping through her shutters, Antjie was amazed to see him again. Everyone was amazed to see him again. But more amazing than his return was his new mood. He kept to himself, stayed away from the store, ate alone in his room, refused to visit Antjie. His attention was on Naoksa, always alongside as she waddled around the settlement continuing her duties till the last moment. His eye never left her, his look protective, yet stern. At night he slept outside her hut (the stone igloo where the ostrich had been caged) and then, as he sensed her time growing nearer, he stayed awake, hunched over a fire, a pot of coffee bubbling throughout the night, his gaze fixed on the black doorway, waiting for any sign or sound that it was beginning.

Through the lack of sleep, the endless cups of coffee, the hours of slowly tracking her movements, he no longer needed to flick his head to banish fears of what was happening in Plungyan or decisions about the future; his consciousness alighted on each present moment, dying as it passed, renewing itself on the next, as though he were crossing a stream with each stepping stone miraculously appearing only when the previous one had dissolved in the water behind him. As in a dream he observed her customs of preparation: a sudden refusal to take sugar on her mealie porridge or in tea, her diligent removal of all fat from meat, her anxiety that no one should pass behind her back, the ritual of smearing herself with soot from any pot before it was placed on the fire.

It happened early one afternoon.

Naoksa was in the kitchen polishing the floor, and Smous was seated outside the door watching two small grey mossies swooping back and forth across the yard with scraps of wool, building a nest under the eaves. His stare had become grimmer as their home took shape. Suddenly Naoksa hurried from the kitchen and into the gardens, Marie and Fleurjie following to the doorway, but making no attempt to stop her. Smous gave a long, heavy sigh, then rose. By the time he reached her hut, she was already setting off across the veld with a stick and her buckskin kaross slung across one shoulder.

It was a hot, windy spring day, with thin clouds casting their travelling shadows across the land, making rocks and bushes leap forward with white edges and black shadows, while, in the distance, the hills beat like a pulse. Naoksa walked with increasing difficulty, yet never slowed her pace, using the stick for support. She grew more and more agitated by Smous's presence – until finally, as they drew close to a shallow ravine of rocks, she uprooted a tuft of veld grass and placed it upside-down in the branches of a thorn tree, glaring at him. He understood and proceeded no further. But as soon as she descended into the ravine, he charged downwind to the opposite side and crawled towards the ridge.

Naoksa was squatting between two boulders, her elbows propped on each, her back towards him, head bowed, neck gleaming, her lower half invisible.

'Np!'

Smous stifled a giggle, thinking, All this fuss and it looks as if she's just come out here for a good old shit. He giggled again, his thoughts freeing for the first time in days. When she hands it to me, he decided, I shall warm it with my body. Is it mine? Doesn't matter, doesn't matter, I shall hold it and hold it and hold it. I need it, I need her, I need them round me, I need a family . . .

Naoksa's moans were carried to him on the wind. He was surprised; Issy said savages didn't feel pain; yet he could clearly see the sweat pouring off her neck and arms, drenching the white cotton of her dress. She writhed and struggled, as though attempting to rise from the torment below, yet unable to, as though being burned alive.

Like my other family, thought Smous, my Plungyan family in their tinderbox houses.

He saw Naoksa's back ripple and buckle. She instantly struggled to her feet. Could it be over? So soon? How many minutes had passed? Or were they hours?

'Right,' Smous whispered and rose from his hiding place. Then he stopped and stared into the ravine, the skin freezing on his face. Naoksa was hacking at something on the ground with her stick. Again and again her arms flew up, again and again she drove the stick down, with merciless force, again and again. He threw himself forward, bounding, stumbling, sliding down into the ravine. She swung round, eyes blazing, and growled, 'Keep away!' The voice was hoarse and ugly, deeper than a man's – a ghost's, a dybbuk's – but he ignored it and lurched over the boulders where she had been crouching.

He expected to find the infant on the ground, mortally wounded, but it was nowhere to be seen. Nor was there blood on the end of her stick, only traces of earth. He frowned. She had been using the stick to break through the hard crust of the veld and dig a hollow, which, now, she was refilling. He glanced round the small area. There was a damp nest of grass, a sharpened reed that had cut the cord, but nothing else. Where was the infant? Then, as he saw Naoksa kick a heap of earth back into the hollow something about the nervous jerk of her foot told him to look closer. Inside the hollow, the surface flickered, like water about to boil. He blinked, stared again. There was another movement, an unmistakable shifting of pebbles, little seepages of sand, the tiny struggle of a living thing below the surface.

Naoksa read his expression and said calmly, 'It is the way.'

Smous stared into the hollow, wondering whether to reach down and brush away the dirt. Just to see it, just to see it! His hands were clenched on the boulder, the earth an arm's reach away, the simplest movement imaginable, but he couldn't shift; his body was capable only of a small, rhythmical rocking, keeping time with the flickering surface in the hollow. Now he saw an edge of skin break through, a finger perhaps, difficult to say, exactly the same shade as the pebbles and grit restraining it. Anything could tunnel through that light film of earth, any living thing, the tiniest insect, yet, somehow it was defeating the infant below. As though urging it on, even as the flickering grew fainter, he rocked harder and harder, wondering whether to reach down, wondering when it would be too late. When precisely? Now? Or now? Was *now* too late – could he still, if he reached down *now*, breathe life back into it? Then he watched Naoksa fill the shallow grave and gradually his own rocking, his own struggle, subsided.

He stared at her face for the first time, and was amazed how tranquil her features were, how smooth her skin, how her eyes shone. This was how she looked the first time he saw her, in the sugarhouse, when her face, although downcast, was so beautiful, its diamond shape perfect.

'It is the way,' she repeated, 'it is how it has always been,' then frowned darkly, 'but you should not have looked on it.'

He shook his head slowly. Extraordinary that she should be able to stand and walk and chatter. Perhaps Issy was right, perhaps savages didn't feel pain. When eventually Smous spoke, his voice was shivering.

'You are much more savage than they told me, much, much more pagan. Actually you're not civilised enough to be a pagan. You are without a soul, like a beast. No. Beasts feel more than you. No beast would have done what you have to its young. Not with it still alive, still struggling. Why do that? A beast, even a beast, could not endure that. God created beasts. God never created you. You can't hear me, can you? When one talks to a beast its ears prick, its eyes move. Your head is dead, it's bones and meat. I could shout at you forever and you'd never hear me.'

She gave a peaceful smile and began to collect her belongings. 'So, now I shall go. But where? There or there? Do you know?' She gestured in different directions and made the sign for home, tracing the movement of a birth into the land.

'Huhh!' he jeered, but then, remembering Issy telling him where the place called Bushmanland lay, pointed dismissively to the north.

'So,' she said. 'Thank you. Long ago, although we had no fight, you gave me a gift.' She brought the illustration of Jonah and the Great Fish from her kaross, handling it with great care. 'Always will I keep this. But I must not go without returning a gift. Please –' She held out the sheaf of dried grasses, her musical instrument.

Smous considered it, then accepted, pretending to smile gratefully, but saying, 'What do you expect me to do with this worthless rubbish, you savage bitch? Damn you forever.'

'It is a good gift, yes?' Naoksa said, pleased by his smile. 'When you play it you will hear me. So.' She slung the kaross over her shoulder, and, using the stick for support, quickly climbed out of the ravine and was gone.

Smous did not glance up to watch her go, to record a last memory of her, but stood smiling to himself, delighted that he had succeeded in cursing her without her knowing. For a long time he stayed there, staring at the ground, still debating whether to uncover the infant, just to see its face, its sex. Then he shrugged and headed back to Middlepost.

Breedt watched the small figure return alone to the settlement, slapping a sheaf of grasses against his leg, and make his way through the gardens to the yard. By the time the Boer reached him, Smous was already burning the grasses, wafting them above his head, adding their sweet smoke to the smell of milk and blood hanging in the air.

'She's gone,' observed Breedt. 'How did you manage that? By the God Jesus, man, I've been half mad with worry. If she'd brought that child back into Middelpos – *oo gonna*! It would have been hard to endure. Thank you, my friend. Thank you for sparing me another terrible deed of bloodshed.' He broke into a grin, his blue eyes twinkling, then clasped his hands over his scalp, scratching it joyfully. 'How did you know?' he asked, chuckling, almost boasting, 'did you see us together also? Hell, do you see *all* my sins?' Now he danced around the yard, which brought Marie and Fleurjie to the kitchen doorway, laughing and lifting their aprons over their heads. 'Oh, my friend, my friend,' panted Breedt, 'you want to see Antjie now? *Antjie?*' Smous shook his head. 'No? Ag ja, surely man . . . *Antjie.*'

He reached out, but Smous pulled away his arm, saying, 'Don't! You're always touching me. Just leave me alone. I have to –'

Breedt frowned. 'I'm sorry, my friend, but you know I don't speak your language.'

They stood staring at one another in silence. Smous no longer felt in awe of Breedt, or crowded by him. He was too familiar now. These people had a covenant with the Lord like his own, were persecuted like his own, deprived of their promised land like his own. That much Issy and Lazar had explained. But there was also a vital difference; something Smous had always seen in Breedt's eyes, but never understood before, a look of defeat. Persecution had defeated him. And that, Smous decided, staring at him intently, that is the difference between your people and mine.

It was a difference he liked.

He shifted from foot to foot, then turned and headed for the veld.

Landing

Home . . . the doorway leading from the road into the kitchen . . .

'Hh-uh,' he murmured and flicked his head.

. . . the narrow passageway, a faint smell of resin, his room, that patch of mould on the ceiling, looking like a beautiful cloud, but now turning black, burning . . .

'Hh-uh, hh-uh.'

. . . his mother and father shouting, the Old Girl stumbling out of her room, Elie leaning against a wall shaking with laughter, everyone burning . . .

'Hh-uh!'

Smous hung his head. Flicking it just made him giddy. His brow was hot and tight, his stomach hollow. When last had he eaten, how long had he been walking? The night was warm and dark, no moon, but thousands of stars, the veld ringing with crickets. He hated their noise – it was how Africa sounded, the earth alive, pulsing, purring, waiting to devour you.

Home, home, home.

Closing his eyes, he yielded and watched the house burning, those familiar rooms darkening and twisting, and his family scrambling onto the road, hair and clothes alight. Soldiers were perched on his father's wagon, doling out the goods to inmates from an asylum; all Her Immerman's thimbles and needles, children's shoes, spices, nuts, every sack and box. A man waved one of the ice-hatchets in the air and shouted something about roasting meat, something about chopping it into pieces the way the sacred forests were being chopped into pieces, and another man shouted something about eating babies and murdering God. How terrible to see them surround his parents, to see how easily his mother's strength could be broken, to see his father, that silly nervous man, fighting like a hero to defend her. And now – how extraordinary to see them now, those people from his earliest memories, who were always there, who were going to live forever, those dear people, it was unbelievable to see them now. How could they lie so awkwardly, with arms bent under and ankles turned over, didn't it hurt to lie so awkwardly? The nicotine on his father's moustache, the dough on his mother's forehead where she wiped her arm earlier, he could recognise these things, but nothing else. Where was her frown, his grins and twitches? *Don't keep hitting them like that, don't keep hitting those faces!*

Smous flicked his head again and again. The images slid back and forth, but stayed. He grabbed his temples and shook with all his might. It was no use; there was no way of clearing his mind, or stifling the horror and grief, and something else, something worse, much worse – an overwhelming feeling of triumph. *It served them right.* At last they were being punished for the scorn they had always shown him, their special intimate scorn. They knew him too well. The family fool, they were so sure of that. 'Only you . . .' his mother used to complain, casting him into the heavens with her triple curse, where he hung, alone, among the stars, 'only you . . . only you.' It had a different meaning now. 'Only me,' he said aloud, mopping his face. Only he had been spared. Surely that meant something, surely God had singled him out. But why? What was he to do, where was he to go?

He stared at the land stretching out before him, remembering Issy's words, 'A beautiful young country. A chance for us to take responsibility for once. Shape it our way.' Smous stamped on the ground. Shape this vast black mass? How could he? It was too hard, too powerful, it would have its own way whatever he chose, this sleeping monster with its end-less, maddening heartbeat. 'Trrr, trrr, trrr,' he mimicked, kicking wildly around him. 'Trrr, trrr, trrr!' He stumbled and fell, banging one arm against a stone. 'Yes, poor thing, too bad,' he cried, deliberately striking his arm again, then clutched the bruise and fell back. How magnificent the night looked, great white drifts of stars in a black void. People were singing in the distance, their voices as lovely and pure as the night sky. 'If God lived on earth,' Smous whispered, 'all his windows would be broken.'

He began to smile, then hesitated. Where was he, which part of the veld? What was he kneeling on? He sprang to his feet and peered down. It could be here – the child, her child – here in the black ringing earth beneath him. He shifted from foot to foot. If only she hadn't done that terrible thing he would have a family now, a new family, his own family, not ideal but it didn't matter. They would have been better than nothing.

Digging his hands in his pockets, he set off through the darkness again, teeth gritted, puffing and sighing. Why did he let Naoksa go? He should have hurt her first, struck her, cut her, burned her, made her burn and bleed as his parents were burning and bleeding. It would have been all right, no one would have minded. These were people who buried their young alive. Issy was right. They were primitive beyond belief, a peculiar form of life God had put on the surface of the world just before He created mankind. Bushmen. Plant-men. That was it! She smelled like a plant, a bush; to touch her was like touching dry leaves or bark; it must be their way to bury their young in the ground like seeds, and let them lie there, apparently dead, until the next rainfall when they would burst through the surface like the flowers – but yellow, ugly, stunted flowers.

He stopped in his tracks, unable to believe his eyes. The horizon ahead showed clearly against a bank of stars, flat and still, except for two human silhouettes slowly growing out of the earth. They were rocking back and forth, hugging one another, their rhythm like the pulse coming off the veld; it was as though they were connected to the land, as though it were breathing through them, flexing them back and forth, back and forth. They were murmuring and moaning, but the sounds were not human; they were the sounds of the veld before the rains: the wind rubbing the bushes, dry and rasping, and little clicks, like stones skimming the surface.

Smous swallowed hard, several times, to unblock his ears.

> ' . . . dream tree rests in our cheeks
> The young moon rides – come – the beer is foaming
> Are they come?
> Are they . . . ?'

Could this be the same song he heard a moment ago in the distance? He narrowed his eyes and, for a moment, thought these were children from the schoolhouse, or rather their ghosts, before he recognised April and Klippie. Was it possible? He felt a shiver go up his spine. Issy was right, he was right – savages didn't feel pain. April had been deafened and blinded, his son mutilated and outcast, yet here they were, still creeping onto the veld at night to chant their strange song, the cause of so much trouble, to chant those questions, one after the other lifting into the air like beckoning fingers. What did the words mean? *Da – da – daa? Da – da – daa?* What unholy forces were being sucked from the earth as they knelt on it, rocking to its rhythm, singing with its voice? *Da – da – daa? Da – da – daa?*

Disease. Lazar said everything here was diseased. Smous wiped his hands. They were slimy. He stumbled, clattering the loose stones. Both figures swung round, the blind man moaning with surprise. For an instant the light from the stars swept over their wet cheeks, bared teeth, and Klippie's huge startled eyes. Smous flicked his head. These were not people he knew, these were witches or warriors in black masks, briefly lit by the stars, then vanishing, dissolving back into the night: all except Klippie's eyes.

'Oh, my brother,' the youth said, offering his hand, 'I'm glad it is you. Come and be with us. Our hearts are sore.'

But Smous had already turned and fled. He ran so fast the night tore into pieces round him, wild black pieces, and the veld tore under his feet, its black surface shredding, the corners lifting, flapping into the sky. And the moment itself, this moment in time, came adrift, and the past, the present and the future caught together like stray threads and meshed, with him running, always him running and always a crowd chasing, and always a night filled with torn black pieces, smoke and spears, banners and flags; him running and a crowd chasing. Not people but shadows, dark ghosts with hundreds, hundreds of arms reaching out of the dark night to take hold of him, to drag him down into their dark earth, to bury him in their eternal darkness.

'God,' he cried, finding a tiny, icy voice in his throat, 'save me – save me, God!'

In the next moment the lights of Middlepost appeared only a few hundred yards ahead, and he saw a fire, candlelit windows, a circle of oil lamps on the road, and heard the cries of children playing.

Pouring with sweat and muttering thanks, he stumbled into the settlement.

The people were gathered on the road in their usual way, farmers from the district seated round the Breedts on an assortment of rocking-chairs and stools, but nothing else was familiar. Their faces were gleaming and raw, and as the children tumbled in and out of the shadows they shrieked like mad things. The air was spicy with the smell of meat and smoke; a goat had been roasted over the fire and dogs crunched at bones round every chair. Strangest of all, Antjie was there. Antjie, out of her room, sitting among the others? Smous had not seen her for weeks and was surprised how much her skin had cleared; yet, like everyone else, her eyes were red, her grin lopsided and wet.

'Ah, my friend, boomed Breedt, rising and spreading his arms, their ginger hairs matted, 'come and join us. Hell, now you look done in. He walks with the hyena's hind legs, nê? Can a person offer you some coffee?'

This produced a chorus of guffaws. Smous frowned as he watched

Breedt pour something from a dark bottle into the coffee before handing it to him. He took a sip and closed his eyes. That taste. Shaking his head, he emptied the cup onto the road.

'Hey – best Afrikaner brandywine!' cried Swanepoel close to his ear, the man's breath hot and sharp. 'Much better than the Bushman piss your hell-baked Redneck friends used to bring in.'

'Celebration . . .' said Breedt leaning into his other ear, 'celebration because my Antjie is getting better, and –' he winked at Smous and dropped his voice, 'other things to celebrate also, hey, my friend?' He tried to pour another slug of brandy into the empty cup and, when Smous resisted, laughed through closed teeth. 'It's all right, all right . . . sent Marie and them all to their huts. It's our little secret – they mustn't know, you hear? Mustn't tell them.' Breedt's face was extraordinary, his heavy features crumpled and pasty, yet radiating peace.

'How can he tell anyone anything?' purred Antjie, cooling herself with a fan which made wisps of her blond hair glow against the firelight. 'He can't speak so how can he tell anyone anything?' She turned, swaying, to Smous and spoke in Yiddish. 'I say to her father – you, stupid, stupid. You . . . no . . . talk, ja?'

Smous glared back, his neck prickling. He lurched forward, then steadied himself and glanced down, expecting to find a crack in the road It was level. Strange. He peered into his cup. It was empty. Yet he hadn't drunk anything. Perhaps it was a fever. On a nearby wall a flickering shadow was trying to attract his attention He pretended not to notice, fearing it would turn into the stevedore from the dockyards, the first savage that he saw, stepping from a doorway, bringing the darkness with him. Now Smous pretended not to hear when the shadow said, 'No, no, I'm not him – I'm the man with a mouth full of Good Hope, the man who was given another day by God . . .' Smous coughed loudly to silence the voice, then noticed Antjie watching him through half-closed lids, lolling in her chair, head back, the tip of her tongue slowly pushing open her lips. For a long, long moment he stood facing her, before turning to the others.

> 'Da da da-da – daa – da da da-da
> Da – da – daa?
> Da – da – daa?'

It felt like he was singing his barmitzvah again, singing in a thin, shivery voice to an assembly of puzzled faces. The children stopped playing and gathered round, while Mevrou Breedt looked away, the first to recognise the tune.

'Da – da – daa?
Da – da – daa?'

As the other leaned forward, their curiosity deepening, Smous pointed to the veld and imitated figures dancing around a fire, stamping their feet, waving their arms like apes, howling to the sky.

'Da – da – daa?
Da – da – daa?'

It was Swanepoel who finally made a move, staggering to his wagon and digging among the sacks on the back. 'Right, my people,' he called over his shoulder, 'who fancies a little old sport under the stars tonight?'

There was a moment's silence, then Breedt gave a loud, deep-throated moan, a hungry savage noise which the other men echoed, running to their wagons, carts or horses, finding shotguns and whips. 'Reminds me of times during the war,' whispered one of the women wistfully as they collected the children and retreated into the house. Antjie was the last to go, steadying herself against the door-frame and glancing back to Smous; an approving, bloodshot glance that cut through him.

The men had formed a line on the road, some hopping from foot to foot, rubbing their noses like boys, others trying to shake off their drunkenness, while the dogs, catching their excitement, began to leap in the air, grinning and snapping. Now a cheer went up as Breedt lurched from the store with his shotgun and Swanepoel allowed him to take the centre.

'Shush . . . shush . . .' Breedt cautioned and all obeyed.

Then Reukes whispered, 'Hang on a minute, must just have a piss first . . .' Laughter broke out again as he struggled to balance the shotgun under his chin, fumbling with his buttons, the stump of his missing arm jerking faster as his need grew more urgent.

'Come on man, hurry, come on!' the other men urged, sniggering, making him panic more.

'Ag, what people, let's just go – go, *go!*' Swanepoel cried impatiently, and ran into the veld with mad swaying strides, heading in the direction Smous had shown. Whooping and baying, the men and dogs followed, Breedt in the lead, Reukes at the end, splashing his knees and boots. He tripped over the colossal figure of Naude who had already fallen, then the two struggled to their feet and, heaving with laughter, disappeared into the night.

Alone on the road Smous held his breath for several moments. How quiet it had become, how dark. The fire had been extinguished and the oil lamps carried deep into the house, leaving the windows gaping blackly in the whitewashed walls. Behind him a horse blew its lips and stamped, gently bumping its cart against another. For the first time tonight Smous felt calm, and although his brow still burned it was not unpleasant. He marvelled that his arrival had changed everything, sending the women into the house and the men into the veld; and now everything was so peaceful. Perhaps Issy was right about this too: perhaps you could make things happen here, shape things. Smous turned in a circle, looking at the darkness, remembering how, fifteen minutes earlier, it seemed to tear apart, a nightmare of smoke, spears and banners. He shook his head and smiled. What had been frightening before was ordinary and beautiful now. Life in this place was ordinary and beautiful. Like Plungyan before the troubles started. It must be kept that way.

His spine prickled. That noise from the veld, that shivering chime, he didn't mind it now. If you listened carefully it was a soothing, thrilling noise, the pulse of a million tiny bodies breathing, chewing, copulating, crawling across the surface of the land, bringing it to life, shifting it slightly. He glanced to the ground. Perfectly level. Strange. Now he saw a star shoot across the sky, then another, and another. They were alive also, giant swarms shifting the heavens. He gasped, for now there was no doubt: the world was leaning into its tumbling, twisting fall. But somehow, amazingly, he kept his balance, treading, hopping, dancing, as oceans and continents swept underneath him, the Americas, the islands of Great Britain, the great mass of all the Russias, his native Litva, and Africa, Southern Africa, the Cape Colony, Middlepost . . .

He blinked and was surprised to find himself lying on the road, hands clutching the earth. Above, stars spread to infinity in every direction, but just by stretching up and outwards he could hold them all in his arms; as when, long ago, he was small enough to nestle in a basin of sweets, and he opened his eyes to find the universe filled with treasures, scent and light, him at the centre and everything else within reach.

'Yes,' he murmured now, 'it was true, it was true!'

A Note on the Type

The text of this book was set in a film version of Ehrhardt, a type face
receiving its name from the Ehrhardt foundry in Frankfort. The original design
of the face was the work of Nicholas Kis, a Hungarian punch cutter known to
have worked in Amsterdam from 1680 to 1689. The modern version of Ehrhardt
was cut by The Monotype Corporation of London in 1937.

Composed in Great Britain

Display typography and binding design by
Mia Vander Els